PRAISE FOR S.T. GIBSON

"A story as intimate as it is decadent, a delightful romp through occult society, grounded by all-too-human characters, the power of love is a real and vibrant force in this story and its effects are profound. Sincerity is scary and Gibson aims to thrill."
Elizabeth Kilcoyne, Morris Award finalist for *Wake the Bones*

"With characters as vibrant as the story is twisted, Evocation *is the start of a bold new saga — daring, pulpy, and delicious."*
K. M. Enright, author of *Mistress of Lies*

"Gibson has crafted a meditation on abuse, grief, and the shadows of past lives which delves into the liminal space between what we desire and what we deserve, and interrogates the trust between those who have hurt each other more deeply than can ever be erased — all as it offers characters who will be indelibly inked on your memory, bound together by secrets and bargains stronger than death itself."
Laura R. Samotin, author of *The Sins On Their Bones*

"Dazzling and compelling from start to finish, S.T. Gibson's Evocation *crackles with magic and the strong chemistry between its three leads."*
Morgan Dante, author of *A Flame in the Night*

"Romantic and delectable, Evocation *is an entrancing start to a new series by S. T. Gibson. If anyone can make you root for three intricately crafted characters, it is Gibson. David, Rhys and Moria have ensnared me, I will be making a deal with the devil, just to get book two in my hands."*
Ben Alderson, author of *Lord of Eternal Night*

EVOCATION

S.T. GIBSON

ANGRY
ROBOT

ANGRY ROBOT
An imprint of Watkins Media Ltd

Unit 11, Shepperton House
89 Shepperton Road
London N1 3DF
UK

angryrobotbooks.com
twitter.com/angryrobotbooks
Give the Devil his due

An Angry Robot hardback original, 2024

Cover by Eleonor Piteira and Alice Claire Coleman
Edited by Eleanor Teasdale
Tarot Card descriptions by Adam Gordon
Set in Meridien

ISBN 978 1 91520 268 0
Ebook ISBN 978 1 91520 274 1

Printed and bound in the United Kingdom by CPI Group (UK) Ltd, Croydon CR0 4YY.

9 8 7 6 5 4 3 2 1

To everyone in search of real magic.

The hanged man

CHAPTER ONE

DAVID

David pulled up to the haunted house ten minutes before he was expected, because arriving late was for amateurs and getting there too early was for interns. He used three of those minutes to sit in the Audi and review case notes for an upcoming deposition on his phone. Technically, it wasn't six yet, which meant he was *technically* still on the clock for his day job. Not that he ever really clocked out of working as a prosecutor for the city of Boston. He just spent his nights expanding his vocational horizons.

He had been juggling full-time work and a thriving private occult practice ever since graduating law school, not to mention weekly secret Society meetings, and he would rather donate his entire fortune to charity than walk away from any of it. David was like a diamond, forged under pressure and bound entirely in hard, cutting edges.

At two till, David straightened his collar in the rearview mirror, ran a hand through his wavy bronze hair, and locked up his car. Tonight's client was an eccentric heiress with a penchant for the occult and a recently dead husband, which was right up David's alley. He could be in and out before eight, with time for a workout and an hour or so answering work emails before bed. It was his ideal type of day: packed to the brim with meaningful, lucrative work and centered entirely around himself. The only thing that could possibly make it better was a round of athletic sex, which was off the table for reasons relating to David's lack of interest in almost all the men in Boston and his ironclad marriage to his work, or a stiff drink, which was off the table for reasons related to David's sanity and general well-being.

The widow lived in an ivy-covered Brookline brownstone with black-shuttered windows closed tightly to the world. David had to knock three times to get an answer, and when the door finally opened, it was only an inch.

"Who's there?" a reedy voice from inside demanded.

David tried – to no avail – to peer inside the darkness of the house. "David Aristarkhov. We spoke on the phone?"

"David who?" she pressed.

David flipped open his wallet and thumbed through the glossy cream business cards work had given him until he came to a few embossed black cards hidden in the back. He slipped one free and held it out between his fingertips through the crack in the door. The silver script gleamed like a knife under the bright spring sunlight.

Spirit Medium and Psychic Intuitive.

"I don't know," the woman said after a moment. "I've changed my mind. I don't know if my Levi would want me to try and contact him after all this time. Come back tomorrow. We'll see how I feel then."

Cold feet, then. Typical. There was no way he was cutting his losses and driving back to Fenway now, though. Not now that he was wired after a long week on the job and ready to, quite literally, raise the dead.

"Miriam," David said, every syllable deliberate. His voice had the timbre of smooth, polished brass, without a trace of anything less than all-American. It was a voice curated for conveying utmost surety and bulldozing anyone who got in his way. "Why don't you just open the door a little bit, and you and I can talk about it?"

There was a long pause, but then the widow obeyed him. People usually did, when he asked nicely. It was one of the innate, uncanny abilities that had been with him since childhood, like mediumship or perfect pitch.

The door swung open to reveal a wizened but glamorous woman in her seventies, wearing a purple silk headscarf and large tortoiseshell glasses. She took David in appraisingly, flicking her eyes across his wood-inlay summer Rolex and monogrammed cufflinks. He was still dressed for his day job, in his bespoke shirt and slacks that cost more than what most men paid for their wedding suit. The Aristarkhovs had money so old you could have exhibited it in the Hermitage: vodka-exporting, fur-trapping, wartime-advising money. Champagne-in-the-box-seat money. Discreet-exit-from-the-public-eye-when-wealth-became-unfashionable money. David had never been interested in denying himself any of the comforts his inheritance provided.

"I just don't know if I'm ready to talk to him again, is all," she said, a little quieter.

David gallantly took her small hand between his own, pressing gently. He was better with the dead than he was with the living, but he could feel the apprehension wafting off her like a perfume gone sour. Best to lay on the charm a little bit to put her fears at rest.

"That's what I'm here for. You wouldn't have called me if we weren't meant to do this together. It will be wonderful, I promise. Now why don't you invite me inside?"

She nodded absently and stepped aside, muttering something about being willing to try anything once. Entry secured, David dropped his pleasantries at the door and strode past her into the house. She stared at him as though baffled at how quickly she had let down her defenses. David simply gave her a wry smile over his shoulder.

It was whispered that a long time ago, before Martin Luther had even written his treatise and plunged Europe into holy war, an Aristarkhov made a deal with the Devil. One thousand years of servitude for an apprenticeship in the art of persuasion, with a crash course in the occult arts thrown in to sweeten the pot. It was difficult to say whether there was any truth to the claim. But it was true that David's grandfather had been gifted entire stables of thoroughbred horses simply by asking for them, and that his father stole his prima ballerina mother away from her debut in *Giselle* by draping her in his coat and telling her that a car was waiting outside.

David rolled up his sleeves, revealing the thickly inked *monas heiroglyphica* tattooed on the inside of his right arm. It was a sigil meant to represent the principles of alchemy distilled into universal power. David had gotten it when he was young and drunk on his own invincibility, but of all the occult symbols he could have chosen to get marked on him forever, it wasn't the worst option.

He spread his fingers, testing the aura, air pressure, and electrical currents of the room. The familiar cold malaise of dead energy curled around his fingers, lighting up the psychic intuition in the base of his brain. His whole body relaxed into the sensation, comforted by the familiarity of restless ghosts.

"I'm going to need a quiet room to work in and an object that belonged to your late husband," David said, "and a sparkling water, if you have one."

David Aristarkhov didn't believe in the Devil. But he was certainly willing to work with everything his birthright had given him.

An hour later, David was holding Miriam's hand in a dimly lit room while she wept gently. A glass of water – still, not sparkling – sat untouched on the table between them, along with David's phone, facing up, black screen on display. David only lugged around a crystal ball when he was doing a group séance at a private event. Today, the dark mirror of his iPhone worked perfectly well to scry into and decipher messages from beyond the grave.

"Levi is only restless because you're having so much trouble letting him go," David said, the script smooth and rote in his mouth. "He'll be able to rest easy once he knows you've settled into life without him. And then he'll stop rearranging the furniture while you're asleep. These things just take time."

Miriam dabbed at her eyes with a handkerchief. "Will you ask him if he misses me where he is? Please?"

David resisted the urge to roll his eyes. This was always the million-dollar question, and the answer was always something along the lines of "yes and no," but he asked it anyway, turning his attention down on the black screen. A familiar drowsiness filled his limbs as his consciousness drifted deeper into an intuitive state, his mind opening wider.

He was born to do this. It was as natural to him as breathing.

All at once, David was knocked back by a psychic blow to the head. He reeled, eyes stinging, and his teeth ground against each other painfully.

David had been put in his place by spirits before. He had been scratched up by poltergeists, dragged around the room by demons, tortured with nightmares by the dead who refused to let him rest until they could. It took a lot to make him uncomfortable, and even more to scare him. But now he was battling back a terror so big he felt seven years old again, frozen by the bedside of a mother dying terribly and slow.

David gasped, ripping his hands out of Miriam's. He felt like he had been doused in freezing water, and he shivered uncontrollably as cold passed through him in waves. His vision went indigo at the corners, tightening into a claustrophobic tunnel, but then he was out of it again, taking in so much light and color that his eyes hurt.

Something spoke to him, so close that he knew it had to be coming from inside his own head.

SON OF ANATOLY

Whatever that was, it had nothing to do with Miriam, or with the ghost of her dead husband. This was something entirely new. It felt like he was channeling a spirit directly, only he hadn't invited this one in. The voice had simply asserted itself and expected him to listen.

"Is everything alright?" Miriam asked. She looked like she was going to pat his shoulder reassuringly, and David would rather die first. He pulled together a smile and glanced down at his watch, angling his body away from any of her pity.

"Everything's fine. But unfortunately, it looks like we've reached the end of our time together. Do you want to book a follow-up session?"

Ten minutes later, David left the townhouse a few hundred bucks richer and considerably shaken up, though he took care not to show it on his face. He had put Miriam at ease with some well-placed jokes and flattery, total child's play, and had gotten out before she'd realized anything was wrong.

David loitered outside his car to have a cigarette, turning his phone over in his hands as he sucked down the nicotine-laden smoke.

He nearly dismissed it entirely. He almost headed home to shake off whatever funk he was in and turn his attention back to the next case on his to-win list.

But something nibbled at him, burning in the back of his skull in the same spot that acted up when he was near a murder site, or on the precipice of making contact with the dead.

There was an opportunity here – for connection, for reaching out and seizing a moment that might not pass by him again anytime soon.

He pulled out his phone and scrolled through his messages until he found Rhys's name.

He had to scroll back pretty far.

David's thumb hovered over the name, his palms suddenly clammy. His heart leaped into his throat, pounding a rhythm in his jugular. This wasn't exactly a good idea, but it was the best chance he would have at making contact for a long while.

He and Rhys didn't have real conversations, not these days. They avoided each other at social events and sniped at each other occasionally during Society meetings, rarely venturing further than to ask the other to pass the ceremonial salt during a spirit summoning. David had made a promise, after all. He had sworn to keep his distance, to let Rhys live his own life outside of the realm of David's influence or interest. They were supposed to be acting like perfect strangers.

Not like two men who had been as close to each other as blood and breath, once.

David decided, with a lick of pettiness flaming behind his ribs, that he was done keeping his distance. It had been six months since the incident. If Rhys wasn't ready to talk now, he was never going to be.

David shot off a quick text.

What do you know about possession?

The Chariot

CHAPTER TWO

RHYS

Rhys McGowan stood with feet planted, pointing his flame-bladed dagger into the heart of the ceremonial circle. His flawless Latin chanting echoed clearly through the darkened room. Twelve white taper candles of exactly the same height flickered on the ground in a ring of beckoning light.

He had been preparing for this evocation for nearly a month: blending resins into an incense that the spirit would find pleasing, meticulously chalking out the proper magician's seals onto the hardwood floor, and taking so many ritual baths he was sure he would smell of frankincense for weeks.

The temperature in the room slid downwards as shadows stirred in the study's darkest nooks. Something moved in the corner of his eye, but Rhys didn't let himself get distracted. He was used to the scare tactics these things used when they didn't want to show themselves fully. Summoning was all about the follow-through, and he was willing to stand here chanting for an hour if it got him what he wanted.

Realistically, this sort of ritual was well within his realm of expertise. The spell was a classic, lifted from *The Lesser Key of Solomon*, and he had pored over the instructions for summoning, binding, and bending the demon to his will so many times that he could recite them in his sleep. Still, he liked to be prepared, and the grimoire lay open to the correct page at his feet.

As Rhys commanded, an entity began to take shape within the circle. Slowly, darkness clung to darkness and grew into a light-swallowing swirl.

Primary source texts indicated that today's spirit favored a classic black mass manifestation, so as shadows began to clump together over the chalked triangle used to trap spirits, Rhys knew he was doing his job right.

He doubled down on his intonation, leaning into the binding words that would render the spirit powerless to harm him. Initial contact was for making an entity amenable, whether through cajoling or threats, to one's wishes. Rhys had spirits at his disposal that he could summon with simpler methods. But he was in the market for a new demon to round out his stable, and nothing beat the feeling of accomplishment that came with dragging something onto the material plane for the first time.

He had been scared out of his mind by spirits before. He had taken ill after conjurations gone wrong or woken up to find every stitch of furniture in his house turned upside down. But he always kept coming back for more. No matter the promises he made to himself or to his wife, he could never stay away for long.

As a result, he had gotten very, very good at this.

The spirit strained against its bonds, but Rhys was stronger. He splayed his fingers and drove it down with divine names, compelling it into submission.

The thrill of bending something ancient and undying to his own will coursed through Rhys like electricity. He wondered, not for the first time, if this counted as something he ought to confess to before Mass. But then again, there was a long tradition of holy men subjugating the powers of darkness with divine names, blessed water, rosaries, and more. So Rhys was in good company, even though he would balk at being called holy himself.

Rhys's cell phone trumpeted out a text message notification, shattering his focus.

His shoulders sagged, and the entity within the circle made a rumbling sound like laughter that raised the hairs on the back of his neck. Rhys fumbled with the incantation, eyes flipping desperately down to pick up his place in the book, but he could already feel the spirit straining against the cage he had been weaving around it.

He was losing his grip on it.

The spirit wiggled free from its bonds and disappeared. Nothing but the scent of wick-smoke and a clammy feeling of dread was left behind.

Rhys swore softly under his breath. His head fell forward, chin hitting his chest, and he rubbed at the back of his aching neck.

There was a Saturday wasted.

Drawing a lazy sigil through the air with his fingers, Rhys closed the spiritual doorway his circle had opened and shut the ritual down. Then he stomped over to the window near his desk and yanked open the curtains, letting clear April light into his study.

Stuffed bookshelves, crystal decanters, and gaudily framed pinned butterflies all vied for attention, jostling against dark paintings in the Flemish style and sticky notes reminding him to return his library books, or call his mother. A vase of irises valiantly battled with patterned china on the small breakfast nook table, and a taxidermy meerkat stood at proud attention on one of the shelves. Rhys was nothing if not a maximalist.

He blew the candles out one by one, careful not to disrupt the magic circle underfoot. Then he swiped a finger over the phone left foolishly out on the desk.

David.

Rhys furrowed his brow and disregarded the notification.

He shouldered through the door and headed towards the kitchen, disappointment clinging to him like a cloud. Missing the mark always stung. But he might be able to find time Sunday afternoon to try again. That was, if annotating his article on land deeds purchased by single women in twelfth-century Wales didn't take too long. Specializing in medieval Welsh history hadn't turned out to be very lucrative, and it hadn't turned into acceptance into a Master's program, but it was good enough for a certification in special collections and an associate position at a small university library. The spirit he had summoned to boost his charisma during the interview process hadn't hurt, either.

Moira was in the kitchen, of course, holding court at the banged-up wooden table. She trailed her fingers across an elaborate spread of tarot cards, ombre purple nails gleaming, while another woman looked on. Moira wore her black kinky hair loose around her shoulders, and the sunlight streaming in from the window made her brown skin glow.

"Looks like you're in a bind," Rhys's wife said in her sun-warmed drawl.

The client, who Rhys recognized as one of Moira's many acquaintances, leaned further over the table. Rhys couldn't recall her name. In addition to the smorgasbord of women from college she kept in regular contact with, Moira had an uncanny knack for befriending baristas, hairdressers, yoga instructors, and pretty much anyone else who crossed her path. Her clients liked to whisper that it was the intuitive psychic energy she radiated, but Rhys knew it came from a deeper, more potent magic: her natural aptitude for putting people at ease.

Moira glanced down at the calculations scribbled into her composition notebook.

"You're starting at a disadvantage with all his Piscean energy clashing with your Sagittarius heart center. You both share a Mercury in Libra, so y'all might be able to work through your differences with clear communication and a commitment to seeing things from both sides. But the cards are tuning me into a couple of red flags, I'm sorry to say."

"Just what we need," the client muttered. A plate of gingersnaps and a glass of iced tea sat in front of her. "Go ahead and give it to me. I wouldn't have come here if I didn't want to know."

Rhys opened the cupboard above his three coffee makers and retrieved a bottle of homemade cardamom syrup.

Moira hooked her hair behind her ears and slid a couple of cards closer to the client. She had dusted off her box of crop tops last week to celebrate the start of spring, and was currently wearing one crocheted from baby-pink yarn.

"The two of swords illuminates inner conflict, and the nine of swords lets me know that you've been losing a lot of sleep over whether or not to leave this guy. You've been carrying all that anxiety around in your body, and it's coming out in nightmares and nervous habits. You've been dealing with this all alone?"

The client swallowed and nodded, eyes a bit glassy. Moira made a knowing hum.

"I can sense that isolation. But look over here at the three of cups. See these three girls dancing and cutting up, having a good time? That's showing me all the relationships in your life that are so full of love and support. You can lean on them."

"You're gonna tell me to leave him, aren't you?"

"Sugar, I can't tell you to do anything. All I'm here to do is relay messages from the Divine and help you explore potential options. There is no right and wrong in this room. Just potentials."

Rhys scooped ice out of the freezer by hand to avoid the belligerent rattle of the dispenser, then poured himself a glass of cold brew. He tried to slip out quietly without disturbing the session further, but Moira threw a glance at him before he made it to the door.

"Can I get a second opinion?" she asked.

Rhys drifted behind Moira's chair, settling a hand on her shoulder, and she tipped her head back for a kiss. She smiled against his lips when he obliged her, enveloping him in the familiar intoxication of her sandalwood and rose perfume.

Rhys leaned over Moira's shoulder and ran his fingers across the swirling watercolor illustrations arranged on the table. These were Moira's cards, more abstract than his classical deck that lined up nicely with traditional accordances. But he was learning, slowly, to speak their language of death, rebirth, and transformation. His eyes leapt from card to card, minding reversals and major themes as he pieced together a story from symbols.

It was not a happy one.

"You've got to leave him," he pronounced. "Seriously. He's never going to be able to give you the affirmation you need. Also, it looks like he's shit at paying his bills on time."

Moira held out a consolation gingersnap to her client, who took it with shaky fingers.

"I'm sure this is a lot to process," Moira said, securing her notes with a star-shaped paperclip. "Sleep on it. Call your girls and ask for their honest opinion."

"Must be nice, living with someone who gets your hobbies," the client said, surveying Rhys curiously. "I didn't know your husband was a witch too."

He opened his mouth to start in on a lecture about semantics, about how witchcraft generally referred to ancestral practices rooted in the home and the needs of a community, and how what he did traced its magical lineage more to monasteries and mystery cults. Instead, he settled.

"Actually, I'm a sorcerer."

"Is that the male version?"

"No, there are male witches. The title refers to what kind of magic you do; gender is irrelevant."

Moira's painted lips tugged up into a private smile as the client struggled to follow.

"But you do magic, like her. You can read tarot cards and stuff."

"And more."

"So you're a witch."

Moira leaned conspiratorially over the table to her friend, eyes sparkling. "That's right. He's even got a coven."

"Oh my God," Rhys groaned. "For the last time, it isn't a coven!"

"Sorry, sorry," his wife said, hiding her smile with a sip from her iced tea. "My mistake. It's a very secret boys' club. No girls allowed."

"It's an occult fraternity," Rhys said crisply.

"Oh, I get it," the client said, easing into familiar territory. "My brother was in a fraternity at UMass. Aren't you a little old for that?"

Rhys kneaded his brow while Moira laughed. Arguing was useless.

He bided his time as Moira hugged her client and walked her to the door, and as she accepted her cash payment with you-shouldn't-have graciousness. She always managed to make a skilled service come across as a goodwill favor, and she refused to raise her rates despite Rhys needling her about competitive markets and calculating her per-hour value.

When she returned to the kitchen, flipping bills between her fingers, Rhys shot her a warning look.

"You're mean."

"Little old me?"

"Yes, you," he insisted. The fight was already slipping out of his voice.

"No, I'm sweet."

"Sweet, huh?" he asked, looping an arm around her waist. He pulled her in close enough to feel her warmth against him, see the microscopic shimmer she mixed into her makeup sparkling on her cheeks.

She kissed him slowly, reddening his mouth with her lipstick, but he didn't care. She tasted like mischief.

"Shouldn't you be summoning demons?" she murmured.

"Demon got spooked and took off."

"Was I being too loud?"

"No, I was an idiot and left my ringer on."

Moira fixed his hair, smoothing the dark curls out of his eyes. He probably looked paler than usual after a long winter spent barricaded indoors with his books.

"Who was it?"

"No one." A heartbeat passed, the longest span of time he could comfortably hold a lie to her in his body. "David."

She hummed her disapproval, and Rhys leaned back against the hard, cold countertop. Moira wasn't the type to leave old connections unsevered, and she had a hard time understanding Rhys's ability to carry on professional correspondence with David. Especially after what had happened the last time he paid them a visit.

"I didn't answer," Rhys said.

"You're grown; I'm not going to tell you what to do. What did he want, anyway?"

"Nothing. Something about demon possession. He's baiting me."

"This is why I don't fool with the dead. Someone asks you to call up dear departed grandma and the next thing you know, you're hip-deep into some dark stuff. You haven't texted each other in what? Six months? I told you he'd crack eventually."

"David isn't exactly a paradigm of self-restraint."

"He's got no boundaries, is the problem," Moira declared. "This is why he'll make a piss poor High Priest."

Rhys gave her an affronted look. "Have a little faith, please. The votes aren't even in yet."

"He's a legacy, and that club of yours runs on nepotism. You know I support you, baby, and you'd make a fantastic High Priest. But you shouldn't expect David to go down without a fight."

"I'll try to keep that in mind," Rhys said, and pressed the heels of his hands to his eyes. They ached from peering at tiny type in a darkened room, but the pain was familiar. He would need glasses before he was thirty if he kept on like this.

"You were in there for two hours," Moira said, voice a little softer as she squeezed his free hand. "Why don't you take a break?"

"I've still got a lot to clean up, and notes to take. Do you have any more clients today?"

"I've got a man coming in looking for a money-drawing spell tomorrow, but I'll need to do my prep work tonight. Moon's in a mighty fine position for abundance."

"We'll have dinner together afterwards, then, I promise. Italian? My treat."

"You're bribing me with breadsticks to get me off your case."

"I am."

Moira took a long drink of his cold brew. "I'll let you. But one of these days, you're gonna hit your limit, Rhys McGowan."

"I like being busy. You knew this when you married me."

"And I consider it my God-given duty as your wife to make sure you don't run yourself into the ground."

He took his glass back, kissed Moira on the cheek, and slipped out of the sunny kitchen. The door to his study lay open before him, inviting him back into familiar darkness. "You can tell God I'll review his demands and get back to him later. For now, I've got spirits to summon."

The hanged man

CHAPTER THREE

DAVID

In the all-encompassing whirlwind of twelve-hour days in the courtroom, the attorney's office, and in private clients' living rooms, David almost forgot about the text entirely. It had only been a little indiscretion, a way to test the waters. If Rhys wasn't biting, fine. It wasn't as if they could keep avoiding each other outside of Society meetings and pretending they didn't know each other during conclave ritual circle forever. Rhys would cave eventually.

But on Thursday a week later, as David shouldered open the door to his condo, his phone buzzed in his briefcase. He tossed the briefcase on the marble-topped kitchen island and let the call ring through while he rummaged through the sparse refrigerator for a pre-portioned dinner. It was probably one of the interns calling with a fire that wasn't his to put out. Or Leda, holding up her end of their unending game of sibling phone-tag. The voicemail notification, however, took him by surprise.

While the plate rotated in the whirring microwave, he flicked his phone on to speaker mode. Rhys's voice filled the airy emptiness of the pristine condominium as the sun set over the skyline out of the window.

"David. We talked about this. I asked for space. I'll reach out when I'm ready."

That was it. No timeline about when they could start talking normally again, no indication of how Rhys might be feeling about any of it. Just a curt message to enforce the embargo.

David stabbed a fork into his chicken breast and steamed broccoli. He shouldn't be surprised. Rhys knew him better than anyone. He knew when David was goading him.

Nudging aside a Barney's shopping bag he had picked up on his last mindless trip to Copley but never unpacked, David sank into his leather sofa, laptop in one hand, dinner in the other.

This high above the city, the noise of Fenway couldn't reach him, so he was left in peace to sort through the dozens of tabs he had left open. They were etymological, mostly, researching the transmission of that name which had been burned into his brain at the séance last week. He hadn't had an episode like it since then, but he hadn't felt quite like himself, either. There was a fuzzy sort of film over his psychic intuition that made him second-guess the messages he channeled for clients, and he suspected his abilities still hadn't recalibrated themselves since he accidentally picked up on something he wasn't supposed to.

Or alternately, he'd picked up on a message that someone very badly wanted to get across to him. He wasn't sure which possibility was more concerning.

David had been sifting through references to spontaneous possession for days to no avail. Any resources he found were distinctly Catholic in nature, which were of less use to him than any of the rambling conspiracy theories he might find on a garden-variety occultism Discord. He had also made a few wire transfers to leading occult scholars in Berlin, Shanghai, and Prague in the hope to fast track an answer, to no avail. It always irritated him when throwing money at a problem didn't make it go away. Lorena might know something, but she was sure to be slammed this time of year with spring equinox orders. He was on his own with this one.

This was not David's wheelhouse. He specialized in contacting the dead and was serviceable with home blessings and hauntings. Possession was another matter entirely. And David was sure it was possession, or as sure as he could be about that sort of thing. It felt so similar to the times he had allowed himself to become ritually possessed before, either at a Society ritual or during one of his father's séances; only this time, he hadn't invited the spirit inside him. Nothing had ever overtaken him like that in the past.

He was so engrossed in thought that his dinner went cold on the table beside him. When he finally glanced down at his watch, he hissed through his teeth.

He had lost track of time. There would be no gym for him tonight, not if he wanted to make it to the Society meeting.

David devoured the rest of his dinner in three bites, then snatched up his coat. He promised himself, not for the first time, that he would play nice with Rhys tonight, no matter how satisfying it was to get a rise out of him. If David wanted any sort of answer to the possession question, he shouldn't press his luck.

The Society hall was in Cambridge, within a stone's throw from Harvard Yard. Unlike the lineaged Freemasons or undergraduate social clubs that met in stone buildings guarded by wrought-iron fences, the Society favored discretion. The main entrance was beneath a Cantonese restaurant, down a grimy flight of stairs that seemed more likely to lead into a college dive bar than anywhere else.

David rapped crisply on the door. It slid open two miserly inches. A pair of rheumy eyes peered at him behind the chain pulled taut across the opening.

"Password?" a man asked.

"Gerald, I helped get your daughter out of her DUI; I think we're well beyond this now."

The guardian huffed and slammed the door shut, but a moment later, metal clunked, and the door was opened.

"Welcome back, Mr Aristarkhov," the Society's ancient footman said, his wispy white hair stirring in the breeze of the AC. Gerald had been there before David had been initiated and would probably be there after David retired. He was an artifact of grander times, when secret societies would employ staff at their séances to refill the glasses of enraptured onlookers. Currently, one staff member to answer the door, run the coat check, and serve drinks with the utmost discretion was all the Society could afford. But the High Priest liked to think that with time, new members and new money would find their way into the brotherhood's ranks, and the staff would grow. Gerald was, in this way, aspirational.

David slipped off his blazer and held it out on two fingers. Gerald made it disappear into the coat closet.

"Shall I hold your keys?"

"That won't be necessary. How is she, anyway? Sherry?"

"Oh, better now, but you know how it is. Hard to keep someone off the bottle once they have a taste for it."

David made a disgruntled sound in his throat, then brushed past Gerald and slipped beneath the draped curtain that separated the foyer from the clubhouse.

Despite relatively small square footage and a lack of natural light, the clubhouse had an antiquated grandeur that even David, with his taste for the modern, could appreciate. Overstuffed armchairs sat atop oriental rugs, and the bulbous sconce lighting along the wall evoked the Victorian without going full set piece. The paintings on the wall showed off autumnal pastorals and hunting scenes. A long wooden table along one wall offered light bites of meat and a spread of miniature pastries that looked stolen from a megachurch coffee hour.

It was a love letter to the idea of a gentleman's club, of what they were supposed to have been like before wing night at sports bars and neon-lit strip clubs had taken over.

Most of the men – retired bankers and middle managers and professors – mingled freely throughout the room. There were twenty on a good day, closer to ten on most. At the turn of the twentieth century, occult orders had been the height of fashion for any young man of means. In the past, the Society had been a center of political might, a place for power brokers to discuss the future of cities and even nations. But now, they tended to attract eccentrics and social climbers, people who were either all-in on the promise of attaining universal secrets or simply there to hob-nob. David, who had been raised in and around occult societies, didn't fall into either camp. He was totally disillusioned with the concept of supernatural enlightenment, knowing damn well that most people used magic to secure mundane boons, and there were very few people in any given room that he ever felt the need to impress.

Put simply, the Society was a demon-summoning social club, and while everyone had their own reasons for bending spirits to their will, they were all united by self-interest and a desire for comradery. In this way, an occult fraternity wasn't much different from a Greek one. David had never been in a college frat, but he had been in a men's acapella group at Williams, and that was basically the same thing.

David's crowd was already congregated in their usual spot: a conspiratorial semicircle of chairs in a far corner. In the winter, the fireplace would cast a cheery glow on the corner. But now, three men talked in the dim light cast by a standing lamp.

David caught the flash of dark eyes and the curl of mussed black hair as one of the men glanced briefly over his shoulder. He sighed. Rhys had beat him there.

David noted the cluster of men having an animated discussion amid a low-lying fog of tobacco. Cameron Casillas, a theology professor at a nearby divinity school, was nodding gravely while the older men went on about the rising price of oil. Cameron was generally grave. All the older men were smoking acrid cigars. Cameron puffed away at his meticulously packed wooden pipe, his Princeton haircut slicked back against his skull.

David snagged a bottle of Perrier from the refreshment table and crossed the room to their usual corner. Cameron followed, sweeping into an ancient loveseat while David stood, doing his best to look blasé.

Rhys glanced up at him from his seat in his favorite red velvet armchair. He looked as he always did: slightly underfed, terminally scholastic, and two weeks overdue for a haircut. But his eyes were just as ferociously intelligent as ever, the set of his mouth just as doggedly determined. Rhys was a man who would not be moved about many things: his punctual arrival to Catholic Mass no less or more than eight times a year; his conviction that one ought not be seen out of doors in a t-shirt and jeans after the age of twenty; and last year's decision that David Aristarkhov was in his black books, with all non-Society socializing privileges revoked.

"David," he said coolly. "How was the deposition?"

"No worse than expected," David said, and knew better than to go in for the light air kiss he had picked up during summer break in Italy and sometimes used to greet intimates. Currently, that number had dwindled to, well… his sister.

Nathan Vo, he thumped amicably on the shoulder, and Antoni Bresciani, who stood at Rhys's side with a glass of bourbon in hand, got a firm handshake.

"We're talking Bardon," Antoni said. A Harvard business grad from a large Italian family, Antoni was also an amateur weightlifter who could probably bench press David, despite being barely 5'5". He had been initiated less than a year ago but had quickly found his place in the quintet of younger men. They were a subculture within a subculture, and it was unlikely any of them would have been friends if they hadn't been introduced through the inscrutable inner workings of the brotherhood. But age gave the five a bond that monthly brunches and gossip-swapping strengthened.

"Didn't he write *Initiation into Hermetics*?" David asked, bringing his cigarette smoothly to his lips. "He's a bit woo-woo for me. Very into awareness of the higher light, or whatever."

"Theurgy is so much more than that!" Antoni said. "I only got my hands on the book a few weeks ago, but if you're patient with it, it'll blow your mind. Autosuggestion, astral projection, clairaudience, it's all there."

"Theurgy," David said, barely managing to get the word out without a bit of a sneer. Self-perfection through union with the divine had never been very appealing to him. He had always been able to get in touch with much more interesting entities with the snap of his fingers. That was, of course, what made him such a valuable asset to the Society. His keen second sight was essential in the ritual workings that helped the ambitious men of the order cajole spirits into helping them through divorces, or securing political office, or getting out of parking tickets. As an adept scryer, David could talk any sorcerer through any ritual, because he could actually see the spirits being summoned, even when they didn't choose to manifest on the corporeal plane.

"Isn't that more Cameron's ballpark?"

"I've worked through *Initiation into Hermetics*," the professor replied casually.

"All of it?" Antoni exclaimed.

"Doing inner work is just as important as knowing how to stage a ritual," Rhys cut in. "A truly great sorcerer has to be able to master both."

"How about you focus on all that self-knowledge, and I'll summon the dead and we'll see who gets the farthest?" David said.

Rhys leaned back in his chair, shaking his head. He didn't agree with David's no-frills methods, and David chalked that squeamishness up to early exposure to Catholicism. Antoni and Rhys were formalists, though Rhys had the obsessive focus of a scholar while Antoni had the gluttonous, cherry-picking appetite common in new occultists. Cameron followed a psychological model, insisting he was more interested in building moral fiber than in causing magical shifts in the world. And Nathan... Nathan was in it for the camaraderie.

The venture capitalist leaned forward in his seat, a forgotten martini going lukewarm in his hand. The second-youngest member of the society at twenty-four – Antoni was twenty-two and Rhys held the lifetime record for being inducted when he was only nineteen – Nathan had a relentlessly upbeat air that would have been annoying if it wasn't so goddamn genuine.

"How's the necromancy business?" he asked David. His broad, Californian accent made everything he said sound particularly laid-back.

"Booming, as always. How was the honeymoon?"

"China was China, but that was just visiting family. Cyprus was phenomenal."

"And married life?"

"I love it. Kitty keeps me on my toes."

"I'll bet she does," Antoni said into his glass, and David shot him a wicked smirk.

Rhys was not amused by the banter, and glanced down at his watch. "When are we going to start?"

"God knows, with Wayne running things," Cameron said. Their High Priest was not known for his punctuality. "He's probably gearing up to give us another lecture on recruiting new blood."

"Ugh," Nathan groaned. "Evangelism."

"Maybe if he started reading the ten applications a year we get from qualified women we wouldn't have to rehash this discussion every week," Rhys said, bringing his drink to his lips. It could have been gin, or water. He always had a knack for temperance.

"Don't start that again," David sighed. "I'm too old for another controversy."

"If you ask me, Wayne's retirement can't come fast enough," Rhys said with a frown.

"You're saying you could do better?" Nathan asked, scandalized eyebrows shooting up towards his hairline. How he had managed to survive this long in a Society run almost entirely on backroom deals and scheming, David had no idea.

"I'd be sure we start on time, for starters," Rhys replied.

"You know you have my vote," Antoni said.

David wasn't surprised by the show of support. Induction into and advancement through the Society wasn't just determined by how well a man performed in his evaluations. At least two thirds of the active members had to vote in favor of any candidate, which led to its own rash of controversies. Most recently, there had been an argument over whether or not transgender men could be inducted. Nearly all the brothers had favored amending the bylaws, but a handful of the older men, the kind who liked to brag about having gay friends but still voted Republican, had dug in their heels, resulting in a stalemate. David, Cameron, and Nathan had refused to drop the issue, but Rhys in particular had gone to bat for Antoni, who had demonstrated immense natural talent and ironclad resolve to advance his skills during his evaluations.

In an impassioned speech – sketched out on little notecards, no less – Rhys had managed to sway enough of the fence-sitting members, and the bylaws had been amended. Since then, the two men had become fast friends, bonding over their Southie upbringings and their shared passion for dead languages. Antoni, never one to back down from a challenge, had soundly changed the minds of almost all his detractors, and shamed the most bigoted one into quitting the Society altogether. He would put Rhys's name down for High Priest without hesitation.

"Don't encourage him," David responded. "Think of all the homework he'd give us."

"I don't think there's anything wrong with making sure everyone in this Society is actually progressing in their magical practice and not just showing up to brownnose," Rhys said. "Or do you want it to devolve entirely into an Elks Lodge situation?"

"I just think the High Priesthood should go to someone with the sort of social prowess it takes to command a room like this," David said. "Someone with a natural magical aptitude who's been in the occult community for decades."

"Someone like you?"

"Your words, not mine."

Rhys was excellent at controlling spirits; that much was true. He could read Latin, German, and Greek, and could pick up new magical techniques so fast it was frightening. But he was still young, and too radical in his views to sit well with the older set. David, at nearly thirty, had mellowed out enough to gain the respect of the senior members. He came from an aristocratic background that bestowed ample social graces and family connections. Rhys, for all his intelligence and politeness, still radiated an ambitious middle-class energy that made old money nervous.

"I wouldn't mind seeing that," Cameron said. Something like a smile touched his lips when he met David's eyes.

"You're both getting ahead of yourselves," Nathan reminded them. "Wayne could just name a successor, and then no one would have to vote."

David let out a derisive laugh. "Wayne won't."

"Not in a million years," Rhys echoed. "There'd be another schism."

"He can't afford that. Not with the membership numbers looking so abysmal."

Wayne's booming laugh echoed from across the room, and David glanced over his shoulder to see the graying white man thump someone on the back. Wayne wasn't the worst High Priest the Society ever had. He even managed to keep out of the usual embezzlement accusations and sex scandals that seemed to afflict men his age and certain status. But things had stagnated, and everyone could feel it. The vultures had started to circle. There was talk of absorbing the Society into a larger, more established occult order, or bringing in someone out of Boston to whip them all into shape. Neither improved David's chances of advancement.

Wayne began to round up the men, ushering them towards the doors that separated the clubhouse from the inner sanctum where the Society did their ritual work. This was their cue to congregate. Nathan and Antoni abandoned their glasses and stood, drifting into the crowd meandering towards the day's encounter with the ephemeral. Cameron followed, and David had just fallen into step behind him when Rhys caught up, causing David to slow.

"Moira has a client who might be interested in talking to you," Rhys said. "They want a séance."

"You could just give her my number, you know," David said, doing his best to extend the olive branch. He didn't dislike Rhys's wife, not strictly speaking, and he knew from her reputation that she was one of the city's best readers. Magical competence was enough to make him respect anybody, even if he didn't exactly want to cozy up to them. "I can be nice."

"I somehow doubt that."

"Did you get a chance to think about my text?"

"I've been busy."

All of David's goodwill evaporated. "So, we're adding lying to our status quo list now? Does that mean I get to take pretending to like each other off?"

"You don't have to blow everything out of proportion. Either take the client or don't; I don't care either way."

David's temper sparked, but he smothered it down. There would be no reasoning with Rhys here, where they were surrounded by other people. Still, he was running out of patience for the injured, icy shoulder Rhys kept giving him. How many times did he have to say he was sorry? It had been six goddamn months.

But David didn't press as they slipped through the door into the perfumed darkness of the inner sanctum. He knew his chances of stealing a word during the ritual were zero, since Rhys attended to their cosmic playacting with rapt attention. He liked to insist he wasn't as religious as he used to be, but David knew that Rhys's moralistic affliction had only gotten worse with age. Confession or ritual bath, eucharist or the cup of initiation, it was all the same.

Conversation fell to a hush as the men reached for their wine-red robes, hung up neatly on a rolling rack, and pulled them on over their clothes. Rhys chatted quietly with the others, but he didn't meet David's eyes.

David scowled as he retrieved his robe, Nathan blithely talking his ear off about Cyprus. As far as David was concerned, if Rhys wasn't willing to play nice, David didn't have to obey the rules either. He hated apologizing, as a general rule, since he didn't often believe himself to be in the wrong, but a grand gesture along those lines might be the only thing that would help the situation.

A house call had gotten him into this mess. Maybe another one could fix it.

The High Priestess

CHAPTER FOUR

MOIRA

Moira Delacroix hummed to herself as she dusted off each piece of amethyst, rose quartz, and citrine in her crystal collection. The windows of her meditation room were thrown open to the balmy weather, welcoming in equinox breezes and the smell of evaporating morning rain. Moira's grandmother had taught her to respect the equinox as a powerful day of rebirth and new life, and it was a perfect time to clean out the clutter of winter.

Moira swept candle stubs and incense ash into a garbage bag. She and Rhys had set upon the townhouse as soon as the dishes had been cleared from breakfast, and as lunchtime approached, they were nearly done with the top level.

"Why do we have so much stuff?" Rhys called from the bedroom, a distant clatter following his voice as he knocked something over.

"Because you can't drive past an estate sale without pulling over."

Rhys appeared in the doorway in teal chinos and a rumpled button-down, with a smudge of grime on his nose. Soon, the sun would bring back the smattering of freckles across his face, the ones that made him look much younger than twenty-six if he smiled. But now he was wearing his usual vaguely dour expression.

"I like antiques," he huffed, dumping an armful of throw pillows on the ground. "And you have too many pillows. They're going to smother us in our sleep."

Moira gathered the puffs of sea foam cotton, teal velvet, and lilac suede to her chest.

"But they're so pretty!"

"They can be pretty in your meditation room. Pick two for our room."

"Four."

"Three, and I'll let you keep the pink one."

A knock at the front door cut off their negotiations. Rhys turned to head down the stairs, doing his best to arrange his hair into some semblance of order.

"I've got it. It looks like you're on a roll in there."

"So, four?" she called after him from the landing.

"Three!" Rhys demanded, but laughter broke any resolve left in his voice.

Moira chuckled as she began re-introducing her meditation room pillows to their exiled bedroom brethren. It could be anyone at the door: a walk-in tarot client or the UPS delivery man with another international order for Rhys.

Moira froze when she heard Rhys's voice, crisp as an ice storm and devoid of his usual courtesy.

"Absolutely not."

"You weren't taking my calls, and I was in the area."

She knew that voice, buttery and plying.

Moira's skin turned to steel.

"That's no excuse for showing up on my doorstep," her husband continued. "I asked you for space."

"It's been half a year. You're pushing me out."

"I have every right to."

"Rhys?" Moira called out, voice a little higher than she would have liked. "Who is it?"

"No one!" Rhys called back. He immediately dropped his voice out of audible range, but Moira could still follow his irritated rhythm.

"I thought we agreed on civility," the other man said, apparently not caring whether she heard him or not. "The civil thing to do would be to invite me inside."

This was all Moira could stand. Wiping her hands off on a dust rag, she marched out onto the landing at the top of stairs.

David Aristarkhov stood in her doorway, looking poisonously at ease with his sunglasses on, hands tucked into the pockets of his navy blazer.

He slipped his sunglasses into his breast pocket and glanced over Rhys's shoulder, eyes alighting on Moira. They were a pale green that would have been pretty on a nicer face.

"Are you going to invite me in?" he asked Rhys.

Rhys's shoulders sagged and he stepped aside.

"Ten minutes. That's all I'm giving you. Don't expect coffee and finger sandwiches."

David slipped into the foyer, taking in the framed portraits and cityscapes on the wall. Rhys couldn't afford much genuine art on his associate librarian's salary, but he had an eye for convincing fakes. Moira did her best to brighten up Rhys's tastes for heavy furnishings with cream-colored backsplashes and potted plants, and they had found an equilibrium between historic charm and shabby chic. But David was a blight on her Eden, filling the space with his blinding arrogance and the sharp scent of his bergamot cologne.

"This had better be good, David," Rhys muttered. "You had better be on death's door or about to tell me I'm getting promoted to High Priest. I'm serious."

"I assure you," David said. He probably thought he sounded suave, but to Moira he just sounded like a used car salesman. "Intruding on your evening is not my intention."

"Don't do that," Rhys snapped. "That Aristarkhov charm thing. I can tell when you're doing it, and I hate it. Just shoot straight with me and then get out of my house."

"Ms Delacroix," David said. At least he was respecting the fact that she had elected to keep her name after marriage, something many men overlooked. It felt like a gesture of kindness. Moira didn't trust it. "I hope I haven't come at a bad time."

Moira fumed. The last time David had stepped foot in her home, he had accused her of witching up a thoughtform to torment her husband. David hadn't been entirely off base; the dark entity banging cupboards and stealing sentimental keepsakes *was* a thoughtform, a mass of negative energy brought to life by the unkempt emotions of its magician-creator. But it had been made by both Rhys and Moira, accidentally, over many months of refusing to discuss problems in their marriage.

Moira and Rhys had spent the next six months making painstaking progress towards healing. They were working on their communication.

Things were getting better. And more David was the last thing their marriage needed.

She gave David the eyes her grandmother had always given her when she was in deep trouble. She hoped she looked forbidding, even in wide-legged overalls and the silk scarf around her hair tied in a big bow.

"No better than any," Moira said.

"What are you doing here, David?" Rhys asked.

"I came by to apologize."

Every line of his Rhys's body went taut as a violin string.

"Apologize? No, no. You don't apologize to anyone. Being a dick about being right is your whole *thing*."

David glowered at him. "Easy."

Moira rested her hip against the banister, settling in to watch the boys go at it. She had been raised by Southern women and a chivalrous father. She was fine letting her husband rise to her defense as much as he pleased before she laid into David herself.

"I invited you into my home," Rhys went on. "I gave you everything you asked for, and you completely betrayed my trust."

"You asked me for my professional opinion about a haunting," David clarified. "Judging by the evidence available to me at the time, a thoughtform seemed like a viable explanation. I wasn't wrong."

"That doesn't put you in the right. You upset me, and you insulted Moira, and we nearly killed each other fighting when you left. It took us an hour to figure it out, and by then it was almost too late."

David shrugged, trying to look sympathetic. It didn't sit right on his features.

"Does that mean I'm not allowed to apologize?"

Rhys turned from David with a sharp *tsk* through his teeth. "I'm done with this. If you're dead set on apologizing, apologize to Moira."

David eyed her lazily, a snake debating whether or not its would-be prey was worth the energy it took to slither out of the sun. Moira pulled herself tall as a cypress and eyed him right back. She wasn't positive apologizing was even a thing a man like him could do, as it involved making himself smaller so that someone else could take up space. He probably hadn't had much practice in his life.

To her surprise, David approached the stairs, pausing with one foot up on the first step. The gesture was oddly gallant.

"Go on," she said, Southern accent sweet as strychnine. "Impress me."

"As I understood it," David began, "you took offense to some… allegations I made last fall."

Moira snorted and tossed her head.

"It's possible I was a little hasty in my diagnosis of the problem," David went on. "I'm sorry if you felt singled out or bullied."

Rhys lingered close as a shadow to David, arms crossed over his chest. He looked like he had half a mind to drag David back out of the house and throw up a couple of nasty wards to make sure he never got back in.

Moira descended the stairs, and kept advancing when she reached David's level. He took an unsure step back. Confidence flickered off his face for only a fraction of a second, but it still felt like a victory.

She always told her clients that forgiveness wasn't about the person who wronged you; it was about freeing yourself from resentment and moving on with your life. Her distaste for David was an old companion, a stubborn grudge she nursed in private. But Rhys didn't have many friends, certainly not ones that had stuck by him as long as David had, and she knew she had no right to take that away from him. She might be ready to make peace with David's existence, but not his attitude, and only on her terms.

"I don't forgive you."

David blinked. "Sorry. You… don't forgive me?"

"No, I don't. I have no indication that you actually feel any remorse, and moreover, I'm under no obligation to give you my goodwill even if I did. But I might be more inclined to believe you if you tell me why you're actually here. What do you want, David?"

"I wanted to apologize."

"You wouldn't have come all the way out to Jamaica Plain for an apology. I know you've been trying to contact my husband. What's going on?"

David glanced over at Rhys. "I was hoping we could talk alone," he said.

"What do we have to talk about, David?" Rhys sighed.

"Fifteen minutes. That's all I'm asking."

"Whatever you have to say in front of my husband, you can say in front of me," Moira said. "Just spit it out, already. You're damn near close to wrecking my Saturday."

David took a deep breath, as though what he was about to say pained him physically. "I'm, uh… a little, how shall I put this. Unwell."

"Unwell," Moira repeated slowly.

David's shoulders were tight with discomfort at having to show weakness. Moira felt a touch guilty for enjoying the sight, but not enough to deny herself the pleasure of reveling in it.

"And Rhys is the only person you could think to come to when you're feeling unwell, is that it?" she prodded, twisting the knife a little.

"I had thought that *you* might offer a second opinion, actually. I hear such good things from your clients." He gave her a smile, one that might have charmed the pants off someone else, but she saw it for what it was: Desperation.

No matter how much she might not want to admit it, Moira was curious. And her curiosity, as her mother always used to tell her, could rival any cat's.

"Fine," Moira said crisply. She turned from him and started down the hallway. "Stop hanging around the doorway; y'all are making me nervous. There are chairs in the kitchen, and coffee. You can have your fifteen minutes there."

The kitchen was hazy with steam from the bisque bubbling on the stove, and thick with the scent of oregano and bay. Dragon's blood incense, sweet and musky, lingered in the air as protection against negative energy.

Rhys cleared her flower cuttings and his abandoned glasses of iced coffee from the table. David lingered in the doorway, almost looking spooked to step onto the tile.

"Haven't you ever been in a kitchen before?" Moira asked dryly. "Or does your personal chef handle that?"

David's eyes flashed in irritation, but then his expression was smooth again.

"No, I'm just taking it all in. Is this your office?"

She glanced around at the hand-labelled jars of herbs, flavored honeys, and graveyard dirt sitting out on shelves, and the witch's ladders tied with colorful thread in the window. She had stuffed the little room with all the plants it could hold, mostly ones with medicinal properties mentioned in rootwork lore. It was her effort to recreate her grandmother's garden, as well as she could this far from the fertile soil of sweltering Georgia.

She imagined what David's workspace might look like. There would probably be crystal balls, and spirit boards, and all those other methods of communicating with the dead that her mother had strictly forbidden her from using growing up.

Not that it kept the dead from trying to reach out to her, anyway, but David didn't need to know that.

"Suppose so," she said.

Moira handed Rhys two floral mugs and nodded towards the coffee pot, nudging him towards hospitality. He was as tightly polite as any New Englander raised by strict Irish parents, who hadn't been brought up in an entertaining household.

Rhys poured coffee and a swirl of cream into David's cup, then slid down into a chair while Moira discreetly set out a plate of coconut meringues. Store-bought, because David didn't deserve the custard pie chilling in the fridge.

"Unwell, huh?" Rhys said.

David settled against the side of the island but couldn't quite bring himself to take a seat.

"What do you know about demon possession?"

"What kind?"

"The Catholic kind. Is there anything to it, or is it just something priests say to scare altar boys into going to confession?"

Rhys blinked at him, unamused. "You open up your body to the dead and goetic spirits and God knows what else every Thursday in conclave. How can you even ask if it's real or not?"

David waved Rhys's words away with a breezy gesture.

"I'm not an open door. I play host and then, when I'm done, I send the spirit back to where it came from. I'm always in control."

Rhys shot him a dark look, then drained half his coffee cup in one swallow. "If you want my opinion, possession against one's will is possible, but it's rare. You need a very spiritually weak host, a powerful entity, and the right environment and timing. It's always because someone has some sort of contract with the demon, or because they're channeling for a certain time under certain controlled circumstances. Even if that wasn't the case... I don't know, I feel like there would have to be someone pulling the strings."

"Why are you so interested in this, anyway?" Moira asked.

"I was with a client recently and I got a little bit more than I bargained for. It was one of your referrals, actually." He smirked in a way he probably thought looked friendly. "Better than the last one you sent my way, though. He cried the whole time I was trying to get hold of his dead wife. So distracting."

Moira bristled. There was something about the thin layer of disdain glossed over most everything he said that got her hackles up.

"Sorry, do you just want me to send you the bereaved who can behave themselves? Or should I stick with the ones who are willing to pay your exorbitant fees?"

"*Moira*," Rhys said, halfway between a warning and a plea.

David laughed brightly. "Two-hundred and fifty an hour is hardly exorbitant, in our line. What are you charging, anyway? You do all that energy healing stuff; you should be going for at least that, if you're as good as your clients say."

"I *am* good," she shot back, scandalized that he was trying to get her to discuss hard numbers in mixed company. "And I know what it's like to live paycheck to paycheck."

"So why keep that up if you don't have to?"

"*David*," Rhys said.

"I'm being nice!" David exclaimed, looking absolutely martyred. "I told you I would do my best to be nice, didn't I?"

Moira turned abruptly to deposit her dishes in the sink. She wanted David gone, but her father hadn't spent thirty hours stitching her cotillion dress so she could throw good raising out the window whenever she felt like it.

Rhys caught Moira gently and tugged her back towards the table, nestling his arm around her waist. She smoldered in silence, but his reassuring closeness dampened her anger.

"Let's get back on track," he said to David. "Plenty of people think they're possessed the same way plenty of people think their houses are haunted. It's rarely the case; you know that. So, you were with a client. Then what happened?"

David rolled his shoulders. "Something… grabbed me. I don't know how else to phrase it. It's like when I channel a spirit in conclave, only I didn't decide to open myself up to it. One second I was fine, and the next second I was seeing stars. I haven't felt right since."

"And you're sure it wasn't the ghost you were talking to?"

"Positive. It felt entirely different."

"What did it feel like?"

David flexed and unflexed his hands at his side, searching for the right words. "Old. Malignant."

"Demonic," Rhys supplied.

"Your word, not mine. But I've seen a lot of wild shit in my life, and I'm not going to take demon possession off the list just because I don't understand it. This is your playground, Rhys." Moira got the impression that whatever David was about to say next was only happening with great effort. "Listen, I'd love your help diagnosing the problem. I'm happy to pay consultancy rates."

"No way."

"Why not?"

"Because I don't want to, David, and because I'm busy. I'm sorry you're having trouble with your mediumship, but that's not my responsibility. If you really need help that badly, call a priest."

David looked like he would rather swallow tacks than get on the phone with the Church.

"That's it, then? Just, no?"

"I can say it again if you'd like."

Moira chewed the inside of her mouth. A thought, as bold as it was petty, was bubbling up inside her. "How old are you, David?"

David was so taken aback by the question he answered without hesitation. "Twenty-nine."

"You're probably in your Saturn return. It's a particularly tough astrological transit that can bring up all sorts of issues about ability, identity, and life purpose. It's been known to mess with intuitive people especially badly." Moira ran a hand lightly through Rhys's curls, her mind whirring. "Baby, go get me my charts."

Looking dubious, Rhys pushed himself up from the table. He disappeared from the kitchen with a parting glance at David, which was probably meant to bring him to heel. The little room was chillier in his absence, despite the fragrant steam still rising from the stove.

"Want to let me in on what you've got in mind?" David asked.

Moira wiped the powdered sugar off her fingers with a tea towel, then put her hands on her hips. "Giving you that second opinion you asked for."

"Why would you do that?"

"Because I don't like seeing anybody getting harassed by nasty entities, no matter my opinion on the person." It wasn't entirely a lie, but she wasn't about to admit she also wanted the pleasure of showing him exactly how good she was at what she did. The men of the Society liked to say they respected all magical paths, and that they recognized that power could take many forms. David, however, had never had the opportunity to really see her at work, to taste the magic that had been handed down to her from her mother and grandmother. She might not know her way around a goetic circle, but she was damn good with the stars. "I can do your natal chart, if you want. If there's anything in there about facing a health or spiritual crisis right about now, I should be able to see it. Unless you're the type who thinks astrology is just a party trick."

"You're still angry," he said, like he was noting something for the court record.

"Fit to be tied, if you want to know."

She did not in fact, want him to know, but as much as she might want to radiate effortless cool in his presence, she had never been good at hiding her emotions.

David helped himself to a bit more coffee and cream as though this were his own house. When he spoke, it was in a tone so light it had to be calculated.

"Is this about my having dated your husband, or about my accusing you of cursing him?"

"Don't flatter yourself," she shot back. "It's the second."

"You really do hold grudges, don't you?" He nodded and took an introspective sip of coffee. "I think that's fair."

She glanced over at him in suspicion, but if he was pulling her around, his face didn't show it. As a matter of fact, David seemed entirely unbothered by her disdain. Admiring, even.

"I mean it," he went on. "I crossed you, so you can hold a grudge as long as you like. When people embarrass me, they're on my shit list for life, and sometimes on the ground with a broken nose first."

She had assumed that David had never felt embarrassment, that he floated from social hierarchy to social hierarchy, impervious to insults and gossip. He certainly carried himself like that was the case. But maybe that was just more grandstanding.

David drained his coffee, and Moira reached out instinctively to take the empty cup from him. As she did so, their fingers brushed, and a tiny crack of electricity sparked between them.

David's skin was hot, almost like he was fighting off a fever. Unbidden, a rush of emotion coursed through Moira's fingers and up her arm. As a born intuitive, this was one of her many abilities: to be able to pick up someone's feelings simply by touching them. But she rarely felt anyone's emotions with such supercharged clarity, so strong and clear that it made the hair on the back of her neck stand up.

David snatched his hand back, staring at her in bafflement.

"You shocked me," he said quietly.

Moira folded her hands and fixed him with her most compassionate gaze. She suddenly felt in control again. "You don't have to be nervous around me."

"I'm *not* nervous," David said, with so much petulance he almost sounded like a teenager. "How long have you been able to–"

Rhys returned, his arms full of notebooks and star charts. He dumped them on the table, and Moira sorted through the huge rolls of indigo paper that cataloged the night sky. Rhys had also brought down the dingy plastic star finders she had stolen from her high school, and the stacks of spiral-ring notebooks where she meticulously recorded eclipses, new and full moons, and of course, birth charts.

"I'll need your place and time of birth," she said, making the executive decision to sweep whatever had just transpired between her and David under the rug. There would be plenty of time to turn it over in her head later. "Date too, of course."

David pulled a pen out of his pocket and jotted the data points down on a nearby sticky pad. Rhys sidled up to his wife, his fingers brushing over the top of her wrist in a silent question. Unlike David, his anxiety was faint and indistinct, more a suggestion of a feeling than anything else.

"I know what I'm about," she said to him, too quietly for David to hear. Rhys nodded, and that was that.

"The placements of the planets at the time of someone's birth exert influence over their temperament," Moira said. "But they continue to exert influence over us during the rest of our lives. Our bodies are seventy percent water; the moon pushes and pulls on us, and sometimes we get caught in planetary crossfires. Astrology has material benefits. If you know what's going on in your client's stars, you know what's going on with them."

"Alright," David said. "Do it."

"Happy to. But it's an involved process, and I need to run my numbers. I wouldn't suggest hanging around here waiting."

"What's your turnaround time like?"

"A few days, if I clear my schedule."

"Beautiful." David pulled out his wallet and flipped it open. "What's your fee?"

Rhys shot up from his slouch against the kitchen counter, nearly swatting the wallet out of David's hand. "We don't want your money, David."

"Uh, I do," Moira said, baffled by her husband's hair-trigger reaction. She thrust her open hand out between the two men. "It's one-fifty."

David scoffed. "For a full natal chart? You *are* undercharging."

"I didn't ask you for business advice, I asked you for one-fifty."

David peeled off two hundred-dollar bills from a neatly clipped stack and placed them in Moira's hand.

"Call the extra fifty a tip for taking a walk-in. Maybe you can buy Rhys a sense of humor."

"Well, this has been loads of fun," Rhys said acidly. "But your fifteen minutes are up, and now I think it's time for you to get the hell out of my house."

"I'm going, I'm going," David said, already halfway out of the room. He threw one parting glance over his shoulder to Moira, surveying her spread of materials on the kitchen table. "Thank you for your time, Ms Delacroix. I look forward to hearing from you."

With that, he was gone, the front door swinging shut behind him. Rhys seethed in silence and watched him out the kitchen window.

Moira didn't say anything until the purr of the Audi had disappeared down the street. "You can't tell that boy anything."

Rhys killed the rest of his coffee, and grimaced. "You're preaching to the choir."

"How many times are you going to cut him off just to let him back in again?"

"You're the one that invited him into the kitchen."

She worried at her thumbnail with her teeth. "Is it wicked of me to want to show off a bit?"

"Of course not, little goddess. It's good for him to realize that there are people besides him who know what they're talking about."

"I wouldn't get my hopes up about that," she said with a sigh. She seated herself at the table, settling in for a long session of filling in logarithm tables and cross-checking planetary placements. "You have terrible taste in friends. And in men."

"You go through a couple of near-death experiences with someone in college and suddenly you're stuck with them for life."

"Is it him that's stuck on you, or are you stuck on him?" she mused aloud.

Rhys gave her a startled look, bringing an affronted hand to his chest. Moira smirked right back.

"You're going to give me gray hairs," he said. "Both of you."

"I keep you young, Rhys McGowan, and you know it. Now get outta here and let me earn my two-hundred dollars."

Rhys stole a kiss, then left her to lose herself in the familiar sea of trigonometry, astronomy, and divination.

The hanged man

CHAPTER FIVE

DAVID

David stood on the steps of the courthouse, lighting up a self-congratulatory cigarette. A supernatural knack for persuasion was a handy asset to have as a prosecutor. And as a result, David rarely lost cases, but he liked competing with himself anyway. He had wrapped closing statements in under three minutes, a personal record, and walked away with an easy conviction. Now he had an hour or so to kill before he had to start getting ready for another séance with a client. He narrowly avoided double-booking himself on some days, but it was better than sitting around idle with nothing to do but listen to himself think. David had been born and bred to achieve, and nothing made him happier than working. Even if work didn't come quite as easily these days as it had in the recent past.

David hadn't been able to shake off the cold, sick feeling that had overtaken him when his mind was intruded upon. It rose up in his throat whenever he channeled, and he was starting to get tension headaches when he communicated with the dead for more than a half hour or so. Group séances, which had once been a buffet of praise and parlor tricks, now sapped him to his core.

It had been nearly a week already, and he had never heard back from Moira about the natal chart, which was probably just as well. He still wasn't convinced celestial alignments were of any use outside of cheap pick-up lines, and owing Moira Delacroix favor was not a position anyone should put themselves in lightly. The witch may be sweet as peach cobbler, but she kept meticulous records. She had a reputation in Boston for mending marriages, forging friendships, and whipping up spells that would make anyone's in-laws fawn on them, but she also knew her way around a hex, and was imbued with such a strong sense of cosmic justice that David could see why people were wary to cross her. She remained, to David, something of a mystery. She was effortlessly kind and gracious, but there was a streak of electricity undercutting her energy that David recognized intuitively: power calling to power. He highly suspected that she was capable of much more than the services she advertised, and there was already plenty on her magical menu.

He also didn't like the way she had been able to read his emotions with one fleeting touch. He preferred his feelings under lock and key, not flayed open for the world to see.

His phone rang just as he was turning to go fetch the Audi from the garage and drive to his next appointment.

Rhys. Thank God.

David pulled the phone to his ear. "I was starting to think you weren't going to call."

"I called you when I was good and ready," Moira said. "But if you're gonna be cross with me, I'll hang right up and keep this natal chart to myself."

"Ms Delacroix," David said, sounding more taken aback than he would have liked. "Why are you calling me from Rhys's phone?"

"You mightn't have picked up a call from a strange number."

This, he had to admit, was fair. Still, his skin felt itchy and tight at the forced conversation with his ex's wife. He only started things like that on his own terms. He had done his best to give Moira a wide berth ever since she had started dating Rhys, not really wanting to know her more deeply than was politely necessary. They tended to avoid each other at Society functions, and he had only had a private conversation with her once, on her wedding day, when he had awkwardly excused himself from the party. Weddings, with their open bars and obligatory glasses of champagne, were hard for anyone trying to stay sober, and doubly hard for anyone having to watch their college sweetheart marry someone else.

"Where's Rhys?" he asked, trying to keep his voice light.

"Out and about somewhere, I don't know. Probably picking up wine for dinner; he can't abide reds in warm weather, and we're out of white."

She was taking deep, slow breaths every few sentences, speaking in a falling lilt on the exhale. There was the gentle rustle of cloth in the background.

"What are you doing over there?"

"Sun salutations."

The thought of Moira flicking him onto speakerphone while she went through her morning strength-training routine was enough to short-circuit something in his brain. Was she taking this seriously *at all*?

"Do you think you could… not?"

"Yoga helps me think."

"Then think; I only have a few minutes."

"Funny how all those live-in tutors don't seem to have taught you any manners."

If David was an unstoppable force, Moira was an immoveable object. There was something infuriating about her self-possession, her unshakeable poise. David typically liked people who carried themselves with a sense of authority, and under other circumstances, he might have liked Moira Delacroix immensely. She was smart, she was powerful, and she had a poison wit, all qualities David appreciated. But he hated having to ask for help from anyone, least of all his ex's new wife, so in the here and now, he simmered with irritation.

"If you get to do yoga while we're on the phone, I don't have to be sweet about it. This is a business call, isn't it?"

"That it is. So, let's get to business, shall we?" There was a little grunt and sigh on the other end as Moira changed positions, maybe pushing herself into a plank. By the sounds of it, she was holding that plank without losing her breath. Moira was composed entirely of soft, rounded lines, but David was getting the impression that she could probably keep pace with him in the gym during cardio day. "First of all, you're a double Leo with a Virgo moon. Appearances are everything to you, but so is meticulous attention to detail and material security. You're only comfortable when you're at the center of attention, performing."

David bristled, and he considered lobbing another barb her way, but he swallowed it down. Nice. He had promised to be nice.

"There have been a lot of chaotic transits in your chart lately, playing havoc with your emotional well-being and gut instincts," Moira went on. "You're likely to catastrophize any little thing. So that tells me it's possible you're reading too much into things, jumping at demons where there aren't any."

"This is a false alarm?"

"I didn't say that. I said your instincts are a bit raw right now. You're smack in the middle of your Saturn return, as I suspected. The planet of duty is transiting back to where it was when you were born, causing tension in your sense of self and purpose. If there are life lessons you've refused to learn up until this point, they're gonna come back to bite you."

David pressed his mouth into a thin line.

"So, the cosmos is conspiring against me. Is that all?"

"About all you can understand."

David smiled tightly. "Well, it's been a pleasure."

"Oh, mutual. I'll send Rhys over with the full write-up to the next Society meeting; I just wanted to deliver the spark notes myself. Don't keep him too late this week; we have a movie date."

"Have a nice day, Ms Delacroix."

David let the line go dead and sucked down the rest of his cigarette. He tamped down the disappointment in his chest about there being no easy answer to his predicament written in the stars, or about Rhys not being the one on the other end of the phone. They had shared everything, once, bouncing supernatural theories and spiritual experiences off each other until they reached some climax of enlightenment. It had worked exceptionally well until it had all burned to the ground.

David retrieved another cigarette from the carton and scrolled through his contacts until he found Leda's number. It was nearly one in the afternoon. If he was lucky, he would catch her just as she was waking up.

The phone rang four times before anyone picked up.

"Hey," he said. "Welcome to the land of the living."

"Welcome to the land of calling people back," Leda quipped in her voice like smoked velvet. David heard fabric rustling in the background, and the low murmur of a man's voice. One of Leda's boyfriends, probably. "I was starting to think you'd disowned me."

"Oh, I'll get around to it eventually. How's life? Still leading astray the souls of America's youth?"

Leda chuckled, followed by the metallic flick of a cigarette lighter. "Last night was college night, and it was a raging success, so I guess so."

"How are things at the club?"

"Good, good. Allston's a happening neighborhood to be in. Nowhere is New York, but I'm willing to forgive Boston."

Leda was the owner of a nightclub on the other side of town, an expansion of her already lucrative success with a sister club in Greenwich village. She had been splitting her time between Boston and New York for almost four months now, and David had still only gotten around to having dinner with her once. Family wasn't his strong suit, and both Aristarkhov children had an independent streak a mile wide. Still, it was rare that his sister stopped touring long enough to be found in the country, much less in his very own city, and he knew he should make more of an effort.

"That's good," he said awkwardly. He never knew how these things were supposed to go.

"How are things with you?" Leda asked, switching on to speakerphone.

"Oh, you know," David said, sucking down his cigarette. He tapped his foot, debating whether to tell Leda anything about what had been happening to him. Childhood instincts to confess everything to his older sister swelled up, but he tamped them down. "Fine. Work's busy, but fine."

"What about your other job?"

"The séance business is booming. There are always grieving widows and rich party kids looking for a taste of the supernatural. How's the cult leader business?"

"I've told you before," Leda said, with a wicked laugh, "it's more of an ecstatic sect. And it's going great; I had five people over for a ritual last Friday night and a couple of them stuck around to make me breakfast in the morning."

David made a generalized listening sound, since he could never tell when Leda was being serious, being salacious, or just messing with him. He settled on messing with him for this round, then sighed.

"Well, I just wanted to touch base. You know. It's been a while."

"It has. Come by the club some weekend; we'll do a VIP room, the whole nine yards."

"I appreciate it, but I'm working this weekend."

"You work too much, David. I miss you."

"I miss you too," David said quietly, almost afraid of being overheard by anyone who worked in the courthouse. He kept his feelings for his sister close to his chest and he wasn't good at talking about them, but he did care.

"I'll let you get back to work," Leda said breezily. "You sound busy. But don't be a stranger, alright?"

David nodded. It was easier to be in person with Leda; the phone calls always felt forced. "Great. I'll take you out for lunch sometime soon. I promise."

"I'll hold you to it. Later."

The call disconnected, and David was left alone on the steps of the courthouse.

The Chariot

CHAPTER SIX

RHYS

Rhys arrived at the Society on Saturday early to soothe his jangling nerves, and camped out in his usual velvet chair in the corner of the hall. Meeting David here had somehow seemed more appropriate than out at a café, but it still felt dangerously close to socializing. That was against the rules he had laid down after his and David's latest falling out, the ones that carefully circumscribed his life and ensured David stayed on the outside of it.

This was just business, Rhys reminded himself. He was just here to deliver Moira's natal chart reading and to discuss a topic of purely academic interest. That wasn't breaking any rules, and that didn't mean that he and David were on good terms.

Rhys's hands itched for something to hold, and he considered fixing himself a gin and tonic from the small but always-stocked bar. He thought better of it at the last minute, partially because it was two in the afternoon and partially because it seemed unkind to drink that early in front of a recovering alcoholic.

He tried not to think about how the motivation behind his restraint was inherently gentle. Friendly, even.

David arrived right on time, sweeping into the room like he owned it. His already golden complexion was set off by a tan he probably acquired sailing with Nathan and Kitty, his hair impeccably set. Rhys's jaw tightened. David radiated aristocratic privilege and generational wealth. Everything Rhys couldn't have, no matter how hard he worked or how furiously he networked.

In a dark, bitter corner of his heart, Rhys hated David for the effortlessness with which he navigated the world. And he hated him more for having the audacity to look *that* good while doing it.

David took a seat next to him. Not across from him, as was their custom when the rest of their set were around, but right next to him, in Antoni's usual seat. Close enough that his knee brushed against Rhys's.

Rhys jerked back from the touch a bit too quickly, earning a scoff from David.

"I'm not going to bite you," David muttered. "And whatever I've got isn't catching. At least I don't think it is."

"We haven't figured that out yet."

"We? So now you're on board with the investigation?"

"Don't get carried away," Rhys said, producing a manila envelope from his messenger bag. The bag was battered from long days and longer nights in the library as an undergraduate, but it was real leather, and full of sentimental value besides. Not that Rhys could afford to splurge on another one.

He tossed the envelope down on the small table in front of them, and David leaned over and began to flip through the contents. His eyes flicked over Moira's tidy handwriting, taking in her sketched diagrams of constellations and her diagnosis of the placements of the stars at the time of his birth.

David studied the pages so intently that it almost seemed indecent to watch him, like Rhys was witnessing something intimate. This close, he could see the flicker of David's eyes behind his heavily-lashed lids, watch the bob of his Adam's apple while he swallowed. This close, Rhys's skin felt hot and too tight.

Rhys laced his fingers together and cleared his throat.

David glanced up at him, pulled back out of his private world. "Am I boring you?"

That flat, sarcastic intonation burrowed right under Rhys's skin, and he scowled at David. "I was curious as to your thoughts, actually. But if you're going to be rude, I can just leave."

They were quickly approaching one of their tipping points, when irritated barbs would either spark into an all-out fight or be accepted into the normal lull of conversation. David looked at Rhys like he might really take a bite out of him, then seemed to think better of things and shrugged.

"It's certainly thorough. I didn't realize astrology got so specific."

"Moira's good at what she does."

David merely nodded, taking in the notes for a few minutes more before fixing Rhys with a perceptive, green-eyed gaze.

"She is, isn't she? But then again, you always had a soft spot for magical people."

Rhys refused to meet David's eyes.

"How did you two meet?" David went on.

This got Rhys's attention. He stared at David, wondering if he had somehow misheard. "Since when do you care?"

"I'm just making polite conversation, Rhys, no need to go on the defensive." David flipped to the next page, running his finger along one of Moira's diagrams. "It was when you were still at Williams, wasn't it? After I graduated?"

"That's right," Rhys said, settling into the story despite his unease around the other man. It was one he had told a thousand times, one he still loved to recount despite present company. "We ran into each other at the same crossroads outside of town, both hoping to do a ritual during a certain cosmic alignment. We needed to kill time before it started, so she invited me into the bed of her truck, and we read each other's tarot cards and shared a bottle of mead. We ended up missing the alignment, we got so lost in each other."

"There's another part to that story though, isn't there? Something about a name?"

Rhys raised an eyebrow. "Have I told you this one before?"

"I might have overheard it once or twice. But I like hearing you tell it."

Rhys blinked, a little taken aback at the flicker of naked honesty from David, usually so above-it-all.

"The ritual I had planned out... It was supposed to reveal the name of the person I was going to marry. I met Moira that night instead, so I guess I got my answer."

David nodded to himself. And for a moment, Rhys thought he might say something else unexpected, something earnest, or even kind. But then David flipped the envelope shut and tossed his head, that same guarded look back in his eyes. "Thanks for playing messenger boy. Was there anything else?"

That 'anything else' felt awfully open-ended, and Rhys wasn't sure what David was getting at. Rhys shifted uncomfortably in his chair, a dozen things to say bubbling up to the surface. He wanted to dress David down for what he had done to Moira all over again, but he also wanted to ask how David had been, and then actually listen to the answer. He wanted to tell David to keep his distance and not get the wrong idea about them being friends again, but he also wanted to make sure that David's condition hadn't gotten any worse. He wanted to put as much space between himself and David as possible, but he also wanted to thread his fingers through David's hair and tug.

In the end, Rhys settled on politics. The emotionally disengaged machinations of Society politics made him feel safe. That was where the world made sense. "Actually, now that I have you…"

"You could have had me anytime. It was you who told me to keep my distance." David said it matter-of-factly, like he was laying out evidence in a court case.

Rhys glowered at him. "You and I don't exactly do well in close quarters, remember?"

David leaned back in his chair and steepled his fingers, probably flipping through his mental book of all the arguments he could dredge up. His favorite ones: the ones that made Rhys look like the bad guy.

"Where do you want to start? The time you walked out on me or the time you tried to kill me in conclave?"

Rhys didn't take the bait. "I'm not looking for a fight, David. We might not be friends, but I don't have any ill will towards you. If I did, I wouldn't have let you into my house. I would have hexed you six ways to Sunday instead."

"See, those sound like fighting words to me."

Rhys took a deep, steadying breath and leaned in closer to David, shrinking the gap between them. David's eyes flickered to Rhys's mouth for a millisecond.

"I'm worried about you," Rhys said, voice low. His stomach did a somersault, telling him that he was treading into dangerous waters. He *should* keep his distance. He should pretend not to care. "You show up to my house, talking about demons? That's not like you. Have you been having any more of those sick spells?"

"Spare me the sympathy, please. You know I don't go in for it."

"Then tell me what's really going on here."

David's eyes flashed with annoyance, but he didn't make another smart comment, or excuse himself to leave. That was a small victory in and of itself. Rhys couldn't remember the last time one of their conversations hadn't blown up in his face.

"I'm not sure," David said. He smoothed his hands over his eyes, and looked very tired all of sudden.

Had he been sleeping? Old, treacherous instincts to soothe, to offer David a soft place to land when he bottomed out, welled up inside Rhys. It would be so easy to touch him, in this dark corner of the room with nobody paying attention to them. He could reach out and squeeze David's knee, or spread his palm against his thigh, or...

No, Rhys chided himself internally, guilt making him feel suddenly sick. *None of that.*

"I've been turning it over in my head, but none of it makes any sense. And there was something else. Something I didn't mention before. A name." David's gaze darted over to Rhys, almost like he was second-guessing what he was about to say, but then he gave over his secret. "Whatever took over during the séance spoke to me. It called me 'son of Anatoly'."

"Your father's name was Evgeni."

"I know. But I've been mulling it over, and I realized that I *have* seen that name before. A long time ago. In the library at the house on Beacon Hill."

Rhys felt his eyebrows creep skyward. "You're going back there?"

"Sounds like I have to, if I want to figure this out. I was thinking this weekend, maybe."

Rhys's voice softened, perhaps more than he wanted it to. He spoke before he could stop himself. "You don't have to go if you don't want to, David."

David gave him a wry look. "I thought we weren't friends."

Rhys caught himself and drew back into his seat. Stupid. It had been stupid to show his hand like that; he didn't know what he was thinking.

You can never think straight when you're around him. You know better than this.

He took a long drink of his water to cover his embarrassment, then steered the conversation back into more comfortable waters.

"You're right. I want to talk about the Priesthood."

This caught David's attention. He took in every inch of Rhys, trying to sniff out a motive. Rhys didn't blame him. He wasn't a liar – there were more elegant ways of getting what he wanted – but Rhys did very little without an ulterior motive. Even charity miraculously ended up benefitting him in the long run.

"I won't pull my name out of the running, if that's what you're asking," David said.

"I wouldn't dream of asking you," Rhys said, showing his teeth when he smiled. "Running unopposed would make me look weak."

"Speaking of opposition, you'd better watch your back. Antoni might be your friend, but he's hungry. He'll swipe the crown right out from under you if you give him half a chance."

"It's not Antoni I'm worried about. When the time comes," Rhys said, crossing his ankle over his knee and trying to look at ease, "will you kneel? Or should I be expecting a coup?"

Every Society brother took a knee and swore fealty to the new High Priest during the ascension ritual. It was a dusty old bit of pageantry, but like most rituals, it held weight for Rhys.

David retrieved a cigarette from his pocket and placed it between his lips, smiling to himself. Rhys hated that imperious curve to David's mouth. He hated its surety and arrogance, and he hated the way he still couldn't help but admire the shape of it.

"I won't put this organization through a schism," Rhys said firmly. He didn't know if he was trying to threaten David or plead with him. He just knew it was important that they get on the same page about this, and quickly. "I won't do it."

"No need to worry about a coup," David said finally, smoke pluming from his mouth. The familiar scent of David's brand of cigarettes stung Rhys's nostrils, transporting him back to a time when everything that was dear to him smelled like that. "Because it's you that will be kneeling for me, McGowan."

Rhys opened his mouth to reply, but his attention was diverted by a movement over David's shoulder. Wayne had appeared out of his office and was in conversation with another one of the older Society brothers over by the fireplace. David followed Rhys's line of sight and then gave a Cheshire grin.

"Daddy's home. Do you need to run on over and pay obeisance?"

Rhys grimaced at him. "Some of us worked for the connections we have, David. I wasn't born with a crystal ball in my mouth."

Wayne's eyes fell on them both, and Rhys felt a cold jolt go through him, as though he were a child with his hand caught in the cookie jar.

"Trouble," he muttered. "Three o'clock."

David shot one more surreptitious glance Wayne's way as the High Priest began to make his way across the room to them.

"I'll let you handle this one, I think," David said, pushing up to leave. "You're so much better at getting lectured than I am."

"David," Wayne said, settling a hand on his shoulder. "I wasn't expecting to see you here today. Could I speak to you in my office for a moment?"

Rhys smiled at David with serene self-satisfaction. It was obviously not he who was in for a lecture.

The hanged man

CHAPTER SEVEN

DAVID

The High Priest's office was a small room off to the side of the inner sanctum with an old-school frosted glass window and a brass plate on the door displaying Wayne's title. The wooden desk inside was covered in books and binders of financial records, spells, and God knew what else. David didn't even want to think about what a mess the inside of the filing cabinets behind the desk must be; there were probably membership records in there dating back to the Society's inception in the swinging sixties.

Wayne gestured to the worn, black leather armchair that sat across from the desk, and David took a seat. He had been in here plenty of times before, whether it was to be reprimanded or congratulated, and he always lost himself in fantasies of how he was going to redecorate. At least two of the walls were coming down to bring in more light, and he was going to swap out all the heavy furniture for minimalist pieces.

Wayne poured himself a dram of Scotch from a nearby decanter and swirled it around thoughtfully in his glass. He knew better than to offer David a drink, even though it had taken quite a while to get that message through to him. When David had been a drinker, he and Wayne would spend hours shooting the shit at a local distillery with some of the older Society brothers, talking politics and economics. David was one of the few men in the Society who could float between the older set and the younger set effortlessly, but he felt like his influence was somewhat diminished now that he couldn't show up at the bars.

"I didn't realize you and Rhys were so..." Wayne sorted around his vocabulary for a moment. "Convivial."

"He owed me a favor," David said, lacing his fingers in front of himself. "Just business."

"Of course. And I trust there's nothing else going on between you two, considering Rhys's recent marriage?"

"Of course not." David ground his molars together. "Not for years."

"Good," Wayne said, nodding thoughtfully. The gesture clearly communicated to David that the conversation was far from over. "David, we've known each other a long time."

"Yes, we have."

"I remember going to one of your father's séances and seeing you at work for the first time. You couldn't have been more than fifteen, but you had such an immense gift. And an immense attitude."

David couldn't help the smile that pulled at his lips. He always warmed under praise, even though he suspected Wayne was buttering him up in preparation for asking a favor.

"Maybe so."

"Yours is a once-in-a-lifetime talent, David. It was only natural for you to follow in your father's footsteps and join the Society. It's been my great pleasure to watch you grow and progress in your studies, and all before you turned thirty." Wayne rattled the ice cubes in his glass thoughtfully. "Now, Rhys... Rhys is another matter."

David knew better than to interrupt, even though heat was crawling up the back of his neck. He'd rather climb out the window than discuss Rhys with Wayne.

"I've never met someone so ambitious, or so sharp," Wayne mused. "That boy sees everything that goes on around him: never forgets a name, never misses a detail. Bringing him to that first Society meeting was probably one of the greatest gifts you ever gave me."

"I'm happy to hear it," David said, working hard to keep the disdain out of his voice. When he had invited Rhys to a Society meeting with him all the way back in college, he had thought he was showing off to a wide-eyed freshman boyfriend with an amateur's interest in the occult. He didn't realize he was letting a fox into the henhouse, cementing his greatest rival's place right next to him.

"I don't think it's any surprise to say that you're the two brightest stars the Society has to offer," Wayne went on, finishing his Scotch. "The older guys respect you; the younger men look up to you. But when you two work together, things get… volatile."

David swallowed hard. He had heard a version of this speech before, when Wayne had hauled David off Rhys in the middle of a drag-out fight. They had gotten into some shitty immature altercation in the middle of the summoning circle a few weeks after the breakup, Rhys acting as sorcerer and David as scryer, and it had escalated so badly that Rhys had set his spirit court on David. David had responded by wrestling Rhys to the ground. Not David's finest moment.

Neither of them had ever put their hands on each other when they were dating, not even during their worst screaming matches. But with the bonds of love and loyalty worn away, it was so much easier for hatred and violence to take their place. By the time Wayne tore them apart, Rhys's lip was split, and David had a bloody nose. Not that David really cared; he had gotten his nose broken in schoolyard fights twice before, and there was very little plastic surgery couldn't fix. But it hurt worse, somehow, coming from Rhys.

"I hope I can rely on both of you to maintain a professional distance," Wayne said, rattling the ice in his glass pensively. "It would be the greatest honor either of you could give to me, and to what we've all built here together. Oil and water don't mix. Do you understand what I'm saying to you?"

"Yes, High Priest," David muttered, suddenly unable to meet Wayne's eyes. He felt eighteen years old again, guided by Wayne's firm hand on his shoulder away from self-destruction.

Wayne smiled, and the expression made him look warm and jolly. "Good." He laid a finger aside his nose. "And when I make my choice for High Priest, I assure you that I'll pick someone who understands tradition. The way business ought to be handled."

David's chest swelled with pride. That was him; it had to be. Rhys was always trying to pass new motions and introduce new ritual texts, and the younger set loved him for it. But David had a family name no one could argue with and the decorum to match. He would restore the Society to its former grandeur, not propel it forward, open throttle, into ruin.

"Thank you, Wayne."

The two exchanged a few minutes of pleasantries before David dismissed himself into the cool hallway. He clenched and relaxed his hands at his side, burning up with electric energy.

His. The High Priesthood was his.

Rhys was still sitting out in the meeting hall when David passed by, scrolling through his phone. David didn't bother saying goodbye.

It took David almost a week to make the congested drive into the Beacon Hill district. He told himself it was because he was busy at work, not because he was nervous about setting foot in the house again. He tried to ignore the gnawing sense in his stomach that he was working on borrowed time, and that whatever had spoken to him out of the scrying glass wasn't done with him yet.

David considered slipping in through the back door, so as to avoid getting the neighbor's hopes up about an Aristarkhov returning to the neighborhood and upping their property value, but he didn't want the house to realize he was afraid of it. So, he shouldered through the front door as thoughtlessly as he used to in high school, even leaving it slightly ajar behind him.

The emptiness of the home rushed up to meet him, cloying and desperate for attention. The scent of wood polish and dusty damask and stale liquor dried in the bottom of crystal glasses rushed into his nostrils.

David didn't allow his eyes to alight for too long on any stick of furniture, or any face staring out at him from any hanging portrait. He breezed through the foyer with clinical efficiency, taking the stairs at a brisk clip.

If he didn't make eye contact with anything, the house might stay asleep, and grant him a few more minutes of peace.

The library was on the second level, opposite the rooms where David had wasted hours banging out piano exercises or smoking joints or sifting through the piles of designer clothes he left for housekeeping to hang up. He didn't bother to visit his old bedroom. He had rescued what he wanted already: the vinyl records and the letters from his sister, sealed with neon stamps that charted her trail through Munich, Florence, Morocco. The only things of real value left in this house were shelved in alphabetized rows in Evgeni's study.

Evgeni's private collection of esoteric texts had drawn colleagues from all over the world. David's childhood memories were full of visiting occultists who had long ago abandoned the armchair, stern-eyed men in tweed jackets or ties. David had been forbidden from speaking to them, unless he was leading a séance; and even then, Evgeni hovered over him. David sometimes glimpsed them smoking with his father in the library, or caught a whisper of their cologne, lying in wait for him in the kitchen when he scrounged for breakfast before school. The foreign, fading scent of spruce pine or lemon balm irritated his nose, and the thought of strange men milling around his house at night, holding private conversations in rooms a stone's throw from his own, made heat crawl up the back of his neck.

David tossed the memory aside as he shouldered into the library, ignoring how small the cavernous room still made him feel. He didn't allow his eyes to linger on the dark corners where he had liked to sulk with his headphones on during rainy days. Instead, he moved straight to the floor-to-ceiling bookshelves that held more of the Aristarkhov fortune than any bank account or investment portfolio.

Notoriously meticulous, Evgeni had devised his own categorization system for his library, which David had never bothered to learn. Psychic ability was inherent to David's being, and he didn't need anything in a book to tell him how to talk to ghosts. He conducted his own occult experiments – under Evgeni's watchful eye, of course, or in the secret attic rooms where he and Leda had played during those sparse years of companionship – and came to his own conclusion. He had never given a damn what a dead Renaissance alchemist thought of it.

Now he ran his fingers across the shelves, muttering to himself. As far as he could tell, the books were broken into sub-genres and then alphabetized, but no thought had been given to language, or for arranging the titles in a pattern anyone but Evgeni could parse.

There were books here that men had killed for, books that had been smuggled out of war-torn countries or acquired in under-the-table gentlemen's agreements to the tune of a few million dollars. That wasn't even including the ones kept under glass in a nearby display case, crisscrossed with lead bars and lacquered with a bulletproof coating. But those weren't what David was looking for. He had something more inconspicuous in mind, something he couldn't get anywhere but inside this house.

The temperature in the room slid down a few degrees, and one of the display cases rattled distantly behind him.

David threw a daggered glance over his shoulder. "Don't fucking start."

The library fell silent. David resumed his work, crouching down to peer at the books on the lower shelves. He found a slim section of leather-bound journals wedged next to a collection of Pushkin, the only poet Evgeni had thought was worth the space they took up in the grave.

David freed the journals and dumped them on his father's desk. He remembered being dwarfed by the thing in his childhood, how imposing Evgeni looked, poring over letters at the black walnut monstrosity. But now he fit behind the polished desk perfectly, and the claw-foot leather chair embraced him as he sank into it.

The house took a deep breath and settled.

David leafed through a glossy black ledger and discarded it once he realized it was only where Evgeni had recorded who owed him money. Another catalogued private sales of art and antiques, and was summarily discarded. David had lawyers for all of this, but Evgeni had always been paranoid about involving outsiders in his family business.

The third book offered the answers David had come back to the house for. It was a thin book, wide and flat, with Evgeni's initials stamped into the leather. Inside, David's father had recorded their family genealogy by hand, in branching bloodlines that dovetailed neatly into one another. The sheer volume of names and the level of detail with which their professions and place of birth had been recorded would have made an archivist weep.

David kept flipping, barely touching the pages as he scanned the names and read the tiny scrawl of birth and death dates below them. The chart was aggressively patrilineal, with mothers and wives sometimes only being given first names and a death date, or no name at all.

All the men seemed to have spawned a brood of children before they were David's age, which he couldn't fathom despite the stark difference in life expectancy. He had never wanted children, not to sire or raise or adopt them, despite the bevy of exes who had gotten starry-eyed at the prospect.

David reached the last page, where a collection of boy's names funneled into a single ancestor.

ANATOLY ARISTARKHOV.

No profession. No town of origin.

This book didn't care where he came from, who his people were or what they did for a living. All that mattered was his children, his death date in 1556, and one other date written in bold red ink, about twenty years before his death. David doubted it was a birthdate, since it was rendered so differently from the others.

David leaned back in his father's chair. The study had grown colder, and his fingertips tingled unpleasantly. He glared at the book for a moment, tongue pressed against his teeth as he deliberated. Then he spread his fingers and covered the name of the first Aristarkhov with his palm.

His father hit him first, that unmistakable aura of severity and quiet disdain. Evgeni's residual energy was all over this book, his memory thick enough to choke on. David pressed through the white-hot flicker of adolescent rage that flared up in his father's presence, then leaned deeper into what the book had to tell him.

The dread washed over him first, cold as the pit of the Mariana Trench, and then an awful sense of urgency, hammering in his heartbeat like he had put away three espressos. Behind these names was a terror David could barely hold in his body, surpassing any medieval fear of God. Something reached out for him from within the book, bleeding from the ink and into his skin. It tightened wraith fingers around his wrist and throat and pulled him in tighter, and images flashed through his mind.

Blood on snow.

Beaten gold coins slipping through calloused fingers.

A little boy screaming and screaming.

David came back to himself with a gasp and wrenched his hand away from the book, but something wasn't right. His head was still light, the world was still hazy at the edges and coming in and out of focus. His feet were lead weights; he couldn't feel his hands. Instead of returning to his own body, he felt like he was slipping out of it.

He knew this feeling. It happened when his consciousness stepped aside during a séance to let something else take up residence in his body.

He was being possessed.

He tried to stand but staggered, grasping for the edge of the desk. Hands – his own, or maybe someone else's – grasped for paper, for a bottle of tacky black ink. His ears were roaring louder than Fenway stadium on game night.

Out. He needed to get out of this house.

David lurched against the desk, slamming his hip into the carved wood, but he couldn't feel it. He couldn't feel anything. He careened in and out of his skin on a nauseating tilt-a-whirl, one moment trying to grasp for his car keys, the other moment standing outside of himself, watching himself scrawl frantically with a fountain pen. There was ink everywhere: on his father's desk, on his cuffs, dripping down onto his Hugo Boss shoes.

David made one last effort to wrench himself out of the room, but he only got a few steps before the ground tilted beneath him and his knees cracked against the hardwood. The acrid taste of sulfur burned against his tongue, and then the world went dark.

The Chariot

CHAPTER EIGHT

RHYS

"This is harder than it looks," Rhys grumbled, squinting at the tiny brush in his hand. The butter-yellow varnish came off in a splotch on Moira's thumbnail, and he *tsked* while he tried to fix it. "I'm telling you, I'm a lost cause. You're going to have to take me back to the dealership and trade me in for a new husband."

"But I like that little line you get between your eyes when you're concentrating," Moira said with a chuckle.

They were sitting at the kitchen table, splitting a carafe of steaming pour-over coffee while spring showers pattered against the window. Moira had wiggled out of her hours at the shop and tempted Rhys away from his research on medieval Welsh economics for a Saturday of lazy domesticity. He had cooked feta chive omelets for breakfast and surprised her with a crocus bouquet from her favorite corner store. He knew it wasn't enough to make up for his habit of losing himself to research for weeks at a time, but it was a start.

"What do you want to do after this?" he asked, dipping the tiny brush in the pot of nail polish before moving on to her next nail.

"Oh, I don't know. If it was a nicer day, I'd say we should fix sandwiches and go picnic by the Charles. We could watch a movie, I guess."

"We could," Rhys said, a wicked smile tugging at his lips.

"Or?"

"Or," he said, finishing his work on her nails and pulling her in slowly by the wrist so his breath moved across her lips, "we could go upstairs."

Moira smiled into his mouth as she kissed him.

"I have to convince you to take the day off more often," she said.

Rhys didn't have a chance to reply, because his phone began vibrating insistently on the table. He snatched for it, ready to hit silent and flip it over, but then he registered the name on the screen.

David.

He glanced at Moira, who had simply raised an eyebrow. "I didn't know y'all still called."

"We don't. He texts me when he needs something."

The phone buzzed on, demanding attention, and Rhys moved to cancel the call. Or take it. He wasn't sure what was right in this situation, or what would look right to Moira.

"I'll just–"

Rhys moved to switch the ringer off, but Moira shook her head. "No, you should take it."

"Moira–"

"Something about this doesn't feel right. You should take it."

Rhys pressed one more kiss to Moira's lips before answering his phone. "David?"

It was meant to sound less like an accusation than it did. For a moment, there was silence, and then a distant, "Rhys?"

"Obviously. What's going on?"

He heard the rustle of what sounded like papers, a crash, and then a hissed "Shit!" as David moved around on the other end.

Rhys pressed a knuckle to his mouth and locked eyes with his wife, shaking his head. So far, so inscrutable.

"You alright?" Rhys ventured.

"I just... I'm at Evgeni's."

The first stirrings of nausea swirled in Rhys's stomach. Training told him to reach for the orange bottle of as-needed anxiety meds in his work satchel, but he couldn't move.

"What's wrong?"

"Everything was fine and then... something happened. I don't... I don't remember. Fuck."

"Are you alright?"

"I'm sorry, Rhys, but there's no one. I don't have… I didn't know what to do."

Rhys didn't have an ounce of sixth sense, but he didn't need it to know that something was seriously haywire. David didn't just *ask* for help.

Rhys shot a glance at Moira to confirm his suspicion, but she was already ashen. Wrong. Something was wrong.

"What happened?" Rhys asked.

"That's what I'm telling you, I don't know! I was just here and then everything went dark. Fuck. God. I can't stand up. I think I'm sick. Jesus Christ."

Rhys pulled himself to his feet without meaning to. "What do you need, David?"

"Please come over. You know I wouldn't ask unless… Please."

"I'm with Moira, I can't–"

Moira shook her head and waved him on. *Go*, her flicked wrist said.

On the other end, David had moved the phone away from his mouth, probably pressed it to his chest, and heaved for breath. It sounded like he was on the verge of hyperventilation.

"I'm in Jamaica Plain," Rhys said, trying to remain calm. "Nathan is just down the street from you, do you want me to–"

"No, don't call anyone. I'll be okay. I just need–"

He didn't have to finish the sentence. Rhys knew how it ended, he had heard it a thousand times, on pay phone lines and shouted over thumping club music and sobbed out in parking lots while Rhys tried to drive away.

You. You, you, you, settling around Rhys's neck like an albatross.

"I'm coming," Rhys said, quieter. "I'm coming, alright? Just… hang on. It's going to be alright."

David didn't apologize or say thank you, just let the line go dead. Rhys stood in stunned silence for a moment, heart pounding. Old instincts were warring inside him, battering against the walls he had built to preserve his own sanity. The warmth of their little kitchen seemed all of a sudden oppressively hot, and his nausea worsened.

David could have gotten into absolutely anything when Rhys's back was turned, and he could already be too far gone for Rhys to be of any help. Scenes of potential desolation flipped through his mind like tarot cards: empty liquor bottles, a ritual that called for too much blood, an ambulance screaming through Beacon Hill.

Moira drifted closer to him, nail polish and coffee abandoned. She tipped a tiny white pill out of his prescription bottle and into her palm. "What happened?"

"I don't know. He sounded… I think he had some kind of breakdown. I don't know."

Moira put the pill in his mouth and handed him his cup of coffee. The anxiety was building up under his skin, numbing him like a novocain shot. He would dissociate if he wasn't careful, and he reached out to grip his wife's hand to remind himself that he was real and alive, here with her.

"I'm sorry, I have to go."

"I'm coming with you," she said, snatching up her purse. She was already pulling a knit cardigan over her dress and yanking her phone off the kitchen charger.

"What? Moira, I have no idea what I'm going to be walking into over there. I can't let you–"

"Don't shut me out of this, Rhys." Her voice was heather-soft but her eyes were set harder than steel. "I know the Society usually handles its own problems, and I know what you two have going on is complicated, but I don't want to see you get in over your head."

Rhys's shoulders sagged, and he took his wife's face in his hands.

"Love, please. I shouldn't even be going over there… He's not someone you want to take responsibility for."

"I think you're forgetting that David and I share a referral network. I know how he is."

"If you would rather I not go, say it and it's done. I'll send somebody else. I mean it; if this makes you uncomfortable–"

Moira shook her head, and the blush dusted across her cheeks left shimmery sunset-colored kisses on Rhys's fingertips.

"No, he called you for a reason. And I don't like the idea of you walking into whatever trouble he's in by yourself."

"I love you."

"Damn straight."

Rhys took her face in his hands and kissed her, hard and deep. Her fingers sank into his shoulders, pulling him in tighter, and then she was slipping away, trailing pecks across his mouth and jaw as she headed for the door.

"I'm driving. I want to be able to make a quick exit in case he gives you an anxiety attack," Moira said.

"Pray he's being histrionic and doesn't actually need me."

"That still doesn't seem like a great outcome," Moira said as she held open the front door for him.

Rhys shot a passing glance at himself in the foyer mirror before slipping outside. He looked like he had aged a year overnight. "With David? That's the best of all possible worlds."

The house on Beacon Hill had been purchased by David's father shortly before their move to the states, and had stood abandoned in the years after his death. The brownstone was four stories from street to rooftop garden, tall and narrow with a splashy stone staircase leading to the oak door. It must have cost a fortune, even at the time of purchase. And the fact that David could afford to let the house sit unrented while he burned through his money just a few miles away in his modern condo was a testament to the Aristarkhov's obscene wealth. Rhys couldn't wrap his mind around money like this, no matter how many times he had seen David pull out his black card without looking at the number on the register. Out of principle, Rhys had returned or given away many of the outlandishly expensive watches and blazers David had bought for him, but he still had a few items in his closet that could pay his rent if he ever needed to consign them.

"He grew up here?" Moira asked, glancing up at the forbidding structure from beneath the umbrella Rhys held. Her dress was forties vintage, with a bodice that cinched her waist like a wasp, and she would be distraught if the rain ruined it. He would have brought the Lincoln around closer, but parking prices were murder in this area, if you could find parking to begin with.

"For a while, at least," Rhys said. He had tried to explain the house on their drive over, at least, as well as he could. He wanted Moira to understand what she was getting into. He wasn't sure he had succeeded. "His father immigrated with him from Russia when he was fourteen."

"Mom's out of the picture?"

"She was dead by then." Rhys rapped on the door with a knuckle. Then, when there was no answer, he knocked again.

"It's open," David called from inside. His voice sounded strangely thin.

Moira and Rhys exchanged a glance, and then Rhys turned the golden knob and pushed their way inside.

The interior was dim, lit only by the weak sunlight filtering through the thin decorative curtains veiling the windows. Their steps echoed loudly across the hardwood floor.

"David?" Rhys called.

"Library," the psychic responded, impossibly distant.

Rhys thought about asking which floor that was on, but he was getting tired of playing Marco Polo, so he picked a direction and tried to act like he had been to the house more than once before.

The last time Rhys had been here, it had been half-past two in the morning, and David, emboldened by four highballs and the muggy June twilight, had let them in through the back door while insisting he'd just wanted to see the place again.

Rhys had been baffled by the justification, since David avoided all discussion of his father or the house as a general rule. But David had wandered the lower level for almost twenty minutes, running fingertips over the dusty furniture and singing to himself. There had still been cigarettes in the ashtrays, as though the house had been vacated on a whim. David had stood quietly in the parlor, shivering despite the hot night, and said a few sentences in Russian before swiftly turning on his heel and tugging Rhys out of the house. They had never gone back.

In the here and now, Rhys ducked in and out of the parlor, finding little except moldering pieces of furniture, half-heartedly preserved by sheets. The mess of a house once lived in had mostly been cleared away, although there were still a few books lying open on the floor and cupboards left hanging ajar, giving the eerie impression that the brownstone was not entirely abandoned.

"God," Moira breathed, stepping delicately over a shattered beer bottle. "You said he was rich, but I didn't realize..."

"I don't think I paid for a thing the entire two years we were together," Rhys said. "He tried to get me an Audi for my twentieth birthday and didn't see why I thought that was excessive."

In the end, it was the scent of David's Parliaments that led Rhys up the curving stairs to the second floor, and towards a swinging door that led to the library.

To call the room huge would be an understatement. Floor-to-ceiling black oak bookshelves lined the wall behind an imposing desk, and heavy furniture lounged on high-pile rugs. Rhys knew very little about David's father except that he had been an occultist, but the painstakingly catalogued specialty titles and esoteric memorabilia littering the shelves supported Rhys's initial impression of a man obsessed with his work. Rhys batted down the knee-jerk response to take a closer look at the books, to catalog their contents. He wasn't here for them. He was here for David.

Windows double Rhys's height lorded down over the rain-slicked streets below, and a genuine bearskin was draped in front of a hearth large enough to curl up and sleep inside.

David was seated on the windowsill, a cigarette burning down to nothing in his hand as he gazed out over the city. His slacks were uncharacteristically smudged with something that looked like soot, or paint, but he otherwise seemed to be in one functional piece.

"I was starting to think you weren't going to show," David said. He turned to face them both. Rhys caught an apology in his eyes before they landed on Moira and flickered with uncertainty.

"Ms Delacroix," David said, bringing the cigarette to his mouth and performing a deep French inhale. "I didn't know I was expecting you."

Moira patted the large silk iris pinned into her hair. "Hope you don't mind having another pair of hands around to help. Rhys said you found yourself feeling a bit distraught."

David shot a look at Rhys, trying to draw the other man into their old dance of conversations held entirely in glances. Rhys didn't take the bait, no matter the electric thrill that went through him at the thought of being that intimate with David again.

"Are you alright?"

"Of course I am. Don't I look alright?"

He looked… passable. There was something so off about the sight of David lounging around in the vacant embrace of his despised childhood home that it set Rhys's teeth on edge. More than that, David's usually golden complexion had a sick pallor to it, and he was tapping his knee with his free hand like it was the next best thing to letting his fingers shake outright.

"You sounded like you were staring down the reaper on the phone. What happened?"

"I…" David opened his mouth and then closed it again. He stood suddenly, moving like he was afraid of something spying on him from outside, and drifted closer to Moira and Rhys. "I blacked out."

Terror and rage flooded Rhys's system in one stomach-lurching rush.

The scent of rancid, sticky bourbon invaded his memory, along with the sound of shouts and shattering glass, the ache in his arms as he did his damndest to drag David into a waiting cab. He tasted metal and gin, and he felt like he might be sick.

"Are you... How? When? I swear to God, David, I swear on my grandfather's grave I won't put myself through this again. Find somebody else, I–"

"No, no, no," David insisted, waving his hands in front of his face. Smoke zig-zagged between him and Rhys as his gaze flittered nervously to Moira. "God no, sorry. I wasn't drinking."

The tension seeped out of Rhys's body, but his nerves were shredded now. He was too old for this; he had better things to do than clean up David's messes, sober or not. But he was here, wasn't he? And he had brought Moira. At a certain point, this had to count as courting his own anxiety.

Rhys took a deep breath and steadied himself. "Then how did you black out?"

"I was hoping you could help me figure that out."

Moira drifted from his side, craning her neck up to take in the room. Her eyes came to rest on a gigantic painting of men in seventeenth-century clothes out on the hunt. They shouted at each other from horseback while a dying fox writhed in the jaws of a hound.

"Were you channeling?" Rhys asked, one eye fixed on his wife.

"I... yes, but I don't know who."

"You don't remember who you were channeling."

"No, and I don't remember deciding to start. One minute I was reading, and the next minute I was waking up on the floor."

Rhys took a step closer to his oldest friend. The last time they had been in this house together, Rhys had pulled David back from the brink with a touch on his wrist and a plea to go home and get some sleep. In another life, Rhys would go to him, take David's face in his hands, and look him over to make sure he wasn't injured, or lying. In another life, Rhys would pull him into the secure embrace of his Lincoln and drive him home, then ply him with kisses until the tension melted out of David's shoulders.

But in this world, he just stood – too far away for David to reach, hands stuffed deep into the pockets of his peacoat.

"How long were you out?"

"An hour? Maybe?"

"Mary and Joseph."

Rhys glanced at his wife, hoping for a second opinion, but found her still staring up at that picture. Distress passed over her face in waves.

"Love?" Rhys asked. "You alright?"

Her dark eyes flickered over to him, wary and wide. "I don't like this house, Rhys."

"Hey, I didn't pick it out," David said, a bit defensively. "Evgeni wasn't exactly a man of impeccable taste."

Moira moved towards a richly upholstered chaise lounge, and it was only then Rhys noticed that the ground at her feet was littered with papers. Someone had ripped fistfuls of pages out of an encyclopedia and scribbled on them with punishing pressure. A toppled bottle of black ink was still bleeding into the carpet, and a fountain pen was stabbed through a sheaf of paper.

Moira bent down to gingerly pick up one of the pages.

Rhys peered down at the paper in her hand. Lines of text were layered over each other so densely it was difficult to discern which language was being used, but he caught snatches of Ecclesial Latin and Ugaritic cuneiform. David didn't speak either of those languages.

"You did this?" Rhys asked. "In a trance state?"

David didn't have time to reply, because Moira reached out and grasped Rhys's wrist so tight it was painful. "Look."

He followed her gaze to the papers littering the ground, finally landing on one of the few phrases in English, repeating over and over again in that heavy, dark hand.

The Devil knows your name, David Aristarkhov.

David offered up his palms apologetically. They were smeared with ink.

"I didn't know who else to call," David said.

The door was still open behind them, inviting Rhys back into the world of publication deadlines and bill payments. It would be so easy to turn around, sweep down the stairs with his wife in tow, and close the door on David and his excesses, his self-interest, his constant crises. Rhys and Moira could resume their Saturday, he could lay her down in their bed and luxuriate in her until he felt like himself again, cover her in adoration in the way she deserved. He could resume his policy of not picking up the phone when David's number flashed across the screen, and David could find someone else to talk him down from whatever precipice he had climbed up on this time.

But deeply, in the darkest and quietest part of him, Rhys knew that if he didn't want this, he wouldn't have come. In the still of the library, the arcane writing seemed to hum – an ambient, enticing sound just below audible range that drew him in with the promise of new knowledge. The house felt heavy and oppressive, like a hand squeezing the back of his neck, but the gilt and the antiques spoke his name from the shadows. David was looking at him like they were twenty again, like they might be able to get it right this time, orbiting each other's spheres without burning too hot or swallowing each other alive.

Rhys put his hand out and touched David on the wrist. His fingers came back stained, blue-black smears mingling with the pink blush already on his fingertips.

"You did the right thing."

The High priestess

CHAPTER NINE

MOIRA

Moira spent the next twenty minutes listening to David walk them through everything that had happened, from the voice inside his head to the creeping feeling of dread that overtook him moments before the blackout. He had retired to one of the chaise lounges to tell his tale, looking uncharacteristically delicate. He looked, more specifically, like he might lose consciousness and crash against the ground at any moment. Moira didn't feel like cleaning up a bloody nose, so she perched herself on the arm of the chaise lounge as a precaution.

Rhys stood framed by the walk-in fireplace behind him, arms crossed over his chest.

"So, you think whatever knocked you out was the same thing you felt during the séance?"

"That's my best guess."

"And the last thing you did before you lost consciousness was look through that book?" Rhys asked, moving towards the desk. David pushed himself up off the chaise.

"I wouldn't touch that if I were..."

His voice trailed off as he swayed dangerously, any remaining color draining from his face. Snagging his elbow, Moira guided him back down into a sitting position. The gesture felt stiff and foreign, but David looked about two seconds away from unconsciousness, so she had to commit to it now.

"Don't try to stand; you're green in the gills," she said.

"Then it's not my fault if that thing takes the legs out from under him," David grumbled.

Pages rustled softly as Rhys peered through the book, handling it with an archivist's care. He flipped the thin paper with his pinky finger.

"Rhys is blind as a bat when it comes to second sight," Moira said. "I'm sure he'll be fine."

Despite what a well-established fixture he was in Boston's occult community, Rhys had no inherent supernatural ability whatsoever. The voracious appetite that had spurred an adolescent Rhys to beg his priest to teach him to perform the miracle of the Eucharist was the same one that drove him to devote himself to ceremonial magic. When you didn't have the advantage of uncanny intuition or the ability to speak with the dead, you had to be twice as good as everyone else.

"I still wouldn't go poking around in that book if he asks you to," David said.

"I don't ask Moira to scry for me," Rhys said, never glancing up from the book. The twin furrows between his eyes were especially visible in the dim light of the study. "Ever. Our practices are separate."

"Seems like a waste of a perfect match, doesn't it? Sorcerer and psychic?" David ran his tongue over dry lips. "Some people spend their entire careers trying to find the right person to partner with."

Rhys flicked a warning to him with his eyes. Moira could sense that this was an old argument, one neither Rhys nor David would be wading into.

"Those people don't have marriages that come first," Rhys said.

Moira laid the back of her hand against David's forehead. He looked ruffled by the uninvited touch, a cat that had gotten its nose wet, but he allowed it. Whatever had him in its throes made him more amenable to her presence. She liked him better this way.

"You're sick," she pronounced.

"Tell me something I don't know; I haven't felt this nauseous since the morning after the Halloween party my sophomore year of college."

"No, I mean psychically sick."

It was a catch-all term for getting a bad high off low vibes or being left wrung-out after channeling something nasty, but it was the best language she had to describe what she felt. David was clammy to the touch, and there was something rancid beneath his blinding golden energy. She could pick it up like the smell of death under expensive cologne.

Moira indulged herself and took a moment to scan his emotions as well as his health. It was just a little indiscretion, slipping underneath his skin to find out how he really felt about her. She was probably never going to get this close to the inscrutable David ever again, so it was a breach of privacy she had a hard time feeling bad about.

She half-expected the hot irritation of jealousy, or the possessive prickling of someone who didn't like their things being touched by outsiders, but neither were present.

To her great surprise, she picked up a cold wave of something far better hidden.

Fear.

What did he have to be afraid of, with her in this house?

"What kind of psychic safeguards do you have in place?" she asked.

"None," David said flatly. "And I'll thank you not to read me without my consent."

Moira snatched her hand away, face flushing with heat.

"Moira," Rhys groaned. "We've talked about this; it's invasive. And David, don't..." he waved vaguely, exhausted by having the two of them in the same room, "be an asshole."

"Wait a minute," Moira said, shaking off her embarrassment long enough to register what David had just said. "You have *no* safeguards? That can't be right."

"Depends on what you mean by safeguards."

"Circles of white light, prayer caims, Florida water, trance meditation? Methods to keep your energy in and the energy of things that want to hurt you out?"

"I get five hours of sleep, go to the gym, and don't talk to anything I don't feel like talking to. I know you two are like, really religious–"

"Gotta love the way you say that like it's a dirty word," Rhys said with cutting sarcasm. "Didn't miss that."

"Spiritual, whatever. That stuff has never worked for me. If something pesters me, I tell it to fuck off. No woo needed."

Moira rolled her eyes and muttered, "Lord."

"Are you serious, David?" Rhys asked, kneading his brow.

"Why are you looking at me like I sacrificed your firstborn?"

"Because you're a whole fool," Moira cut in, a lick of anger flaming in her stomach. She wanted to be shocked that a man so careless had managed to rise to such a position of supernatural prominence, but she was too familiar with the nepotism and lineage-worship of occult circles to be surprised. "You're lucky you aren't dead if that's how you've been carrying on all these years. It's a disrespect to the spirits you work with, and to the clients who trust you to keep them safe."

David looked like he had half a mind to ask Rhys to come to his defense, but Moira's husband shook his head, unsmiling. In the end, David was smart enough not to snap back with any pithy remark.

"I'm not trying to disrespect anyone," he said. "I'm just trying to answer your questions."

"You don't do *anything* to protect yourself while you work?" Rhys asked, and now it sounded more like an interrogation, like he might be ready to haul a couple skeletons out of the closet. "Nothing at all?"

"Sometimes I'll wave some incense around the room for show if it makes the client feel better. I'd rather just do away with all the theatre and get down to channeling. Rhys, you know how I work; you've lived with me, for God's sake."

Something that had been pulled tight inside Rhys snapped. Moira braced herself for the thunderstorm.

"I always assumed you were doing protective work behind the scenes! You led me to believe that you had everything under control–"

"I *did* have everything under control!"

David tried to stand again, and Moira pushed him back down, this time with a little more force.

"Rhys," she warned.

"You know the pains I took to make sure I was prepared *every time* we worked together," Rhys went on. "To keep myself safe, to keep *you* safe. I brought you into circles that took me *days* to construct. I tried evocations with you I would never have attempted with anyone else. I trusted you with my life!"

"I don't know why you're making this about us. You knew what you were getting into with me, and you made it clear when you left that you couldn't handle that."

"This is not about us, David; this is about you, and how you never take these things seriously enough. Which I'll remind you was a glaring issue on the few occasions I actually–"

"Don't be nasty, either of y'all," Moira snapped. She realized she was digging her nails into David's shoulders and retracted them slightly. "I did not tramp all the way out here in the rain to watch you two go at it like cats in a bag. Rhys, if that's all this is gonna be, I'll send an Uber back for you when you're done."

"Moira," Rhys began plaintively, but she waved his apologies away.

"Don't make me chide; it wears me out," she said. David shot Rhys a satisfied smirk, which Moira intercepted. "I'm not on your side, either. Stay focused on the problem at hand and spare me the attitude. Humans need rest. It's part of our natural rhythms."

David stared at her like she had just started speaking Latin. "You seriously think self-care can help me now? I was just *possessed*."

"Maybe because you don't do enough self-care," Moira said.

"Can we move on, please?" David asked. "To something remotely helpful?"

"We *are* trying to help you. We wouldn't have driven all the way into the city if we weren't serious about wanting to help. But you've got to cooperate."

David glowered at the ground, looking for all the world like a petulant child while Rhys paced a tight circle around the desk to cool down. Moira was surprised they had lasted two years together without killing each other. Hell, she was surprised they had lasted twenty minutes in this house together with her.

When Rhys spoke, it was with his eyes closed. As though not looking at David would help him feel less furious.

"You're sure this isn't just someone you channeled for a séance who never stopped hanging around?"

"Positive."

"Or a spirit we called up during a Society meeting that decided to follow you home? You could have picked something up just from exposure; God knows we have our hands in some pretty dark stuff on any given week."

"I would be able to recognize something like that instantly. Whatever this is, it's new, and it came from inside me."

"And you're absolutely *sure* this isn't just stress? Or a family history of mental illness manifesting?"

David's eyes rolled back so far they almost disappeared into his head.

"Rhys, come on–"

"I'm being serious! You work constantly, you hardly sleep, you–"

"A little hereditary tendency towards perfectionism doesn't put people on the ground like that. I know what I heard, and I know what happened to me. Look!"

He thrust out his hand, showing the slight tremor through his fingertips.

"None of this makes sense," Rhys muttered. He slipped out of conversation and into dialogue with himself. Wandering legs carried him back over to the bookshelves, drawn by an irresistible force. Moira knew her husband well enough to know that he could easily lose hours, even days, in a library like this. "Perfectly healthy people don't just start hearing voices. We're missing something."

He turned back to the book on Evgeni's desk, flipping through page after page. Words passed his lips in murmurs and mutters, incomprehensible to anyone but himself. He was dissolving into the pages and his own hypothesizing.

Moira sighed. They might be here a while.

She settled down into the armchair across from David, far enough away to not presume familiarity but close enough that she could catch him if he tried to stand.

At the moment, Rhys was no more present than if he had stepped out of the room to put on a pot of tea. Moira very much wished she had a cup of tea to sip, or a cookie to nibble, or anything else to do besides sit with her hands folded and try not to look at David. David wasn't trying. David was taking her in, arms crossed, like she was an armed home invader who had shattered his window and invited herself in for dinner.

"I didn't know you could do that," he said. Rhys didn't even look up, which was just as well. David wasn't talking to him.

"Do what?" Moira asked, trying not to shift uncomfortably in her chair. Her mother always told her she had the Magician's Eye – that intense, perceptive look of magically gifted people – but whatever she had was nothing in comparison to the white-hot pressure of David's gaze. She wasn't sure if she preferred being ignored by him or put under this microscope.

"Read emotions. You did it to me at your house, too, didn't you? You're subtle, I'll give you that. Who trained you? Or did you pick it up by yourself? Can you communicate with the dead, as well?"

She tried to dodge his questions gracefully. This was something she did not like discussing, not even with Rhys. It was family business. Her mother would have a conniption if she knew her daughter was running her mouth about what Meemaw had passed down.

"You know what I do for a living," she attempted. "Don't act so surprised."

"You're a tarot reader and an astrologer. I know damn good readers who aren't psychic, and astrology is just math mixed with psychology. But you've definitely got the knack. You're like me."

"We're nothing alike, Mr Aristarkhov," she snapped back.

God, he *knew*. He could see the touch of death, circling her throat like a necklace.

"What else can you do?" David pressed.

Moira's face warmed. This kind of conversation would not fly at her mother's table, and it wouldn't fly with her now. Even if she was sitting in an abandoned mansion with her husband's ailing ex, some decorum had to be maintained.

"How would you like it if I asked you to share every trick you had up your sleeve?"

David's eyes sparkled. With mirth or malice, it was hard to tell. "You show me yours, and I'll show you mine."

Before she had time to think of a snappy retort, David turned away from her and looked over his shoulder at Rhys. There was a fond smile on his face as he watched the librarian pore over Evgeni's collection. "You're looking at that library like you want to crawl into bed with it," David noted, raising his voice so Rhys would hear him.

"Can you blame me?" Rhys asked. "There are books here I thought I would have to fly halfway around the world to see."

"Help yourself. Maybe whatever's making me feel like shit is in one of those books."

"Maybe," Rhys mused, making eyes at an antique copy of *The Lesser Key of Solomon*.

"You know," David said slowly, and Moira was sure he was getting some sort of idea. That didn't bode well. "You really might be able to find something in there. Certainly more than with a Google search."

"Sure," Rhys said. "But that would take time. Weeks of research, probably, and lists of possibilities to be tested and crossed out. I would need to take a fine-tooth comb to this place."

David said nothing, just smirked at him with a tempting air that spoke volumes. Moira couldn't riddle out what he was getting at, but Rhys seemed to understand immediately.

"Oh, no," he said. "Don't start. I can't, David. Some of us work for a living."

"I'm not asking you to make it a full-time job. I'm at the end of my rope here, Rhys. You're the best occult researcher I know. Take a stab at figuring out what's hounding me, and you can have free reign of whatever Evgeni left in here. Permanently."

All the air left Rhys's lungs in a soft whoosh, and Moira inhaled sharply at the same time. She didn't quite share her husband's passion for antiquarian books, but she understood it. She understood that if you cracked Rhys open, he would probably have paperback pages inside him instead of organs. Books had been his only saving grace through an impoverished, closeted childhood in a too-large family. The magic of the written word, both figurative and literal, had been responsible for all of his successes.

David wasn't just offering Rhys a library. He was offering him the world.

"Baby," Moira said softly. She didn't know if she was pleading with him to take the offer or to walk far, far away from it. The drawback right there, nestled in with all those leather-bound treasures: David. Those were David's books, and they came at the cost of deeper entanglement into David's life. Something Rhys had spent years running from.

"You're serious?" Rhys asked.

"As a heart attack. Catalog it, cross-reference it, take it home with you, I don't care. Just help me figure this out. Hell, point me in the right direction and I'll take it from there." His voice took on a slightly darker tone, diminished somehow. "I can't be sick, Rhys. I can't."

Rhys turned to stare at the floor-to-ceiling shelves, bringing his hand up to touch his mouth. Moira's heart was beating so hard in her chest she felt sure that David must be able to hear it. If she told Rhys to refuse, she would never forgive herself. But if he waded right back into the middle of David's life and tried to save him from himself, she wasn't sure if any of them would survive it. It had almost killed Rhys the first time. He had told her, the same night he swore that he would never let David set foot in their house again.

Apparently, this was a week for breaking promises.

"I... I'll have to think about it," Rhys managed. He looked at Moira, and his face was pale and desperate. God, when was the last time she had seen him want something so badly? The moment he first saw her in her wedding dress, maybe.

"What's there to think about?" David asked, pushing himself up to his feet. A bit of color had come back in his face, and although he winced, he was able to stand just fine. "All I'm asking is for a couple hours of your time."

"This is more than a couple hours of work."

"Then I'm asking you for a professional favor, and I'll compensate. Come on, Rhys. For God's sake, don't leave me to figure this shit out on my own."

Rhys plucked up his peacoat and shrugged it on. *We're leaving*, his eyes told Moira. She quickly began to gather her purse and umbrella off the floor, happy to get out of this awful old house with its oppressive, stale air. She hadn't been able to breathe right since setting foot inside.

"I need to think," Rhys repeated. "Let me talk to Moira about it."

"Don't worry, I've got something for her, as well."

Moira couldn't help the scoff that rose up in her throat. "What do you have that I want?"

"Do you really want to have that conversation right here, now?" David asked. He flicked his eyes over to Rhys and then back at her. She didn't speak this language, but she got the impression he was passing her a note to show that he knew something Rhys didn't. Inviting her into a secret.

"I don't know what occasion I'd have to see you again," she said crisply. "Anything you want to say, you'd better say it now."

David fished another cigarette out of his box of Parliaments. He lit it, and took a long drag, looking at her squarely. This was more like the David she knew: haughty, self-assured, and ready to make a deal.

"You can do more than you let on to your clients. A lot more. You *see* things. You hear them. But you pretend like you don't. Why?"

"Leave her alone," Rhys said. "She's allowed her privacy."

"I can handle myself, Rhys," Moira said. She arched an eyebrow David's way. "You think I don't know what I'm doing, is that it? That I need you to ride in on your white horse and save me from my uneducated ways?"

"No. I'm the one that needs you."

This threw Moira for a loop. She couldn't say she ever imagined finding herself in this position. It seemed like a trap. But her ego was purring, begging to be stroked, so she ventured, "Need me how?"

"You said it yourself, I've got no defenses up against anything that wants to hurt me. Maybe, *possibly*, I was foolish to go so long without them. If you know anything about how to protect myself from more of those blackouts, I'd be happy to hear it. But I know you're a busy woman and you're a professional whose time is valuable, so I'm offering you compensation."

"You'll teach me to channel the dead in return?" she said flatly. So far, he wasn't dangling anything she wanted badly enough to deal with him for long periods of time.

David smiled, a whisper of triumph touching his lips. "Or show you how to make them shut up. Dealer's choice."

She tried not to let him see how much that bit rocked her. Did he really have the secret to peace and quiet, stowed away somewhere inside him? Could he really make the voices go away, disappear the long-dead figures she caught staring at her in grocery lines and salon chairs? She had wanted that, begged for it, for years. She didn't think there was a way out. She thought the best she could do was just keep her eyes closed and press her hands over her ears and wait for the visions to go away. But now...

"You're bluffing."

"I'm not. I've got my back up against a wall here, so I'm offering you what I have. It's not a lot, and it's probably worth a lot less than what you've got to teach me, but I'm good at what I do. You know that. You could be too."

Moira pressed her lips tightly together. "I'm not a babysitter. I don't want you rifling around in my spiritual practice for tricks you can cherry-pick, making a God-awful mess of things as you go."

"Is that a 'no'?"

"That's an 'I'll think about it'. Rhys?"

He nodded and crossed to her, knowing when her light usage of his name actually meant *you've got five seconds to get going before I leave you behind.*

"Are you safe to drive?" Rhys asked David. The words sounded old and stale in his mouth.

David's eyes glimmered with disappointment, but otherwise he didn't let it show. "I'm feeling better now. You'll consider my offer?"

"I will."

"We both will," Moira said, already striding towards the door. "But don't call on us at home again, please."

"Wouldn't dream of it. Rhys?"

Her husband stopped at the door and tossed one last glance over his shoulder.

"Yes?"

"Thank you."

Rhys just nodded, then followed down the curling stairs after her.

They didn't speak again until they strode out into the drizzling, gray day and filled their lungs with good, clean air. Immediately, the headache pounding at Moira's temple cleared.

"He wants you, so he'll take us both as a package deal," she said as her heels clicked across the pavement. She didn't know if she was furious or impressed. "Make us both offers we can't turn down, so we'll support the other's decision."

"I know."

"He sure is one smart son of a bitch."

"I know."

"And that house… It's damn malefic is what it is. It's got some seriously bad vibes hanging around. You feel that?"

"You know I can't intuit my way out of a paper bag. It just felt like an old house to me."

"Hmm," Moira said, still unsettled.

Rhys glanced warily over at her as he unlocked the Lincoln and opened her door. It was like he was seeing something in her for the first time. "What did he mean, Moira? About you seeing things?"

Moira bit her lip. Once Rhys was seated next to her, she covered his hand with her own and looked him square in the eye. Honesty, her mother always said, was the cornerstone of a marriage. But it was also a heavy and unyielding thing to carry around with you.

"There's something I've been meaning to tell you."

The Chariot

CHAPTER TEN

RHYS

Moira didn't like having serious conversations in the car, so Rhys drove to her favorite vegan ice cream shop in the Brookline neighborhood. She ordered two heaping scoops of taro ice cream sprinkled with carob chips and cherry boba and studiously worked through them in a booth in the back of the café. Sweets were her security blanket.

"Do you remember Meemaw?" she asked at last, apparently out of nowhere. Rhys was eating toffee gelato drowned in rich espresso.

"Of course."

Rhys didn't know how he could forget the small old woman who had beckoned him over to the kitchen table the first time he'd met her family. Moira's father had met him at the door with a friendly handshake, and her mother, taller than Moira was, had emerged from the kitchen to envelop him in a hug. He thought he'd handled all the touching pretty well, considering he came from a family where that was only appropriate at weddings and funerals.

"He's got The Eye," the aging matriarch had pronounced, looking him over. "He's got plenty of scruples, too, which counts for something in this life. Respectful. Smart as a whip. But oh, he's *hungry*. Wants the whole world on a silver platter." She arched an eyebrow at her granddaughter. "You like that?"

An impish smile had crossed Moira's face. "Yes, Meemaw. I do."

Moira's grandmother had given his hand a squeeze. "Well alright, then. Looks like we're gonna have a wedding."

She had died just last year, and Moira had been quietly but utterly devastated. Millie Delacroix had taught her granddaughter how to make a proper galette, how to embroider a pillowcase and deliver a baby goat and let her *yes* be her *yes* when she made promises. Moira's accountant mother, Margo, had taught her plenty too: how to calculate natal charts by hand and braid hair for pocket money and balance a whole household's zero-sum budget. But Moira's grandmother passed down the most precious family knowledge: rootwork spells and West African folktales carefully preserved by shared community memory.

Moira took another bite of her ice cream, chewing miserably.

"Love," Rhys said, lowering his voice and putting his head close to hers. "What's going on? You're scaring me."

Moira brushed her nose against his, and he kissed her cold, sweet mouth. "There's just…" She sighed. "There's a lot. Have you ever wondered why I don't work with the dead?"

"You said it was for ethical reasons."

"Oh, it is… I just… I had some bad experiences when I was a little girl, too."

Moira had never mentioned any of this, and they had had heated discussions over the last year about being honest with each other. But this didn't sound like a lie coming to the surface; it sounded like something personal, potentially a site of distress. So he listened without passing judgement or saying a word.

"I've always been intuitive, you know that. I know what people need without asking; I can feel what they're feeling, even if I don't want to. But what I've never told you is that it's not just live folks. Sometimes, it works… on dead people."

"Dead people," Rhys repeated slowly. The information filtered through his existing knowledge of his wife, coloring and informing every single conversation they'd had about spirit work. "You mean you can feel the feelings of… dead people?"

"Sometimes, if the feelings are strong enough. Other times it's just little impressions. Sounds. Glimpses." All the fastidiously applied lipstick she had put on before doing battle with David was gone, eaten away with the ice cream. "Once, after Meemaw died, I woke up and saw her standing in our room, clear as day. She came and sat on the edge of the bed and smiled at me, and I know I wasn't dreaming, Rhys. It's not the first time something like that's happened."

Rhys swallowed hard. He wrangled down entities that would love to see him skinned alive on an average Thursday night, but demons, at least, made sense. They followed rules, they wanted things, they could be tricked or bribed into working for you. Ghosts were a different matter entirely. They lingered like watercolor washes over a painting, always just out of perceptibility but heavily, heavily felt. Ghosts were ripples of trauma echoing through the living world, reminders of horrible deaths and broken hearts and long, dark passages to realms Rhys wasn't ready to contemplate. He had never seen a ghost and didn't care to.

Moira was summertime and cool bed sheets against flushed skin and a wholesome meal straight from the oven. Everything she touched bloomed: flowers, babies, grown people. Moira was so tied up with verdant life that it was almost impossible to wrap his mind around the thought of dead things clamoring to speak to her.

"Baby?" she asked. It was hardly more than a whisper.

Rhys shook himself out of his staggered daze. This wasn't about him. There would be time enough to process the ramifications on his image of her later. Now, Moira was frightened and desperate for affirmation, holding open the delicate shell of her heart to reveal a dark, secret pearl. He couldn't blow this.

"I still love you," he said quickly, bringing her hand up to his mouth. "You're still my wife."

"But you're scared of me," she said, voice trembling. Her brown eyes filled with tears.

"No, no! Why would I be scared of you? Is this something *you're* scared of?" he asked.

"Yes," she said, and the floodgates opened. She curled up into his jacket and sobbed.

Rhys's jaw tightened. He didn't do well with public displays of emotion, but he slid his arms around her and let her cry anyway.

Rhys smoothed back her hair and kissed her forehead.

"I'm not angry you didn't tell me. But you could have. You know that, don't you? I would have listened."

"I know," she sniffed. "But I don't like talking about it."

"Then you don't have to."

Moira groaned and put her face in her hands, wiping off her tears. She daubed at her face with a napkin, doing her best not to disturb her mascara.

"But I *need* to. I can't ignore it anymore. The more I ignore them, the harder they try to get my attention. I thought I had all these imaginary friends, when I was a little thing. I didn't realize that boy on the swing set had been dead since the eighties, or know why the little girl who played with me in the sandbox at school was always there waiting for me. When I told my momma about it, she went white as a sheet and told me in no uncertain terms that spirits were nothing to fool with, that we didn't touch that sort of magic in our house. She was only trying to protect me. I promised her I would stay away from it. But it won't leave me alone."

She sagged against him, emptied. He wasn't strong enough to lift anyone, much less a woman as sturdily built as Moira, but he wanted terribly to scoop her up in his arms so she wouldn't have to walk the hundred feet to their car.

Rhys heaved a heavy sigh. "And that's where David comes in."

"I don't want his hands in this. But he might be the best chance I have. He's the most powerful medium on the east coast, and we just happen to know him. It's hard not to see that as a sign."

Rhys could feel the strands of an invisible net drawing closed around them both, tighter and tighter. They were on the brink of something they could both walk away from, in theory, but probably wouldn't be able to. His stomach churned.

One smart son of a bitch was right.

"Do you think he could do it?" Moira asked. "Show me how to get a handle on this?"

"Yes. That isn't the same thing as it being a good idea, or him being nice about it. But, yes."

She nodded numbly, eyes not really fixed on anything. He was shocked he hadn't noticed the strain this was taking on her. But she flittered from client to client and from spell to spell like a busy bumblebee, always buried in her work. And if he was being honest, he didn't emerge from the dark cavern of his study and his research half as much as he should to check on her. This was how things this big fell through the cracks.

"Are you going to help him out?" she asked quietly.

"I don't know," Rhys said, even though he knew damn well that he would commit crimes for an hour alone with those books. David knew that too. It had been checkmate the instant Rhys had seen the library. "Are you?"

"I need to think about it."

Rhys nodded and pushed away the rest of his affogato. Moira's skin had taken on an ashen undertone he didn't like. She needed rest, preferably tucked into bed with a hot mug of tea.

"Can I take you home?"

"Yes, please."

"Come on, little goddess," he sighed, rising from the table. She let him lead her back onto the street by the arm, and they both tried to ignore the heavy certainty hanging in the air around them.

The wind of their lives was shifting course, blowing towards the unknown.

The hanged man

CHAPTER ELEVEN

DAVID

Brunch at Santiago's was a monthly ritual for David's clique. Santiago's was a trendy fusion bistro that served bottomless mimosas and the best eggs Benedict in the city. The restaurant had buttery leather booths tucked into dim corners that were perfect for gossiping. But today, they were dining al fresco at one of the wrought-iron tables that lined the exterior. David was nursing a San Pellegrino on ice with his shades on against the late spring sun while Antoni verbally processed his decision to ghost his most recent almost-boyfriend.

"I feel like I'm in the right. At least… I'm definitely not in the wrong here."

"It depends on what you mean by 'in the wrong'," Nathan said, adding a handful of raspberries to his mimosa. He had been doing much of the active listening and advice-giving up until this point, since that wasn't really David's forte, and Cameron had been distracted through their first round of drinks – daydreaming about writing an academic rebuttal to some dead theologian, probably.

"I'm asking if what I did was shitty."

Nathan looked pained. "Uhhh… do I think it's shitty? No. Do I think it's the nicest thing to do to someone? No."

Antoni crossed his arms over his chest. "What does that even mean? I'm looking for a yes or no answer."

"I think it depends!"

"Why are you asking him?" David demanded, begrudgingly involving himself in the conversation. If he left it alone, Nathan would hedge for a half hour until he roused Antoni's temper. "He couldn't make a decision if you put a gun to his head, *and* he's straight."

"Hey," Nathan protested. "I'm the only one here who's married. That counts for something. At least I think I'm the only married one. Cameron?"

Cameron made a vague, noncommittal noise that suggested that the idea of marriage was preposterous to him. No one had ever been able to figure out if he was seeing anyone or not, but for some reason it was hard to imagine.

"Antoni, I won't hold your hand about this," David said, dismissing the question with a wave. "Every time I see you, it's the same thing. You're sure there's not someone else you're hung up on who's getting in the way of you connecting with Grindr randos?"

Antoni kicked him under the table, shooting him a daggered glance with his eyes. David had certain suspicions about who that might be, but it wasn't his place to say. That didn't mean he wouldn't poke the bear, however.

"I'm asking for real advice, David."

"I'm not gonna give it. What was wrong with this guy anyway? Same as the last one?"

"Nothing was necessarily *wrong*; everything was fine and then he just started getting really attached and was trying to plan months in advance with me, and I started getting really claustrophobic, you know, and–"

"Same as last time, case closed," David said.

Antoni fumed, but then he caught sight of something past David's shoulder and gave a sigh of relief. "Rhys, thank God. Settle an argument for us."

David tensed. This wasn't possible. Rhys had not been to brunch in six months. Not since the fight.

David turned around. Rhys McGowan approached the table with his hands tucked into the pockets of his peacoat, dark curls tossed by the wind. He came to a stop next to their table and tucked his sunglasses into his jacket, and David still wasn't entirely sure he wasn't hallucinating. This was all strictly off limits. David had gotten brunch in the divorce, by default, when Rhys had started making excuses for why he hadn't been showing up.

"Sorry I'm late," Rhys said. The lateness wasn't strange. Rhys was always the last one to arrive, either because of the commute in from Jamaica Plain or from his sporadic Sunday church attendance. What was strange was that he was here at all. Nathan and Cameron shared a meaningful look as Rhys took a seat between them, but no one commented on his sudden appearance.

David caught the scent of candle wax and incense as Rhys swept past him and intuited that Rhys had just been kneeling in some chapel moments before. David suddenly wanted a mimosa, or three. The craving hit him like a freight train, but he swallowed it back down along with a few swigs of sparkling water.

The table went right back into their old rhythm, Nathan passing Rhys the drink list while Antoni launched into his crisis of the week. The kid never missed a beat.

"Is it wrong to not call someone back after you've been seeing them for two months, give or take?"

"Who is it this time?" Rhys asked. "Guy or girl?"

"Does it matter? Just some guy I've been hanging out with."

"Romantically?"

"More or less."

"Of course it is; who raised you? Always do someone the courtesy of a call when you want to break something off."

David's mood swung from awestruck to irritated on a dime. Who did Rhys think he was, re-inserting himself back into their lives like he had never left, like he hadn't been stringing David along with his inscrutable list of boundaries for six months? He really thought he could just slot himself back into his usual seat and pick up conversation right where he left off, even though David was banned from setting foot in his house?

"Why?" David shot back. His father had always said his attitude was the cause of all his problems, and it tended to rear its head when he needed to shut up the most.

Rhys poured himself a glass of water from the decanter in the middle of the table. "It's the right thing to do. And Antoni, if you feel guilty about it, that's your conscience telling you that you've done something wrong and that you need to apologize. It sounds like this is keeping you up at night, so there's your answer."

"That's Catholic bullshit," David said. "Nine times out of ten, guilt is just internalized shame holding you back. If you don't like what you did, don't do it again. But don't beat yourself up about it."

Rhys fired a warning shot with his eyes but didn't rise to the challenge, just buttered himself a piece of artisanal focaccia.

"If you really want my opinion, Antoni," Rhys continued, as though David hadn't even spoken, "if you aren't ready to have a serious conversation with someone you're seeing, you aren't ready to be seeing him. You keep having these opened-ended flings and then freaking out when the other person tries to take them somewhere. Be more intentional from the start."

"Bullshit," David repeated with a dry laugh. Now he was remembering why Rhys drove him up the wall when they didn't have the veneer of professionalism between them to keep things civil. The moralizing, the endless judgement of other people. "Dating should be about having a good time with somebody else."

Rhys spared David a withering glance. "And how's that been going for you recently?"

Nathan leaned further across the table, nearly putting his body between the two men. He had always played referee, even back in the days when Rhys and David's spats were the product of living together. Cameron would always delicately remove himself from the situation, and Antoni usually took Rhys's side, the little bastard, but Nathan strived to be impartial.

"It's been a while since you came to brunch," Nathan ventured carefully.

"I've been busy," Rhys said smoothly. "Everyone is making their final thesis rush on the library, and I haven't had enough time for my own research. I've been trying to get my work out there more. Publish or perish, you know."

Only Cameron had any sort of understanding of the demands of academia, and he nodded sagely.

"You know, Kitty's been missing you," Nathan said. "We should all go out on the boat sometime."

Rhys's eyes skimmed over Nathan's face, so fast that someone who wasn't David might have missed it. He was gauging whether or not he wanted to accept this peace offering. Nathan hadn't handled the blow to their social circle well. He wanted everyone to get along, and he wanted everyone within arm's reach of him at all times, for cocktail hours or sporting events or crisp walks across Harvard yard to find a decent cup of coffee after Society meetings. Nathan's heart was too big for his own good, and he wore it proudly pinned to his chest like a wartime medal. Rhys was, by all accounts, a private and retiring person, suspicious of enthusiastic overtures of friendship. An invitation like this the instant he showed back up at brunch would probably be too much for him, and he would probably find a polite way to wriggle out of it.

"That sounds great," he said, much to David's surprise. He was making an effort, then. Actively working to reintegrate himself into their shared world. "Have Kitty phone Moira and we'll hash out a date." He even smiled when he said it, in a way that made Nathan beam right back with his sunset-strip grin.

"So," Rhys said, settling into his seat as the waiter poured him a glass of champagne and orange juice. "Besides boats and dating, what have we been discussing lately?"

This opened the floodgates to a torrent of occult chatter as everyone tried to fill Rhys in on what he had missed. Antoni was still working through Bardon to great success, with a diligence that David was surprised to see in a sorcerer so young. Cameron had been cross-analyzing some infernal names in various texts, which made Rhys's ears perk up, and David listened in silence as the two men swapped linguistic theories about the origins of summoning formulas. Nathan, as usual, was just happy to be there, and bounced between thread to thread without missing a beat. He was infinitely flexible in a way David could never be, filling the air with chatter. David couldn't help but feel a little jealous. He was a social maverick, sure, but there was always a sense of performance to it. Nathan seemed genuinely at ease around damn near everybody. It reminded David of Moira, of her proclivity for making friends out of every stranger.

"David," Rhys said, snagging his attention. "Will you take a walk around the block with me?"

David set his glass down definitively, staring at Rhys as though he had just proposed they go halfsies on buying a casino together. "Now?"

Rhys just gave a take-it-or-leave-it sort of shrug. Nathan politely pretended not to notice the negotiations going on, but Antoni looked outright offended.

"You just got here, Rhys. You disappear for the entire winter and now–"

"Let him go," Cameron said.

Antoni fell back in his seat, seething, but he didn't say anything else. Rhys reached for his wallet.

"I've got it," David said.

"No, you don't," Rhys replied, and tossed what he owed down on the table. David added a few larger bills to the pile, enough to cover the table's tab, but he was hardly paying attention. Rhys was here, and he wanted to talk to him privately. David didn't know whether he wanted to punch Rhys in the mouth or cling onto him for fear that he was just going to disappear again, but either way, he was having fits. Quietly, of course. Subtly, so as not to give Rhys the satisfaction of knowing the effect his presence had.

A temperate spring breeze hit them as they stepped onto the street, and David quickened his pace to keep up with Rhys's stride. David was taller and his legs were longer, but Rhys walked with mercenary intentionality. David had no idea how this was supposed to go. Was he supposed to wait for Rhys to speak first, or volunteer some kind of apology? He felt like he had apologized more than enough. If Rhys was here, walking alone with him on a sunny afternoon, then his most cardinal rule was already broken. They were already socializing outside of a Society meeting, and that meant David could barrel through any other taboo he wanted.

"Antoni is going to be pissed at you," he said. "You show back up for ten minutes, get his hopes up, then break his heart."

"Antoni's fine."

"Antoni idolizes you. He's been mad at me for keeping you away from him ever since you cut me off. You know we go to the same gym, right? He refused to spot me for a month after you stopped showing up."

"You don't think he has a crush, do you?"

"How should I know? Not my business. Besides, if he's pining after anybody, it's not you, and we both know it. I think he's just pissed you pulled a disappearing act."

"Well." Rhys wrinkled his nose as they crossed the street and walked alongside a string of ivy-adorned brownstones. "Maybe it was wrong of me to cut everyone out for so long."

There wasn't the shadow of a joke on his face, but David sometimes had trouble telling when Rhys was joking even when the punchline was right in front of him.

"I expect you to tell him that. I don't want to be your go-between."

"I will. But I've been meaning to talk to you. This seemed like the easiest way."

David realized he was holding his box of cigarettes, rotating it around in his fingers. Rhys made him nervous when he was like this, reticent and unpredictable. David's fingers itched for his lighter.

"Do you mind?" he asked.

"Go ahead."

Rhys slowed to a stop beneath one of the beech trees shading the sidewalk so David could light a cigarette. Then, to David's great surprise, Rhys nodded at the carton. "Can I trouble you for one?"

The muscles in David's neck tensed. He felt as though he were being invited into one of those old carnival games: step right up and stick your hand in the shadowy vase and you might pull out a prize.

Or a snake.

"You haven't smoked since college."

"For everything a season, right?"

David retrieved a cigarette from the box and held it out to Rhys, who placed it between his lips expectantly. David wasn't much for chivalry, but Rhys hadn't lit his own cigarette the entire time they were together. Rhys hadn't allowed him to get close enough to touch him, much less help him nurse an old vice, since their falling out six months ago. It was hard to say if this was an invitation or not, but David took the chance and brought the tiny flame up to Rhys's face. He lingered there long enough for the cigarette to catch, not knowing if he was going to get his hand bitten off.

Rhys drew the smoke into his mouth ponderously, watching David with hard eyes and a curious tilt to his head. It reminded David of a bird. A crow, maybe.

"How have you been? Any more blackouts?"

David gulped down his own cigarette, not relenting until the smoke burned the inside of his lungs. It was how he had learned to smoke at fourteen, right before his father carted him off to America and dropped him in some prep school where he wasn't allowed to even look at a cigarette. He still snuck them, smoking them behind dumpsters and faculty cars like they were going out of style.

"No, no more of that."

"But?"

A cool, stray wind blew in from the south, catching the smoke out of Rhys's mouth. They weren't all the way to summer yet, and David wasn't all the way sure he wanted Rhys to know the extent of things.

"I'm still feeling… off. Sick, like Moira said. I'm sensitive to every little whisper of psychic activity, but I can't focus on any of it. I feel…"

He grasped for the right words. Rhys waited patiently. David had very little experience precisely naming his emotions. Somehow, that endeavor felt more frightening than the blackouts.

"I'm getting tired way faster than I should. Fatigued and dizzy at work for no reason. And I can't sleep. Can't sit still."

Rhys nodded, then took up his pointed stride again. "We've been thinking," Rhys said, "about your offers at the house."

"I meant them both."

"I know you did. I know what you're doing, David."

"What am I doing?"

Rhys looked like he wanted to answer, but he pulled his punch at the last instant and just shook his head. "I don't have time to take on another huge research project. I'm slammed at the library, and I have barely any time for my own summoning work."

Something sank like a stone right down to the bottom of David's stomach. He wished he was surprised.

"It's fine. I appreciate you thinking it over."

"I'm not telling you no. I'm setting my boundaries."

Boundaries, more boundaries, so many that David thought he might strangle himself in them. Irritation ignited in his chest and caught fire on his tongue.

"I'm not playing fucking emotional Jenga with you anymore. Listen, if it's going to be too much trouble, I'll get someone else. I don't want this to turn into a Thing."

Rhys touched him lightly on the elbow to lead him across the busy street, face entirely unbothered by David's outburst. Maybe he was getting used to them again.

"It won't be. That's why we're talking about boundaries. I'll help you out with this, because I don't want to see you run yourself into the ground and because I would drain my savings account for any one of those books in your father's library."

"And?"

"We can try talking, if you want. I don't know if that will help this whole process or make it worse. But I'm getting tired of being petty and I'm tired of doing backflips to keep our social calendars separate."

"My God, Rhys McGowan, tired of being petty? Somebody hospitalize me, I'm obviously much worse off than any of us feared."

Rhys tried to shoot him a disapproving look, but it morphed into a smirk somewhere along the way. David recognized that smile, half-reproving, half-amused. It had been his constant companion at Williams, through late night raids on the occult section of the library and vodka-fueled quick-and-dirty summonings on dorm room floors.

"I'm not saying things can go back to the way they were, but we can try to figure something out."

"Fine by me. Do you want me to bring the books by your house? I can have them shipped over if you want."

"No, Moira still doesn't want you coming over. She wants to keep all this separate from our home life."

There it was. The catch. The hoop David would have to jump through like a well-trained dog if he wanted any scraps of Rhys's attention.

"Don't you think that's a little ridiculous?" David pressed. "Where else are we supposed to go?"

"The Beacon Hill house. I thought that was obvious?"

"Rhys, you know I hate that house. If there wasn't so much money tied up in it, I would have burned it to the ground as an eighteenth-birthday present to myself."

"It seems ideal. There's plenty of space, nobody to ask any questions, and all the primary documents are on-site."

David snapped another cigarette out of his carton. "I'm just supposed to sit around in dear old Dad's place while you read books? I'd rather die, thanks. I have an apartment, you know."

"I hate that godawful modern monstrosity."

"Easy, it's a million-dollar condo."

"It's an overpriced Ikea showroom. Be reasonable. We're not lugging an antiquarian library up twenty stories for the sake of your blood feud with your dead dad. If we're going to do this, we do it right."

David smoked in sullen silence for the length of the street, bobbing and weaving between the foot traffic until he and Rhys turned another corner. Here, the narrow residential street was quieter, lined with commuter cars.

"Well, if we're going to do this, then I'm going to be honest with you," David said finally, stabbing his cigarette butt out underfoot. "I don't know what her problem is with me. Does she think I'm some kind of homewrecker? Come *on*."

"She doesn't trust you, David. She has no reason to. Frankly, I respect that."

"When have I lied to her? When have I ever done anything shitty except the *one thing* I did in good faith and then apologized for later?"

This wasn't going well. David hadn't intended to bring up Moira, not now. Not ever. There was no way through this conversation that didn't end with him coming out looking bad.

Rhys finished the final puff of his cigarette and put it out in a nearby trash can. "She doesn't know you."

"We've known each other for what, four years? Since before you two got married."

"No, she's seen you around, and sometimes you share clients. She doesn't *know* a thing about you. Not about your history, or your goals, or your likes and dislikes, and certainly not your family."

David recoiled, repulsed. "Why the hell would she? Is she my doctor? My wife? My accountant? Why not just ask for my social security number while she's at it?"

Rhys pinched the bridge of his nose and squeezed his eyes shut. He took a deep, steadying breath. "Listen. How do I say this? You're important to me."

"I'm touched," David said, voice flat.

"Let me finish," Rhys said, holding up a stiff hand. "You're important to me, and she sees that, so she wants to be on good terms with you as well. You two don't have to be friends. You don't even have to understand each other; God knows, you're polar opposites. But she has always been willing to try, at least."

"I didn't notice."

"Because you bulldoze her. You walk all over anyone who doesn't go along with your every whim. You don't see it, but you do. And I know you don't mean it, but that isn't an excuse."

Cold trickled down the inside of David's ribs. Rhys was burning through every bit of his goodwill. "Wow, it sure is honesty hour. I'm not sure if I prefer this or the silence."

Rhys turned suddenly on his heel, and David almost crashed into him. Rhys's voice was steady, but his eyes blazed. "I love her, David."

"Christ, you nearly barreled me over. Don't be dramatic, nobody is questioning–"

"I'm not done. I love Moira all the way to hell and back. I love her more than money, more than my own pride and ambition. That woman is my home, and I am more than willing to prioritize her – vehemently, if need be. If she tells me she needs something to feel safe, she gets it. End of story."

David jutted his chin out combatively, but he knew better than to tangle with Rhys on this. He had been on the receiving end of that honed, blind devotion before, and he knew how far Rhys would go to follow it.

"And what does she need now? A cozy conversation about our feelings over tea and cookies? Sorry Rhys, but that is just never going to happen."

"She just wants to come along with me to Evgeni's house."

David barked a laugh. "To what? Chaperone me?"

"Help, if she can."

This gave David pause. With the way this conversation had been careening, he'd assumed Moira had zero interest in taking him up on his offer to show her around the spirit world. If she had any other opinion of him besides hatred, Rhys was doing a poor job of conveying it.

"She actually wants to work with me?"

They rounded another corner, Rhys falling in behind David as they slipped between an apartment building and construction scaffolding.

"She hasn't decided yet. That's between the two of you. But she's amenable to spending a little more time with you so she can figure it out."

"Is this the part where you tell me to stop trying to involve her in my scary, immoral necromancy?"

Rhys came to a stop, and it was only then David realized they had merely circled the block. They were right back where they started, on the corner outside Santiago's. At the other end of the outdoor seating area, the three Society brothers carried on their conversation over a second round of drinks.

"That's not my call to make," Rhys said. There was something pleading in his eyes that threw David off balance. "This is her choice, and I know you aren't trying to hurt her. Just... be careful. She's got a lot of shit she hasn't worked through rattling around in her head, and no offense, but so do you. I don't know what happens when you put two people like that in a room together with ghosts, and I don't want to see anything bad happen to either of you."

David sifted through all the smart comments he could make in response before discarding them wholesale. Instead, he just nodded somberly. Rhys was a chronic killjoy and worrier extraordinaire, but for once, his fears might be founded.

Rhys gave a jerking nod in response and started to move away towards his car. "We'll come by this weekend. Does eleven on Saturday work?"

"Fine with me."

"Thanks for the cigarette and the walk."

"We managed to go about..." David glanced at his watch, "ten minutes without shouting at each other. Call Ripley's."

"Don't get cocky," Rhys chastised, but that smirk was back. "This whole thing is just me doing you a favor, alright? Don't expect anything else."

"You're not my type anymore, anyway," David said archly, even though he knew Rhys wasn't talking about sex. He was referring obliquely to something far more precarious and frightening: Friendship. Real openness and trust with each other.

David's chest tightened, old fight-or-flight instincts kicking in.

"Sure," Rhys said, and waved at him, half-dismissal, half-farewell, as he slid into the Lincoln.

The High priestess

CHAPTER TWELVE

MOIRA

They arrived at the house on Beacon Hill ten minutes before eleven with a tray of Dunkin' Donuts coffee and a bag of apple fritters in hand. Moira had picked out an eighties, drop-waist ivory dress for the occasion. Its big, puffed sleeves made her feel powerful. Everything about David made her feel like she was too soft, and she hoped the outfit would help to combat that preemptively. Her hair was pulled out of her face into simple, no-nonsense twists, and cherry lipstick was slashed across her mouth like a stoplight. Rhys had also gone out of his way to dress presentably. He had dug a button-down out of his closet that was less rumpled than the rest and reached for his good, shined shoes and an assortment of filigree rings. Rhys's style of dress had become more subdued since he started working at the library, but deep down he was still a sullen teenager armoring himself against the world with black clothes and smudged eyeliner, and Moira was still the contentious art student desperate to stand out in a sea of conformity.

"We go in, we get out," Rhys repeated for the third time that day. "Home in time for dinner."

"Right," she said, and rang the doorbell.

No one answered, but a window a story above them was thrown open.

"Library," David called down. "Door's open."

The distant sound of music filtered down to the street as Moira tentatively pushed open the huge door and stepped inside. He was playing something raucous enough to fill a stadium, bombastic and yet comforting, like her favorite vintage T-shirt.

The eighties music fit her perception of him, but only if she tilted her head and took it in from a forty-five-degree angle. There was still something charming about the surprise.

They followed the wail of electric guitar up to the library, which David had already taken over with his own brand of organized chaos. Certain books had been hauled off the shelves and arranged into stacks with sticky notes plastered to the top, and a tea table had been dragged out into the center of the room. A portable record player was sitting on top of it, along with a twelve-pack of sparkling water and a carton of cigarettes.

David was sitting cross-legged on the ground with legal correspondence spread out around him, two highlighters in hand as he drained a sparkling water. Moira couldn't recall ever seeing him in anything less formal than a blazer, but he was wearing an honest-to-God T-shirt and jeans. Granted, they probably cost more than she was willing to spend on a month's groceries, but she was still thrown off balance by the sight. For a second, he looked half his age.

"You're early," he said, not looking up at them as he finished scribbling something in the margins of a printout. "Traffic wasn't terrible coming into the city, I hope?"

"No," Rhys said, setting down the coffee and donuts on the tea table. "Can I turn this off, please?"

"It's about the most inoffensive record I have in the house. You're lucky I didn't break out the Whitesnake."

"It still stresses me out. I can't work with all that shouting going on."

"Well, we're at an impasse then; I can't work in silence."

Moira retrieved her mocha from the tray and handed David the large coffee with cream.

"Ah, caffeine, my old friend," he purred. "You're a peach."

"We brought donuts, too."

"No, thanks. Those don't fit my macros. I'm a little tied up down here, but why don't you kill the record before hubby has a fit?"

Rhys stripped off his jacket and rolled his eyes. He was more anxious than he looked, Moira could tell, but he was making a great effort to appear comfortable and in-control.

"I'll meet you in the middle if you can find something mellow and turn it down to a decibel level that isn't an assault on human ears," Rhys said.

"Let Moira do it, then," David replied. "I'm sure she knows how to cater to your delicate sensibilities."

Moira was so used to David barely acknowledging her existence that she was caught off-guard by this snippy, bantery version of him, a version that needled Rhys openly and called her 'peach.' This, too, was some sort of defense mechanism, she was sure. A second line of protection after his above-it-all, alpha-lawyer façade was pierced. She didn't know if he was inviting her into tentative good graces, or laying a trap of mockery for her to walk into. But she didn't have anything better to do with her hands, and this house still made her nervous, so she crouched down next to David and began to flip through the crate of vinyl albums at his side.

"I'm not sure what is all in there," David admitted. "Can't vouch for my taste at eighteen. The Crosely isn't the best quality either, but it's better than quiet."

Moira's fingers deftly flipped through the battered cardboard cases. David at eighteen had a taste for, well... No taste at all. All of the albums were belligerently over-the-top rock bands. And a couple of early aughts pop albums. Nothing that Rhys would find at all palatable.

"You must have been a terror," she said. "Did you torture your family with this stuff?"

David shrugged one shoulder. "My dad forced me to learn classical piano from kindergarten on, so everything at the opposite end of the spectrum was a breath of fresh air." He caught her eyeing a Britney Spears album and said quickly, "Some of those are my sister's."

Moira pressed her lips together to keep from giggling. He wasn't as good a liar as the law degree would suggest.

"I didn't realize you had a sister. Older or younger?"

"Half-sister. Seven years older."

She retrieved the only album she recognized that probably wouldn't drive Rhys up the wall.

"Is Fleetwood Mac okay?" she asked her husband. Rhys, predictably, had been drawn by the magnetism of the books, and was examining the stacks left out on the table by David.

"Fine," he said, peering at one of the sticky notes. "How do you have these organized, David?"

"I grabbed every bit of family history I could find, and then pulled out whatever Evgeni had about psychic ailments or attacks. I wasn't sure what you were looking for."

"Honestly, I'm not sure either. Did you draw up that list of symptoms like I asked?"

David held up a lined piece of paper, ripped out of a notebook. "I've decided that if it turns out that I've got some kind of malignant brain tumor, I don't want to know. Just let me drop dead in peace."

"Don't even say that. And I'm not any kind of doctor, so if you have any reason to think you might be sick, I want you to take yourself to your physician."

"Yeah, yeah. Let me know if you find anything. I've got a ton of reading to do."

"No rest for the wicked, huh?" Moira said, retrieving an apple fritter from the bag and tearing it into bite-sized pieces. "I guess lawyers don't get days off."

"This *is* my day off," David said, gesturing to his designer jeans. "No clients, no office hours, no court time."

"And all that reading is just…"

"Homework. Gotta bill those hours."

"Here I thought Rhys worked too much. You're sure you're not hungry?"

David tossed down his highlighter and stood, pressing his hands against the small of his back and stretching.

"I'll eat later. I would, however, like to talk to you."

Moira crossed her arms and felt her eyebrows shoot up to her hairline.

"It's possible," David began, "that you and I got off on the wrong foot."

Maybe it was the sheer improbability of the situation, or the bubbling stress of being cooped up in this creepy house with her least favorite person, but Moira couldn't help it. She threw her head back and laughed. "Oh sugar, you're gonna have to give me a minute," she said, almost cackling at the thought of it all. "The wrong foot? Oh, my stars. Let's not pretend that you and I like each other very much, Mr Aristarkhov."

"And yet, you're in my father's house."

"Alright, so I came with my husband on a business trip. What about it?"

"You came back because you want something from me. Are we going to be honest about that or just pretend?"

"David," Rhys warned, but he was too distracted flipping through the books to finish his rebuke, like a parent cut-off mid-lecture by a pressing email.

Moira found she wasn't bothered. If anything, this fight was overdue. "You've got a streak of mean in you as wide as the Atlantic; did anybody ever tell you that?"

David didn't seem bothered by this accusation. "I don't really care what people think of me; I care about getting down to the bottom of things. The truth isn't always nice, Ms Delacroix. No point in acting like it is."

"And what do you suspect is down at the bottom of me, huh?"

The floorboards creaked overhead, and David's eyes snapped up. Not an uncommon sound in a house as old as this, but he was paying close attention. The creaking sounded again, this time from another place. Like someone was moving around upstairs.

Startled, Moira looked to David for an explanation. He scowled up at the ceiling in annoyance.

"Rhys?" she asked, her voice coming out thin and high despite every attempt to sound casual. "You hear that?"

Her husband glanced up from the book. He had been examining it so closely that his nose was nearly pressed to the pages.

"Hear what?"

"Listen."

They listened silently for a few agonizing moments. Then the creaking came again. This time, there were heavy, thudding footsteps to go along with it. There was definitely someone else in the house with them. Had David neglected to mention a live-in housekeeper? Or had someone broken in to go rooting around for valuables?

Just as Moira opened her mouth to ask what they should do, Rhys shrugged and made his pronouncement: "See? Nothing."

Moira felt like she had been doused with cold water. Nothing? How could he say it was nothing when someone upstairs was so clearly making a racket, getting up to God knows what?

Rhys turned back to his research, leaving Moira stunned. Was she losing her mind? Had she hallucinated the whole thing? But David...

David was watching her with keen interest. He was a little pale, but his eyes burned with every bit of their usual vigor. "That's very interesting," was all he said. Then, before she could question him further, he swung his attention back to Rhys. "Any luck?"

"I just started, David; it's going to take me days just to get all these records in order. Find some way to entertain yourself. Put somebody in jail or something. You're good at that."

"I've got a better idea," Moira cut in. This was not going to devolve into the Rhys-and-David show. Not on her watch. "Why don't you tell me who let you get away with not learning to psychically protect yourself? That's what we're here for, right? To keep our bargains with each other. I didn't come all the way out here just to watch you highlight case notes."

David surveyed her warily, slouching against the upholstered chaise lounge. "In that case, it was my father. He brought me up in the occult community. He didn't seem to think protection was that important."

"Brought you up? How old were you? When you started training with him, I mean."

"I dunno, five? He knew how to look for the signs."

Moira felt her face soften despite her best efforts. She tried to imagine him as a child, wide-eyed and golden-haired, his tiny hands being placed on a planchette by grown magicians eager to see what he could do. She had heard of children that young being trained to keep their eyes and ears open for the dead.

They usually didn't grow up quite right.

"That's a lot of pressure to put on a kid."

"Well, I'd rather be exceptional than average. Pressure is part of the package."

There was something about that statement that stuck in Moira's intuition like a needle pricking her finger while she mended a dress. It was the kind of warning sign that would make her skip a bus she had a bad feeling about, or place a call to a friend when she got the sense the strange man walking behind her might be following her home.

"Okay, then. First things first, I'm teaching you how to ground."

"Sounds terrible."

"Which is exactly why you need to learn. Come on over here, indigo child."

Moira moved to one of the antique couches and hefted two large damask throw pillows onto the floor. She arranged herself cross-legged on one and gestured for David to do the same.

"Lesson one in How Not to Be a Spiritual Danger to Yourself and Others," Moira said crisply, "is how to root yourself in your own body, no matter where you are."

"Sounds like meditation," David said, eyes narrowed. There was a hard set to his shoulders that reminded Moira of a teen mouthing off to a lecturing principal. "I don't do that sort of thing."

"Why not?"

"I don't see the point in sitting still and not doing anything useful for hours at a time just so I can feel good about myself."

"You don't see the point in it, or you're afraid of it?"

David barked out a laugh. "Afraid? Sorry, what?"

"Lots of people are afraid of being alone with themselves," Moira said with a shrug. "They're afraid of what they might find out about themselves, or they're terrified that the world will stop turning if they step away from the day's to-do list. Pretty common hang-up, actually."

"I'm not *hung up;* I just don't want to waste time learning some stupid breathing exercise when I could black out at any second."

Not just scared of siting still, then. Terrified. She had gotten this kind of pushback from clients dozens of times. Generally, defensiveness was a clear sign they weren't ready for her services. They had to start wanting to help themselves first. But this time, sending the client away to chew on some tough lessons wasn't an option. David was here, and in danger, and locked into a three-way pact with her and Rhys. She was going to have to forge on ahead, problem client or no.

"Listen to me. I know you don't see value in this, but it's the best way I know to help you. That was my half of the bargain, and I'm going to stick to it. It's not your fault no one told you how to protect yourself. But now you have the chance to learn."

David's eyes were still hard with suspicion, but he uncoiled from his fighting stance. "Fine. But you're up next, Ms Delacroix. And I'm not going easy on you."

"Fine. My daddy raised me not to shirk hard work. Now close your eyes. Don't fuss. Just do it."

David managed to obey while conveying to her with a quirk of his eyebrows that this entire exercise was ridiculous. If it helped him to cooperate, she was willing to tolerate a little attitude.

Moira tried to bring her awareness into her own body, attending to the rhythm of her own breath like there wasn't a dozen other things fighting for her attention. The fiery competitive streak David roused in her, the clammy feeling on the back of her neck this house gave her, the concern for Rhys's emotional well-being circling in her stomach like an anxious cat... She tried to let it all go and sink deep down into this moment.

"I want you to become aware of your own body, from the crown of your head to the soles of your feet. Feel where it's pressing into the wood floor underneath you. Sink into that point of contact and just take a deep, steadying breath. Breathe into the bottom of your belly, all the way down into the ground, if you can."

David, to his credit, did as he was told. Moira waited for the rise and fall of his chest to become deep and regular before she went on.

"Now visualize all your excess energy, all the stress and spiritual electricity of the day, sinking down through you into that floor. You walk around all day absorbing it from other people, other places, other spirits. Just let it go. Trust that you're enough, and that you don't need all that heaviness clinging to you. Let it go."

A ripple of some emotion – confusion, maybe – furrowed David's brow. Moira sat in perfect stillness, observing him so closely that she caught the faint tightening of his mouth, the shallow scoop of constricting breaths. He was running up against that fear, whatever it was. The concept of letting go might be enough to get under his skin; David went through life with his fingers tight on every rein and gearshift.

"There's no timeline on this," she said, a little softer. "This isn't a test. Take all the time you need."

Moira managed a few steadying breaths before something above her rattled, creaked, and crashed to the ground. She gasped, nearly jumping out of her skin. Rhys was shuffling through papers in the distance as though nothing had happened, apparently deaf to the strange noises. David was still sitting with his eyes closed, face placid.

"That's so fucking annoying," he murmured.

Moira clapped a hand over her pounding heart, fear burning so hot within her it came out as anger. "What the hell is going on in this house?"

David opened his eyes with a dramatic flutter. "You're a smart woman; put two and two together."

"I didn't come here today so you could make fun of me."

"I'm not making fun of you," David said, and now he was the one who sounded offended. Was he really so oblivious to his own nastiness, or did he think he was showing her some kind of tough love? Perhaps to a child raised on cruelty and impossible expectations, that's the only kind of love he could recognize.

"Well, the way you're acting doesn't feel good," she shot back, refusing to let him get away with bad behavior, childhood trauma or no. "Do you understand that?"

"I do," David said, sounding slightly chastened. "Listen, Ms Delacroix, I... appreciate the effort you're putting in here. I'm trying to put in effort on my end, too."

He hoisted himself up onto his feet and held a hand out to her. Moira stared at it for a moment in fury, then conceded and let him pull her to her feet. Standing, they were nowhere near eye to eye, but Moira felt for the first time that he was appraising her on equal footing, as a force to be reckoned with.

"Congratulations," he said. "You passed your first test."

Moira didn't withdraw her hand. She held him tight and looked him in the eye the way her father did when making a deal with a client that he suspected might renege.

Then, inexplicably, she felt David nudge her gently, energetically, through the point of contact. She might have missed it if she hadn't been paying attention, like brushing shoulders with someone in a hallway. But she *was* paying attention, and she noticed the way he sent a faint pulse of reassurance into her fingertips. If he had spoken some soothing platitude aloud, she probably wouldn't have believed him, but there was no Aristarkhov artifice in his touch. Moira could only sense his emotions for a flicker of an instant, but it was enough: he didn't like seeing her so scared.

Moira probably should have dropped her hand then, but curious as ever, she pressed the issue. She squeezed his fingertips ever so slightly, sending him a clear emotional image of her iron resolve, her refusal to back down or be underestimated.

David snatched his hand back and slipped it into his pocket, as though he had been burned. Behind them, the record came to a scratchy end, filling the room with silence.

"Come back next week and we'll talk about it," David said.

"That's your move?" Moira asked, her fingers still warm from his touch.

"That's my move. Thanks for the lesson."

He turned his back on her and flipped the record over. Then he lowered himself back into his sea of paperwork. Moments later, David was a million miles away.

CHAPTER THIRTEEN

DAVID

The next time he was supposed to go meet Moira and Rhys at Beacon Hill, David woke up with a splitting headache. It felt like five vodka sodas on an empty stomach and two hours of sleep, though he was coming up on three years sober and was the most well-hydrated person he knew. Either the psychic sickness was getting worse, or he was dying. David wasn't entirely sure which one he preferred.

When he shouldered open the front door to the Beacon Hill house, hands full of car keys and a cardboard tray stuffed with lattes, the house didn't put up a fuss. If anything, it almost seemed happy to see him, like he was a king restoring order to a domain long left to grow fallow and wild. He didn't like that.

Rhys and Moira were in the library, shoving open the huge bay windows to let in a spring breeze. Moira loitered close to the windows, breathing in the fresh air and wearing some kind of floor-length orange paisley Charlie's Angels number. An amber dragonfly pendant gleamed on her throat.

"Wasn't sure if you were going to show," she remarked. She looked a little short of breath, which didn't surprise David. How she managed to breathe at all in the evil atmosphere of this house, he would never know.

"Why wouldn't I? I confirmed the date with you."

"You sent me a Google calendar invite called 'training' with no description. I wasn't entirely sure what to expect."

"Well, we're all here now," he said. Pleasantly, he hoped. He was going to be diplomatic today. He was going to keep it together and stay in control. This was his house, after all. He should start acting like it.

He held a latte out to Moira. "I stopped at Tatte on my way down and it seemed rude not to bring you anything. You like sweets, right?"

"I suppose. What is it?"

"Your new favorite."

Moira brought the coffee to her lips and sipped delicately. David generally avoided drinking his calories, but this was one of his favorite cheat meals. Strong espresso and frothed milk mingled with the decadent taste of honey, cardamon, and sugared pistachio.

"Oh my God," she said, eyes round with delight.

David felt a pulse of self-satisfaction go through him. He didn't actually have many reasons to be nice to people in his daily life, but he hadn't been able to stop thinking about what Moira had said to him the last time they were together. She had thought he was mocking her. David was appalled to find that he actually cared that he had insulted her, and even more appalled to find that he wanted to make amends.

Emotional entanglements were tricky, most often not worth the headache and heartsickness they induced, but if Moira was going to do her best to help him, he should do his best to show his appreciation to her.

"Rhys?" David held the third cup out to him. "Before you ask, no, it isn't a triple shot, because your heart is gonna burst one of these days and I'm not aiding and abetting."

"I won't say no to caffeine," Rhys said.

David dumped his coat and briefcase down on a creaky loveseat. He gestured Rhys towards his father's sprawling library. "Well, we'll leave you to it. Work your magic. Literally or figuratively, I don't really care which."

"Where are you two running off to?" Rhys asked, glancing nervously between David and his wife.

David gave Moira a sweet smile, and she couldn't have looked more wary. Amazing how she could freely offer him kindness without making any preamble towards trusting him as far as she could throw him. It was a skill he was jealous of. All the charm in the world, and he still couldn't fabricate a kindness that anyone believed.

"She hasn't been given a proper tour of the house yet. It isn't quite Southern hospitality, but I was brought up to make sure guests knew their way around."

"I never got a tour," Rhys said, almost sounding offended.

"You were never a guest. Ms Delacroix?"

David offered her his arm. He was in shirtsleeves, and he could feel her warm touch as she wrapped tentative fingers around his bicep.

"Suit yourself," she said. "Lead the way."

They ambled through the second floor of the home, their steps leaving ghostly footprints in the dust. The portraits on the wall scowled down at them. Whorls of oil paint, thick and dark as blood, ate up all the light in the room.

David spoke without looking at her, a small smile tugging at his lips. "You're nervous." Her anxiety was a thin thread pulled taut under his skin, emanating from their point of contact. He chased it with his mind, trying to root out the heart of her. "Don't worry, I'm not taking you up to my gothic attic to murder you."

"And you're trying very hard to keep a calm mind and not give me anything," Moira replied. "But you aren't actually relaxed."

David grinned, glancing down at her. She kept her gaze fixed ahead of her, never breaking stride.

"You can pick up *layers*. That's fantastic."

"All I do is pay attention to the way people are feeling, even when they don't say it outright. It's nothing special."

"I beg to differ. You're empathic. Genuinely. I could hold hands with someone in a darkened séance room for an hour and only be able to pick up the littlest threads of dread or anger. The strong emotions. But you're a maestro."

Moira shrugged. "Thanks, I suppose. But you shouldn't be walking me through this place. The air's no good; I feel like I'm breathing in mold spores or asbestos or something."

"I promise you'll be safe."

"I'm not worried about me; I'm worried about you. You're sick as a dog. If I were you, I would get far away from this house, or any other place that agitates whatever you've got going on inside you. I can feel it circling you like shark, waiting to bring you down."

David untwined their arms, shoving his hands into his pockets. He turned on his heel to face her, trying to maintain his self-possession. "What about auras? Can you see those?"

"No. Can you?"

"Sure."

Moira pursed her lips. "What does mine look like?"

David wasn't expecting that one. She'd asked it with such an open curiosity, a little bit of marvel in her eyes. How could she do this sort of thing for a living without it losing every ounce of glamour? David had stopped being impressed by magic tricks years ago. But maybe he could do one more for her. It couldn't hurt anything, and it might make her trust him a little more.

David unfocused his gaze and looked slightly beyond her in that sweet spot a few inches from her shoulder. Looking at people this way gave him a headache even on the best days, and it wasn't helping his migraine, but it was worth seeing if he was still capable of such a small thing. As a child, he had picked up auras without having to try, but the human eye didn't like taking in so many wavelengths at once. He flexed the muscle often enough that he could usually still pick up a shimmer of color here and there, if he tried.

"Sort of a pinky-purple," he declared, blinking a few times to clear his vision. "On the lavender side more than magenta."

Moira looked down at her fingertips as though she too might see a glow. "Huh. What's that supposed to mean? Open-heartedness, right? Or creativity?"

"Oh, I don't know. If you ask me, they don't really mean anything; they're just energetic vibrations most people can't see. I would just make up something that sounded nice when I worked in Lorena's botanica. Then I was twenty bucks richer, and the client felt that much better about themselves."

Moira stopped short. "You worked for Lorena Vargas?"

Every occultist in Boston knew that name and spoke it with a mixture of reverence and justified intimidation. Lorena was the city's premier supplier of occult paraphernalia, and a revered priestess of Santeria. If you had a magical problem no one else could fix, you went to Lorena. If you wanted to get your hands on obscure spell ingredients or needed a reference for a spiritual teacher who wasn't accepting initiates, you went to Lorena. She also just happened to be whom David had gone to for homework help and friendship advice, once upon a time.

"She practically raised me. Evgeni sent me to her shop after school, hoping a job would keep me out of trouble and teach me a little work ethic. She was always waving her palo santo around me and making me sit through reiki healing sessions. She likes adopting stray kids."

"It sounds like she was trying to teach you basic self-defense. Maybe if you had listened to her more, you wouldn't need me. You two keep in touch?"

"Not really."

"You should. And you should thank her. That's your homework."

"Can do," David said, even though he knew he wouldn't. He hadn't talked to Lorena in ages, and he hated awkward reunions. David gestured to the narrow dark halls winding through the townhouse like a tangle of snakes. "This floor is mostly bedrooms. I slept on the opposite side of the house from the study. Not very interesting."

Moira pushed up on her toes to peer over his shoulder into the darkness. "It was just the two of you alone in this big old house?"

"Trust me, space to get away from each other was nice. After you." David nodded down the curling staircase that led to the lower floor of the house, and they descended towards the intricate marblework pattern on the floor.

"And you think whatever I can do is more useful than reading auras?" Moira asked.

"The dead always have their uses, Ms Delacroix. How long have you been seeing ghosts?"

"Since I was tiny. I tried to tell my mother about it once, but she wasn't having it. I just stopped trying to tell folks after a little while, and then I tried to stop seeing them all together."

"How?"

"Any way I could. I would shut my eyes, slap my hands over my ears, say nonsense over and over again until I couldn't even think straight. If I saw somebody I thought might not be... really all there, I just looked somewhere else. Like averting your eyes from sin in the Bible. Eventually, you train your brain not to pick anything up."

"Muscles atrophy over time if you neglect them. But some people are born gifted."

"I bet you've been told that you're gifted since you were old enough to sit upright, huh?"

They came to the bottom of the stairs, and David quirked an eyebrow. "I thought I was asking the questions."

Moira smoothed the long skirt of her dress, looking innocent as a daffodil. A daffodil with a taste for secrets and a merciless mind.

"Well, that *is* why I came all the way out here, isn't it? We can't very well help each other if we don't know anything about each other, can we? And I've been so forthcoming with my personal details."

David screwed up his mouth like he had just tasted something sour, but nodded. "What do you need to know?"

"You could start by telling me what the hell your family was into," she said, strolling leisurely at his side through the high-ceilinged living room. David barely remembered what the furniture looked like under the sheets; he had just told the cleaning company to put the house into hibernation.

"Most of the money comes from international trade and investing."

"Rhys said y'all were rich; he didn't mention the library stuffed with long-lost grimoires. Are you, like" – she stole a glance at him, butterfly lashes fluttering – "some kind of occult crime prince?"

David barked a laugh. He had almost forgotten that his childhood wasn't normal by any stretch. "Barring a better word. Although, in my family's defense, we've only ever been tangentially involved in crime. We don't have any direct ties. None you can prove, anyway."

"I take it magic goes way back in your family."

"Centuries," David said, leading her into the kitchen. It was big enough to prepare a banquet in, open-plan and decorated to early-nineties tastes, down to the track lighting and ugly oak cabinets. "You don't get as established as we are without practicing magic for a long time, or without doing it very well. My father was on a first-name basis with some of the most influential occultists in the world; they were always coming through the house to smoke cigars or trade spellbooks or borrow money. Oftentimes, I would host séances. Evgeni liked showing me off."

It was impossible to keep the bitterness out of his words. Moira's mouth formed a soft, concerned *O*, poised with a question, but David wasn't in the mood for any kind of sympathy.

"My father knew what he was dealing with when I was born," he went on. "He made sure I had access to the right resources and teachers."

"And what was he dealing with?"

"A prodigy." There was no pleasure in the word, just a cool statement of fact. It felt like slow-melting ice in his mouth. "Parlor is on your left. And now, if you don't mind, I'm done talking about Evgeni."

They had emerged back in the airy foyer, right at the base of the stairs.

Moira looked around her, craning her neck up to see the dark beams of the ceiling. "Fine. But I'm not done with you yet. You're a hard man to get alone and I don't intend to waste the opportunity."

"Easy, your husband's not around. Don't say anything you wouldn't want him to hear." Flirtation, slippery and glib, came easily. It was his favorite way to wriggle out of hard conversations.

Moira swiveled to face him, chin jutting out sharply. "Are you trying to *charm* me, David Aristarkhov?"

She spat the verb out of her mouth like a bite of rotten fruit. David sucked air through his teeth. He had miscalculated, but he had to commit to the bit now.

"No, I'm *being* charming. I'd like to posit a semantic difference between the two."

Anger shadowed her face like thunder clouds rolling over the horizon. "You try to butter me up and I'll march myself right out of this house and never come back. I'm not some cocktail waitress you can bat your eyes at for free drinks."

David blinked the playful light out of his eyes. Fine. If she was going to get her hackles up about everything, he didn't have to sugarcoat himself. "That Aristarkhov charm never worked on Rhys either. It works on everyone else. Judges, bartenders, doesn't matter. What gives?"

Moira wrapped her arms around herself. She looked half-frozen, even in long sleeves. "I'd wager Rhys liked you too well to go in for it. When you love somebody, you only want what's real. Even if it's less pretty than that first date sparkle."

David smiled at her, genuinely this time, with that bitter quirk to his mouth that an especially poetic ex had once compared to the lemon twist in a martini.

"Don't tell me you're getting soft on me, Ms Delacroix."

Moira put her hands on her hips and stared him down. Her face was carved from stone, her orange lipstick set into an unimpressed line. David couldn't help but smile wider. He didn't appreciate spinelessness in people, or bravado they couldn't back up. But her unflinching ability to stare down an opponent impressed him.

"I'd rather swallow a live crayfish than harbor one soft thought in my heart for you," she said. Slowly, deliberately, with niceness that stung. "I don't go in for it because I can smell a liar at a hundred yards. And any man who can turn from nasty to sweet that fast is nothing but one big forgery."

David clapped a hand over his heart, reeling with the delight of an insult aficionado. "Absolutely *merciless*. You'd make a good defense attorney."

"Are you trying to compliment me?"

"Yes," he said, and walked past her. He positioned himself in the eye of a large slab of marble that looked like churning clouds frozen in stone. "This should be about the center of the house. Come here for a second."

"Why?"

She seemed off-balance and a little tired. The energy of the house was wearing her down, but he needed her present and alert for a few minutes more.

"I want to test a theory."

Moira took a few wary steps forward, and David mirrored her with steps back until her wedge heels were right over where he had just stood.

"Let's see if you're any good with houses," he said.

"You want me to try and read this whole house?"

"If you can."

"I don't know how," she muttered. She stuck out in the gaping maw of the antique foyer. An orange lick of flame lighting up the lifeless wood around her.

"I suspect you've been reading the house without realizing it for some time now. Just try to relax," David said.

"I'm never relaxed when I'm here," she said. She didn't add *when I'm around you*, but he heard it loud and clear.

David moved behind her and raised a hand over her shoulder, pointing straight ahead into the gloom of an unlit hallway.

"Pick a point to focus on," he said. "Let everything else fall away. Just look right there and breathe."

This was one of Evgeni's methods, most often employed when a school-aged David had been too wound up to see straight, much less to see beyond the veil of death. Sometimes Evgeni would dangle a pocket watch in front of the boy, or spin a top, anything to capture his focus and induce a trance state. David knew darkness worked just as well. Darkness drew the eye and enfolded the mind, quieting conscious thought. David's habit of closing his eyes during a séance wasn't just for show; it was a mental trick to help him slide into the right frame of mind. If Moira played along, she should feel like she was falling into the dark, pulled in gently but irresistibly.

"How does that feel?" he asked.

"Better."

He waited until her shoulders dropped down from her ears and her breathing deepened. Then he brought his palms up over her eyes, close enough to feel the warmth of her skin but not close enough to touch her. Another one of Evgeni's tricks, to kick her consciousness down into an ever-deeper state. David's stomach twisted a little at the thought of training anyone the way his father trained him, but he reminded himself that Moira wanted to be here, that she was consenting to every step of the process. It wasn't the same.

"Close your eyes," he said. "Breathe with the house. Tell me what you see."

He stepped back and settled against the staircase banister to watch. A tiny furrow appeared between Moira's brows as she listened intently.

"I don't know..." she murmured. "Everything just feels cold. A little sluggish."

"It's not a lived-in house. It's lethargic. Go deeper."

Moira took a deep breath, and her fingers spread at her side, fanning out to search the atmosphere for any energetic messages.

"I'm cold," she said. "And a little dizzy. But I think... I don't know." Her face turned from side to side as she tried to riddle out the mysteries of the house.

"Something isn't right about the place. Something's... off. Like rot underneath the floorboards, or... Oh God." She swayed a little, pressing a hand to her breastbone. "Oh, that's not nice at all."

Moira's lip wobbled, and David pushed himself up from the banister, heart kicking into high gear. He never knew what to do with criers.

"God, it's so bad," she said. She gasped for air in gulps, dancing dangerously close to hyperventilation. "It's just this ugly malice, pressing down on me from everywhere. I'm scared. I can't breathe."

David rushed forward and grabbed both her hands.

"Moira. Open your eyes."

She shook her head rapidly, lost to terror. Her fear coursed through him like the one line of blow he had tried at a freshman party, all jitters and nausea and crushing helplessness.

"It's alright, you're safe. Moira. Listen to me. Open your eyes."

Her round brown eyes flew open, glassy with tears, and her grip on David's hand tightened so much it was painful. That was proof she was present and fighting, proof she hadn't lost herself somewhere in the dark underbelly of the spirit of this place. She tangled her fingers through David's, and he squeezed to show he was real and there with her.

"Moira," he said, for the third time. It was enough to break the murky spell around her, like magic words in a fairy tale.

She looked straight at him and took a shaky breath.

"This house," she said quietly, "is not fit for man or beast. There's something wrong with it."

"I know." David ran his thumbs in unconscious, soothing circles over the delicate bones of her wrist. When he'd been small, Leda used to rub circles into his back to help him stop crying. David hadn't cried in years, but the gesture stayed with him, an incantation against emotions running wild.

Moira stared at him with an awful understanding shining in her eyes. "What happened here?"

"Plenty," David said, quieter. He really hoped she wouldn't try to talk to him about it. He hated talking about it.

"Your father... You two didn't end things on good terms, did you?"

David laughed. Her gentle hedging made the horrors of his childhood sound like a sitcom.

"We didn't end anything; I came home from school one day to find my father in his study, dead from a heart attack. I took his black card, bought myself an Audi, and threw a party in the house so big the neighbors called the cops. I didn't cry over him. Evgeni was a controlling, mean-spirited son of a bitch. And yeah, he beat the shit out of me."

He spat the last sentence out flippantly because it never got easier to say out loud. But she didn't need to know that.

Moira released his hands and laced her fingers together, doe eyes full of so much compassion. She was pretty like this, pretty like the old picture of his mother he kept in his wallet, the one where she was giving the camera a faint Mona Lisa smile that belied gentleness and good humor.

That prettiness made David want to lock himself in his old room until Moira left.

"I don't want you to think that Rhys ever said... I didn't want to jump to any conclusions. But this house is..." She shivered in the oppressive malaise.

David led her lightly by the elbow away from the center of the home. He had barely ever touched her before now, but suddenly it was easy to press his fingers lightly into her skin and send a pulse of reassurance straight into her heart. Easier than saying it out loud.

"An energetic black hole two murders shy from a hellmouth," David supplied. "It doesn't take a very strong psychic to know there's something off about this place, and in my estimation, you're more than competent. Rhys might not notice anything, but he's got the intuitive aptitude of a Roomba. He just looks at this house and sees comfort and money and status, everything they aren't exactly handing out on the street corner in Southie."

"David?" Rhys's voice floated down from the second storey, echoing like a memory. "Where did you two run off to? I found something."

Rhys appeared at the top of the stairs, leaning over the banister to peer down at both of them, and froze. He looked like he was seeing a ghost, not a man and a woman standing so close to one another they could be mistaken for old friends. Maybe that was what made the scene so shocking.

David released Moira's elbow as though he had been caught shoplifting. "What is it?" he called.

Rhys blinked, a bit dazed, then waved David up the stairs. "I think you should come have a look at this. Both of you."

David looked back to Moira, who was standing ramrod-straight, dabbing the tears from the corners of her eyes with a lace handkerchief. She sniffed and brushed past him, her shoes clicking along at a brisk clip.

"You heard him. Let's go see what he's found."

David followed behind her carefully, just in case she swooned. There was no telling how she would react to that much negativity in one go, and while he wasn't feeling chivalrous enough to carry her bridal-style up the stairs, he wasn't going to let her crack her head on the hardwood, either.

There were books of various sizes laid open-faced on the desk in the study, meticulously marked with sticky notes. A number of notebooks had been sectioned off and marked as well.

David didn't look at Rhys when he passed by, but he heard the other man slip over to his wife.

"Are you alright?" Rhys asked quietly. David pretended to study the dense academic writing of one of the books as though it meant anything to him. Eavesdropping was not a good look. "What did he say to you?"

"Nothing, I just got spooked is all. It's this damn house."

"Are you sure?"

"We'll talk about it later," she said, with the sound of a fleeting kiss.

"What am I looking at, Rhys?" David asked, a little too loudly.

Rhys appeared at his side, eyes lit up with the thrill of discovery. "A common thread. I think. I started by going through the family tree you showed me and then moved on to Evgeni's ledgers and journals. I found something. A name."

Rhys pushed one of the giant reference texts across the desk to David. The text was minuscule: a list of demonic names thought to be linked to the same entity. One was circled in blue ink. Not by Rhys – he would probably rather come out as bisexual to his mother than deface an antiquarian book. Whoever had marked this off had come before all of them.

David squinted to read the name. "Baelshieth?"

The syllables slipped through his teeth like oil, like something that might leave a stain behind. He didn't like it, but he didn't recognize it, either.

"Wait for it," Rhys said. He bustled around the desk, showing off another dog-eared page where the name showed up in footnotes, then a clothbound edition of some turn-of-the-century spiritualist's scribbling. The infernal name was written clearly in the margins next to a section on maintaining relationships with entities through offerings. The handwriting was thin and heavy, and David recognized it immediately.

"Evgeni."

Moira pushed herself up onto the edge of the desk, crossing her legs primly. She was still a little shaken, but she was bouncing back.

"Those are your father's notes?" Moira asked.

"And there's more," Rhys said. He was breathless with excitement, cheeks flushed pink. Rhys only had two elements: occultism and archival research, and he was deep into both. "Look here."

Rhys thrust out a palm sized leather notebook and David read the noted section.

Cross-reference with Sumerian text. Possible connection to Baelshieth?

He could almost hear his father's voice, clipped and brusque. David shrugged. "They're research notes, so what? He did a lot of research. I don't even recognize that name. It doesn't sound real."

"But it is plausible. You know how these names get bastardized as they're passed down, but this one is reminiscent of Semitic linguistic patterns. I need to make sure it's not someone trying to retroactively add a constructed name to the record; it wouldn't be the first time, but–"

"Rhys," David said gently, pressing the book back into his hand. "What are you going on about?"

"I've found six references to this already, *six* separate times your father went out of his way to mark some obscure name that I've never heard of. Doesn't that seem strange to you?"

David remembered Rhys pacing their apartment, running through demonic names and associations on flashcards while his medieval history homework lay untouched. He counted them like sheep at night when he couldn't sleep, determined to ace his initiation exam and climb the ranks of the Society as quickly as possible. David couldn't think of someone better acquainted with the widely accepted names on the spirit court.

"I just don't see what it has to do with my feeling like shit. Or the voice in my head, remember that? The reason we're here?"

Rhys shrugged expansively. "It's like looking for a needle in a haystack, and I don't even know what needle I'm looking for. He marked the name everywhere he found it, underlined it, highlighted it, circled it. You told me to keep an eye out for weirdness; that's weird."

"Maybe," Moira said. She didn't sound convinced.

Rhys pushed away from the desk and rubbed the back of his neck. He looked like he hadn't slept in days, and David wondered if he had been working on this little research project off the clock. It was very like Rhys to get laser-focus obsessed with solving any problem that crossed his path; he had been notorious for all-nighters back in college. David just never expected his problems to be important enough to Rhys to earn that much attention. Not anymore, anyway.

"Hey," David said, peering into Rhys's face. "Don't spiral. Let's just... stay focused, alright?"

"It's a lot to sort through," said Moira helpfully. "You're doing a good job, baby."

David couldn't imagine where she was finding the energy to be encouraging. Then again, Moira could probably be bleeding out from a knife wound and still stop on her way to the hospital to tie a toddler's shoe.

"Fine," Rhys muttered. He had caught the scent of something and wasn't going to let it go, David knew that much. "But I'm going to keep an eye out for it in the library records."

David thumped him on the back. "Knock yourself out. As long as you figure out what's making me sick so I can burn it out of my system and get on with my life."

"Speaking of which," Moira said. "I think it's time for another lesson."

"Oh yeah?" David asked, turning towards her. All the vulnerability he had seen moments ago was gone, replaced with her usual courteous but firm bearing. "In what?"

Moira smiled, and that smile told him that she was done playing along with his experiments for the day. Now, it was his turn to be uncomfortable.

"I think we'll start by visualizing a white protective light and then incorporate some deep, steadying breaths."

David groaned. It was going to be a long day.

CHAPTER FOURTEEN

MOIRA

The Beacon Hill house, despite all its grandeur and empty rooms, got claustrophobic fast, and Moira needed to sort through her thoughts with someone who wasn't her husband or David Aristarkhov. There were any number of people she could call for good advice: her mother, her gang of ride-or-die friends from Rhode Island School of Design, even the girls she worked with at the vintage shop. But she needed someone who understood the incestuous intricacies of the Boston magical scene, and someone who was clever enough to think two steps ahead of whatever the hell David was up to. That left one woman.

"I knew there was something strange going on between you three," Kitty Vo said, sipping her espresso delicately. The skirt of her white tea-length dress swung around her calves as she and Moira walked briskly through Boston Common. It was the first truly warm spring day, flirting with the promise of summer. The two women had met for coffee on Kitty's lunch break, and now, with the usual compliments and pleasantries dispensed with, were right down to business.

"It's certainly not a situation I expected to find myself in," Moira said. "But it's like I said, we couldn't walk away. What David had to offer was too good."

"And you hate watching people suffer," Kitty put in. "Even if that person is David."

"Right," Moira sighed. She swirled her iced mocha, rattling the ice pensively. "Do you think it was wrong of me? To agree to help?"

"There's no wrong or right with a man like that. There's just getting everything you can get out of him. I had no idea you were a medium, too."

Moira wrinkled her nose. She had always defined her abilities in opposition to mediumship. 'Witch' was a cozy, familiar term, passed down from her mother and grandmother. Witches helped their communities: they healed sickness, mended relationships, and divined the future. Mediums made their living in the shadows, preying on the emotions of the bereaved and dragging the recently deceased back from the grave for impromptu family therapy sessions. She had been taught from a young age to look both ways before crossing the street, refuse candy from strangers, and not keep the company of mediums.

"Let's not get ahead of ourselves," Moira said. "Just because I see dead people doesn't mean I *want* to. I don't want to start hosting séances like David. I just want a little peace and quiet. David seems to think that by strengthening that psychic muscle, I'll be able to block out the dead more easily. I hope he's right."

"David might be a dick, but he's not a charlatan," Kitty said, in that careful, airy tone she used with her clients when convincing them to sign on to an upsell. "I do believe he helps people, in his way. Maybe you could too? You're already a powerful witch, Moira. You aren't afraid of your other gifts, so why run from this one?"

Moira shrugged one shoulder, suddenly feeling a bit put on the spot. Interrogating why exactly she was afraid of the dead meant doing some serious shadow work, and wrestling with the legacy of her parents, who were loving, if complicated, people. She wasn't sure she was up to the task quite yet.

"You don't need to make yourself smaller in order to be worthy of blessings, God knows those boys in the Society don't. They truly believe they deserve to get everything they want, and the universe responds in kind," Kitty pressed. "They don't care about what other people might think of them, so why should we?"

"I still want to be a good person," Moira said.

"Being a good person is overrated, if you ask me. Have you talked to your mother about this? I know you two are close."

Moira nibbled on her bottom lip. She usually told her mother everything, and she looked forward to their twice-monthly Sunday calls. But she had spent so long trying to quash down the glimmers from the great beyond creeping in at the corners of her life that she had forgotten how to talk to her family about it. There were some things her mother simply wouldn't understand. Taking lessons from a medium was at the top of that list.

"I think this is something I've got to handle on my own. I'm twenty-four already, right? We've all got to grow up and make choices without parental input sometimes."

"Well, what has it been like? Working with David?"

"Eye-opening for sure, but also frustrating. David is... I don't want to sound unkind..."

"Moira, you're *too* kind sometimes. There's no love lost between me and that man. David Aristarkhov is exactly what's wrong with the Society. He's a spoiled, overpowered nepotism case."

"I remember your holiday party dust-up."

Kitty snorted. "He was bragging about himself for the thousandth time. Somebody had to put him in his place, and I had a couple of martinis in me. If I had any say in the situation, he would be completely out of the running for High Priest."

Moira gave Kitty a knowing smirk. "Sure, like you don't have *any* say in the situation."

Everyone knew Nathan had only started showing up to the Society because he was trying to meet more young professionals in the area, and Antoni, God bless him, thought it had been a good idea to invite some guy he had approved for a bank loan to his demon-summoning club. Moira knew full well that every suggestion Nathan broached at Society meetings was actually Kitty, whispering in his ear. She was the stronger magician by far, and had been running a booming occult business long before getting married to sweet, sunny Nathan.

Kitty was one of Boston's premier interior designers, known for her integration of traditional feng shui with sleek minimalistic interiors. The daughter of prominent Chinese American businesspeople with a strong family tradition of geomancy, she was the jewel in their crown, the child that excelled in both business and magic while making it all look chic. Nathan was their great concession to her, but they seemed happy to indulge his wandering investment whims and lack of any coherent career path because he came from a good family and made Kitty happy. Incandescently so.

"It's not my fault the Society doesn't induct women," Kitty said with a shrug. "I have to leave my mark in less direct ways."

"Why do you even want in, Kitty? It's just a bunch of boys in robes doing dusty old rituals trying to land jobs or protect their assets during a divorce. What you do is so much more interesting, and it actually helps people."

Kitty cast her eyes over the Common as they strolled, taking in the picnicking young lovers and tots racing after squirrels.

"I want access. Proximity to power. And I'll never say no to more cross-training. In this day and age, flexibility keeps you relevant. Could you imagine what I could do with my skills if I also knew how to summon and control the kind of spirits the Society has access to? That's why I want Rhys on the throne. I know he'll change the bylaws. David will just kowtow to the sexist old guard."

"And what would Rhys get in return?"

"Loyalty, my dear. The scarcest resource around."

Moira sucked her teeth. "You can wade into that political nightmare if you want, but I'm just fine on the outside. I like calling the shots and running my own business. I never was good at falling in line and taking orders."

"Maybe so, but you could be good at giving them."

"What are you saying?" Moira asked, a premonition creeping across her skin. She gave a little shudder. Her grandmother had always taught her to pay attention to the tingling presence of her sixth sense. As far as a divination practice went, it wasn't as aesthetically impressive as astrology or tarot, but her hunches had never led her astray before.

"Whoever the High Priest is married to has a certain influence. Wayne's wife was never interested in the role, and she's not an occultist. But you..."

"Kitty, please don't try to pull me into any power games. You and Rhys are two peas in a Machiavellian pod."

"And you're sweet as can be," Kitty said. "One of the many reasons I enjoy your company. But I'm no fool, Moira. I know how hard you work to earn the respect of those playacting men in the Society. I'd wager it would feel pretty good to have them groveling at your feet for a change."

Moira had never considered herself a very ambitious person. Ambition, she had been raised to believe, was not ladylike or Christian. But she couldn't deny the tingle of excitement raising the hairs on the back of her neck at the thought of appearing at Society events on Rhys's arm, wearing a metaphorical crown as her chosen consort. She could just imagine the way the older men who never gave her the time of day would gag and gawk to see her elevated to such a station. The way they would fall over themselves to kiss her hand and whisper their requests in her ear. And she, who never forgot a slight or forgave a person who didn't deserve it, would delight in denying them.

Moira shook herself out of the fantasy with a little gasp. It was very unlike herself, to wish for such things. But then again, she had been acting less and less like herself lately. She felt like there was a whole other woman germinating deep inside her, poised to break through to the surface and bloom like a poisonous flower.

It should frighten her, probably.

She found she was only eager to meet this new woman.

"Moira?" Kitty asked.

"Sorry," Moira said, shaking off the last dregs of her daydream. "I've just got a lot on my mind, these days."

"Is this about Rhys and David?"

"How do you mean?" Kitty lowered her voice, despite the fact that nobody in the open expanse of the Common was eavesdropping on them. Kitty always lowered her voice in the presence of a potential scandal. "There's nothing... going on there, is there?"

"Going on?"

"I mean, in the past it's been all too easy for them to get tangled up in each other. Are Rhys and David seeing each other again? I won't tell Nathan if they are, I promise. I just wonder."

"Rhys and I are married," Moira said with a thin little laugh. Something in her stomach clenched and fluttered at the thought of David and Rhys *together*, which was ludicrous, it was impossible. And yet, a strange, giddy sensation swept through her, part jealousy, part simmering intuition, part... Moira wasn't quite sure. It almost felt like excitement, but that was all wrong, wasn't it?

"Plenty of people have open marriages," Kitty went on. "Nathan and I are closed at the moment, but I had a standing arrangement with my last boyfriend. I thought you and Rhys might be the same. That he and David had a sort of on-again-off-again thing."

"They're on-again-off-again, alright," Moira said with a snort. "One minute they're attached at the hip and the next minute they're fighting like cats and dogs."

"Interesting," Kitty said with an innocent glance over her Prada sunglasses.

"Are you trying to say Rhys has been running around behind my back?"

"Absolutely not! I have no reason to believe it and I don't think the man even has it in him to hurt you like that. All I'm saying is that he and David have history."

"I can handle David Aristarkhov," Moira said. A few weeks ago, it would have been a bluff. But she was starting to learn what made David tick, and she was confident in her ability to fiddle with the clockwork of his mind. "And my marriage is rock solid."

"I'm happy to hear that. I just worry about you, Moira. Your heart is so big, and I never want you to be taken advantage of. Don't let David take more than he gives."

"I won't," Moira said, bumping shoulders amicably with Kitty, and they continued their promenade through the park, turning their faces up towards the sun.

"We can talk more at the Society benefit gala in a few weeks," Kitty said. "You are coming, aren't you?"

"We'll be there. Rhys won't miss an opportunity to shake hands and make an appearance as the upstanding Society member he is. Thank God you're going, Kitty. I never know who to talk to at those things."

"They're a drag," Kitty said with a blithe laugh. "But we can find a corner to gossip in. In the meantime, promise me that you'll watch out for yourself. Sex or no sex, getting into bed with your enemies is dangerous."

"I promise," Moira said, the wind catching in her hair and ruffling the coils. "And I wish you all the best on your machinations to break into the Society. I hope to see your induction ceremony someday."

"And I very much hope to see you on Rhys's arm as the High Priest's wife, someday. I know you don't want the title, Moira, but you'd be great at it. You have a good head on your shoulders, you don't suffer fools, and you're a stronger witch than those men give you credit for. You could bring them all to heel, if you wanted to. Especially after mediumship lessons from Boston's own prince of the occult."

Moira offered her coffee cup to Kitty in a toast. "To getting what we deserve, then," she said.

Kitty's pink lips spread into a smile of perfect professional understanding. "To just desserts, my dear."

The High priestess

CHAPTER FIFTEEN

MOIRA

The fourth week they were all supposed to meet up, David sent over a brief note to Moira's cell, obviously dictated with speech-to-text, apologizing for having to work through the weekend. Apparently, the judge was incompetent, and his co-council was intransigent.

"David cancelled," Moira said, not looking up from her gala dress, which she was expertly hemming at the kitchen table.

"Looks like it's just you and me today, kid," Rhys said, pulling a tray of freshly baked brioche out of the oven. He was a decent cook, but he could probably sweep the bread week of any season of Bake Off.

"I assume you're gonna want some time in your study to cross reference that demonic name?"

"I actually thought you and I could spend today together," he said, deftly halving a bun and slathering it with butter and raspberry jam, just like she liked. "Maybe get out of the house."

Moira opened her mouth with a mischievous gleam in her eye and Rhys fed her a bite, then let her suck a spot of jam off his thumb.

"Well if we're going anywhere, I'm going to need a shower," she said. "Care to join me?"

"I was hoping you would say something like that."

Half an hour later, Moira was freshly showered, liberally perfumed, and well-pleasured by Rhys's deft fingers. She hummed to herself as she pinned her favorite bamboo doorknocker earrings in place and shimmied into a matching linen crop top and culottes set that flattered her midsize frame. She had put on weight since living off goldfish crackers and the cafeteria's free iced tea (never sweet enough) in college, but she loved the body she lived in, and so did Rhys, so she didn't mind. Rhys actually opted for some color, for once in his life, and paired his dark chinos with a pale green shirt that complemented her outfit. Walking on his arm out to the car, Moira felt desirable and spoiled for love and otherwise invincible.

They brought a picnic lunch out to the banks of the Charles, and Rhys painstakingly arranged the brioche buns and dried apricots and Babybel cheese wheels on the blanket so that Moira could take an aesthetic photo for her Instagram page. She snapped one of Rhys when he wasn't looking, because he was just too handsome in his sunglasses and tousled hair, and she snuck it in at the end of her social media carousel.

After their miniature feast, Moira reclined with her head in his lap and drowsily listened to the sounds of children playing in the distance. Rhys alternated between trailing his fingers along her bare shoulders and dropping kisses to her forehead.

It was, in a word, perfect.

"I love this," she said, rubbing a dandelion stem between her fingers. "Quiet time with you."

"I love it too," he said, giving her a lingering kiss on her mouth. "I'm sorry I've been so busy lately. I just get so caught up in what I'm doing, and I lose track of time."

"It's okay."

"It's not okay," he said, guiding her chin up gently so he could look her in the eye. "You're the sun in my sky, Moira. You should always come first. Work, research, the Society... it should all be secondary."

She could tell from the tight way he was holding his jaw that he was more upset by his actions than his words suggested. She pushed up onto her elbows and cocked her head at him. "Sometimes life gets in the way. Lord knows I can get swept up with my clients and you don't see me for the whole day. But I appreciate being prioritized, as much as you can."

A question tingled on the tip of her tongue. Another day, when she was less sure of herself, she might not have asked. But she felt safe and secure, in this moment, so she posed it. "I talked to Kitty last week. She seemed to think there might be something going on between you and David."

Rhys blanched. "Something romantic?"

"That seemed to be her idea."

"Love, you don't believe that, do you? Whatever lies between David and I is strictly professional."

"Come on. I'm not accusing you of cheating, but even you can't really believe that."

"What do you mean?"

"David is a force of nature. He's got a way with people, and he's charming, for better or worse. He's... compelling."

"Don't tell me you've got a crush," Rhys said with a wry smile, but there was a touch of panic underneath the expression.

Moira arched an eyebrow, unable to resist batting her husband around like a cat with a mouse, just a little bit. "Would that make you jealous? Imagining me with him?"

"Of course," Rhys blustered, but Moira knew her husband well enough to know that he also found something about the image enticing. "But that's never going to happen. We're married, and David only dates men. As far as I know, anyway."

"I'm only pulling your leg, sugar."

"Right," Rhys said, but his shoulders sagged in relief. Moira was tempted to press on that relief a little, to worry at it like a loose tooth, but she resisted the urge. One step at a time. "There might be some lingering... energy there, I won't lie to you. But I remember what dating David was like. Unless he becomes a different person overnight, I don't want anything to do with that. And moreover, I would never do anything to jeopardize what we have."

"But you're allowed to have friends. You know that, right?"

Rhys harrumphed. "I've got you and I've got my Society brothers. Who needs more friends than that?"

"Don't be prickly. I'd love to see you let yourself have a little more fun, sometimes. There's more to life than research papers and summoning circles."

"You're probably right."

She reached out and squeezed his hand. She couldn't read him as well as she could read David; Rhys was a fogged mirror, where David was a plane of clear industrial glass. But she could feel the love he had for her, emanating from him like his favorite cologne.

"Speaking of David," he said, clearing his throat. "There's something I've been wanting to ask you too."

"Go ahead."

"These sessions the two of you are doing... Do you think they're really helping? I'm protective of you, Moira. I know David can be a lot to deal with, and I don't want him crawling around in your head unless you're sure this is good for you. Say the word, and I'll call this whole thing off. Your health and safety come first. I'm serious."

Moira reached up to brush a stray wisp of pollen out of Rhys's hair. All around them, joggers and cyclists made use of the footpaths, taking in the dazzling way the light reflected off the water.

"I can take care of myself, baby. And yes, I think the sessions are helping. My intuition is getting stronger, but it's also getting easier to control. Besides, David isn't so bad, once you dig under all the posturing. Some days, I almost like him."

Rhys's eyebrows shot up. "No way I just heard you say that."

"I'm a woman of mystery," she said, settling back down against his lap. "You never know what I'm gonna do."

"And if you reach a point where you can totally block everything out, will you choose to walk away from that part of yourself?"

A single cloud passed across the sun overhead, shadowing Moira's face. She gnawed on the inside of her mouth until she tasted iron. A good person wouldn't be tempted by the promise of power. A good person wouldn't spend hours turning a possible version of themselves over in their head, a version who was influential, respected, maybe even a little feared. A good person wouldn't be propelled forward by such reckless curiosity, a bottomless appetite to *know*.

Maybe Kitty had been right. Maybe, when you got right down to it, Moira wasn't as good a person as everyone thought.

"Well. Sometimes I don't know what I'm gonna do either," said Moria.

Rhys, God bless him, left it at that. He just held her and watched the ducks on the Charles paddle by, and that, in its tender simplicity, was enough.

The High Priestess

CHAPTER SIXTEEN

MOIRA

David wasn't the most hopeless student Moira had ever had, but he was close.

David was powered entirely by flat whites, hubris, and a pathological need to push himself beyond his limits. Moira had never met someone who slept so little or worked so hard and looked so effortless doing it. She wasn't sure which seemed more exhausting, constructing two parallel high-pressure careers or maintaining the image around them. Although that seemed to be getting increasingly difficult as his condition progressed. Every time she saw him, he seemed a little more diminished, a little more rubbed raw. He didn't need to say it out loud for her to know the blackouts hadn't let up.

She was just going to have to convince him to loosen his death grip around productivity to get him to accept them, even if that meant breaking a few fingers.

"If you don't close your damn eyes, I'm going to blindfold you," Moira said.

David was sitting in a circle of amethyst, rose quartz, and selenite crystal in the second story hallway of his father's home. Rhys had banished them both from the study, claiming that their bickering was making it impossible to get any work done. Moira indulged his snippy attitude, since he was cross-referencing fourteen texts in three languages. Listening to your wife and your ex debate the magical properties of various crystals probably wasn't conducive to research.

"I don't see why that part is necessary," David said. He was dressed for work, and he did look a little ridiculous sitting cross-legged on the ground in Brooks Brothers slacks. Good. He needed to stop taking himself so seriously.

"You know why. It's about focus. It's about surrender."

"Gross," David muttered, but he closed his eyes all the same. He took a deep breath, and Moira nodded her approval. She was sitting just outside the circle, across from him, within grasp if necessary.

Moira trailed her fingers over the spiky contours of her favorite amethyst geode, lovingly transported all the way from Jamaica Plain. She had built this crystal grid to emanate and magnify feelings of deep peace, healing, and self-compassion, exactly the sort of re-charge a drained psychic would need after a long day of work. And David's life, it seemed, had been nothing but a series of those.

"How does that feel?"

"Like dunking myself in warm bathwater."

"Not so bad, is it?"

"I hate baths. They're inefficient."

Moira made an offended sound, but then she realized that David was grinning, doing his best to hold back laughter.

"I'm kidding," he said. "You have to learn when I'm teasing you."

"Well, you're on the record as a genuine asshole, so that might take a while."

"Noted."

"Back to the task at hand; are you getting anything?"

David shrugged. "Not really. The energy isn't uncomfortable, but none of that love and light you promised is getting through."

Moira chewed on her lip. Should she have incorporated more clear quartz to boost the properties of the other crystals? Had she leaned too heavily on selenite, which could be soporific if overutilized? Her eyes landed on the labradorite on his left hand.

"Give me your ring," she said. "I've got a suspicion it's cancelling everything out."

"This?" David asked, covering his ring with his hand. His eyes were still closed, a concerned expression creasing his brow. "I never take it off."

"Exactly. I've got you sitting in a ring of downers while you're wearing an upper. Hand it over."

David grimaced but unscrewed his ring and dropped it into Moira's hand. The moment the skin-warmed crystal hit her palm, a rush of energy flowed through her. She felt wide awake and revved up, strong enough to face down any challenge. It hit her like espresso on an empty stomach and left her feeling similarly queasy.

"This is how you feel all the time?" she asked, slipping the ring onto her thumb for safekeeping. "I feel like I could fight a catamount. Or pull a twelve-hour shift."

David absentmindedly rubbed the pale band of skin where his ring had been. "I'm getting a little spinny," he said. "Could I have my ring back, please?"

"Not yet. Ground like I taught you. You can handle this by yourself."

David pressed his palms into the wood on either side of him, leaning into the point of contact. In a few minutes, the concerned lines between his eyes smoothed over, and he was breathing evenly again.

"How does that feel?" Moira asked.

"Good. I think. Quiet. Soft, sort of. Warmth, right through here." David pressed splayed fingers to his sternum. "But weird. I don't know what to do with myself."

"You don't have to do anything. You just have to receive. That's the point."

Just as David was about to reply, there was a deafening crash from down the hall, loud enough to shake the floorboards. Moira yelped and her go-go boots kicked over a couple crystals, breaking the circle. David's eyes flew open.

"Rhys–" Moira began breathlessly.

"That wasn't Rhys," David said with a glower. He pushed himself to his feet and stepped out of the circle, staring down to the other end of the hallway. "Wrong wing."

"What do you mean?"

David stood frozen for a long minute, flexing and unflexing his hands at his sides. Then he came to some sort of conclusion and hoisted Moira up by a strong grasp on her wrist.

"Come with me," he said.

Moira bristled, tugging her hand free. He hadn't hurt her, but she wasn't used to being touched by him. And she definitely wasn't used to being ordered around.

"What for?"

David stared at the floor, gripping one of his hands in the other as though he couldn't trust them not to act of their own accord. "Please just come with me," he said quietly.

She could barely hear him, and after a moment of total bafflement, she realized that he wasn't ordering. He was begging.

Moira wrapped her fringed shawl tight around her shoulders. She had chosen a suede miniskirt that morning because the sun was back in Boston with a vengeance, but she always caught chills in this house.

"I'll go with you. But you don't look so hot."

"I don't feel it. But I have to handle this now. Or I'm never going to."

Moira wasn't entirely sure what he was talking about, but she nodded. David led her down a dark corridor she had not yet explored, the one that led to the majority of the home's bedrooms. He made his way through the dim space like a man walking to the guillotine, mouth set in a resigned line. Moira shivered as the temperature slid further downwards.

David swung open one of the heavy oak doors, and Moira stepped inside a bedroom that was perfectly pristine except for the contained chaos of a toppled armoire. It must have been beautiful once, and heavy, but now it lay in a heap of splintered wood and shattered glass.

Moira looked back at David, who stood in the doorway with palms braced on either side of the doorframe. He was white as a sheet.

"I wasn't allowed in this room," he said. "It's just strange, is all. To see you there."

"Whose room is this?"

"Evgeni's."

David stepped through the threshold, his loafers sinking into plush, forest-green carpet. The room favored deep greens: emerald and juniper and matte pine scattered among the wood furnishings. It was probably supposed to feel elegant, or evoke some fir-strewn countryside she had never visited. But all the green struck Moira more serpentine than anything, like a snake coiling around their legs right where they stood.

David yanked the sheet off one of the huge oil portraits hanging off the wall, sending a shower of dust sparkling through the air. A man who could only be Evgeni scowled imperiously out from the frame, with a judgmental gleam in eyes as hooded and green as David's.

"Ms Delacroix," David said, as though he were introducing her at a society ball. "My father, Evgeni Aristarkhov: occultist, millionaire, hardass, and son of a bitch extraordinaire."

Moira took a curious few steps towards the painting, eyes fixed on the unblinking visage. Even in death and captured behind a gilded frame, he raised her hackles. She felt like she was being weighed and measured, evaluated as deficient in some way. She decided immediately that she hated that man, and hatred had never been an easy thing for her to muster.

"Was he always like that?"

"Pretty much. Still is."

Moira turned to face David, a question on her lips. Then, the penny dropped.

Moira gave a little gasp. "Oh my God. I'm such a fool, I should have seen it. The house–"

"Still his." David gave a wiggle of his fingers that could only be called congratulatory. "Now you know why I hate it here so much. That, and the Addams Family vibes. Would it have killed the designers to put in some subway tile or an open plan kitchen? Jesus Christ, it's gloomy."

She all but scurried across the room to him, wanting to get as far away as possible from the shattered furniture. She had lived in a haunted house before, during the terrible few months when she and Rhys had been terrorized by a tulpa of their own making. It wasn't an experience she ever wanted to go through again, even if this ghost wasn't hers to put back in the ground.

"Your dad's still hanging around here, isn't he?"

"Parts of him. The nasty parts. So, most of him."

"That's why I can never get warm in here, and why I'm getting headaches all the time. How can *you* stand to set foot in this place?"

"Necessity. And the knowledge that it pisses him off."

He was being glib, but spiting his father couldn't be worth the memories. It wasn't worth walking into halls that his father still roamed freely, never sure whether something was going to shatter, just to put him back in his place.

Moira reached out to cover his hand with her own, but he withdrew from her touch.

"Listen Ms Delacroix, I mean this in the kindest way, but I'm really not a guy who gets into his feelings with other people, okay?"

"And if you ask me, that's half your problem. Have you ever attempted an exorcism? Or tried talking to the ghost?"

"Whenever I try, it's more of a one-way shouting match than a conversation."

Moira sighed. "Fair enough. It might be worth trying again, but not today. You look like you're on death's door. Let's get out of this drafty old room and go find Rhys."

David turned towards the door, but he had no sooner taken a single step than the bedroom door swung shut with a slam. Hard enough to send a cold gust of air over Moira's face. She yelped and almost toppled to the ground, but David hauled her up by the wrist again.

The distant sirens of panic started wailing in the back of her mind, growing louder and louder. It was impossible to tell if the terror was coming from her, or David, or both of them.

"David, let me go. I need to think straight."

"Really wish I could," he said, fingers still wrapped tight around her wrist. He was standing close behind her, his blind fear feeding into her at the point of contact.

One of the paintings, a dreary wind-lashed landscape, began to rattle. It shook violently, as though caught up in an earthquake, and then crashed to the floor. Moira squealed as the frame shattered, and David pulled her in tighter. He was beyond scared, he was paralyzed, wracked by the sort of mind-numbing fear only experienced by children cowering from monstrous parents. The sensation reminded her of one summer when she had almost been drowned by the younger girl she was trying to save from floundering in the pool. If he didn't let her go, they were both going to be swallowed alive.

"You need to let me go," she said.

"If I let you go, I'm going to have a panic attack," he said through gritted teeth.

"And if you keep holding on, you're gonna drain me of all my sense and then neither of us will be calm."

"We're getting out of here. Coming here was stupid; I don't want you in a room with him."

"For God's sake, he's haunting your house! You can't just keep on ignoring him. We're both here now, aren't we?"

David spun her around, never breaking contact, and slid his hands up to clutch her shoulders. "*Listen to me.* You see this?" David ran his tongue over his teeth and tapped with his thumbnail on an incisor one shade whiter than the rest. "Fake. The real one got knocked out when I got smart with a client whose husband was cheating on her. My dad hit me so hard I concussed myself on the tile floor. He made me clean up the blood while he called our orthodontist. You do *not* want to piss him off."

Moira pried his hands off her shoulders and latticed their fingers together, squeezing tightly. "I hear you. That's an awful thing to do to a child, and I think it's a miracle you lasted eighteen years living under that man's thumb. But he's your father, not mine. I'm not afraid of him. He doesn't have any power over me."

"I don't want you getting hurt."

Moira weakly tried for a joke, if only to lighten the mood. "Since when do you care about little old me?"

"You know damn well I care," David bit out, and Moira was shocked to find that there was no lie in the energy thrumming from his palms.

She took a step into the center of the room. A porcelain and gold clock flew petulantly from the bedside table and shattered at her feet. David rattled the doorknob, but it wouldn't give way.

"This is my problem," he said, voice rising in irritation. "I need to handle it myself."

"Just let somebody help you!" Moira snapped, surprised at her own venom. She had handled him diplomatically for so long, but this was not the time to be delicate.

David sagged against the doorframe and covered his mouth with his hands. There were beads of sweat pooling on his forehead.

"He's going to kill me," David moaned. "I am never going to get rid of that bastard; I'm going to die in this godforsaken house just like he did."

"No," Moira said. "No one is dying today, do you understand me? Now I need you to pull yourself together, indigo child, because I can't handle him and take care of you at the same time."

David swallowed hard and nodded, still pressed flush against the door. He looked half-wild and anemic, but he was upright, and she had nipped the fatalism in the bud before it spiraled out of control.

She took a few more steps into the center of the room, kicking aside debris.

"I've had it up to here with your antics. You're trying to get a rise out of us, is that it?" She did her best to sound confident, even though her voice was shaking. "What are you doing, still hanging around here? Nobody wants you, so you better get on gone to where you're going. I don't care where, but you can't stay here."

Three coils of wallpaper were ripped ceiling to floor by an unseen hand. Left behind in the exposed, jagged wood beneath were what looked like claw marks.

"Jesus Christ, Moira," David said hoarsely, rushing forward. He stuck an arm in front of her, preventing her from moving forward without actually touching her. "You're gonna provoke him."

"Good! You said yourself he was a bastard."

"He could *murder* you."

"Well, I don't like bullies." She balled up her fists and raised her voice. "You hear that? I don't like you! What kind of sick person goes around terrorizing babies? You beat your own son! Look at him, he's a mess."

"Thanks," David huffed under his breath. He was still pale, but some of his will to live seemed to be returning.

"This isn't your house anymore, Evgeni Aristarkhov," Moira pronounced. She was cribbing from the way she heard Rhys talk to his demons, clipped, authoritative, every syllable a nail in the coffin of their free will. "It's David's by right. And you *aren't alive anymore.* You're rotting in the ground somewhere far away from here. And if you don't take your claws out of this house and go on to wherever you're going, I'll light a fire under you so hot you'll wish you were already in hell."

Every stick of furniture in the room rattled a threat back. Priceless trinkets skittered off surfaces and crashed to the ground. There would be nothing left of this room by the time Evgeni was done with it.

"She's right," David said, voice still a little unsteady. "There's nothing left for you here. You need to leave."

A drawer went flying out of the dresser, almost taking David out at the knees. He stooped to catch it with a huff, then hurled it against the wall. Moira jumped at the sound of splintering wood.

"You can't keep this up forever!" David shouted. "You took up enough of my life when I was a kid, and now it's time for you to fucking leave. There's nothing left for you here. Nobody misses you, nobody is looking for you! It's just me now, living a life that would make you sick. Leave me to it."

The sheets tore themselves off the bed as more paintings crashed to the ground. The room was a minefield of falling objects and ruined finery, and Moira yelped at every new crash.

"Go to the door," David told her, ushering her behind him and off towards the hallway. "Keep working on that thing until it opens up. We're three stories up; there's no climbing out the window."

Moira rattled the doorknob with all her might, even gave the wood a few sound bangs as she hollered for help. It was impossible to say whether Rhys couldn't hear them on the other side of the house, or if the ghost was dampening the noise with some kind of supernatural trick. Rhys had once wandered out of his study after a summoning session babbling that he had been locked in there for hours, calling her name.

David stepped across the ripped silk and shards of china, crushing them underfoot. He stood in the center of the room and addressed his father, heedless of the flying projectiles.

"I don't belong to you anymore," David snarled. His face was beautiful and terrible, a sneering imperial bust carved from marble. "And neither does this place. This house belongs to *me*."

Immediately, the pillows and bits of broken furniture flying through the air came thudding to the ground. All the rattling and creaking subsided, until all Moira could hear was her own gasping breaths echoing through the room.

"The door," David said hoarsely.

Moira tried it again, and this time it gave way so easily she nearly tumbled out onto the hallway. David followed close behind and slammed the door shut on the room.

Forever, probably.

He stared at her for a moment, looking almost pained. Then he took a step forward and pulled her into a tight hug.

Moira was so shocked she almost lost her breath. His aquatic cologne stung her nose with unpleasant notes of lemon oil and sea salt, and she couldn't help the instinctive suspicion that this was some kind of trap, but it quickly became apparent the gesture was genuine.

She tentatively lifted her arms and slid them around his shoulders. Moira could feel the rabbit-quick heartbeat in his neck pressed against the sensitive skin of her inner arm, and she held him until it slowed. Gratitude, the kind that would probably tie David up in knots to speak aloud, flowed between their flush bodies and wrapped Moira up in a heady daze. It felt like warm summer rain, dousing her to the skin.

"Now I know why he calls you a goddess," he said, with more sincerity than she thought he was capable of. "Thank you."

"No trouble," she said quietly. "Is he, uh… is he gone, do you think?"

David drew away and stuffed his hands into his pockets, as though suddenly abashed. "For now, at least. Maybe for good."

"Good. Fuck him." Moira liked to avoid the coarser swear words unless they were absolutely necessary, but she couldn't think of a more fitting occasion.

David smiled at her, crooked and boyish. "Fuck him," he said.

A wave of bone-deep weariness went through her. That would be the exorcism catching up with her. "I'd like to go find Rhys now, I think."

"Me too. Let's go."

He led her back down the narrow, dark hallways of the house until they came once again to her wrecked crystal grid. Moira stooped to gather the toppled crystals, cradling a cracked rose quartz point to her chest.

"I'm sorry about that," David said. "I'll help you clean them up later."

Moira handed him a crystal fragment, jagged as a broken promise, and he turned the gleaming pink stone between his fingers.

"Keep it," she said. "It's a gift."

For a moment, she thought he was going to give her one of his breezy lectures about not really being into crystals, especially not rose quartz, but then he pocketed the stone without protest.

"Let's go see if Rhys made any headway."

CHAPTER SEVENTEEN

RHYS

Rhys was hunched over Evgeni's desk behind a barricade of books. He had spread out as much as possible without disturbing the ledgers, the fountain pens, or the ceremonial dagger displayed in a decorative holder the business mogul had left behind. Working at Evgeni's desk felt strange, like slipping into a coat that was two sizes too big for him, but Rhys was making do. At the moment, he was taking notes on his phone and in a battered Moleskine simultaneously, working at the speed of light.

Found it. He had found it.

"No rest for the wicked?" Moira asked, appearing through the massive doors.

Another time, Rhys might have asked her what she and David had been getting up to. But now, everything that wasn't his research was fuzzy and faded at the edges, eclipsed by the brightness of a breakthrough.

"I found it," Rhys said, tossing down his pencil. The thrill of discovery crackled over his skin, making Moira's dark eyes all the lovelier, David's haughty mouth all the more perfect for its cruelty. "The primary source for the name. Remember, Baelshieth?"

"Come on," David groaned. "It's a red herring, Rhys."

"No, it's not. It's important, I *feel* it. Your father kept referencing some sort of primary document that he was comparing all his research against, and I'm sure it's in this study somewhere. I've opened all the books, checked the back of the shelves for loose paper, but it's here. Trust me."

"Baby, it's a big study," Moira sighed. She sounded exhausted, like she had just wrestled a bear. "And it's an even bigger house. You'll be looking for weeks."

"No, I'm close, I just… It's like it's on the tip of my tongue, I just can't quite get it right. He would have kept it here, someplace private to him, someplace he knew nobody else would look…"

Rhys sagged against the desk, hands pressed flush against the wood as he thought. Then he straightened, features illuminated with revelation. "How long did you say this desk's been in your family?"

"Ages," David said. "It was commissioned by a great uncle or something. Evgeni dragged it around with us wherever we moved. Why?"

Rhys ran his fingers along the contours of the desk, feeling out every lip and divot for imperfections. He was man possessed, aflame with single-minded pursuit.

"What the hell's gotten into you?" David asked.

Rhys ignored him, squatting down in front of the desk and peering up at the underside of it. He rapped along the belly of the desk with his knuckles, listening intently. The dull knocking of solid wood was his only reward.

"You've completely lost it," David said, throwing himself down onto a chaise lounge. He covered his eyes with a hand.

Rhys hit a spot that echoed deep and hollow.

David sat back up.

"Is that some kind of compartment?" Moira wondered, wandering over to the desk.

Rhys's roaming fingers slowed, finessing into every darkened corner of the elaborate piece of the furniture. He pressed and prodded until something clicked into place.

An otherwise invisible compartment on top of the desk hissed and popped open. It was a shallow, nondescript drawer, covered by a perfectly fitted piece of oak attached by hidden hinges.

A flush crept across David's face as he swung his legs over the chaise lounge and approached the desk. Rhys tried not to notice his closeness, the way the dusting of pink across his cheeks made him look alive and excited and warm to the touch.

"Evgeni was private, but he didn't keep secrets from me," David said. "I was raised to know the location of every safe in the house, the contact information for every offshore banker who managed our quieter investments. There was no point in hiding anything from his successor. At least, I thought so."

David leaned over the desk and looked inside the compartment, his hip brushing against Rhys's thigh. The touch jolted through Rhys, and he tried to ignore the warm bloom of arousal in his stomach. This wasn't the time. It would never be the time, but especially not now.

Rhys dug his nails into the palm of his hand and mentally ran through a Hail Mary to distract himself.

David scoffed through his nose. "It's empty. Just a hollow drawer lined with marbled paper."

"It's probably a stationary compartment," Moira said, pushing up onto the edge of the desk and crossing her legs. Her miniskirt rode up further on her thick thighs, and Rhys couldn't help but trace the movement with his eyes, despite the circumstances. He hadn't slept well or eaten right in days, too consumed by his research, and now he was starting to fracture. He was desperate to touch his wife, desperate to be closer to David, and so, so miserably ashamed for wanting all that at the same time.

"No," Rhys murmured, running his hand along the inside of the compartment. He tried to steady himself, to focus on the task at hand. "This is custom-built to keep a secret. Can I have your pocketknife?"

Moira reached into her purse and produced a multitool on a resin handle with pressed flowers set in it. Rhys used it to slice a thin line around the perimeter of the marble paper, moving with a conservationist's care.

He peeled it back to reveal a neatly folded document, pressed almost perfectly flat beneath the compartment's lining. It was still crisply folded and pristine, without a whiff of mold, though Rhys had no idea how long that thing had been in there. Judging by the splotched ink and the yellowed edges, a very, very long time.

Rhys unfolded the document, then furrowed his brow. "Of course. David, can you read this?"

David moved in closer, peering over Rhys's shoulder at the spindly handwriting. "I can read modern Russian, not creepy, ancient, handwritten Russian."

"Do your best, please. And be careful with the paper."

The paper was feather-light in Rhys's fingers, and he could easily imagine it dissolving to ash under his touch. But the dark and the dry of the desk had preserved it well, and the document kept itself together as David held it up to the light streaming in through the window.

"It's a legal document, I can tell you that much. It's dated and it's got signatures at the bottom."

"What's the date?" Rhys asked, his heart galloping in his chest. He hadn't been this excited by something in ages, and he felt drunk on success. This is what they had been looking for during the last few weeks, and Rhys had found it. He had swept into David's life and done the impossible, and now David was looking at him like he was the second coming. Rhys's chest swelled with pride. Nothing felt like David Aristarkhov looking at you like that. Nothing.

"1514," David said.

"Holy hell," Moira breathed.

David peered at the writing, squinting at the garbled script. "Whoever wrote this thing up did it in a hurry. There's plenty of words I can't make out."

"Just try," Rhys said, crossing to David's side. One of his hands hovered between David's shoulder blades, perilously close to making contact. He needed to get a hold of himself. He was getting swept up in the thrill of the hunt. He wasn't thinking.

When he was feeling particularly cynical, Rhys said he had only fallen in love with David's money, not the man himself. It wasn't exactly true. But at eighteen, being looked at by someone of David's status like he was worth something, like he deserved to be taken to Gucci and flown first class to Italy for spring break, had been intoxicating. Loving David had felt a lot like drinking, actually. Like tottering on the edge of a blackout.

Right now, Rhys could still taste the hangover.

David made a choked noise, sounding somewhere between amused and enraged.

"What is it?" Moira asked, appearing at his side. She brushed her fingers along his knuckles, and David, surprisingly, didn't draw away. He just stared at the document as the color drained from his face, too flabbergasted to put his usual distance between Moira and Rhys.

Rhys was reminded of a church triptych as they stood there holding their breath, waiting for David's translation. Three figures with their heads bowed together, hoping for revelation.

"No," David pronounced, folding the paper closed and tossing it onto the desk. "Absolutely not."

Rhys felt like he would chew through one of the room's heavy damask curtains if David didn't tell him exactly what was written down there. Against his better judgement, he let his hands settle on David's back, smoothing a line up the fine linen of his shirt. His skin was warm beneath the fabric, his muscles tense. On David's other side, Moira jostled closer. Rhys could smell her perfume, intoxicating as ever, see the enticing gleam of her glossy lips. She was always the sort of perfect that defied description, but right now she seemed closer to a deity than a human woman. He ached to pull her close and bury his face in her neck.

"What does it say?" she pressed.

"David," Rhys said, leaning in to look David in the face. His green eyes were wild. "Tell us what it says."

David stepped forward, breaking the tight circle of their bodies, and paced a dazed, wide ring on the imported rug. He chuckled, raking his fingers through his hair, then shook a finger at the page like it had gotten the best of him.

"He wanted me to find that. He left that there to fuck with me. No getting rid of him, not ever."

"*David,*" Moira said, flapping her hands. "You're making me dizzy, what on God's green earth is in that thing?"

"It's a contract," David spat out. "*The* contract. The goddamn Aristarkhov deal. He mocked it up."

"Wait a minute, the deal with the Devil?" Rhys said, advancing a few steps towards David without even thinking about it. This was an old dance, one he knew the steps to, talking David down by rooting him to his body, to the here and now. "You told me–"

"It's a fairy tale. A fable made up by people who couldn't stomach my family's success. People hate the rich, Rhys, so they gossip."

"People hate inequitable distributions of wealth," Moira corrected. "And landlords."

"Why would your father forge a historical document just to mess with you?" Rhys asked.

"Who knows!" David exclaimed. "To keep me on my toes, as some sort of training exercise? I don't know!"

"Will you please just tell me what it says so I can take down a translation?" Rhys pressed. "Even if you think it's a fake."

"I *do*."

"It could be important, David. Humor me."

Rhys flipped open his leather messenger bag and retrieved a notepad and pen. David refused to touch the paper, but he leaned over the desk and read aloud what he could make out. The language was stilted and archaic, and he kept losing every fifth or sixth word, but he could parse enough of it. The terms were general and matched the folktale, a human soul bartered for powers of persuasion and guidance in the study of sorcery.

"What's the demon's name?" Rhys pressed. "I'm sure it's there, it has to be…"

"Baelshieth," David spat. "Don't you dare gloat."

Victory rang like a church bell in Rhys's head, but he swallowed his good cheer. David was distraught, and Rhys was starting to worry about him.

"What are the terms of the deal? Specifically."

"These terms are set in exchange for the youngest Aristarkhov heir. Or something like that."

"Youngest? That doesn't make any sense," Moira muttered. "Rather defeats the point of an heir, doesn't it?"

"Anatoly was the youngest of seven sons," David replied. "The demon wanted to make sure he didn't swap his soul out for one of his brothers'. Demons will squabble over contract terms until they wear you down. They're like corporate lawyers."

"But Anatoly is dead, David," Rhys said gently. His fingers itched to grasp David by the shoulders, to steady him and make him look Rhys in the eye. "So are all of his brothers. There's no reason for Baelshieth to be hounding you if he already got the soul he was after."

David threw his hands into the air. "I don't know what you want me to say! That some medieval demon is knocking me out trying to suck my soul out of my body?"

"I'm simply acting on the evidence presented to me," Rhys said.

"Don't take words out of my mouth," David said, jabbing a threatening finger in Rhys's direction as he yanked up his coat.

"You need to take this seriously, David. You asked me to find out what was going on with you and this looks like writing on the wall."

"And how exactly am I supposed to take it seriously?"

Rhys took a deep breath, bracing himself for the backlash. If there was one thing David hated, it was being told to slow down. "You need to stop working so hard. I would put your mediumship practice on hold, for starters, maybe take a couple days off from work. Go visit your sister, or get out of town, anything that would help you rest…"

David shook his head rapidly, brushing past Rhys on his way to the door. "Never going to happen, Rhys. I need air."

"Hey, hey," Rhys said, catching David as he passed. David froze as soon as their skin made contact, every muscle taut. Rhys circled his slender fingers around David's wrist, applying steadying pressure.

"Let me go," David said, voice deathly quiet. But he wasn't pulling away. He was standing so close that Rhys could feel his breath tickling at the collar of his shirt, making the hairs on the back of his neck stand on end.

Rhys swallowed hard and slid his hand along the underside of David's wrist. He rubbed a tiny circle into the palm of David's hand with his thumb. The effect was immediate. The tension melted out of David's shoulders. If Rhys was a better man, he might have felt guilty about pulling such an old trick.

"Stay," Rhys said, and David's breath caught in his throat. The world felt suddenly wonderful and dangerous, like standing in the middle of an electric storm, and Rhys allowed himself the guilty indulgence of letting his eyes travel over David's face, from his strong brows to his cleanshaven jaw. The last time they had been this close, they had been in bed together, mapping the contours of each other's bodies with fingers and mouths.

"I can't…" David began, but the rest of the sentence died on his lips. Rhys waited, feeling for all the world like David had cracked open his ribs and was cradling his heart in one hand, very gently. David shouldn't have that effect on him, not after all these years. But Rhys was too far gone to turn back now, and he would accept having to confess the illicit thoughts racing through his head the next time he saw his priest if it meant a few more moments of refusing to let David go.

Moira drifted over cautiously, as though approaching a spooked bird, and settled her small hand on one of David's shoulders. Her touch broke the taut line of sight between David and Rhys, and David's eyes snapped over to her.

"When's the last time you ate anything?" she asked.

The last bit of fight left David's body in a shaky rush. "I don't remember," he admitted.

Moira pulled her cellphone out of her purse, clucking her tongue. "I'm ordering Thai. Sit down, David."

"I–" he began, his last attempt at an argument.

"Don't run from this," Rhys said. "Whatever's going on, we'll figure it out together, alright? Promise me you'll try."

David withdrew his hand. It might have been a delusion of Rhys's overheated brain, but he thought he felt David trail his fingers along Rhys's, making the contact last as long as possible.

"I'll try."

"Let's all just have something to eat and take a lap, alright?" Moira asked. "I think there's been more than enough excitement for one day. I want you both to take the night off. Witch's orders, you hear me?"

David covered her hand with his own for a moment, and that surprised Rhys most of all. The balance between them had tipped, and something new was taking shape, something he didn't have words for.

Moira pressed David gently down on the chaise lounge by the shoulder, effortlessly, with so much grace it was breathtaking. He bent under her touch like a sapling under punishing rain, and Rhys was left winded by David's wordless submission.

He had bent that easily for Rhys once too.

"Fine," Rhys said, his chest tight with so much guilt and longing he thought it might kill him.

The dining room was imposing and too large by half, so they threw pillows on the ground and sat around one of the coffee tables in the library. Moira sent Rhys to the corner store to pick up a pack of Singha beer and a liter of sparkling water for David, and by the time he got back, Moira was unpacking takeout containers of pad Thai and green curry, arranging them just so on the table.

An hour later, Rhys was full and satisfied, leaning back on his pillow with his long legs tucked up underneath him. The light outside the house was low and orange through the big windows, wrapping them all in a sunset glow. Moira knelt close to David, cradling his hand.

"I don't think I believe you've never had a palm reading before," she said.

David laughed, the sound a bright ribbon in the darkening room. "I'm serious!"

"Well, I'm not the best at it myself, so don't expect the moon and stars."

"I'm a complete novice, so I'll be impressed by whatever you do."

"And what do I get in return for my trouble?" Moira asked, her dark eyes sparkling. She radiated the gleeful mischief of a child trying to wheedle sweets out of an adult.

David laughed again, and Rhys couldn't remember the last time he had been treated to so much of that irresistible, golden sound. David barely smiled these days, let alone laughed.

"I'll teach you some Russian, how's that?"

"Aw, come on, that's his out for every trade," Rhys said, unable to repress the smile crawling across his own lips. He had been wound so tight for the past weeks, wrapped up in so much research that he could barely remember what day it was. But Moira hadn't been kidding when she told him and David to take the day off, and putting him at ease had always been part of her particular magic.

"I think it's a fair trade," Moira decreed, and then leaned forward to peer at the lines etched into David's palm.

Rhys watched David watching Moira, noting the soft curve of a smile on the medium's lips. Something between David and Moira had shifted that Rhys couldn't quite put his finger on. But the ice between them had definitely melted, and the resulting effect was startling. Rhys couldn't think of two people more opposite than David and Moira, but when they weren't sniping at each other, they fit together surprisingly well. It sent a strange ache through him, to see them so comfortable together.

"A strong head line straight across here," Moira said. "That indicates a sharp, analytic mind. And there's a little hiccup in your life line, but otherwise it suggests a long, full life. I don't see any children in your future, but I do see love throughout your life."

"Is that so?" David asked, arching a playful brow.

A troublemaking grin spread across Moira's face. She was up to something. "Oh, yes, I see a man in your past. Dark and handsome." She shot a sly glance to Rhys. "Though maybe not very tall."

Rhys blanched. "Moira," he pled. He wasn't sure he could live through the embarrassment of his ex and his wife discussing his past relationships in his presence.

Moira turned back to David's hand, resuming her work. When she spoke, it was with a calculatedly blasé tone. "What happened between the two of you, anyway? Or am I not allowed to ask?"

David's eyebrows shot up towards the ceiling, and he looked over to Rhys for an out. Rhys just shrugged, as baffled as David was. Moira did what she wanted, and she did it with a bluntness that was hard to wriggle away from.

"Hasn't he told you?" David said, his smile faltering.

"Not much. I don't have to tell you he's private. Hm, your fate line is a little faded. That could mean you'll change professions often, or that you'll divert from the career path your family laid out for you. So. Why didn't things work out?"

Moira was very deliberately asking David, not Rhys, even though she knew full well she could get the information out of her husband much easier if she had asked in private. She was testing David, seeing if he would shoot straight with her or clam up at the first mention of the past. Maybe she was testing Rhys, too.

David thought for a moment. This was the part where he would usually find a way to shift the blame onto Rhys, or act like the breakup had been no big deal instead of a shattering event that had wounded both of them badly. Rhys braced himself to be pissed about whatever it was David came up with this time. But to his great surprise, David was honest.

"I drank too much. I was out of control, and I was bound and determined to take the people closest to me down with me. You couldn't tell me shit; I was twenty-four and thought I was invincible. Rhys had every right to leave."

"It wasn't all you," Rhys heard himself say, to his even greater surprise. This was usually territory he would rather burn to the ground than cede to David, but the long day and Moira's searching eyes took the fight right out of him. "I was controlling. You needed me to listen, and I tried to micromanage you instead."

"Yeah, you always had a thing about being in charge," David said, breaking the somber atmosphere with a salacious smirk.

Rhys nearly choked on his beer, and Moira cackled with laughter.

"Alright, alright," Rhys said, feeling the tips of his ears burn red. "That's enough of that. My turn."

Rhys leaned over the table and presented his palm to Moira, who took it between her hands. David watched with an amused expression, his green eyes studying Rhys in a way that made Rhys feel like he was on display, somehow. Like he was an artifact in a museum that existed for David's careful perusal and appreciation.

Rhys tried to ignore the feeling and studied his own palm instead.

"See anything interesting?" he asked, as though Moira hadn't read his palm a half dozen times before. She would sometimes laze in bed with him, tracing the lines in his skin and naming them off as though she was cataloguing constellations.

"Let me look," she said. "Oh, a strong, defined fate line. This is a man who knows what he wants and how he's going to get it. A strong mount of Jupiter here, beneath the index finger. That indicates a born leader."

"What's this one?" David asked, leaning over the coffee table to trace one of the lines in Rhys's palm with his little finger. The sensation sent a shudder up Rhys's spine. Moira's finger joined David's, tracing the spot where one of the lines split into two clear forks.

"Could represent a heart divided. Or someone with two great loves."

When Rhys looked up, he found that Moira was giving him that heavy, meaningful look her mother would call the magician's eye. She wasn't just speculating; she was making some kind of prophetic pronouncement.

"Interesting," David mused, withdrawing his hand. Rhys couldn't read his expression because his eyes were downcast, shaded by short, thick lashes.

Both David and Moira were so close, close enough that Rhys could smell the vestiges of oat soap clinging to Moira's skin and see the details of the fine stitching on David's cuffs.

It would be very easy to kiss them both, if he wanted to.

The thought flickered through his mind like lightning, shocking and momentary, and it terrified him. He closed his fingers and pulled his hand back on his side of the table, sitting on his heels.

"Thanks," he said quietly.

"Alright," Moira said, turning to David. "Now teach me something."

David tapped her beer bottle and named it in Russian, simple syllables that she was able to repeat without fumbling.

"Good!" David exclaimed. "That's beer."

"Give me a harder one," Moira said with a grin.

David touched the underside of Moira's chin with his knuckle and said something else, a string of sounds like water rushing over rocks. The word settled low in Rhys's stomach, and he swallowed dryly. He had always enjoyed the sound of David speaking Russian, maybe more than was strictly decent.

Moira tried to repeat the word and mangled it. David repeated it slowly, savoring every sound, and his eyes flickered over to Rhys for a fraction of a second. Rhys, for his part, studied the bottle in his hands.

Moira finally managed to get to word out, and David beamed.

"Good! We can work on your accent."

"Was that the word for woman?" Moira asked.

"No, it's one of the words for pretty."

Moira's hands flew over her face, covering a bashful smile, and David jostled his shoulder against hers with a laugh. A sharp pang went through Rhys's chest. This was David at his best: charming without any ulterior motive, kind simply because it pleased him to be, and Moira at her most radiant, confident, and gracious.

A strange emotion rose up inside him as he watched the two of them joke with each other. It almost felt like jealousy, but that wasn't quite right. It was more like longing, although he had no idea what it was that he wanted so badly. Maybe just more of this: companionable chatter in a drafty old library with the sun setting outside. Real friendship and the tentative bloom of affection, without any sort of sarcastic edge or undertone of argument. Rhys had spent the last few years of his life believing that any proximity between he and David was a toxic thing, a web of cruelty that other people got caught in. Now he wasn't so sure.

Before he could investigate his feelings further, Rhys's phone rang. The caller ID took him off guard.

"Excuse me," he said, clambering to his feet. "I need to take this."

Moira and David waved him away, and he ducked down one of the dark hallways leading away from the library. Rhys found an alcove to lean against and cleared his throat, then answered smoothly.

"Wayne."

"Hello, Rhys! I hope I haven't called at a bad time. How are you? Are you alone?"

"I've got some privacy, yes," Rhys said, pressing back further into the alcove. "I'm a little tied up at the moment, unfortunately, so if you need me to come by Cambridge and unlock–"

"No, no," Wayne said. "Nothing like that. I wanted to talk to you. I'm so sorry I couldn't do this in person, but I couldn't wait to speak to you any longer."

Rhys's heart did a two-step. He was either in serious trouble, or he was about to get the best news of his life. Rhys leaned his head out of the alcove and looked back towards the library. Moira and David were wrapped up in private chatter, their heads bowed close together, oblivious to his conversation.

"I'm listening."

"I've made up my mind and I picked a successor. I know there was some contention about that, but it's within my rights, and I want it to be you, Rhys."

All the air left Rhys's lungs in a rush. The close, dark hallway spun and then righted itself again. Wayne was still talking, Rhys realized.

"You're the best and brightest of any of us, Rhys. The Society needs someone with vision, someone who can lead us into the 21st century. I believe that man is you."

"Thank you," Rhys said, pressing his fingers to his mouth. His heart galloped in his chest. "I don't... I don't know what to say."

"Just say you're up to the task. That's all I ask."

"I'm up to it," Rhys said automatically. There was no thinking about it. There was no turning Wayne down. He had been working towards an accomplishment like this his entire adult life, and he was swept along on the heady euphoria of success.

"Good man," Wayne said warmly. "Come by the Society tomorrow and we'll discuss the logistics. And Rhys? Please don't discuss this with anyone else, at least not yet."

And just like that, the conversation he had been waiting for since Wayne's retirement announcement was over. Rhys stood in the darkened hallway for a moment, stunned.

When he returned to David and Moira, he found them sitting shoulder to shoulder on the floor. Moira was leaning forward with her palms on her crossed knees, talking animatedly about something, and David was watching her with an amused quirk to his mouth. There was a genuine fondness in his eyes that Rhys hadn't seen in ages, one that the psychic would be quick to deny if pressed about it, probably. But Rhys knew what he was looking at. Friendship. Genuine, impossible affection between two opposing energies. The sun and the moon orbiting each other in perfect synchronicity.

Pain shot through his ribcage. He knew that feeling. He had felt it at eighteen, when David had smiled brazen and wide at him while they chalked out their first summoning circle, and he had felt it again at twenty-two, when Moira had teased him in a dirt crossroads about his style of magic.

It was, he realized with creeping horror, love.

"Why are you hanging around the doorway?" Moira asked. "Come here and help me finish this beer."

"And help me with this curry," David said, leaning back on his hands as leisurely as a prince lounging around his castle. "I'm stuffed."

Rhys opened his mouth to tell them everything, to confess that he had just been awarded the highest honor he could think of through some stroke of celestial benevolence. But David was smiling at him with that same fondness that lit up his face when he looked at Moira, and it was enough to nearly send Rhys to his knees. The moment David found out that Rhys had been named High Priest instead of him, his gaze would shutter and ice would glaze over his countenance until there was nothing else but bitter haughtiness. All the progress the three of them had made would be undone, all in the name of Rhys's boundless ambition.

He couldn't do that to David. Not here. Not now.

He would tell him later. But not like this.

"Sure," Rhys said, swallowing back the maelstrom of emotions gathering in his throat. "Scoot over and make some room."

The High priestess

CHAPTER EIGHTEEN

MOIRA

Summer descended upon Boston all at once. One day, there was still a chill in the air, and the next, the students were out in full force in board shorts and sundresses, and all the neighborhood bars had their windows thrown open to the world. Moira spent her free afternoons working in the nearby community garden, or meeting up with old friends from RISD for mimosas and oysters, or strolling down the main thoroughfare of Jamaica Plain with Rhys on one arm and a bouquet of flowers under the other.

Saturdays remained dedicated to sessions with David, who, true to his word, had helped her hone her psychic intuition to a fine point. He hypnotized her with swinging pendulums and guided her through visualizations, all with his trademark mix of brashness and the weird but wonderful sense of closeness that had started to develop between the two of them. She was becoming less frightened of the phantoms she saw lurking in empty seats on the T, or of the strong senses of emotion she picked up from the various establishments she walked into. When a mournful ghost child tugged on her skirt in the supermarket, she didn't even cry out. She was getting stronger. Braver.

On the second Saturday in June, Rhys had a fire at work (some professor had spilled an entire cannister of – strictly forbidden – coffee in the special collections room) and got pulled back to the library. Moira expected David to cancel on her, but instead, he asked her to meet him somewhere entirely new.

"What are we doing on Newbury Street?" she asked, striding alongside him in platform wedges that made her legs look miles long. David was wearing Ray Bans and a breezy linen shirt that practically screamed 'I summer in Capri'. "I thought you hated crowds."

"I do," David said, weaving through the throngs of tourists queuing up for fancy brunch or window shopping at overpriced boutiques. "But crowds mean energy, and energy means ghosts. Consider this your final exam."

"Oh, we're giving out grades now?" Moira quipped. "In that case, I'd say you're currently hovering at a B minus in spiritual self-defense."

"Give me a break," David said, but he was smiling, that crooked grin that Moira had come to associate with jokes, and verbal sparring, and everything that felt quintessentially David. He placed a light hand between her shoulder blades as they weaved to avoid a woman with a stroller, and Moira was surprised at how easily she ceded to him, how they fell into perfect step with one another. "I figured we'd get a little lunch, do a little people-watching, and see if we can spy any ghosts. Nice way to spend a Saturday, right?"

"The stuff dreams are made of," she said sarcastically, but found to her surprise, that the prospect of spending an entire afternoon alone with David Aristarkhov, once the makings of her personal hell, now didn't sound bad at all. It almost sounded, well, enjoyable.

"Are you charming me?" she said suddenly. If he was laying it on her, she would shove him into the nearest trashcan and train herself right back home.

He raised his eyebrows at her over his sunglasses. "Right now? No way. Trust me, if I was trying to charm you, you'd know it. While effective, that little party trick isn't exactly subtle." His grin broadened. "Are you feeling charmed by me, Ms Delacroix?"

Moira snorted, and David laughed, and that was that. They fell into an easy rapport of chatter, sometimes discussing things as mundane as the wares in a nearby shop window, or the fragrant blooms on an overhanging tree, and it all felt impossibly, magically normal.

Moira, who had heard plenty about David's flair for trying to buy people's approval, wondered if he had booked them some eye-wateringly expensive restaurant for lunch. But instead, to her delight, he led them to a food truck parked on the curb outside a jam-packed bookstore. It was so pedestrian; she didn't think he had it in him.

David ordered two carnitas tacos while Moira pushed up on her tiptoes to read the chalked menu. Seeing the trouble she was having, he snagged a paper menu from just inside the truck and passed it to her.

"Coming right up," the man operating the truck said with a big smile. "And what will your wife be having?"

The tips of David's ears turned pink. "What? Oh no, no you've got us wrong."

"You're blushing," Moira needled.

"I've been on Nathan's boat; I'm sunburned. Listen, we're not... I'm gay, and she's–"

"Got standards," Moira put in, rescuing him from the awkward interaction despite the pleasure she took in watching him flounder.

"Ouch," David said, pressing a melodramatic hand to his heart.

"Come on, now," Moira said as she sifted through her coin purse stitched with butterflies for the proper number of bills. "You're not my type."

"That's right, you prefer brooding former emo kids."

"Be nice," Moira chided, but she was giggling so much it undercut any bite in her words. "An al pastor burrito for me, please."

"Two waters, as well," David said, bumping her aside with his hip and using his height to swipe his card before she could pay.

Ten minutes later, they were seated on the steps of the Boston Public Library, enjoying their Mexicali and the sunshine.

"Cities are spiritual vortexes," he narrated, his green eyes watching passersby closely. "They draw in life, but they can also trap death. The more crowded a location is, the more likely ghosts are to be drawn to the energetic signatures of the living."

"Do you reckon the ghosts don't know they're dead?" Moira asked. "So, they go on gathering in the usual places, acting like they're alive?"

"Maybe, maybe not. It's possible they're stuck in a loop, repeating actions that came easily to them in life. Waiting for the bus, tending to children, tidying up the house... Following the path of least resistance, if you will. So," David said, cleaning his hands with a napkin and polishing off the rest of his water, "do you see any ghosts around here?"

Moira glanced out to the street before them, and the tiny park and stately church beyond. There were people jostling around as far as the eye can see.

"I don't know, David. This place is pretty crowded."

"Exactly. Think of it as a spooky little game of Where's Waldo. Just give it a shot for me, alright?"

Two months ago, David asking her to do anything 'for me' would have been enough to make her eyes roll back in her head. But now, she found she did want to try for him. He had tried for her, after all. It was only fair.

"Fine, but you've got to give me a hint. How many ghosts do you see right now?"

"In my direct line of sight? Four."

"Goodness gracious."

"Don't focus on the numbers, just focus on the energy. Block out all the noise and hone in on what you want. You can do this."

What I want. Moira didn't spend a lot of time thinking about what she wanted. She was usually too focused on other people's needs, always placing her own desires dead last. If you talked to her mother, it was her best quality. If you asked Rhys, it was her worst.

What do I want?

Moira closed her eyes and quieted her mind. Right now, she wanted to be strong. She wanted to look right through the veil and see, truly see, what was in front of her. She was done running from herself.

I want to see what's really out there in the world.

When Moira opened her eyes again, she did so with a medium's deliberateness. She scanned the bustling groups of people slowly, parsing faces and posture, and then let her gaze drift to the margins of the crowd, where some figures stood stock still, or paced in idle circles. One of them, a woman Moira could at first only glimpse out of the corner of her eye, began to take shape. She wore a mournful expression and a high-necked Edwardian gown. Her skirts drooped behind her, tarnished with mud and debris.

"I see her," Moira breathed.

David perked up at that. "Who? Tell me."

"The woman in the park. It looks like she's waiting for a cab, or a carriage."

"Waiting for someone who isn't coming," David said with triumph. "I see her too."

"Will you hold still for me? I want to try something."

David looked wary, but he did as he was told. Maybe he was finally learning to trust her.

Without looking away from the woman, Moira reached out and settled her hand on David's knee. Bolstered by his energy and his psychic prowess, the watery outline of the woman firmed into a deliberate shape, and little details, like the pale-yellow color of her hair, and the tear tracks on her face, coalesced. The woman looked around more and more fanatically, and then, as though making some awful decision, she rushed headlong into traffic.

Moira tore her eyes away from the scene moments before a car trundled right through her. When she looked back, the woman was gone.

"Repeating the same thing over and over again," Moira said. "You were right."

David wasn't looking at the ghost. He was staring at Moira with open wonder. "How did you do that? Did you just–"

"Siphon off a little of your power to give myself a boost? I hope you don't mind."

"Not at all," David said. His hand hovered over hers for a moment, then he seemed to think better of it and tucked it away into his pocket. "That's a gamechanger."

"Haven't you ever worked with another medium before?" Moira asked. It was the first time she had referred to herself as such out loud, and the word still felt awkward in her mouth, but she could get used to it.

David shook his head. "No. My father used to tell me that opening myself up to other people was a recipe for disaster. He said I was too volatile."

"Your father was wrong about a lot of things."

"He sure was," David said, and then, swung the lens of the conversation away from himself and back towards Moira. Typical. "Does this mean you're actually thinking about using your powers? Not just smothering them into silence?"

Moira thought about it long and hard. She had spent so long abiding by her mother's rules, she wasn't even sure what they were supposed to be protecting her from anymore. A life lived in close proximity to death was a complicated one, but that didn't mean it was wicked or wrong. Maybe her mother had just been trying to protect her daughter, and now, Moira was old enough to protect herself.

And more than anything, that curiosity burned hot and bright at the heart of her. She was tired of averting her eyes and keeping herself small. She wanted to unfurl her wings and see how far she could fly.

"I think so," she said. "I want to learn everything I can about them, for sure. And maybe, when I'm ready, I can use them to help other people."

"Just don't steal my clients," David said, but he was grinning wide. Proud. He was proud of her. Moira shouldn't care about something like that, but she felt warm and fuzzy all the same.

"To the victor the spoils, Mr Aristarkhov."

"So, what comes next in these lessons? What do you want to learn? Say the word and I'll make it happen."

What do I want?

She wanted to be fearless and heedless and maybe a little dangerous.

"I want you to teach me how to channel the dead."

"Oh my God!" David said, clapping his hands together in pleasure. "I was waiting for you to say that. We're going to have such a good time. You're going to be an absolute psychic terror when I'm done with you."

Moira grinned back at him. She liked the sound of that.

"Are you coming to the gala next week?" she asked, bumping shoulders with him.

"I never miss it. Wayne notices who shows up and who ditches. Gotta keep a good face on, you know? Are you coming?"

"Of course. Can't leave Rhys to manage the sharks by himself. You should sit at our table with us. It wouldn't be the same without you."

"Deal," David said, sticking out his pinky to her. Moira was amused by the childlike display, but she hooked her little finger through his all the same and gave a determined shake.

She could feel his delight as clear as day, and it bloomed in her chest like a flower.

The hanged man

CHAPTER NINETEEN

DAVID

Galas were not David's scene. They were boring and drawn-out, and reminded him too much of formal dinners his father used to demand he make a surly, necktied appearance at. But he did his best to show up every year, if only for an hour or two. It was one of the Society's few decent opportunities to network, and the older set always looked favorably on younger men who showed up for charitable causes.

It helped that David made the largest contribution to the benefit every year, with enough zeros to be impressive but not enough to shame anyone who wasn't rich enough to play real philanthropy ball.

This was his second year turning up at the gala sober and determined to stay that way, but it was his third arriving with what felt like the aftermath of a blackout night drinking, and David thought this was wildly unfair. If he was going to sit through an entire gala sober and listen to aging CFOs give speeches, he thought he ought to be rewarded for his efforts with good health. But no such luck.

He woke up the night of the event around the time the sun was setting. Light hurt to look at, he could barely handle the street noise out his window, and every time he tried to stand, he was hit with a wave of nausea. David had felt like he was dying plenty of times in his life, but this one *ranked*.

When he finally managed to clamber out of bed, he had been assaulted by spirit sickness so bad it had put him on the floor. His vision went black at the edges, and danger screamed in the back of his mind. He had clutched his aching temples while in a fetal position on his bedroom carpet, suddenly freezing cold as though he were standing out in a snowdrift. Any thought that tried to form was mangled and incoherent, a jumble of English and Russian.

All David could do was wait for it to pass, then get into the shower fast enough that he could pretend that the tears of pain leaking from the corners of his eyes were just droplets from the showerhead.

Eventually, he managed to get himself dressed, despite the numbness in his fingertips that made small buttons impossible. He wanted to ditch the whole event, maybe curl up on the couch with an entire bottle of white wine and drink until the sun came up. But skipping out on the gala wasn't an option. He had to make an appearance and look good while doing it.

He wore Armani, black-tie friendly with gunmetal silk lining. It was crisp, timeless, sharp as a knife without being showy. His labradorite ring, family crest pinky signet, and Louboutin red-bottom loafers were the only other accents he needed. He felt like he had just pulled himself up off the bathroom floor of one of those cramped gay bars he had spent so much time in during college, but at least he looked like himself.

The event was at a rented hotel ballroom slightly out of town, so he drove himself and arrived a tasteful forty-five minutes after the doors opened. Wayne and his crew were already there, and David gave them a warm nod as he got his bearings. He would drift over and make conversation after everyone else had a couple drinks in them, pressing his sober advantage. If he nailed this night, the High Priesthood was as good as his. There was nobody else with his skills and connections, not even Rhys.

Instinctively, he scanned the dimly lit ballroom for Rhys and Moira. Neither were anywhere to be found.

Antoni and Cameron were here, however, seated at a back table and swirling glasses of brown liquor. David fished an off-brand sparkling water out of a brass tub of ice and went to join them.

"Look who's back from the dead!" Antoni exclaimed.

"Who said anything about dead?" David asked, sliding in beside him.

"Come on, nobody's heard from you all week," Cameron said with a thin smile. He wasn't wearing his glasses, and the bare face gave him a keener, sharper appearance. He almost looked handsome this way. No, not handsome. Cunning. David had a bad habit of conflating the two. "I don't think I've ever seen you miss a Society meeting."

"Not since I got here," Antoni put in.

David inclined his head in response. He had missed a Society meeting before, actually, but that was because he had been stupid and twenty-three, and because Rhys had been doing something unethical to him in the Ancient Egypt section of the library.

"Work's been crazy," David said lightly. "Where's Rhys?"

"Not here yet," Cameron supplied. "But Antoni just texted him. Hopefully he shows."

"This whole night is going to be boring as hell if he doesn't," Antoni muttered, polishing off his bourbon.

"Agreed," David said, crossing his ankle over his knee. "What's been going on with you two? Cameron, anything new?"

Cameron rubbed his freshly shaved chin. "There's been some really interesting developments in the field lately, actually. Some scuttle out of Yale about a potential third century Q source that mirrors the Johannine text closely. I'm not convinced, myself."

David nodded dutifully, completely glazed over. Then he turned to Antoni. "What about you? Any batshit developments in the dating department? You're always an interesting gossip mill."

Fire flashed in Antoni's eyes, that telltale temper rising to the surface. "I'm not that much of a fuck-up." He glowered down at his empty glass for a moment, rattling his ice, before he gave into the temptation to spill. "Although, I was hooking up with this guy in Brighton for a while, but then I found out he still lives with his parents and I'm not sure how I feel about *that* one. That's not unreasonable, right? I think…"

David didn't hear the rest, because the door on the other side of the ballroom swung open to usher in Rhys and Moira.

Moira captivated with every step, dressed in a figure-hugging eggplant gown. It was pure seventies glam, and between the disco eyeshadow and her teased halo of hair, she wouldn't have looked out of place on Robert Redford's arm. Wives pinched their husbands to get them to stop staring at her, but David couldn't stop looking at Rhys.

There was a severity to his face that David wasn't used to seeing outside the ceremonial circle, his gaunt features set off strikingly by the dark hair. He was wearing a wine-colored velvet blazer and a white oxford shirt, one button undone to show off the Saint Michael medal winking from the hollow of his throat. The shoes didn't match the outfit, but David would forgive him that.

He looked like a king.

"Excuse me," David said, abandoning his water at the table and leaving Antoni hanging mid-tale.

Moira and Rhys slipped effortlessly through the crowd, exchanging pleasantries and smiles with whoever they passed. They looked so perfect together it made David sick. He was compelled to be close to them, to start a conversation or... something.

David pressed through the crowd of aging high-society girls and middle managers as the pair found a seat at an empty table. Rhys swept Moira's hand up and kissed it, then stood suddenly and disappeared into the crowd.

When David reached the table, Moira was alone, sifting through the contents of her beaded purse. David lowered himself silently into the seat beside her, and savored her surprise when she looked up.

"I didn't think you were coming!" she exclaimed. "I texted you this morning to confirm but I never got a text back."

David smiled despite himself. He was getting used to her wide-eyed expressions, and enjoyed how openly she displayed her emotions on her face. It was refreshing. "Well, I never pass up an opportunity to scandalize."

Moira waved a finger off in the direction Rhys had gone. "I think he went off to chat up Wayne. Society business."

"Of course."

"You're welcome to wait with me until he gets back. I think he'd be happy to see you."

David thrummed his fingers against the table, thinking. Sitting around killing time was not a good look. That would make it seem like he had nothing better to do than wait around for Rhys's beck and call, like he had been feeling his absence over the last week too sharply. Not an option.

David pushed himself to his feet and held out a gallant hand. If he was going to try to catch Rhys's eye, he was as well do it while looking busy, and he and Moira were overdue for a serious conversation. Two birds, one stone.

"Ms Delacroix, would you do me the honor?"

She stared at his hand. "David Aristarkhov, are you asking me to dance with you? Here in front of God and everybody?"

"That's generally what people do to entertain themselves at these sorts of functions," he said, doing his utmost to lay on the confidence even though he didn't feel any of it. He didn't feel like he was inviting her to dance, he felt like he was handing her one of his vital organs and asking her to hold it for him while he ran errands.

Moira smiled. "Fine by me."

She let him lead her onto the floor properly, by the arm. The dance floor was sparsely populated, but not bare enough to be embarrassing. David picked a quiet spot in the corner, and Moira assumed the position effortlessly, her hands resting lightly on his shoulder and in his palm. Their sway was an unadorned approximation of a dance, an excuse to speak privately.

"Aren't you gonna tell me I look pretty?" Moira asked. "That's usually how most boys open when they ask me to dance."

"'Radiant' was more the word I was looking for," David said, and he didn't even need to sprinkle in any charm to make the sentence ring true. "Love the dress."

"I tailored it myself."

"Ah, that's why everything you wear fits you so well."

"Daddy taught me right. And so did fashion school." She evaluated him with shrewd eyes. "I'm happy you felt well enough to come."

"I didn't say that," David admitted, turning her in a gentle circle around the floor that would have passed any junior prom decency test. "I spent the morning sick. Everybody here is lucky I showed at all."

"You should be home in bed," Moira said. There was genuine concern in her eyes, freely given, without a second thought. David knew she wasn't lying because he would have felt the guilt jump under her skin like a faulty pulse.

"I'm sorry if this sounds rude," he said, because they had to address it sometime, "but you've had every reason in the world to be unkind to me. And yet you always choose to be graceful. Why?"

"Are you suggesting I've got some sort of ulterior motive?" She moved effortlessly, gliding along the floor as she pulled him in wider and wider circles. She was attracting appreciative attention, and as they made another turn, David thought he caught the gleam of Rhys's eyes over the shoulder of another Society brother.

"Maybe. You're smart enough that I'd applaud you for having one."

"My aims and designs are my own. But why isn't it enough for someone to be kind to you? Not all strength comes from pissing brimstone and spitting fire. I'm nice to you because it pleases me to be, and I'll keep that up until it ceases to please."

"Fair enough."

"You changed your tune about me pretty fast, too. You're not just being sweet to me to get to my husband, are you?"

It was a joke, but there was a steely thread of true inquiry underneath, and David's heart stuttered. He didn't think he had overstepped any boundaries, and he did his best to deal with Rhys and Moira on their own individual terms, but Moira was perceptive. She would see any lingering feelings in the microexpressions that snuck to the surface when Rhys was in the room.

And she would feel his true emotions, and if he was lying to her, through the touch of her hand.

Damn. Clever woman.

David swallowed, his throat suddenly dry, and chose his words carefully. "Any kindness I've extended to you has been on your own merit. And I've never tried to come between you and Rhys."

"Neither of us would let you," she said, a little smugly. Then, softer, "But between is different than close. You can be close, you know."

Adrenaline hit his stomach in a sickly rush, and she must have felt it. What was she saying? Was she offering…? No. There was no way.

"I'm not following," he said, doing his best to keep his voice level.

Moira shrugged, suddenly not able to meet his eyes. She fastened one of the tiny buttons at his cuff that he had missed.

"It's just that whenever I feel like we're getting closer, you pull away. You and I don't have to be best friends, but I don't hate you, David. I don't hate having you around, either."

David squeezed her hand gently. He was bad at verbally reciprocating feelings, but he hoped she felt it. "I'll keep that in mind."

"Good. Now are you gonna keep rocking me back and forth like we're at a church function or didn't anybody ever teach you how to dance?"

"You know how to dance?" David asked, with surprise. "Ballroom?"

"I placed very well in my cotillion, thank you."

"Foxtrot?" David pressed, an old lick of childhood mischief sparking to life in him. He tried to contain himself these days, but there was nothing he loved better than creating a spectacle. The music wasn't right for a foxtrot; it was some recycled tired top forty hit. But he could make it work.

"Well, they ain't playing a waltz, are they?" Moira shot back.

David broke into a grin, shifted into proper position, and swept her into the dance with a delight that bordered on ferocious. Moira let out a peal of laughter, following with quick, agile steps. David hadn't danced ballroom much since his teens, but it was like riding a bicycle, the body never really forgot. He thought he was decent at it, but he could barely keep up with her. Moira swept along the floor like she had been born and raised to it, arm held high, neck arched gracefully. He spun her on a tight fulcrum, and her dress swirled around her ankles and snapped against his legs.

She was a terror on the dance floor. David loved it.

He led her in one of the foxtrot's standard twirls, and she kicked her heel up with a little flourish as she came back into his grasp.

"Show off," he said, and swung her into a low dip. Moira squeaked in surprise, grasping him tighter, but recovered quickly.

"Then what do you call that?"

"I'm not going to drop you," David chuckled. "*Can* you waltz, by the way? That one's my favorite."

"Better than you, I bet," she said, quirking a challenging eyebrow as she came back into the starting position, pressed nearly flush against him.

In that moment, David knew exactly why Rhys loved her.

"I think you and I are going to get along just fine," he said. He would have followed it up with a footwork variation to see if he could throw her, but the music cut off abruptly. Wayne was mounting the small stage with a glass of champagne in hand, fiddling with a microphone.

"Oh, I'd better go," Moira said, looking suddenly fretful. "Thank you for the dance. Come say hello after?"

"Sure," David replied, even though he wasn't quite sure what 'after' she was referring to. Moira picked up her skirts and scurried off, leaving a trail of floral perfume behind her. He found himself a nice quiet table in a corner to watch the proceedings from.

David had sat through one of these speeches every year and they always went the same: a rambling reflection on the accomplishments of the year and a warm commendation of everyone's wonderful work giving back to a good cause. Previously, they had only been interesting because they kicked off the half of the night where everyone would start drinking in earnest. Now they were just dull.

However, Wayne veered off the usual script pretty quickly.

"I don't have to tell you all that this has been a rocky year for the Society. We've faced challenges in all arenas. But as always, the Society looks to the future, and we raise each other up along the journey. Leadership has always been one of the top qualities we search for in our induction exams. Every one of you have demonstrated the potential for greatness. It is my great pleasure to recognize that excellence here tonight."

David leaned forward slowly in his chair, every nerve on end. The High Priesthood. Wayne loved pomp and circumstance; of course he would do it here.

"The young man we're here to celebrate exemplifies the values of this Society: resourcefulness, curiosity, mastery of self and mastery of his work. Since his induction, he has been one of the most dedicated and reliable members of this Society, often going above and beyond the call of duty in order to take not only his practice, but everyone else's, to the next level."

David swallowed. It was really happening. Wayne was talking about him, about all the tips and tricks he had lifted from his father and gifted to the Society.

God, he needed this. He needed a win.

"It has been my deepest pleasure to mentor and work alongside this young man, and it's an even greater pleasure to present him to you now as my chosen successor. I'm so happy he was able to be with us tonight. He'll be taking over administrative duties effective immediately, with a formal ascension ceremony to come, of course. We don't pass up the opportunity for a ritual here."

Crisp-collared waitstaff circulated the room, passing out fizzing flutes of champagne. David's mouth watered, but he waved the waiter away when he came close. He wasn't going to ruin his own celebration by relapsing.

Wayne gestured somewhere off stage, smiling warmly. "Rhys, would you come up here please?"

David's blood turned to ice in his veins, freezing his heart solid.

Rhys took the stage elegantly, somehow managing to look resplendent and humble at the same time. He was perfectly at home standing on that stage, bathed in white light and applause. This was everything Rhys had ever wanted, crystalizing together in one perfect moment.

David felt like he was looking into a funhouse mirror.

Wayne handed off the microphone to Rhys. "I'm looking forward to getting to know you all better as your High Priest," Rhys said, the title dripping from his lips like honey. "This is truly an honor I don't take lightly."

Rhys raised his champagne, admiring the way the light turned the bubbles to liquid gold.

"But tonight, I want everyone to enjoy themselves. Celebration is the greatest defiance in the face of death, and if there's anything we do here, it's tilt the natural order of the world in our favor. So tonight, death has no dominion here."

He had definitely written this speech in advance. The bastard. He had known. For how long? David ricocheted from emotion to emotion with a velocity that made him sick. Rhys was well within his rights to keep the succession decision private, and Wayne had probably asked him too. Why did David even expect to be one of the first people Rhys called with news, anyway?

Rhys tilted his glass down to Moira, lingering at the corner of the stage with her own glass of champagne in hand and a beatific smile on her face. His chosen queen.

"Cheers," Rhys said, and clinked glasses with Wayne before taking a self-satisfied sip.

David wanted to storm out to his car and smoke through an entire pack of cigarettes, or walk circles around the block until he was too tired to think through all the ways his life had gone wrong. But he was rooted to his seat, aching and numb all over.

Nothing. He couldn't feel anything.

The staff were circling again, offering champagne on gleaming trays to anybody who hadn't been served the first time around. David's ears were assaulted by the ringing of glasses and drumbeat of claps. Something that had been bottled up tight, festering inside him for months, exploded in his chest.

David snagged a glass of champagne from the nearest server and put half of it back in one swallow. The bubbles stung his tongue, tiny pinpricks of sweet poison. It tasted like apple rot and freedom.

Making up his mind, David finished the rest of the champagne as everyone else toasted, oblivious.

His world came crumbling down around him to the sound of applause.

CHAPTER TWENTY

RHYS

Rhys was swallowed up in the attention of well-wishers the moment he stepped off the stage. He shook too many hands to count, had a dozen business cards slipped into his pocket, listened with tepid interest to half-baked ideas about what direction the Society should take under his headship. The atmosphere was equal parts rabid and restrained, courteous and conniving, and a weaker man might have been overwhelmed.

Rhys felt right at home.

Moira also experienced a surge in interest, mostly from the older brothers who had never bothered to learn the name of her business and wives who had whispered about how much skin she had shown at the Christmas party. Rhys made a mental note of every one of their names, separating them out from the people who had always welcomed her like goats from sheep. Though Moira insisted she could handle herself, he had always done his best to shield her from the disapproving glances of some of the older men, the type who would balk at being called racist but would never bring a woman who looked like Moira home to meet their families. The chances of any of the Johnny-come-latelies getting a request granted from him were abysmal. If he had his way, they would be edged out of the Society within six months. Still, he enjoyed watching them listen with rapt interest to stories about her tarot practice and compliment her vintage jewelry. Let them fawn. She deserved every drop of worship.

David was nowhere to be found. Rhys had only caught one glimpse of him the entire night, when he was leading Moira through one of the prim dances Rhys never had the coordination to learn.

Moira was the blinding sun at the center of the universe, overshadowing everything else, but somehow her radiance was only accentuated by David's cool, silvery light. Rhys had felt a strange mix of anguish and longing, watching them wing their way around the ballroom like celestial bodies. Not jealousy, exactly. Something softer and more treacherous.

David was probably sulking in the bathroom with a cigarette. Rhys felt a stab of guilt about not telling him ahead of time, but he hadn't had much choice in the matter. Wayne had insisted he keep the succession decision secret until the announcement, and Rhys had no idea how to broach the topic with his oldest friend anyway. Truth be told, Rhys hadn't said anything because he was a coward, and because he was selfish, because he had wanted to wring every drop of goodwill out of his and David's barely patched relationship before it broke open again. The idea of watching David shatter twice, of telling him privately and then watching him react at the gala, had been too much.

Rhys decided to be at peace with his choice, no matter how much guilt he felt.

He was passed around from table to table, conversation to conversation, for what felt like an hour before he was able to catch his breath. His head was swimming with new schemes, new ethical quandaries to take into consideration as he weighed just how much nepotism he was going to incorporate into his term as High Priest. Some of the guests had already started to trickle home, buzzed and satisfied that they had done their charitable duty for the year. Rhys left Moira to the conversation about gardening she was having with Kitty and wandered off for water.

He retrieved a bottle and leaned against the wall of a shaded alcove in the corner of the ballroom. It was a gaudy addition to the room, carved like a seashell, but it was quiet and allowed him to view the proceedings with a little privacy.

Almost.

"Caesar is dead; long live Caesar," David said.

Rhys turned to see David slouched against the wall, twirling the stem of an empty champagne glass in his hands. It was common for him to drink water from wine glasses at formal events, just for the aesthetics of the thing.

"Can I join you?" David asked, gesturing with his glass to the bit of spare room left in the alcove. Rhys nodded and David sidled in beside him, their bodies angled towards each other.

"Congratulations on the Priesthood," David said. "I'm thrilled for you."

Somebody else probably would have bought the lie, but Rhys knew David too well. He caught the thickness in his voice, the cutting flash behind his eyes. David wasn't thrilled. He was on fire, with half a mind to burn something down.

"Come on," Rhys said. He should be worried about that wild look, the fight that could ensue. But he was just relieved David was talking to him at all, that he could stand him well enough to linger close in a dark, quiet corner where no one could see them. "You could probably kill me right about now."

"I *could* kill you right now," David said, ferocity a bright, golden ribbon on his tongue. "You should have told me."

"I should have."

"But I still mean what I said. You're the best chance this Society has of dragging itself kicking and screaming into the twenty-first century. They don't deserve you."

He always seemed the most himself, the most quintessentially *David* when he didn't hide his excitable temperament. He had been an impetuous child prone to emotional outbursts, and he probably would have grown into a much more expressive man if Evgeni hadn't done his damnedest to beat it out of him.

"I appreciate it," Rhys said quietly. "I'm really very honored. I'm going to do my best to steward the role well."

David laughed, haughty and blithe. "Spare me the speech, Speaker of the House. You're living for this. Come on. Look me in the eyes and say it doesn't feel good."

Rhys met David's eyes. They passed over his face, his mouth, his collarbone and back up again with a near-physical weight, searching for any sign of deception. The gaze sizzled along Rhys's skin, burning away any pretense at faux modesty.

"It feels *phenomenal*," Rhys said, leaning in closer. "Did you see the way the old guard came to pay respects? Last week they couldn't even be bothered to remember my last name."

"I did," David said. "Power looks good on you."

A live-wire jolt went all the way down Rhys's spine. The same thrill that accompanied just barely pulling off a summoning at the edge of his ability. His whole life with David had felt this way, once upon a time, like barreling twenty over the speed limit without worrying about the inevitable crash.

Rhys shifted in place, studying his glass of champagne intently. It was suddenly very hard to look David in the eye.

"I'm glad you're here," Rhys said. "I didn't know... I wasn't sure if you would want to see me, after you found out."

God, why was it so hard to get the words out? He was a grown man, secure in himself and his boundaries. But he felt nineteen again, like when David had taken Cunnigham's *Wicca: A Guide For The Solitary Practitioner* out of his hands in the student coffeeshop line and told him if he wanted real magic, David could show him where to get it.

"Why wouldn't I want to see you?" David asked.

David seemed fidgety, like he was having a hard time standing still, but his attention was laser-focused on Rhys. For once, there didn't seem to be any artifice in what he was saying.

"I don't know," Rhys muttered. "It's been nothing but close calls and high drama for a month. I wouldn't blame you for being exhausted of me."

"I've never been exhausted of you."

"David, come on–"

"No," David snapped. Almost snarled, an animal shine on his wet teeth. Rhys couldn't decide if David looked more like predator or prey. "Not even then."

Rhys's face felt suddenly hot. Probably the celebratory champagne people kept pressing into his hands.

"I just can never figure out if you want to be my friend or not," Rhys said, the truth bubbling up out of him. "That's the exhausting part."

David let out a bark of laughter, discarding the empty glass on a nearby table. His mood was a swinging pendulum cut from its mooring. Rhys had no idea what David was going to do next.

"Is that what this is?" David asked, looming a little closer. "Friendship?"

"Why does that question sound like a trap?" Rhys shot back, his pulse roaring in his ears.

He didn't step back. If anything, he welcomed this confrontation.

David made an anguished sound, then caught Rhys's face between his hands and kissed him.

It was an act of tenderness that bordered on violence, David's mouth on his, his fingers in his hair. Rhys's whole body went taut, suspended in time and space by the impossibility of the act.

He grasped David's wrists with every intention to free himself but somehow ended up pulling David closer, ceding to the kiss.

Rhys's lips parted, and the tip of David's tongue scalded against his own.

He tasted sugar, something distinctly floral, and then, unmistakably, the tell-tale burn of alcohol.

Rhys grabbed David's lapel and wrenched him away, holding him in place. He had never understood the expression 'blind with rage' until that moment. Anger flowed through him so fast and hot that for a moment, everything went dark. When he came to, he was still holding David, who looked startled and so, so stupid.

"Easy tiger," David said with a nervous laugh. "We're in public."

Rhys threw him against the back of the alcove. The wall was only a few inches away, but he still hit it hard enough to rattle.

"You're *drunk*," he hissed, spitting out the word. It was the foulest blasphemy he could conjure.

David's mood careened towards nasty. "So, I had a few drinks," he snapped. "So what? Don't get all pious on me."

The whole ballroom tilted at a nauseating angle. Heat flooded across Rhys's face and chest, and he was horrified to find that he very much wanted to hit David.

"Rhys," David said, suddenly slick and cajoling. "Come here. It's fine, I'm fine; it's not a big deal."

"I trusted you," Rhys snapped. His voice was rising, maybe loud enough to be heard over the music. Time was melting away, past and present blurring together in a nauseating swirl. He felt like a teenager, he felt ancient, he felt like he was stuck in some distant god's sick sense of humor with no chance of escape. "And you made me into your fucking enabler *again*. Jesus Christ, how many times are we going to have to walk this road? I can't believe... You never change."

Fate had never been an appealing word to him before, but right now it felt like this was the only life he was ever going to have, getting screwed over by David Aristarkhov again and again.

David tried to circle his hand around Rhys's arm, but Rhys threw him off with considerably more force than was necessary.

"Do not touch me," Rhys spat. "Never again, do you understand me? *Never.*"

"Rhys," David pleaded, voice splintering. Good. Let him break. Rhys wasn't going to be there to pick up the pieces.

"I'm calling you a cab home. Stay here."

Rhys stalked out of the alcove, and David disobeyed of course, hot on his heels like a dog. Rhys swirled around and thrust his finger into David's face. He was shaking, he realized. From grief or rage, he didn't know.

"I can't trust my hands around you right now, David. If you follow me, I swear to God I won't be responsible for what I do, I—"

"Rhys?"

It was Antoni's voice, tentative and unsure. Rhys whirled around to find the younger man staring at him.

"Antoni," Rhys breathed. The anger left him in a rush, and then he realized how anxious he was. The world was jittering around him, his nerves threatening to vibrate him into the stratosphere.

"I was just, uh…" Antoni fumbled. "Some of us were going to hit the bar after this, and I wanted to ask if you would come. A lot of the guys want to buy you a drink."

David stared at Antoni, horrified, and then brushed past him without another word. He would probably never let Antoni speak to him about the moment ever again.

Rhys turned to follow him but ultimately opted to do damage control first. He did his best to keep his voice level. A High Priest always maintained control.

"How much of that did you see?"

"Uh…" Antoni's eyes darted nervously from Rhys to the party and back again. "All of it."

Rhys clasped Antoni's shoulder and squeezed.

"You can keep a secret for me, can't you?"

"Of course. Rhys, whatever you need—"

"Go enjoy yourself with the other guys, I'll catch up with you later. Will you text me the name of the bar?"

"Sure. Is David alright?"

"That's all I need right now, Antoni," Rhys said, and gave his shoulder an encouraging slap before slipping off into the crowd to find David.

He should let David go. He knew that, rationally. But there was a wronged, self-righteous fire in his belly that drove him forward. David was not going to get away with this, not after everything else he had done. He wasn't going to self-destruct on company time and make a scene of it during a night that, by all rights, belonged to Rhys.

He found David, predictably, by the bar, slipping the bartender a drink ticket in exchange for a double vodka soda. Rhys didn't even know where he had gotten the ticket. He always became suddenly gifted at sleight of hand when he was covering up his habits.

Rhys had to get a hold on his temper and handle this carefully, otherwise the backlash could be explosive. David had already proven he was willing to go way off the rails to get a rise out of him.

Rhys stood close to him, discreetly covering David's hand on his drink with his own.

"You're done for the night. I'm calling you a car."

"You can't make me get in it," David said, shrugging him off. He brought the glass to his mouth and took a brazen swallow. The glass came back half empty. Rhys forgot how fast he could put liquor away, especially when no one was looking. "Give the messiah complex a rest."

"How many of those have you had?"

"None of your damn business."

"That's it," Rhys said tightly. "Give me your keys."

Rhys tried to reach into the interior pocket of David's jacket, but David caught his wrist and scowled.

David leaned in close to speak, and his breath smelled like acetone. "Why won't you just let me have this? I can't have *anything* with you, can I?"

Rhys stared down David, and this was the worst part. Looking at someone he had known for years, someone who had been closer than his own family to him, once, and seeing a stranger.

Rhys lowered his voice and threaded steel through it. There was only one way out of this night. And it was going to hurt. "If you do not cooperate, I will humiliate you so badly, so *soundly*, in front of every single person here that you will never be able to show your face in a meeting again."

He didn't have to give specifics. There were a dozen ways that he could do it, and his tone told David that this wasn't a bluff. Rhys was really willing to drag David out into the middle of the room and run a knife through his deepest, oldest fear, of losing face in front of other people. It was cruel, and Rhys knew it. But it was effective.

The wild light in David's eyes dimmed into dull, simmering hatred, and he released his grip on Rhys's wrist. Rhys retrieved the keys to David's Audi and his cell phone, just in case he decided to call someone he shouldn't. Rhys wasn't even sure who that would be, since he was standing right there with David, but it was better safe than sorry.

"Let's go," Rhys said. "I'm driving you home."

David's mouth curled into a miserable twist, and he huffed a sigh that made his shoulders collapse.

"Rhys. Please."

This, too, followed the usual progression from erratic to angry to pitiful. This was usually the moment in the narrative arc of a bender where David would cling to him, call him baby, beg him not to be angry. The trick to getting past it was to not empathize with David's misery or to blame himself for letting it get this far.

The trick was to not feel anything at all.

"Let's go," Rhys repeated. "I'm not going to ask again."

CHAPTER TWENTY-ONE

MOIRA

Moira was deep into conversation about the precise week in November one should plant tulips when she felt her husband's presence behind her. He smiled politely at Kitty as he settled his hand over his wife's shoulder, but Moira knew right away that something was wrong. There was a tightness in his jaw and a dark cast to his features that spelled trouble.

"What's up?" she asked quietly, swiveling to look at Rhys. David was standing a few feet away acting like he wasn't eavesdropping. He couldn't have looked more miserable if he had swallowed a frog. Something was definitely wrong.

"Nothing," Rhys said, too lightly. He leaned down near her ear and added in a low voice, "I'm going to drive David home. I'll be right back for you. Forty-five minutes, tops."

"Why?" Moira demanded, swiveling even more to try and get a good look at David. "What's happened?"

Rhys gave Kitty a tight smile. Ever perceptive, Kitty gathered up her clutch and excused herself.

Once she was out of earshot, Rhys added, "David's drunk. I'm going to make sure he gets home safely."

Moira moved to push up from her chair, head swimming with awful possibilities. She had been lucky enough to be raised in an environment free of the specter of addiction, but she knew people in David's position didn't relapse for no good reason. They had to be pushed.

"David, honey, what *happened*?"

David covered his face with a hand, unable to look at her, and Rhys blocked her path before she could go to him.

"I don't want a scene. Please, just let me take care of this. I know how to handle him."

"Don't be cow-headed," Moira said, snagging up her purse. "What, are you supposed to drive and talk him down at the same time?"

"You don't have to take care of him—"

Moira shot her husband a hard look. "I want to, Rhys. When will you learn I don't do a damn thing in this life unless I want to?"

"Jesus Christ," David groaned when he saw her coming towards him. "Just don't, please. I'm not in the mood for a lecture."

"I'm not gonna lecture you," Moira muttered, threading her arm through his and leading him discreetly towards the ballroom doors. Rhys followed close behind, shooting Antoni a pointed look as they passed. "Do you want me to wait with you for a cab?"

"If we call him a cab, he'll just go to a bar," Rhys muttered. There was a bitter, dark cloud around him that only got more pronounced as they got further from the noise of the ballroom. He was absolutely livid, angrier than she had ever seen him, angrier than she knew he was capable of getting. But it was a quiet, cold kind of anger, and that scared her the most.

"Get in the car, David," Rhys said, unlocking the Lincoln as they approached.

David slid sullenly into the backseat as Rhys held open the passenger side door for his wife. She opted to duck in after David into the backseat.

"Scooch," she ordered. David looked at her with bleary bafflement but duly scooted to the other side of the car. His eyes had a wet, red look in the streetlights.

Rhys gave her a skeptical glance through the rearview mirror as he revved the engine. *I know what I'm doing*, her eyes responded.

David's apartment building looked like any of the other glass and metal structures that jutted out of the overdeveloped modern parts of the city. They were indistinguishable from banks and coworking spaces, and Rhys hated them precisely for their clinical sheen. But he seemed to know his way to this one perfectly well, not even having to glance at the GPS.

There was barely a stick of furniture in the gleaming, anonymous lobby, and what seating there was looked futuristic and pointedly decorative. Moira felt sure that security would get called if she actually sat on anything.

"Night, Robby," David said to the concierge, doing a bad job of trying to sound upbeat. The suited man behind the counter swept a watchful eye over Rhys and Moira but said nothing as they waited awkwardly with David for the elevator.

Moira had assumed her husband would drop David off in front of his building, but now she saw that he really intended to deposit David at his condominium. It felt extreme to her, a little invasive. But maybe Rhys had reason to believe it was absolutely necessary.

She didn't expect him to follow David into his house. But when David swiped the card to get into his apartment unit, Rhys stood by expectantly, glowering with his hands shoved in his pockets. This was an old routine, she realized. One only they knew the steps to.

The condo felt awful, but a different kind of awful than the house on Beacon Hill. This house didn't feel haunted. It didn't feel lived in at all. Moira got the impression she was walking through a beautiful morgue. Clean, soulless lines accentuated a kitchen that seemed more showroom than dinner-party ready. Everything was rendered in cool tones of white, gray, black, and dark blue.

David shrugged off his jacket and tossed it onto the ground near the couch.

"Are you happy now?" he demanded, unfastening his cuffs.

Rhys said nothing, only clinically swung open kitchen cupboards and drawers. He even went so far as to rummage through the freezer.

"There's nothing there," David snapped. He looked unsteady on his feet, like he needed an IV drip and a twelve-hour nap to feel anywhere close to human again. "I don't keep any liquor in the house."

"Go to bed, David," Rhys said, deathly quiet.

"This is my house; I'll do what I want," David shot back, speech ever so slightly slurred. If Moira hadn't been around him when he was sober, when every single gesture and word was carefully weighed against optics and the politics of power, she might not have even been able to tell he was drunk. "Give me my keys."

"I'll leave them out for you to find in the morning. Is your therapist's number still the same?"

David's face was a mask of hatred and misery, so contorted Moira could barely recognize him. "Your world's perfect now, huh? Everything just like you designed. But I don't fit anywhere, so I've got to go."

"You're being dramatic," Rhys said, voice frighteningly emotionless. He had entirely shut off. "You're embarrassing yourself."

"Then why don't you just leave me alone to fuck my own life up? I didn't ask you to get involved."

Rhys's temper snapped like a dry twig. "You involved me!" he yelled. "You pulled me into your life, and you asked for my help and then you fucked with my head! What else do you call the stunt you pulled back there?"

"I wasn't trying to fuck with your head!" David shot back, matching his volume. "The one time I'm honest with you, and you think that I'm–"

"That's enough!" Moira shouted. Her voice bounced off the blank walls and echoed back at her. She was surprised at herself, and so was David, who jumped in his skin. Rhys stared at his wife, cheeks gaunt.

Moira pressed a hand to her fluttering heart, forcing a deep breath into her lungs.

"You two will not raise your voices around me, do you understand? I can't abide the sound of men shouting and I'll not tolerate it from either of y'all."

"Sorry," David breathed, wiping his mouth with the back of his hands. Rhys just kept staring.

"David, you're coming with me," Moira said, crossing the room with a few determined strides. "It's time for bed."

He left in the direction of the bedroom without argument. Moira following, slowing only to stop beside her husband and hiss, "You had better pull yourself together, Rhys McGowan. Fast."

The master bedroom was, in her mind, a travesty. Barely a scrap of decoration or personal detail to be seen. The unadorned black wood headboard and deep blue comforter looked forbidding rather than welcoming, and the storage space in the room had been designed to keep as low a profile as possible, hiding away suits and undershirts like they were trade secrets. If it wasn't for the few pairs of shoes scattered across the floor and the nest of sheets in one corner of the bed, around which folders and papers were laid out, the room would look entirely abandoned.

David kicked off his shoes and began clumsily unfastening the buttons of his shirt, missing a couple on his way down. Just about the time

Moira was starting to wonder if it would be improper for her to offer to help, he managed to wrench his shirt off. Now wearing just a white T-shirt, slacks, and socks, he clambered onto the bed and curled up on top of the covers.

In the kitchen, Moira could distantly make out Rhys talking in low, urgent tones with someone over the phone. The therapist, she assumed.

Moira eased herself down on the edge of the bed, hands in her lap, staring straight ahead. David didn't move from his position, and the two of them sat like that for a few long, silent minutes. Then Moira reached out to lightly sweep her hand over the hair falling into his eyes.

David recoiled from her touch, curling tighter in on himself. Moira recognized the defensive body language from the kids she had volunteered playing basketball with in high school, the ones who came from broken or battered homes.

"Please don't," David muttered, voice half muffled by the comforter. "I don't want you to read me when I'm like this."

"I'm not going to," Moira said.

David stayed where he was for a moment. Then, he pulled his head out of its tucked position by a few inches.

Moira threaded her fingers through his hair, running her hand along the curve of his skull. Immediately, David edged closer until his head was resting in her lap, facing away from her so he wouldn't have to look in her eyes. Moira kept her word. She didn't try to read him, just smoothed her hand over the forehead of a miserable overgrown boy she had no idea how to help, feeling very tired and very useless. She didn't have anything to say to him, so she hoped her touch was soothing enough.

"What if," David began, his voice hoarse. "I'm not really good at anything at all. Law or mediumship. What if it's this goddamn demon deal, and once that's gone, there's nothing left."

"Don't say that," Moira said. "There's plenty of you that isn't tied up in that deal."

"That's all I'm good for," he muttered, losing himself in some inconsolable spiral. "If I can't work anymore, if I'm not at the top of my game… There's no point. There's nothing left. It's all I'm good for. It's all I know how to do."

"There's plenty left, but nothing you can see when you've got yourself in this state. I need you to sleep, David. Will you try?"

"I'm sorry," he muttered, putting his hand on top of hers to stop the petting. "It was a shitty thing of me to do. I don't know why I did that. You don't deserve that. You deserve so much better than my bullshit."

"What are you talking about, David?"

There was a soft sound near the door, and Moira looked up to see Rhys in the doorway, watching them from a safe distance. He seemed afraid to step foot in the bedroom.

"Time to go," he said quietly.

David shrank away from her at the sound of Rhys's voice, rolling over so his head was on the pillow.

Moira stood, beating the wrinkles out of her evening dress, and slipped out of the room. Rhys flicked off the light and closed the door on David with a soft, final click.

They didn't linger long at the loud, dimly lit gastropub Antoni had chosen to celebrate in. Rhys accepted everyone's congratulations with attentive smiles, but the exhaustion was evident in his eyes. Moira rescued him with apologetic complaints of an early morning and drove them back to Jamaica Plain as soon the well-wishers released them. Once home, the exhaustion hit her too.

"Help me with my zipper, baby," she murmured, one hand braced on the papered wall of their bedroom.

Rhys opened her dress with deft fingers, careful not to let the zipper bite her skin, and smoothed his palm up the bare curve of her back. He kissed the nape of her neck, leaning on her with the weariness of a man freshly home from war.

Moira turned and slid her arms around her husband's neck, looking into his face.

"You've got to let it go," she said, pressing a light kiss to his cheek, the corner of his mouth. "His choices are his own."

"No matter what I do, I keep ending up back here," Rhys said, voice hoarse. "Cleaning up after him."

Moira made a knowing humming noise. "I think part of you likes it. I think even though it causes you pain, you keep chasing that high of feeling needed. But David will be just fine without you playing taskmaster. You can't force somebody to take care of themselves, baby. The only person you can control is yourself."

Rhys gave her a faux disapproving expression. "It's awful late at night to be talking sense to me like I'm a client."

Moira grinned, nudging his nose with her own. "I'll go easy on you, I promise. Come here."

Rhys cradled her face in his hands, and she tipped her head back obligingly for his kiss. Moira's dress slipped off her shoulders and caught around her waist, and she gingerly pulled off his jacket, careful not to crumple the velvet. Her fingers trailed up the curve of his spine through the fabric of his shirt, and Rhys made a soft pleasured sound, deepening their kiss.

Then suddenly, he pulled away.

"I have to tell you something," he said. There wasn't a drop of color in his face.

"What is it?"

"I..." He was frozen, voice stuck in his throat.

Moira raised her eyebrows at him. "Well?"

"David kissed me. I let him."

She pushed back from him a few inches, blinking in a daze. That put a couple of things about their screaming match in the condo into perspective.

"When?"

"At the gala. Before I realized he had been drinking. I'm sorry, Moira, I'm so sorry. I love you so much, you're my entire world, I–"

Moira pressed light fingers over her husband's mouth before he could work himself up any further. He excelled at self-flagellation.

She took a deep breath, willing her pounding heart to slow. A maelstrom of emotions whirled inside her, threatening to consume her. Dismay, anxiety, the butterflies of pure adrenaline. She tried to push them all aside and follow her heart down to her root feelings on the matter. There, in the quiet part of herself she found concern. But also a sense of inevitability. Or puzzle pieces slotting correctly into place.

"It's been a weird night," she said with a soft laugh. She felt strangely light, delirious maybe. "Let's not be too hard on ourselves for one little indiscretion, okay? Anyway, the kiss doesn't surprise me."

Moira shimmied out of her dress and draped it over the back of a chair as she went to the closet to find her nightclothes. She still felt shaky, like she had drunk too much champagne at the party even though she had only indulged in two glasses, and she couldn't breathe quite right. Was she angry? She couldn't tell. Mostly she just felt very upside-down about everything.

Rhys stayed rooted to the spot, staring at her like she had been body-snatched and replaced with a clone. "You're not jealous?" His eyes were wide, waiting for her to burst into tears or start shouting at him.

Moira took off her earrings and heavy necklace, dropping them in a ceramic dish. "Now, I didn't say that. But it's easy to be jealous of a man you don't know from Adam. But I know David now, and he's..." Moira didn't have a word for it. The pang of sweetness that went through her when Rhys leaned over to David to say something soft. The rush of protective affection that had coursed through her when David hugged her tightly in the shadow of his father's bedroom. The sense of power she felt walking flanked by both of them down the sidewalk. "He's just David. I'm no more threatened by your love for him than I am by your love for your mother. Neither stopped you from making me your wife."

Rhys paled. "Love is a strong word."

"Call it what you like. I know it when I see it. And I could see it clear as day between you two from the moment I read your palm at the Beacon Hill house."

"You what?"

Moira tangled her fingers together, scrambling for an explanation. Maybe she should have been more straightforward. But she had no way of being sure if she was making the glimmering threads of unspoken connection between all three of them up. It was hard to tell with David. He was close to her one moment and then gone the next. "I should have said something, but I didn't want to... I don't know. I was worried I was making it up. Or that saying it out loud would ruin something."

"You care about him too," Rhys said, with a strange finality in his voice.

"I do," Moira admitted. "More than I thought I would. Maybe that's why it's hard to be angry at either of you."

"Are you in love with David?"

"I think that's a question better posed by me to you."

He stood there in the middle of the room, flexing and unflexing his right hand and staring at the ground. Thinking intently. For a moment, Moira wondered if she had broken them. They should have had this conversation from the start, from the first time the three of them had been in that house together. She just never dreamed it would go this far.

"How?" Rhys asked finally. His face was positively anguished. "How could you have known when I didn't?"

"Oh, baby," Moira sighed. She went to him and put her hand on his cheek. "For somebody so smart sometimes you really are a little stupid."

Rhys caught her hand and kissed her palm. "David doesn't mean anything to me."

Moira latticed her fingers through Rhys's and squeezed. Hard. "Don't lie. You can have whatever and whoever you want in this life, Rhys. Just don't ever lie to me. Do you hear what I'm telling you? Do you hear how much I trust you?"

Rhys took a deep breath and tried again.

"David means *a lot* to me. But you're my wife." He kissed her with newfound urgency, punctuating each word with a worshipful press of his lips to her mouth, her throat. "My north star."

"Keep going," Moira said, wrapping her arms around him.

"Goddess incarnate. Witch of my heart."

"Are you gonna take me to bed, Rhys McGowan, or are you just gonna keep talking about it?"

Rhys deftly unfastened Moira's bra and discarded it on the floor. He cupped her breasts in his hands, running his thumbs over her taut nipples. A pleasant shudder went up Moira's spine and she pressed their bodies closer together. She tugged at the hem of his shirt, freeing it from the waistband of his trousers.

"My home and final resting place," Rhys said, voice rough with want and desperation.

Moira tugged his shirt up over his head, not bothering with the buttons, and ran her fingers up the familiar lines of his pale chest. She dropped a kiss to the spot right over his heart.

"The important people in our lives might change," Moira said, feeling the kick of his heartbeat against her lips. "But my love for you never will."

"Neither will mine for you," Rhys said, pushing her lightly back towards the bed. He was never rough with her; those weren't the kind of bedroom games she enjoyed. But there was a certain pleasure at being stared at like a treasured possession, like the crown jewels in Rhys's collection. The whisper of objectification made the heat rise in her cheeks.

Moira sank into the sheets, stretching out to offer him the best possible view. "Then we shouldn't keep each other from anything or anyone that we want," she said.

Rhys tugged her stockings down over her knees and then plucked them from her ankles. He circled one of her small feet with his fingers, pressing a thumb against one of the acupressure points in the arch.

"What you're talking about is dangerous," he said darkly.

"I'm not afraid. Are you?"

Rhys's response was to hook his thumbs under her panties and relieve her of them. She watched, comfortable in her nakedness, as Rhys stepped out of his pants and knelt on the bed in front of her.

"I'm cautious," he said, kissing her bare knee. "That's different."

"Then we proceed with caution. Look, we've come to an agreement."

"You're going to make an excellent High Priest's wife," Rhys said with a crooked smile. Moira's heart skipped a beat at the flash of his teeth in the dark. "I love it when you get devious."

"Oh yeah?" Moira shot back with a smirk of her own. "Show me how much."

Rhys lowered his head between her thighs and lapped at the heat he found there. Moira let out a gasp, arching her back off the bed. Rhys made a pleased hum and dug his fingernails into her ample hips to hold her still. She knew his tricks well enough to know that he was spelling his full name with his tongue, marking her as his own in the most intimate of ways.

"Rhys," Moira sighed, tangling her fingers in his hair. She could feel the lust radiating off him like body heat, and it made her stomach do a somersault. Rhys always made Moira feel wanted, but she had not been wanted like *this* in some time. The stalwart tealight of Rhys's desire felt more like a bonfire beneath her fingers, wild and hungry.

Rhys devoted himself to his task with a scholar's single-minded focus, and it wasn't long before her thighs were trembling. Moira gave a little cry as her pleasure crested, once and then twice as Rhys brought her over the edge.

Moira melted back into her bedsheets and held her arms out to her husband, who was over her in an instant. Moira pulled him into a hot, hard kiss. She wanted Rhys closer, she wanted nothing between them but darkness and devotion.

She wrapped her fingers around the length of him and savored the way his breath caught in his throat. She never got tired to this, of peeling back the layers of academic focus and propriety to find the man underneath. Rhys nipped a half-moon on her shoulder, eliciting a breathy giggle from his wife.

Moira rolled over so she was on top of him, his hipbones digging into her soft inner thighs. The warm summer air drifted in through the window and ghosted across her bare skin as she guided him towards her entrance. Rhys dug his fingers securely into her back as their bodies slotted together and found an old, familiar rhythm. Moira let out a shaky sigh as warmth swept through her.

"I'd move heaven and hell for you," Rhys said, pulling her in tighter. "Tell me you know that."

"I don't want heaven and I don't want hell," Moira said, breath coming fast and hot as she rolled her hips. "I just want you."

Rhys thrust into her, his grip on her body merciless. Moira could have purred, it felt so perfect.

"You're going to be a queen, Moira," he said, dragging his mouth across her own as he spoke. His pace quickened, driving her towards another orgasm. He knew exactly the angle to take to pleasure her while pursuing his own gratification. "My Queen. Mine."

Moira shuddered with delight, an irrepressible smile spreading across her lips. She knew exactly what Rhys was when she married him, down to the darkest corners of his insatiable heart. She adored him like this, selfish ambition laid bare by his love for her. Truth be told, Rhys could be a bit of a monster when it came to getting what he wanted. But he was her monster, and what he wanted was her happiness.

She wouldn't change a single thing about him.

"Don't stop," she said. "Keep talking."

"I'm going to give you everything you ever wanted. I'll summon a whole host of spirits to wait on you. I'll buy you diamonds with Society endowment money, I don't fucking care," he rasped. He was approaching his own climax; Moira could feel it in the tightness in his muscles, in the relentless way he drove into her. "I'll make every magician in Boston come to the house and pay their respects to you. God, Moira, I'll do anything. I'll... *God.*"

Moira held him fast as he broke into pieces, filling her with heat and light.

Afterwards, they held each other in the dim, their legs tangled together, sweat cooling on their skin. Moira trailed a lazy line of kisses down her husband's chest, then broke the silence.

"It's not going to be easy, you know," she said in her soft Southern drawl. "Heavy is the head that wears the crown, and all that. The High Priesthood is gonna try to take everything from you. You can't let it."

Rhys circled an arm around her shoulder and kissed the top of her head. She could sense him slipping into introspection, drifting a little further away from her despite how close they were in bed.

"As long as I have you by my side, I'll be fine," he said eventually.

"And David?" she asked, quiet in the dark.

Rhys nudged his nose against her own.

"We'll figure it out together, you and me. That's always how it's going to be, Moira. You and me."

The hanged man

CHAPTER TWENTY-TWO

DAVID

David spent the next four days in a fugue state. One of the worst hangovers of his life blurred together with the spinning head and roiling nausea of spirit sickness. He ignored every phone call that wasn't from his therapist, and answered her questions in as few syllables as possible. Humiliation burned through his chest whenever he thought about the gala and its aftermath. Usually, this was when he would throw himself into his work or hit the gym for three hours until he could barely breathe, much less remember his own failures. But his body refused to allow him to even circle the block without giving out on him, so he confined himself to his bedroom and a steady diet of sparkling water, saltine crackers, and tasteless freezer chicken penne. His stomach couldn't handle anything more substantial, and his id was screaming for another drink to file the edge off the shame, so he resisted the temptation to run down to the corner market for groceries.

He slept through Thursday's Society meeting and couldn't bring himself to care. He didn't have it in him to show his face that week, not when Rhys was sure to be flocked with well-wishers and glowing with favor. He hadn't called, which was fine. David didn't expect to ever hear from him again after the stunt David had pulled at the gala.

He told himself he was fine with that, too.

When his phone did ring, it pulled him out of a black, dreamless sleep.

David flipped over the phone on his bedside table, then groaned when he saw the caller ID.

"Wayne," David said, pressing the phone to his ear.

"David, hello! How are you?"

"Great," David said, pulling the expensive down comforter over his head.

"I couldn't help but notice you weren't at the meeting today. We missed you."

"Yeah?" David asked, trying to make it sound like he wasn't holed up in his bed. He rolled onto his side, looking out his expansive windows to the apartment across the way. The cute young lesbian couple who lived there were having dinner at the open window. David hated them for their happiness. "Who scryed?"

"Cameron. He doesn't have the knack for it, I'm afraid."

Good, David thought. "That's too bad," he said, savoring the schadenfreude.

"I heard you haven't been feeling well."

"I'm fine," David said, pushing himself up into a sitting position. "I've just been working too hard. I took the day off."

"Good, good. Then you'll be up to getting some dinner tonight. Abe and Louie's at eight thirty?"

David passed a hand in front of his face and took a deep breath. "Sure. Sounds good."

Abe and Louie's was a classic white-tablecloth steakhouse in Back Bay, decked out with a heavy wooden bar lit by low golden lighting. It was Wayne's favorite, and he had brought David here once before as a gift on his 21st birthday. David had put away a huge ribeye and three glasses of wine until he was glowing with a merlot buzz and the praise Wayne dished out. It was his favorite kind of memory, where he was the center of attention, being recognized for his hard work, with no whiff of criticism.

Now, he wasn't sure what Wayne's angle was. David had spent the last few days convinced that he had been deposed from his seat as Wayne's favorite by Rhys, and that the current High Priest probably didn't want anything to do with him. Maybe, David reckoned glumly as he pushed his way through the restaurant doors, Wayne had called him out here to let him down easy, to turn him out of the Society in a private, civil way.

But when Wayne saw him, he smiled that same warm smile and shook his hand firmly before pulling him into a one-armed hug.

"So good to see you," he said, as though there was no one else in the world he would rather be taking dinner with. "Have a seat, please."

David smiled in a way he hoped looked friendly, not pained, and swept into the empty chair. The waiter fussed over them both for a moment, but once David had ordered his Perrier and the salmon, he and Wayne were left in peace.

"You look well," Wayne pronounced. "Not sick like they were saying."

"Who's they?" David asked, unable to keep the bitterness out of his voice. "Rhys?"

"No, no. I spoke to Nathan. He said you haven't been feeling much like yourself lately."

David had known Wayne long enough to know when he was working up to an uncomfortable talking point. He cut him off at the pass. "Did he see what happened at the gala?"

Wayne leaned back in his seat and spread his hands. "This isn't an interrogation, David. It's been so long since you and I were able to talk man to man. I thought it would be good to catch up. But yes, I heard you had a bit too much to drink at the gala. It's nothing to be ashamed of; it happens to the best of us."

He wasn't entirely sure how to respond to that. Wayne could never quite grasp that to David, alcohol wasn't an ill-advised one-night stand. It was more like a drawn-out, toxic relationship with a lover who smacked him around but kept him coming back for more.

He didn't ask if Wayne had seen him with Rhys. If that lecture was coming, there was no dodging it, but he wasn't in the mood for quiet sympathy and firm-handed advice. Confrontation seemed more comforting and familiar, so he steered the conversation in that direction.

"Well, as you can imagine, I was a little surprised by your succession pick. It didn't seem in line with conversations you and I have had."

Wayne didn't even have the grace to look guilty. "I never made you any promises, David."

"You led me on."

"I let you know you were at the top of my list, and that was true. But so was Rhys. Surely, you knew that."

The waiter appeared with braised salmon for David and a prime cut of beef for Wayne, and David took advantage of the interruption to let a glower flicker across his face.

"Would it be out of line to say I think you made the wrong call?" David asked once the waiter had disappeared.

"David, come on. You didn't really want the Priesthood."

David stabbed a fork into his dinner with more viciousness than was strictly necessary. "Didn't I?"

Wayne leaned across the table, his blue eyes shining keenly. "You can't look me in the eye and tell me you really wanted to get tied up in all that bureaucracy and red tape. Doing things by the book has never been your strong suit, and while I do think you're a natural leader, you don't do well stuck behind a desk. That's what Rhys is signing up for, and trust me when I say it's a grind."

"I could have done it," David muttered, a treacherous emotion knotting in his throat. He wouldn't get upset in front of Wayne; he refused to. "I would have been fantastic."

"Maybe so. But you would have also been wasted."

David shot Wayne a withering glance. "Spare me."

"I'm serious. Rhys has worked long and hard to get where he is. But you were *born* for greatness, David. It's in your blood. I haven't forgotten about you."

"Oh yeah? What's my consolation prize?"

Wayne chuckled, shaking his head fondly. He had always indulged David's bad attitude, ever since David had been fifteen and mouthing off to his father's friends during a séance. Evgeni had always responded to David's quips with a sharp word or a sharp slap, but Wayne was more understanding.

"How about the role of chief scryer, for starters?"

David refused to let any pleasure show on his face. "I already scry plenty."

"Yes, but I'm talking about putting you in charge of the whole operation. You would have first dibs on scrying any working you want, and you would have more input on the kinds of workings we perform as a group."

David pressed his lips into a thin line. Any other day, he would have been overjoyed with more free reign, and a new title to boot. But now it just felt like a pity promotion.

Wayne raised his water glass in a toast. David remembered distantly that toasting with water was supposedly bad luck.

"You do trust me, don't you?" Wayne asked.

David consulted with himself and found, improbably, that he did. Wayne had been in his life as long as anyone left alive. He used to produce cream toffees out of his coat pockets for David when he visited Evgeni at the Beacon Hill house, and had always readily dished out praise after David emerged, winded and dizzy, from channeling. He had steered David away from total vodka-soaked ruin after Evgeni died, leaving David with millions to his name and zero supervision, and he had been there when Rhys had moved out, leaving David a dejected, jaded mess. David had spent a Christmas with Wayne and his wife in the Alps, for God's sake, of course he trusted him.

"Yes, High Priest," David muttered into his water.

"Not for long!" Wayne said with a grin, jabbing a finger in David's direction. "Soon that title will belong to Rhys. Please do your best to defer to him. I understand that might be difficult considering your history, and what he must still mean to you–"

"Rhys McGowan means nothing to me," David said icily, even though his chest was burning hot. When David felt threatened, he got mean, and when he had been a much younger man, he used to get mean and lie. Apparently, there was no growing out of some vices. "He's a talented sorcerer and scholar, more than fit to lead, but that's where my admiration of him ends. You shouldn't worry about favoritism. There hasn't been any fondness between us for years."

Wayne nodded approvingly. "That's my boy."

The High Priest cut into his rare steak, a dribble of bloody juice running down his knife.

David sat in silence for a moment, and his own appetite – elusive as an unasked question – twisted in his gut. Finally, he gave in. "Wayne, you were close with my father, weren't you?"

"I wouldn't say we were close. Evgeni kept to himself. But we came up together in the Society. He was an excellent sorcerer. A bulldog in the ceremonial circle. He could break any spirit, get them to do whatever he wanted."

David tangled his fingers together under the table, squeezing until his knuckles went white.

"He didn't ever mention any sort of family... deal, did he?"

"You mean that old fairy tale about the Devil?"

David forced a smile. He was talented enough that he knew it looked convincing. "That's the one. I'm just doing a little genealogical research. It's an entertaining tidbit."

Wayne chewed thoughtfully. "He might have mentioned it in passing. Something about your ancestor selling a soul for the power to charm people. I don't remember the details, I'm afraid."

David smothered a frustrated sigh. Another dead end.

Wayne leaned forward, fixing David with a look that usually predicated a lecture. "Now, I'm willing to overlook your absence today in light of recent events, but you know you can't just disappear on us, don't you? Especially now that you're going to be taking on more responsibility."

"I understand."

"Can I count on your attendance next Thursday? The Society needs you. The boys wouldn't know what to do with themselves without you there to set an example."

David was an adept enough flatterer to know when he was being buttered up, but he accepted the compliment all the same. It took the sting out of the dull ache that had been throbbing under his skin ever since he had pulled Rhys into that alcove at the gala.

"Of course," he said magnanimously, a little bit of that old glamour shining through. He didn't feel at all himself, but being asked to make an appearance somewhere and perform his talents helped. That was what he had always been best at, after all. That's what he had been bred for.

CHAPTER TWENTY-THREE

MOIRA

Moira kept her hands busy sorting through vintage denim, cleansing her crystal collection with smoke and sunlight, and occasionally bringing Rhys eggs on toast to make sure he was eating. He spent most of his time in his study, up until ungodly hours working until he could barely see straight. He was smoking again too, late-night cigarettes that strung him out and kept him awake through the wee hours. But she would give him a few days before she reminded him that he promised never to get cigarette smoke in her wallpaper.

Rhys wasn't interested in talking about David, but Moira could tell from the tightness in his jaw and the distant look in his eyes that he was thinking about him plenty. For her part, Moira was worried about the psychic. She had gotten close to David without meaning to, and witnessing his relapse had been unsettling. She didn't like the thought of him coping alone, but she didn't feel it was appropriate for her to reach out unsolicited.

Thankfully, she didn't have to.

Moira was in her meditation room, looking aimlessly out the small window while propped up on cushions on the windowsill, when her phone buzzed gently. She did a double take when she saw the contact name.

David Aristarkhov.

Heart flapping, Moira scrolled to read the message.

Hope all is well over in Jamaica Plain. How are you holding up?

She couldn't help the small smile that pulled at her lips. Her heart had been all but hardened against him after his silence over the last few days, but here was proof that he hadn't deleted her number, at least.

Every day a little better, she typed back, weighing every word carefully. She didn't want to scare him off or let him right back into her good graces with fawning attention. *We're both keeping ourselves busy with work. You?*

Work's fine, he replied, evading giving her any emotional information with his usual slippery ease. *I took the last couple days off.*

Moira gnawed on her bottom lip and tapped her manicured fingers against her phone. David taking time off work was like the U.S. Postal Service ceasing operation: not impossible, but indicative of some larger terrible crisis. If he wasn't working, that meant his condition was worsening. He could only answer emails and take calls from home so long before someone noticed he wasn't operating at maximum capacity, and Moira wasn't sure how forgiving his high-pressure job would be. If David lost his job, she didn't know what he would do with himself.

How's the sick spells? she asked.

Still shitty.

Are you doing your shielding meditations?

If I schedule them into my day, they feel more like productivity and less like I'm getting ready for Lilith Fair.

Moira snorted, rolling her eyes. Still, his particular brand of acidic humor was comforting. That meant he still felt well enough to joke, at least, and that he wanted to make her laugh.

I'm glad you're resting, she typed back, slow and careful. There was a lot more she wanted to say, but she was worried that if she smothered him, he might never come wandering back. He really was like a feral cat.

For nine long minutes, there was nothing. Moira let out a groan, letting her head loll back against the window. She was too old to bite her nails waiting for boys to text her back, even if they were terrible grown ones she wasn't trying to entice into dating her.

Then, David replied. *I'm sorry I was a dick to you after the gala. I don't do well with substances. But that's not an excuse.*

An apology was something she would never stoop to asking for ("queens' crowns slip when they bow to other people," her mother would say) but damn if it wasn't good to hear.

I appreciate you saying so.

If we all live through this goddamn summer, I'll take you shopping to apologize. If I die before then, I'm willing you my vinyl.

Nobody's going to die.

And that was it, the end of their conversation. Moira tossed her phone down on a cushion and lost herself in thought. A few weeks ago, Rhys's eyes had been bright with the thrill of discovery, and David had lavished her with friendly touches and compliments. She had waded into uncertain emotional waters with both of them and found it exciting. Now she felt like she was losing them to their own self-isolating instincts. Rhys had people in his corner who wouldn't let the High Priesthood eat him alive, but Moira wasn't sure if David had anyone to help him fight back his own darkness. It wasn't her business, strictly speaking, but she still cared. He had mentioned a sister, but she didn't feel comfortable calling a family member out of the blue to tip them off to David's condition.

However, now that she thought of it, there was one mutual connection they shared.

It was time to pay a visit to Lorena Vargas.

Lorena's botanica was easily recognizable on the cramped streets of Jamaica Plain by the myriad of colorful statues crowding the windows. Saints rubbed elbows with Aztec warriors and angels taking flight, hovering over Hindu deities and Madonnas of every ethnicity. A sign above the door offered both remedies and consultations.

The scent of Palo Santo hit Moira in a warm wave as she slipped into the shop. Any Boston occultist worth their salt recognized the smell of Lorena's botanica, whether they came to her for oil-dressed candles or to place an order with one of her many mysterious suppliers. The shop looked humble from the outside, but as far as the supernatural was concerned, Lorena's was the center of the universe.

Moira wound through the narrow but well-ordered shelves of rosaries, bundled sweetgrass, and hand-labelled tinctures in little square bottles. There was remedy for everything here: hotfoot powder to drive away sex pests, Saint Expedite medals to hurry up immigration paperwork, road opening oil to dot in the corner of a resume.

"Lorena," Moira sang out, poking her head down another empty aisle. "It's Moira."

"Up here," Lorena replied, voice coming from somewhere in the back of the shop. Moira wandered over to the counter just in time to see her ease herself up from a low chair. She had been plaiting thick ropes of fragrant grass and flowers in a basket at her feet. Her most esteemed saint was set up behind her, a skeletal figure robed in black and surrounded by offerings of flowers, coins, and small bottles of liquor.

"Ah, Moira!" she exclaimed, the lines of her face deepening as she smiled. As always, she wore her long black hair braided with a red silk flower pinned to her crown. "I haven't seen you since you came in for your house blessing bath! How did it work? You let the herbs soak like I told you?"

"Of course," Moira said, reaching over the counter to clasp Lorena's hands in her own. "Your spells are the best in town."

"And don't go forgetting that! You tell your friends and send them to me," she said with a chuckle. She had a warm, rich voice and a low laugh, weathered by a lifelong love affair with cigarillos.

"What are you looking for today?" Lorena asked, wiping the dust of dried flowers from her hands. "Maybe a dominating oil to help Rhys with his new job? Or something to help with conception? No, no, on second thought, you won't have any trouble having babies if you want them. It's just not your time yet."

She said it all so flippantly, but Moira felt a little winded. It was possible Lorena had heard about the High Priesthood from somebody else; gossip travelled fast through occult circles. But it was also possible she hadn't, and she certainly didn't know anything about Moira and Rhys's decision to delay the babies conversation for a few more years. Moira touched her stomach absently. You had to watch Lorena; whatever she predicted came true.

"Actually, I came by to talk to you about David Aristarkhov. You two know each other, don't you?"

"Know each other? I practically raised that brat," Lorena said fondly. "What's he done now? He didn't hurt your feelings, did he? He's got a mouth on him."

"No, nothing like that. It's just that I think he's in trouble, and, well… He had a bad night last week. Now he won't let Rhys or I get close enough to help him."

Lorena arched an eyebrow. "I thought David and Rhys hated each other."

"It's complicated. But I'm worried about him, and I didn't know who else to turn to. Would you please look out for him? Maybe just call and let him know you're there if he needs somebody to talk to?"

Lorena pressed her lips together thoughtfully and nodded. Then, she craned her neck and yelled at whoever was in the back room of her shop, moving boxes around. "Mijo! Bring me my glasses."

"I told you, they're out there," an exasperated male voice responded.

The heavy curtain that separated the back room from the rest of the shop was thrown back, and David stalked through. He stopped dead when he saw Moira, something like fear flickering across his face. He was wearing a Scorpions T-shirt instead of a suit in the middle of a weekday, which meant that either he had come to his senses and taken an extended break from work, or his work had suggested that he do so.

Lorena flapped her hand at David. "Well, where are they? I don't see."

David stayed rooted to the spot for a heartbeat, then snatched up the pair of red glasses buried under a stack of receipts and handed them to Lorena.

"Same place as always," he muttered, unable to make eye contact with Moira.

"You've got a friend here who's very concerned about you," Lorena went on. "You're lucky to have her."

Moira was suddenly flush with embarrassment. She had gone out of her way to drive to the botanic for a man she barely knew.

"I didn't know you would be here," Moira said quickly. "I would never drop in on you like that, I was just..."

David finally met her gaze. Did his eyes soften just a bit, or was she just being hopeful?

"Worried about me," he finished.

Moira nodded helplessly. "What are you doing here?" she asked, hoping she sounded conversational and not like she was interrogating him.

"Doing chores to make up for never calling me," Lorena said. "He just showed up at my door, looking guilty as a dog. He said somebody very wise told him that he owed me an apology for all those years of silence. You've forgotten there are people who care about you, is that it, David? Why don't you run along with Moira and let me work. I've got a lot of orders to fill."

Lorena gave Moira a look that said *you're welcome*, then turned back to her herb bundling.

Moira looked awkwardly at David. "Can I buy you a coffee?" she asked.

The hanged man

CHAPTER TWENTY-FOUR

DAVID

David and Moira walked around the corner to the nearest Dunkin' and ordered an unsweetened coffee with cream and a mocha, respectively. Then they wandered over to the parked Lincoln, and Moira pushed herself up onto the sun-warmed hood of the car.

She leaned back on her palms on the metal, one leg stuck out, one knee bent. "Come over here and sit with me, indigo child," she said.

It wasn't an order, but defying her was impossible. She would just wait him out. Whatever she wanted to talk about, it was best to get it out of the way now.

David pushed himself up onto the hood. He hadn't sat on a car since he was sixteen, trying to impress the older boys who drove themselves to school.

"Is this a diplomatic meeting?" he asked, feeling wary. He still wasn't sure if Rhys had told her about the kiss. Probably. Rhys couldn't keep a secret from her to save his life. Maybe she had called him over closer so she could slap him. She would be well within her rights.

"Not necessarily," Moira said, lolling her head from side to side to catch the sun from every angle. Just like one of her flowers. "Although it is pretty rude to kiss somebody else's husband without asking first."

There it was. This had been coming for a week. Maybe she wanted him alone so she could scream at him without worrying about Rhys trying to pull them apart. That, too, would be fair.

"Have you got anything to say about it?" she asked in a measured voice.

David found, to his great dismay, that he didn't want her to be angry with him. Guilt over his actions was undeniable, as sour and persistent as the aftertaste of a hangover. But there was another twist of pain here, much sharper than the general shame that tailed him for weeks after he did something stupid under the influence. He was sickened by the thought of *who* he had betrayed. Not just Rhys. Moira.

He had grown attached to Moira quietly, without really noticing it and despite all of his best efforts to the contrary. Rhys felt the same way magic did: a dark rush of pure thrill straight into his veins. But Moira was like sunlight after a long, gray Boston winter: he didn't realize how much he craved her until she was gone.

"I fucked up tremendously," he said, shocked at his own earnestness. She made lies evaporate on his lips. "Just, catastrophically. I've been torn up about it ever since, and I know that doesn't excuse my actions, but... God, Moira, I cannot believe I did that to you. Please believe me when I say I'm not trying to come between the two of you. What you have is so special and you deserve each other, truly. I know you and I didn't start out on good terms, but I have the utmost respect for you. You're one of the finest women I've ever had the pleasure of knowing, and I don't..."

He grimaced, searching for the right words. He had no idea whether he was passing her test, or if she was simply biding her time before telling him never to speak to her again.

"Listen, I don't have very many friends," he pressed on. "I'm not good at making them or keeping them. But you make me want to try harder. Rhys and I... We've never been good at keeping our distance, or treating each other well, but I want to try harder at that, too. But I'm not going to go behind your back and I'm not going to do anything to disrespect you ever again, I swear."

Moira extended her hand daintily. David looked at it for a moment, baffled, and then he awkwardly took it in his own.

Moira looked at him over the rim of her sunglasses. "I wasn't mad at you, you know. I just wanted to hear you grovel. Well... okay, I was a little mad, but I mostly wanted the speech."

The tension left David's body like air from a burst balloon. "God," he groaned. "Don't do that to me ever again."

"No promises."

"Be honest. Did Rhys send you to check up on me?"

Moira shook her head. "Rhys doesn't know I'm here. He barely knows what day it is, he's been so busy. I came of my own accord."

"Oh," David said softly. It was easier to fathom Rhys making some kind of political move by sending in Moira than accepting that Moira was here because she wanted to be. He was used to people wanting things from him, not wanting to spend time with him.

Moira fixed him with a hard, perceptive look. "I need to ask you something, David Aristarkhov, and I need you to be honest with me too. You like me on my own merit? I thought maybe I made it up, after you disappeared on me."

David brought her hand up to his mouth and kissed her knuckles, like he was pressing his signet seal onto a legal document. The gesture was entirely thoughtless and uncalculated, which appalled him. But he loved the pulse of earnest hope under her skin, the way the emotion crept into his body through his lips until his stomach was fluttering with it.

"I like you a lot, and that scares the hell out of me. In a different way than I like Rhys, but you're smart enough to have figured that out by now. If we're being honest."

There it was, all out on the floor. A damning confession, if David had ever heard one. But there was no use dancing around the subject of his lingering feelings for Rhys when she had been bold enough to confront him about the kiss. And she deserved to know that he cared about her, against all reason and better judgement. Caring for people was a miserable, bloody business, and it hadn't gotten him very far in life, but it had a way of sneaking up on you.

"Oh, I've had you figured for a while," Moira said.

"Is this the part where you tell me to stay away from your husband? Because I have every intention of doing just that."

Moira shrugged, picking at the sticker on her coffee with her nail. "I told you at the gala, you can be as close as you want to be."

"Are you saying I could rekindle some kind of relationship with Rhys, if I wanted to? Even though you're married?"

"It's a modern age; people have all kinds of relationship structures. But I know things aren't that simple."

"No," David said bitterly. "They're not."

"Just promise me you're taking care of yourself. I don't want to wake up to a phone call saying you've collapsed in a gutter somewhere. I couldn't take it."

"I've got everything under control."

"Rhys and I made a promise to help you figure out what's making you sick. If he won't hold up his end of the bargain, I will."

"You're a good woman. Better than I deserve. But I don't want you getting any more tied up in this than you already are. People that get too involved with me usually end up regretting it."

Moira wrinkled her nose. "I'll get involved with whoever I like. And you forget that you got involved with me too, David. You're stuck with me now."

David couldn't help the smile that spread across his face. So, this was what real friendship was: an immovable object staring you down saying they weren't going anywhere, thank you very much.

"Alright. Stuck together it is."

Moira nodded in satisfaction and then settled closer to him on the hood, tucking her legs up under her and leaning her shoulder against his. David let her, not caring how it looked, and enjoyed the warm press of solidness against him. It reminded him of tight hugs from Lorena or the companionable sling of Leda's arm around his shoulders, the kind of familial closeness he hadn't enjoyed since he was a boy.

They stayed like this for some time, enjoying their coffee and watching the people bustle past. David let himself pretend, if only for a moment, that this was normal. He pretended that he wasn't sick, that he wasn't heir to a family legacy of demons and blood, and that Moira wasn't the wife of a man who probably hated his guts.

He found, to his quiet surprise, that he liked it very much.

The Chariot

CHAPTER TWENTY-FIVE

RHYS

Rhys resolved to put the night of the gala as far out of his mind as possible. He didn't have the mental space for it, not with the totality of the High Priest's duties dumped into his lap. Wayne preferred handshakes to contracts and overstuffed filing cabinets to electronic records, so coming in after him was a much bigger bureaucratic headache than Rhys expected. The drafty High Priest's office was his first undertaking, and he spent long hours sorting through old membership records and trying to parse the sticky notes Wayne had scribbled ideas for rituals on.

Strictly speaking, he wouldn't be High Priest until after his ascension ceremony, but Wayne stepped back right away, offering little in the way of guidance. This, Rhys knew, was part of the challenge of the position. There was no manual he could study to learn how to be a good High Priest; he just had to forge ahead and try to avoid pitfalls.

The transition of power ate up all his free time, with its many official and unofficial meetings. Moira was patient with him at first, gently nudging him towards meals and sleep when their paths crossed, but eventually she got angry.

"If you're gonna keep acting like you don't have a wife, I'm gonna stop acting like I am one," she threatened one day, shouldering her purse as she stormed past him in the hall. She grabbed the keys to the Lincoln, not telling him where she was headed. Not that he deserved to know.

"Love," he began weakly.

"Don't do that. Don't act sweet on me now that I'm mad. I can only take so much of this, Rhys. Eventually, you're going to have to make some hard choices. I'm not saying it's me or the Society, but I am saying that I refuse to go on like this indefinitely. Get your head on straight before you try to talk to me again, please. I'm going out with my friends. Don't know when I'll be back. Figure out dinner for yourself for once."

Then she was gone, the front door swinging shut behind her.

"Be safe," Rhys said miserably to the empty house.

Antoni was a Godsend. He always seemed to be available to help Rhys in whatever way he needed, no questions asked. He stuck around after hours to help sort paperwork in the High Priest's office, and even though Rhys knew Antoni had his own designs and aims, that he was positioning himself as indispensable in order to build social cache with the new High Priest, Rhys also recognized a genuine gesture of friendship when he saw it. In this way, Antoni was there when Rhys finally hit the wall of exhaustion and pressed his hands over his eyes.

"What do you need?" Antoni asked.

"Some goddamn loyalty," Rhys said, tossing the folders back on the desk.

Antoni crossed his arms and sighed. "You've got it, Rhys. From me, anyway."

"I know, I know. But the older guys think I can't tell my ass from my elbow, and the younger set think it's open season on however the hell they want to act. And Moira... Moira is pissed at me." He braced his hands on the desk and leaned forward, squeezing his eyes shut. He wanted to lie down for a long, long time and not wake up until somebody else had sorted everything out. "I need a foothold, I need stability, I need..."

Antoni stepped forward and leaned over the other side of the desk, lowering his voice to that firm, steadying place that had pulled Rhys out of the pit of despair so many times. "You need a second in command."

"I would, Antoni, but you're too young. The older set would eat you alive."

"You think I don't know that? I wasn't talking about me."

Rhys looked up at him, pinning him in place with his dark gaze. "No," he said, his voice rough-edged. "Don't even suggest it."

"You know I'm right. Who else can put everyone at ease in one go? Who else knows you well enough?"

"He's not trustworthy."

"You're biased. Give him a chance."

"Did he put you up to this?"

"Hell no. You think he wants second? If you want him to agree, you're going to have to convince him. But you know I'm right."

Rhys sighed heavily, letting his head drop forward until his chin touched his chest. He felt wound tight as a spring.

"Fine. I'll consider it."

"That's all I would ever ask you to do."

Rhys gave a cynical smile. "You're cut out for politics, I'll give you that. Go home, Antoni. Go see your siblings and enjoy the rest of your night with your parents. I need to think."

Rhys thought about it for the rest of the day. A day of cleaning up Wayne's messes and hearing out every Society brother who demanded an audience and missing Moira so badly it ached. She had stayed out all night after she walked out on him, and even though she had texted him twice to let him know she was okay, and which one of her friends she would be staying with, it still hurt like hell. They managed to patch things up a bit the morning after, but something still didn't feel right.

"Are you upset about the kiss?" Rhys said after they had hugged and apologized and chatted through less stressful things. Testing the waters, realigning their relationship.

"I was mad at you yesterday, not David," Moira said, glancing up from the laundry she was folding on the bed. She handed Rhys a fitted sheet, because she could never get them right, and he folded it crisply. "And I was mad because you couldn't pull your nose out of a book long enough to take notice of me."

"And for that, I'm very sorry. But that's not what I asked, love."

Moira sighed and tossed down a sock.

"I don't know how I feel about it. A little bit of me is relieved, a little bit of me is excited, a little bit of me is hurt, I suppose. It changes day to day. Mostly, I want you close. And I want David close. And I want us all to untangle this godforsaken knot together."

"I swear we will," he said, beating the wrinkles out of one of his folded shirts. All his laundry smelled like the jasmine detergent Moira loved. "But you can always talk to me about how you feel about things, you know that, don't you? I'm going to keep checking in with you from time to time, if that's alright."

"That's alright," she said, sounding so vulnerable.

She looked up at him with those soft eyes, and Rhys couldn't help himself. He leaned in and kissed her. She let him.

Rhys and Moira might be on the rocky road to recovery, but that didn't mean he was out of the woods yet. It was impossible for one man to haul the Society back on track through hard work and long hours alone, and he had been a fool to assume he could do it. Antoni had been right. He needed a second pair of hands helping him out, he needed more inter-Society clout, and most of all, he needed leverage.

He needed David.

Rhys stopped over at Saint Paul's for a few minutes before the Society meeting on Thursday, finding a quiet spot between the pews to kneel down and pray. The glass beads of his rosary passed easily through his fingers as he fretted, losing track of his decade again and again. He was more nervous than he should have been, all things considered. David was the one who had seriously overstepped boundaries at the gala, he was the one who had withdrawn afterward. Rhys held the position of power, and all the authority and respectability it conveyed.

So why did he feel like he was the one about to do something illicit?

He stepped out into the sun just as the church bells rang six overhead, and he called his wife. Moira had taken the evening off, so he wasn't bothering her at work, at least.

"Hey, baby," she said on the other end. She sounded slightly congested, but her voice was kind. "Everything alright? I thought you were in a Society meeting."

"I'm heading there now. I'm thinking of doing something a bit... unorthodox. I want to run it by you first."

"Shoot," Moira said. This was a familiar dance to them. There had been a time when Rhys hadn't made a single move in life, magic, or his career without consulting her first.

"I'm abdicating some of my responsibilities to a second in command. Asking for help."

"Thank the sweet Lord. Finally."

"There's more. I'm thinking of asking David."

There was a beat of silence on the other end of the phone as she thought. "You're sure you two can handle that? David probably won't take kindly to a silver medal."

"I think I can convince him. He's the natural choice, and it would take a lot of pressure off me. It would give me more time. For you. For us."

"I'll admit that doesn't sound bad... Do you think you can bring him to heel? Realistically?"

"I think I need to stop trying to control him and let him do his own thing. Within boundaries, sure, but I'm done micromanaging."

"Wonders never cease." Moira sneezed on the other end, once, then twice.

"Are you sick?" Rhys said, appalled. "Is that why you took today off work?"

"It's just a summer cold; I'll be fine. I didn't want you to worry."

"You let me worry about being worried. Make yourself some tea and get some rest, okay? I'm coming home early tonight. I'll bring you some of that Italian wedding soup you like and a sweet from the delicatessen. You want a cannolo? Two cannoli? Hell, I'll buy the bar."

Moira laughed on the other end, and the sound was a balm on Rhys's soul. How had he lost track of what was actually important in this life?

"If you're okay with it," Rhys said. "I'm going to go talk to him now. Then I'll head home to you, alright?"

"I'm okay with it. And, Rhys?"

"Yes?"

"Don't be late."

With that, the line disconnected.

He found David wrapped up in conversation with Cameron in a cloud of cigarette smoke in one of the corners of the meeting hall. David's green eyes cut over to him as he crossed the room, and as always, the effect was startling. You would think Rhys would have gotten used to being looked at by David, but some things never changed. Even now, Rhys couldn't help the stutter in his heart.

"Could I see you in my office, please?" Rhys asked.

David took a languid drag, taking his time with the inhale. His eyes raked across Rhys, searching him for a motive. "What about?"

Rhys shot a glance at Cameron, who was studying their conversation like he would an exegetical text. "It won't take long."

With that, he turned and started down the hallway towards his office, trusting David to follow.

David made him wait, which wasn't surprising. David was petty enough to wring every last power play he could out of his diminishing station within the Society. With Wayne gone, he was no one's favorite anymore. He was just another brother, and one who had recently called undue attention to himself at the gala. His relapse had become an open secret, one that was evident in the shifty ways the other brothers looked at him.

If there was anything David hated, it was being demoted.

By the time David arrived, Rhys was sitting behind Wayne's desk. *His* desk, he reminded himself. The Society and all its problems were his to handle now.

"David," he said with a sigh. "Come in. Sit down."

"I'm surprised you didn't send your messenger boy to summon me," David said, lowering himself onto the edge of the leather chair across from Rhys's desk. "Antoni's been running around doing all your dirty work lately. You got him on the payroll yet?"

"We're not here to talk about Antoni."

"You look like hell," David pronounced, leaning back in his chair. "Power not agreeing with you?"

"I thought you said power looked good on me," Rhys shot back, the temptation irresistible. Even after all this time, and with the mantle of High Priest heavy on his shoulders, he couldn't resist drawing David Aristarkhov into one of their sparring matches. It felt too good, too familiar.

"Can't hold a man accountable for what he says when he's been drinking," David said with a shrug. "Especially not me."

"How have you been?" Rhys asked, softening his voice. "Since?"

"Sober," David snapped, his eyes flashing. He looked like a petulant prince when he was angry, and the sight always made the bottom drop out of Rhys's stomach. After all these years, he was still weak for David. He should hate himself for that, but lingering affection for his oldest friend had crept in so slowly over the last couple of months that he had already made space in his heart for it. It felt impossible not to be affected by David now, not when he was sitting right in front of Rhys looking like *that*.

"That's not what I meant. Listen, I called you in here because I…" Rhys tried to broach the topic at hand and open negotiations but found he didn't have the heart to. He always thought it would feel good, sitting on this side of the desk with David on the other, but it didn't sit well with him now. "This doesn't feel right," he muttered, and then stood and circled around to the other side. He perched on the edge of the desk closest to David, lacing his fingers together in his lap. They were so close their knees were nearly touching. Up close, he could see the bruised shadows under David's eyes.

"You haven't been sleeping," Rhys noted. "More nightmares?"

David gave him one of his infuriatingly cordial lawyer's smiles. "That's not your concern anymore."

"What if it was?"

One of David's eyebrows raised a fraction of an inch. "What do you mean?"

Rhys plucked up a pencil from a golden tin on the desk and twirled it between his fingers, chewing the inside of his mouth. It seemed best to just lay all his cards out on the table, nerves be damned. He and David were way overdue for this conversation, a conversation in which Rhys was actually honest about how much he needed David, not just as an ally, but as a friend. But saying so in such certain terms felt terrifying, so Rhys couched it in the language of the Society.

"I'm drowning, David. The Society is fracturing under my fingers, and I've barely gotten started. I'm dealing with resistance and backbiting from all sides, and Wayne didn't exactly leave his house in order. I need help."

David narrowed his eyes. "What kind of help?"

Rhys met David's eyes. It was a hard thing to do, and all of a sudden, Rhys felt like he was drowning in green, choking on summer ivy and overgrown grass.

"In the past," he began carefully, "High Priests have appointed a second in command. It would be within my right and covered by precedent. I want it to be you, David."

David crossed his arms. "And what does a second in command do, exactly?"

"Whatever I need him to."

"You're trying to hire me to be your lapdog."

"No, I'm asking you to be my guard dog."

"Say I agreed," David said. "What do I get in return?"

Rhys spread his hands in front of him. "Free reign. You know this Society inside and out. Wayne kept you on a short leash, but I'm not interested in doing that. Form coalitions, dig up new rituals, make staff appointments, advise me, for God's sake. Just promise to back me and defer to my veto if we ever clash. Otherwise, I'll give you whatever you want."

"I want to scry," David said. "Wayne promised me that, and you know I'm the best there is. I don't care who's leading the ritual, I want to scry."

Rhys swallowed. If he granted David this request, that meant they would eventually end up in the summoning circle, back-to-back as spirits swirled around them. Rhys hadn't been in that position with David, hadn't trusted him like that, since their fight in conclave.

"Granted. Just promise me you'll occasionally let someone else into the circle to practice, otherwise no one will advance in their studies."

"Done."

"And if I don't think you're well enough to scry, I have the right to tap someone else in."

"Oh, come on–"

"I'm serious, David. I'm not risking you for the sake of a summoning. End of story."

David glowered for a moment, but Rhys held fast. Eventually, the psychic relented. "Fine. But I want free reign of the inner sanctum. I want to be able to come in after hours and practice or hold breakout circles with members that I choose."

"Done. I'll have another set of keys made."

David blinked, as if he hadn't been expecting the concession.

"Is that all?" Rhys prompted.

David's eyes narrowed. "It's just... I thought you didn't want anything to do with me."

Rhys sighed. Suddenly, he was very, very tired. Tired of arguing with David, tired of standing on opposite sides of a battlefield littered with a thousand unkind words. He was getting too old for it, and it had gotten him nowhere. It was time to lay down arms once and for all. If David wasn't interested in a ceasefire, fine. But Rhys was done fighting.

"I was way too harsh on you the night of the gala. I want plenty to do with you, David. But you're going to have to work with me in order for that to happen."

David watched him with guarded eyes, tilting his head this way and that as though trying to find a fracture in Rhys's earnestness. Rhys didn't blame him. Earnest wasn't exactly Rhys's style, but he was desperate.

And he refused to serve an entire term as High Priest with David sulking around looking wounded, agitating dissenters against him. The clearest way through the thicket of problems that had sprung up around him was to cooperate with David.

"I thought we were supposed to keep our distance."

"Fuck distance," Rhys said, with a conviction that surprised him. His heart was hammering in his chest. This should be strictly political, he should keep his wits about him, but his mouth was forming words without clearing them with his brain. He was too invested in David to keep things professional, and he should have never locked himself alone in a room with the other man. He wasn't strong enough to say no to him. Not after years of holding him at arm's length. "I'm tired of doing this dance. I'm being real with you right now, so be real with me."

David leaned forward in his seat, his eyes searing into Rhys's. All of a sudden, Rhys's blood was singing in his veins.

"Alright, McGowan. Show me real."

Something that had been pulled tight in Rhys's chest for years snapped. He grasped David by the chin, savoring the shock in the other man's eyes. David stiffened, but he didn't pull away. He just stared at Rhys like he had committed some blasphemy, pupils blown wide.

In one intoxicating rush, Rhys remembered what this was like, to have the richest, most powerful, most arrogant man he knew entirely at his mercy. He heard Moira's voice in the back of his head: *you can have whatever and whoever you want in this life, Rhys. Just don't ever lie to me.*

Rhys pulled David closer and kissed him firmly.

At first, David was rigid with shock. But then Rhys trailed his fingers down to David's throat, holding him in place, and the psychic made a small, helpless noise. David always blossomed under a commanding touch.

David's lips parted and he surged against Rhys. In an instant, Rhys was pushed back onto the desk, David's hands braced securely on either side of him. Outside, figures milled past the frosted glass door. Someone could walk in on them at any moment – Antoni, probably, with more papers to sign. But Rhys didn't care. This office was a private world of his own making, one in which he was king. In this world, he got what he wanted, and what he wanted was David.

Rhys bunched his fist into David's shirtfront, pulling him in tight. He couldn't get close enough, couldn't kiss David with enough fervor to get his point across.

This is all we've ever deserved, Rhys was trying to say.

David dropped to his knees with a fluidity that took Rhys's breath away, fingers deftly unfastening Rhys's belt. He was so goddamn beautiful like this, his mouth swollen with kisses, brows knit together in concentration. It was almost impossible to deny him. Just looking at him was agonizing.

Rhys threaded his fingers through David's hair, almost pulling, but not quite. That was an indulgence for another place, another time, when they were able to enjoy each other properly.

"David," Rhys said. "David, David."

He meant for it to be an order, but it came out sounding like a plea. David looked up, green eyes lit from within, and smoothed his hands up Rhys's thighs.

"Not here," Rhys said, voice strained. "Not like this."

Something flashed behind David's eyes – annoyance, or desperation – but then it was gone. He gathered himself together and pulled himself to his feet with that same infuriating elegance, adjusting his cuffs into perfect place. When he looked at Rhys, the fire in his eyes had dimmed.

"What do you want from me in return?" David asked.

"What?" Rhys asked, a little delirious. His head was spinning. He hadn't had a hit of David in years, not really, not on his own terms, and now he was high as a kite on it.

"What do you want from me? In return for my support. Gloves-off realpolitik. That's what this is, isn't it?"

"David," Rhys said on a sigh, fighting the urge to pull him close once again. He had miscalculated. This wasn't strictly political and never had been. He was a fool to think otherwise. "That isn't what that was about–"

"As for what you really want..." David said, brassy voice smooth and unbothered. He was still standing very close to Rhys, close enough to share breath. Rhys pressed his lips together into a thin line, shifting on the edge of the desk. If someone walked in, it might look like they were conspiring or caught in some other similarly compromising position. But he had no desire to move away.

"Sway the older set to my side," Rhys said carefully. His heart was still beating rapidly in his chest. "At least convince them to give me a chance. I just need you to buy me time with them. I'll handle the rest."

"Done," David said.

God, Rhys didn't know if he wanted David more on his knees or like this, cool and commanding. Rhys swallowed dryly. The drafty room suddenly felt close and hot, and he wasn't sure what to do with his hands. He laced his fingers together. "Do we have an accord?"

David stuck out his hand. Rhys took it in a strong, warm grip, and was taken aback when David switched up his grip to slot their fingers together. He pulled Rhys closer, squeezing hard as he gave him a threatening look. "If you screw me, Rhys, I'll end you."

"The sentiment is entirely mutual."

David gave him a sweet smile, then unlocked their fingers and shook Rhys's hand. "Good."

"David," Rhys began, wanting to explain himself, to apologize, *something*. He never got the chance. David leaned in and nipped Rhys's lower lip between his teeth, just enough to sting deliciously. Rhys gasped, hands drifting up to grip David by the biceps, but David had already stepped away.

"I'll hold you to that," David said. Then he wiped his mouth with the back of his hand and disappeared out the door.

Rhys was left flushed and lightheaded, wondering what he had agreed to.

The High priestess

CHAPTER TWENTY-SIX

MOIRA

Moira was holed up in bed with a smutty romance novel and a cup of jasmine tea when Rhys shouldered his way into the bedroom. He was balancing a large paper bag from her favorite deli in his arms.

"Moira," Rhys said. He said her name like an incantation, like it was the only thing standing between him and total desolation.

"You really did leave the Society early," she said, glancing at the clock on the bedside table. "Won't you miss the meeting?"

"I don't care. I needed to be with you," he said.

Moira smiled, warmth spreading through her chest. No matter how far he wandered from her in pursuit of his lofty ambitions, he always knew where home was.

Rhys sank down onto the edge of the bed. He fastidiously unpacked a veritable bucket of Italian wedding soup, two cannoli, and a sugar-dusted lemon square. Moira propped herself up a little more in bed, grinning at the feast.

"What are you reading?" he asked. "Monster romance or more historical?"

"Regency werewolf romance. Best of both worlds."

"And how long have you been sick?" he asked. "No fibbing."

"Just since this morning," she answered truthfully. "It's only a cold, Rhys, really it's nothing."

"Hush and let me baby you," he said, opening the lid to her soup and handing her a plastic spoon. She ate gratefully, the healing soup warming her from the inside out.

"How did the conversation with David go?" she asked.

"He accepted," Rhys said, swallowing hard in a way that told her there was more to the story.

"And?"

"And I kissed him."

Moira's eyebrows crept up towards her hairline. "You two keep doing that."

Rhys looked over to her, agony in his dark eyes. "Are you angry with me?"

Moira snorted, taking another sip of her soup. "Rhys, I told you that you can have whoever you want, so long as you don't lie to me."

"Yes, but that was just a hypothetical. This is real. Our relationship comes first, no matter what other… forces are at play. I want to make sure you're alright."

"You can start by telling me how it happened."

"It was in my office at the Society. I asked him to be my second, and he agreed, and it just… happened. Well, I made it happen."

"You're David's superior now," Moira pointed out, poking at a floating meatball. "That's dancing pretty close to a violation of professional ethics."

"I know."

"That just made it hotter, didn't it?"

"Moira," Rhys said darkly. "Please, take this seriously."

"Oh, I'm being dead serious," Moira said. "If you can't talk about something as simple as sex with me, how as we supposed to talk about something as complicated as polyamory?"

Rhys wrinkled his nose. "I'm not a big fan of that word."

"Too bad. It's a perfectly good word, and I'm gonna use it. Here, I got you something." She reached over to the nightstand and retrieved a hardcover book, adorned with a sticky note that simply said "Read me. In full."

"*Polysecure: Attachment, Trauma and Consensual Nonmonogamy*," he read aloud.

"I read it; it's good. If I'm willing to do my research, you should be too. And I want your ass in therapy yesterday to work on all that Catholic guilt. Those are my terms."

"Terms for what?"

"For you to explore... whatever this is with David. Do you want that?"

"I don't..." Rhys huffed. "I don't know."

"Well," Moira said, sipping her soup thoughtfully. "The way I see it, you ought to figure that out, sooner than later. I'm not gonna be your emotional go-between, either."

"Moira, I would never ask you–"

"I'm just setting down my boundaries, alright? I think it's important that we all do so before this gets any further."

Rhys just scowled. Moira was certain that many of the Society brothers would come to dread that stormy scowl, but she wasn't fazed by it.

"I want... I want too much, Moira. More than I have any right to ask for."

Moira gently grasped her husband's chin in her hand and looked him in the eye. Stubble scraped against her fingers, evidence that he hadn't been able to find the time to shave in a few days.

"You've always wanted the world, Rhys. That's one of the things I love about you. Wanting David is no different. But hear me when I say y'all need to sort this out sooner than later. David is my friend, and I don't want him getting hurt because you can't say where you stand."

Rhys latticed his fingers through his wife's. "Are you alright with this? Really?"

Moira took a deep breath, taking a moment to let her thoughts coalesce. "I'm alright with taking it day by day, together. And since we're coming clean, there's something I need to tell you, too."

"You've met somebody else," Rhys said, a joke undercut with very real anxiety. "I knew this day would come."

"I haven't, at least not in the traditional sense. But I might, someday, and I hope you'd be as open to letting me explore those feelings as I am open to letting you explore your feelings for David."

"That seems fair," he said somberly. "But seriously, what did you need to tell me?"

"David and I have a... physical connection," she confessed.

Rhys blinked at her. "I don't understand."

"David is an intuitive, just like me. We have different specialties, but the skills are the same. So, when I touch him..."

Moira squeezed Rhys's hand, hoping it got her point across. Rhys still looked baffled.

"I can feel his emotions," Moira went on. "I know when he's agitated or excited or upset. And he can feel me right back. It's like having a conversation without words."

"You never told me that before," Rhys said. It wasn't an accusation, but there was a strange sort of hurt in his eyes.

"I wasn't trying to keep anything from you. It was just never the right time."

"No, I'm not cross, it's just... I guess you two really are connected." Now he sounded surly, like a teenager getting left behind to watch the house while his parents went out to dinner together.

Moira made a tsking sound with her tongue. "Do I detect a note of jealousy?"

"Yes, fine," Rhys said through gritted teeth. "I hate how easy it is between the two of you. I wish it was that easy between David and I. Between you and me."

Moira raked her fingers through Rhys's curls, remembering how she used to trim his hair over the bathroom sink when they were college kids with no money between them.

"It only looks easy because we work at it, Rhys. So that's what I'm gonna tell you. Work for what you want."

Rhys looked at her with those impossibly dark eyes, filled with so much longing and ambition that she was suddenly terrified that all the want inside him was going to swallow him whole. But then he blinked, and he was himself again.

"Alright. I'll put in the work. But if you at any time feel uncomfortable or neglected, you tell me."

"I will. I need you here, Rhys, with me. Not all the time, but plenty of the time. I know what the High Priesthood means to you, but you haven't been there for me when I needed you since you stepped into the role. That can't keep on. Do you understand?"

"I do. I won't jeopardize what we have, Moira. Not again."

"You'd better not," she said with a queenly smile. Something about that smile must have lit a fire in him, because he leaned over her and said, "Let me kiss you. I want to make you feel better."

Moira pressed her fingers against his lips. "I don't want to get you sick."

"Then I'll just have to kiss you everywhere else," he said, pressing his lips to the delicate shells of her ear. "Put that soup down. You can finish it after I've finished with you."

Moira giggled, but she did as she was told. She let Rhys lay her back against the pillows, twice as gentle as usual since she wasn't feeling well, and she let him tug the sheets down over her stomach and off her calves. She let him push her dress up around her waist, pull her cotton underwear to the side, and press a lingering kiss to the hot bud between her legs. She tangled her fingers in his hair and let him devour her, savoring every swipe of his tongue, every desperate grip of his fingers in her thighs.

And then, after blissful minutes upon minutes, she let him make her come with a gasp and a laugh.

The hanged man

CHAPTER TWENTY–SEVEN

DAVID

David tapped his fingers in a battle rhythm against the underside of the desk as the defense attorney droned on. He had been sitting in court for four hours already, and the ancient air conditioning units weren't cutting it against the unseasonably warm day. He wanted an ice-cold Perrier and a cigarette, maybe two.

"Could you stop that, please?" Whitney, his co-counsel whispered to him as she inclined her head towards him. It was an elegant gesture, almost entirely hidden from the jury by the fall of her box braids.

David withdrew his fingers and curled his hand into a fist in his lap, heaving his own similarly subtle sigh. The defense attorney was laying it on thick, even doing a show of getting choked up at the thought of the terrible distress his client had endured being accused of robbing an audiovisual store. David found it a little melodramatic for a breaking and entering case… Still, he was bound and determined to send someone to jail today, and he couldn't do that until the other team shut up and let him work. He needed a win, especially after the disorienting kiss with Rhys and the pathetic way he had gotten to his knees in an instant, ready to do anything to earn Rhys's approval and keep his attention. He was a grown man, for God's sake; he should have more restraint than that.

David's scowl deepened as the memory of Rhys's vetiver aftershave rubbing off on his skin invaded his memory. It made him hot and irritated, ready to set something on fire or slam Rhys McGowan against a wall and prove once and for all who set the pace of this relationship.

Whitney leaned in a little closer, her chic Chanel and linen scent invading his space. He had worked with her before, and she was generally an asset: whip smart, nerves like steel, didn't overstep boundaries. Now, however, she was giving him a look that reminded him of Lorena, or Rhys, or anyone else who thought they knew him well enough to meddle.

She scribbled down a message on the legal pad between them, surreptitiously enough that the judge wouldn't notice.

You seem really on edge today.

"I'm fine," David muttered, resisting the urge to roll his eyes as the defense read out a letter penned by his client's estranged daughter.

Whitney scribbled down another note.

You haven't been able to sit still all day. I can hear you grinding your teeth. Do you need to call a recess?

The judge gave David a warning glance. He smiled back politely, then snatched up a pen and wrote his own message under Whitney's tidy handwriting.

We'll be to closing statements soon. I'd rather just get it over with.

The minutes crawled by on bruised hands and knees.

David suddenly felt parched, the inside of his mouth burning hot and dry as the Sahara. He swallowed thickly, willing himself to focus. Maybe he was reacting to the new protein powder he had been mixing into his breakfast shakes.

He finished his seltzer, then leaned over to Whitney's side of the table and nodded at her untouched glass of water. In an emergency, he would settle for still. Whitney looked a little baffled, but she nodded her permission.

David snatched up the glass and finished off the water in one breathless go, Adam's apple bobbing. It banished the sandpapery feeling in his mouth, but it was hard to say if it helped the claustrophobic heat pressing in around.

He pressed the back of his hand to his mouth, waiting for the world to stop tilting on its side. A couple members of the jury were looking at him now. He could feel the eyes burning through his blazer, boring holes into his skin.

Whitney gave him a look that was halfway appalled, halfway concerned. She took up her pencil and left him another note, underlining it this time.

You look like you're about to pass out.

David wrapped his fingers around the edge of the table, willing the world to stop spinning.

I'm not asking, I'm telling, Whitney wrote. *Request a recess.*

David shook his head. They were moments from closing statements. He could do this.

I started this case and I'm finishing it, he wrote back, then ripped the page from the pad as quietly as he could and balled it up in his hands.

If she pushed him one more inch, he would tear into her, and there would be no thought to it, just animal instinct. He was exhausted, and the day was only going to get longer. Being sweet to his co-counsel was not high up on his to-do list.

"Listen, prick," Whitney began, deathly soft, but then the judge's attention was on them both. David pushed himself up into a jelly-kneed but erect position. The defense attorney had wrapped up his spiel and was taking his seat with pleading cow eyes.

"Mr Aristarkhov, is the prosecution prepared to proceed with their closing argument?" the judge asked.

Whitney gave him a look that told him in no uncertain terms that if he went through with this, they would not be working together again.

David took the loss.

"Yes, your honor," he said, buttoning his blazer. It didn't do anything to make him feel less smothered, but it made him feel more put together. Whitney leaned back in her chair, eyes burning, and pressed the statement notes across the table to him with chill crispness.

David paced out into the center of the court, relaxing into his well-worn stage, and glanced down at the paper in his hand. He had been over it a thousand times already, memorizing the rhetorical contours of his parting shot, but the crowded typeset on the page was suddenly illegible. He didn't know if his vision was blurring or if he had spilt water on the page and smudged the ink. Either way, he could barely make out the subheadings.

"Mr Aristarkhov?" the judge prompted. "Are you ready to proceed?"

David threw her a smile. A little too slick and desperate for the circumstances, a little more nightclub bathroom than courthouse. His kneecaps were floating freely, sending a sick feeling right to his stomach. He very much wanted to sit back down, but that was impossible. There would be no losing face. Not now, with everyone watching.

David folded the statement in half and swallowed hard. He could wing it. It wasn't ideal, and it hadn't made him any friends in law school, but it was a skill he could bust out when necessary.

"Theft," he began, reminding himself to project to the back of the house. "Is not a victimless crime."

That wasn't exactly the strongest hook, since he was pretty sure no one was going to fight him on that.

Come on, Aristarkhov, he urged silently. *Think. Adapt.*

"In addition to the financial, material, and emotional damage done to the victim, theft destroys trust between neighbors, weakens community ties, and undermines entire local economies."

Too broad; he was swinging too broad. He needed to bring their focus back to *this* crime, *this* wronged woman.

"Ms Gonzalez is a single mother," he pivoted wildly. "She works two jobs to support her seven year-old daughter and ten year-old son. This shop is the cornerstone of her livelihood, and—"

A lightning bolt of pain shot through his skull, through one eye and up into his cranium. It was searing enough to snatch the breath from his lungs, and he doubled over at the waist, one hand clamped over his eye.

He dimly registered a worried gasp from the jury, the screech of Whitney pushing her chair back in a hurry. The judge was saying something, but the sounds garbled together in his ears until even his own name was unintelligible.

SON OF ANATOLY

The voice rumbled through his head, foreign and oppressive and undeniable.

"Fuck," David said through gritted teeth. "No."

The one journalist in the room clamored forward, shouting questions and wondering aloud if anyone should call an ambulance. And the jury, mortifyingly, was staring at him. Gaping and whispering and looking around with panic in their eyes.

Not here. Not now.

David turned to the judge to plea his way off the floor by any means necessary. Her face swam through the shocked tears that had jumped into his eyes.

"Your honor, I—"

The pain came again, in a sickening one-two punch that sent him gripping a nearby wooden banister for stability. His vision went black and violet at the edges, just like it had done that terrifying day in the study; only this time instead of darkness, he saw a flash of white.

White so high and broad he couldn't see the end of it, until his mind's eye focused on a sliver of horizon in the distance. Snow. He was having a vision of snow blanketing barren, rolling hills. Someone in the fever dream spoke to him, out of sight but close to his ear, in a voice smooth and cool as the ice spheres served in whiskey.

Are you sure this is a sacrifice you're willing to make? I won't ask again.

David felt in his chest the emotions of the person whose dream he was invading, felt the strain it took to keep chattering teeth and pure terror out of the words.

Do I look like a man who's unsure of himself? It's a trifle compared to what you offer. Unless you're nothing more than a common liar.

The strange voice hummed in pleasure, and a wave of bone-deep cold washed over him as the biting edge of a knife was pressed into his palms. There was a sting, and then the steady drip of blackening blood onto snow.

On the contrary. I am the very best.

David reeled out of the vision with a gasp. The blaring fluorescent lights overhead illuminated a courtroom in a disarray: the judge standing to order around the bailiff while the jury moved around in their box like startled pigeons. Whitney was at his side, her strong grip an anchoring presence on his bicep.

"David, what happened? Do I need to call somebody?"

David opened his mouth to brush her off with a soothing explanation.

But for the first time in his life, no words came. He couldn't get so much as a syllable out, couldn't form a single pleasantry or half-truth, not even a white lie. He was left staring at her, exposed in the middle of the courtroom while the journalist eagerly dictated the details of his downfall. He could see the headline now: Hotshot Lawyer Chokes Under Pressure.

"I have to go," he finally managed.

The judge was calling for order, getting more demanding every time, but David couldn't face her. He had already lost the only thing that mattered out there on the floor in front of everyone: his composure. The damage to his credibility was already done and would be served up piping hot in the evening paper. He had to get out of there. Preserve whatever professional dignity he had left.

David snatched up his briefcase and coat, striding down the aisle towards the courtroom doors without making eye contact with anyone. His skin was on fire, either from sickness or humiliation or both. And for a moment, he didn't think he would be able to make it to the door without another episode.

David shoved his way into the men's bathroom, nearly knocking over another lawyer in the process, and locked himself in the stall. He sagged against the wall, gasping for breath. He was either going to make it through this conscious, or he was going to black out and come to an hour later on the floor of a municipal courthouse bathroom. If he was smart, this was the moment he would call someone who understood, who could come pick him up discreetly and take him to a quiet place to ride it out.

David fumbled for his phone and pulled up Moira's number.

It rang through to her voicemail.

David swore. Then, making up his mind, he dialed Rhys.

Under other circumstances, reaching out to Rhys like this would be humiliating. But after the horror show in the courtroom, a greater humiliation wasn't possible. He had handled the worst of his blackouts and stomach-emptying on street corners in college alone, without anyone there to hold his hand or worry about him. If he lived through that, he could live through this.

"Hey," he croaked when Rhys picked up on the other end. "Are you busy right now?"

The Chariot

CHAPTER TWENTY–EIGHT

RHYS

Rhys was in the library when he got the call, elbow deep into a manuscript about Icelandic runestones. His heart leapt into his throat when he saw the caller ID, then plummeted into his stomach when he heard the state that David was in. He punched out of work twenty minutes early, unthinkable on any other day, and threw his bag into the Lincoln, then drove fifteen over the limit the whole way to the courthouse, cursing every red light. David was waiting for him outside, leaning heavily on the banister of the courthouse stairs. Rhys threw the car into park in an illegal spot and swept out of the door.

"I'm fine, I'm fine," David said preemptively, waving Rhys away as he circled his hand around David's arm. Rhys ignored him, guiding him to the waiting car with a firm, steadying pressure.

"You're not. Get in."

"Just drop me off in front of the condo; I can handle it from there. I just can't drive like this. I can barely feel my hands."

"No way," Rhys said, depositing David in the passenger side of the car. "I'm taking you straight to Leda's."

"Rhys," David began, gearing up to argue. Rhys slid into the driver's seat and tensed his hands around the wheel, shooting David a stony look. It was the same look he used to forbid David from ordering a fourth round, or from working until dawn. It sent a jolt of power through him, to have

232

David in his car and under his care, even though he was worried and irritated besides.

"No, you asked for my help and you're getting it. I want you where I can see you and I want Leda to take a look at you. Call your sister, David. And don't sugarcoat things. This has gotten way out of hand."

Rhys didn't know much about Leda, but he did know that she was local, and she was one of the few people in the world David trusted. They had grown up together for a time, and she might be able to talk some sense into him.

David looked like he had half a mind to argue, but he was pale and wan.

"Fine," he said. "What about Moira?"

"What about her?"

"If we're doing this, I want her here."

"I'll call her. You focus on Leda."

His hands shook slightly as he retrieved his phone from his pocket and hit the only number he had on speed-dial.

"Hey, sis," he said when Leda picked up the phone. "It's been a minute."

Rhys drove into the crowded Allston neighborhood, pausing only to pick Moira up at a train stop along the way at six thirty. She made fretful sounds while David caught her up on collapsing in the courthouse, then gave him an earful for letting things get so far. *Good, let her scold him,* Rhys thought. He deserved all that and more for being too thickheaded to accept help when he needed it.

Rhys wrenched the car into a parallel parking spot near the address David rattled off, then opened the door for David, then Moira.

The building David had them stop in front of was not an apartment building or a penthouse, or even a private office. It was a nightclub, wrapping salaciously around the corner and painted matte black from head to toe. A bright red sign towered above their heads, silhouetted by the sun setting in the distance: The Black Swan. A conglomerate of concertgoers smoked and threw back beers on a narrow balcony that wrapped around the second level, their voices carrying easily through the muggy air. Inside, Rhys could hear the distant, steady thump of drums.

"David, I'm not dropping you off at a nightclub," Rhys said.

"Leda owns the club and lives upstairs," David said, looking very tired all of a sudden.

David walked right past the main entrance and buzzed a ringer on a tiny, narrow side door, so unmarked that Rhys almost didn't see it. A moment later, it was opened by a huge man in a tight black mesh shirt. Silver daggers dangled from his ears. The entire outfit would have been comedically overwrought if he didn't seem so committed to it.

"Aristarkhov here for Leda," David said, completely unphased. "Two guests."

Rhys wondered how on earth he knew how to deal with bodyguards, and if it was a byproduct of his carefully calculated unimpressed face or of a childhood spent living under the threat of assassination. It was always hard to tell with David.

The bouncer stepped aside and gestured for them to enter, then locked the door behind them with a resounding clang.

Inside the club, the music was louder, pulsating against the walls. They were in a narrow side stairwell, but Rhys could still hear the wail of electric guitar from the pre-show music being piped in over the loudspeakers.

"This way," the bouncer said.

They had to hike up the stairs one by one because the passage was so tight. Rhys nearly tripped a couple of times in the dim lighting. He was coming up behind David, trying to keep his eyes fixed on the glow-in-the-dark masking tape that outlined each step, when a woman's voice echoed out into the stairwell.

"Look what the cat dragged in!"

A jostle of limbs and a near-stumble later, Rhys was standing at the top of the landing with Moira pressed up against him. The bouncer stepped aside to reveal David, enveloped in the hug of an astonishingly tall woman dressed from head to toe in black. Rhys wasn't sure he knew anyone who even owned leather pants, but Leda looked as comfortable in them as most women looked in jeans.

"David," Leda said, squeezing her little brother to her chest. "You look like hell warmed over."

"I missed you too," David said sarcastically, and took a step back. Leda and David didn't look much alike, except for the strong jawline and hooded eyes that looked sly on David and soporific on Leda. This could have been due in part to the heavy makeup she wore: charcoal with a splash of glitter. Where David's complexion was golden, Leda's was olive, and her teased mane of curls was darker than her nightclub's paint job.

She waved away her bouncer with a sultry wink. "Thank you, Luis. I've got it from here."

He gave her a smile that softened his entire demeanor for one flickering moment. Then he disappeared down the stairs to return to his post.

David arched an eyebrow. "Dating the staff? Really?"

"Technically, I'm not his supervisor, so technically it isn't unethical."

"Technically. What happened to Eon?"

"Nothing." She turned her incandescent attention on Rhys and Moira. From this angle, Rhys could see that she had shaved one side of her head. "Are these your friends?"

"This is Rhys McGowan and–"

"Oh yes, the ex! How could I forget! You fucked David up real bad; I heard all about you after you left," she said with a laugh, and pulled Rhys into a hug. She had to bend down to do it, and he suspected that even out of her platform boots she was six feet tall. "God, I don't blame him. Look at those pretty eyes."

"Leda," David said, flatly. Rhys was too red in the face to respond at all, and Leda had already moved on.

She squeezed Moira like an old friend, then pulled away to take her in, still holding her hands lightly by the fingertips. "And you're Moira, right? I love your shoes! Are they vintage?"

Moira nodded, a little dumbstruck.

"Leda," David said again, sounding incredibly tired.

"Well, come inside. The place isn't exactly tidy, but you're welcome to it; make yourselves at home. David, sit down, you look like you're about to hit the floor."

Leda's apartment, a loft with a sloping roof, was comfortable, by Boston standards. Black leather couches beckoned from atop mandala rugs, and there were three gleaming electric guitars lined up along the back wall. The thick-paned industrial glass windows were draped with sheer crimson fabric, and most pieces of furniture had been painted the same matte black as the outside of the building. It had a sort of relaxed grungy glamour that reminded Rhys of his teenage affinity for *The Crow*.

A tapestry was draped across the arched doorway into a bedroom, spray painted with a white circle from which eight arrows emanated. Rhys froze in the doorway. David nearly crashed into him, and Rhys stepped grudgingly inside. He shoved his hands down deep in his pockets and stared at the painted symbol.

Chaos magician, he thought. He had never met a chaos magician, but he had read about them, and his hardline sensibilities balked at all the nihilism and hedonism in their philosophy.

"Who wants a drink?" Leda sang from the kitchen. There was the banging of cabinets and tinkling of glasses. "David, vodka soda?"

"No, thanks," David replied, dumping himself on the couch.

"Gin, then? I've got New Amsterdam or Tanqueray if you want to be bougie."

"No, thanks," David said again, a little more firmly.

Leda poked her head out from the kitchen. "Oh, right, sorry! Sobriety! I'll pour you an ice water. Moira?"

"I'll take a beer if you have one," Moira said.

"I've got four kinds, come here and pick. Rhys?"

"David didn't say you were an occultist," Rhys said.

Leda slouched against the doorjamb and screwed the lid off a microbrewery lager. "Isn't everyone in this family? I don't have David's psychic eyes, but I do pretty well for myself."

"That's putting it mildly," David muttered. He looked more comfortable here than in the Beacon Hill house, but only marginally so.

Leda eyed Rhys up and down, and somehow managed to make the gesture look lascivious. "I hear you're the big sorcerer on the block now. Ceremonialist, right?"

"I like form and tradition. And to do things right."

"Well, I like to get results."

"Don't start, Leda," David groaned.

"I'm just making polite conversation," Leda said. "I'd like to hear how you guys do things up in that old boys' club. What's a secret society even like? Do you ever get anything done through all that red tape? Or is it really all just orgiastic bacchanals?"

"Nobody's having any bacchanals," Rhys said tightly.

"Your loss," Leda said with a wink. "They're eye-opening."

She retrieved a glass of ice water from the kitchen and handed it to her brother, then felt his forehead with the back of her hand.

"You're running hot. Have you had a fever?"

"I'm just overexerted," David said, waving her away. "I've been working too much."

Moira's eyes flashed in irritation. "Seriously, David? You collapse in court and have some kind of godawful vision, and that's all you can say?

You're impossible; this is why you're so sick. You won't accept any damn help."

Rhys rubbed a soothing hand between Moira's shoulder blades.

"Tell her what's been happening," Rhys said to David. "All of it."

David told her. He started at the beginning and spared no detail, relating the blackouts, the nightmares, the long hours spent in the Beacon Hill house trying to get to the bottom of things. He was just getting to the part about the family curse when a wave of something, either pain or nausea, made him drop his face into his hands.

"I don't feel so hot," he muttered.

"You can say that again," Leda said. "You're practically turning green. Lay down, will you?"

David didn't have to be told twice. He stretched out on the couch, pillowed his arms under his head, and was unconscious in a matter of minutes. Apparently, it had been too long since he slept.

"Poor idiot," Moira said with a mixture of pity and irritation. "I can't believe he let it get this bad."

"I should have brought him to you a long time ago," Rhys said to Leda.

Leda gave a stretch, and her tank top hiked up enough to show a belly button piercing. "Oh, I doubt he would have let you. I only ever hear that he's been in trouble after the fact. It drives me up the wall. But I'm glad you brought him."

Rhys shifted from foot to foot. It was probably fine to leave David here and get back to his own life, though he found that he was hesitant to do so. He didn't exactly feel comfortable in Leda's den, especially not with all the chaos magic paraphernalia lying around, but he didn't want to be rude by running off, either.

Moira, as though making the decision for him, settled into the chair nearest David. She apparently intended to stand watch, at least for a little while.

"Did you and David grow up together?" she asked, making polite conversation as always.

"Oh no," Leda said, gesturing to herself expansively. "I'm just the humble bastard child of a previous tryst. No claim to the famous Aristarkhov name. Evgeni met my mother when he was in Turkey on business. Split shortly after I was born."

"Another glowing endorsement for the man's character," Moira muttered. She reached out to smooth a stray curl away from David's eyes, and Leda followed the touch with an intrigued quirk of her brow. It was an intimate gesture, and it probably didn't fit with Leda's understanding of her brother.

Leda sat down on the other end of the couch and gestured for Rhys to take a seat in the free armchair. Then she settled in, lit herself a cigarette, and started telling her story in a low, lulling voice. "We didn't grow up together, but we did live together for a couple years. I was sixteen, David was nine. Mom figured it was time for her to go off on some Tuscan summer adventure to find herself, and for me to meet my father. So, I got shipped off to two years of Orthodox school in Saint Petersburg. I didn't even know I had a brother until I got there. Evgeni never thought it was important to mention he got married."

"That must have been a shock," Moira said.

"It was hardly the weirdest thing about that house. I had only ever lived in an apartment in Istanbul, and the next thing I know I'm getting dropped off in the snow outside this huge pre-Soviet mansion out in the middle of the woods. Butlers, statuary, a carriage house, whole nine yards. And there's this tiny Russian child waiting for me at the door to tell me that I am not allowed to play with his toys, and that he's a very powerful magician, so I had better watch my step."

Rhys gave a soft snort. David had always had the same winning temperament, apparently. He had to admit, Leda was a good storyteller. And it was obvious from the way she hovered near David, eyes flicking over every so often, that she loved her brother to death. Rhys could respect that, at least.

"Mom said Evgeni was a rich eccentric with quirky hobbies. She didn't mention they included casting spells to insulate his international accounts from stock market crashes. The things that went down in that house were *wild*. But I figured out pretty quickly why she shipped me off: for Evgeni to whip me into shape." Leda smoked ponderously, tipping her head back and blowing a couple of smoke rings. She was savoring their attention, drawing out her story to build tension. This was where Rhys saw the most resemblance between David and his sister: their irresistible impulse to perform.

Rhys was suddenly reminded of something David had said about Leda, one of the few details he had let slip about his sister. *She's a powerhouse*, he had said, with a sort of reverence in his voice that Rhys didn't think David was capable of. At the time, he thought he had been referring to Leda's musical aptitude, but now he realized, David had always been talking about magic.

Rhys had looked at Leda and only seen the chaos star and the smudged makeup and assumed she was a novice, more attracted to the aesthetics of magic than the practice of it. But when he set aside his prejudice and looked again, he saw the fire of pure, unadulterated power in Leda's eyes. It was so bright it almost hurt to look at.

"Unfortunately," Leda said, sucking her cigarette down to ash, "Evgeni's lessons didn't really stick. I preferred to walk my own path, and I got reprimanded for mixing and matching magic traditions and making up shit on the fly. And I snuck out a lot to go to rock shows and shoplift, so we never had that cozy daddy-daughter relationship. But David was a much better student. The prodigy. His *heir*." She finished her cigarette and stabbed it into an ashtray with a bitter twist to her mouth. "It didn't spare him any of Evgeni's brutality, though, poor bastard."

Moira opened her mouth, probably to supply some gentle change of subject, but then Leda's front door opened a few inches. Her bouncer stuck his head in, looking much less intimidating now that they had all been vetted.

"Sorry to interrupt," Luis said.

"No worries," Leda said, pushing up to her feet. "Is everything alright downstairs?"

He glanced at his watch and glowered. "Band's late. People are starting to get rowdy."

"What about the opener?"

"Never showed. We've already broken up a couple of fights down there. Kids are trying to climb on the stage and shit. Are we good to send Eon and the rest of the band out there?"

Leda beamed at him with a love so pure and saccharine, Rhys almost wanted to look away. "Sure, pet. Tag them in. And bring them back up with you afterwards."

Leda tossed her hair and wiggled her shoulders as Luis disappeared into the hallway.

"Isn't he so dreamy?" she mused to the room. "Retired MMA fighter. Such a softie. He cooks me Brazilian food all the time and he's phenomenal in bed."

Rhys was so embarrassed he wanted to crawl out a window. But he managed to keep a stiff upper lip and ask a polite question. "He's your boyfriend?"

Leda gave a devilish grin, and Rhys caught the unmistakable whiff of some bedroom dynamic that probably came with a contract and a collar. "Something like that. If you stick around long enough, you'll meet Eon, too."

Rhys flicked a glance to his wife. This was probably the most polite time for them to take their leave, but just as Rhys was opening his mouth to excuse himself, David stirred.

"Ouch," David muttered, and coughed miserably.

Rhys was on his feet before he realized it, moving towards David with single minded concern. Leda watched him with keen, hawkish eyes as he lingered near David, wanting to touch him but not sure how to go about it, or whether the gesture would be welcome.

"How do you feel?" Rhys asked.

"Like I got hit with a freight train," David responded, struggling to push himself up into a sitting position.

"You can stay the night if you want," Leda offered, patting her brother's knee. "I've got the Murphy bed in the next room. Just don't drive like this, for God's sake. Tonight, rest. Tomorrow, we'll figure something out to help you."

"Thank you for taking care of him," Rhys said. "Moira and I should probably…"

David grabbed Rhys's wrist before he could go anywhere.

"Stay," the psychic said, with a such simple, naked need in his voice that Rhys was taken aback. "Just for another hour or so. Please."

Rhys swallowed and nodded, savoring the steadying pressure of David's fingers around his wrist.

"Sure, David. Whatever you need."

"You're all welcome to stay for dinner," Leda said, sweeping to her feet. "Fair warning, it gets a little rowdy in here after dark. People like to come pay their respects after the show."

"I don't care," David said. "Just don't send me home where I might pass out and crack my head on the tile and not be found for days."

"Don't even say that," Moira said, giving a little shudder.

"I'll order something to eat," Leda offered, plucking up an honest-to-God landline phone off the wall. "Pizza work for everybody?"

The hanged man

CHAPTER TWENTY-NINE

DAVID

David slept through most of the show downstairs. But once it was over, people started trickling into the little apartment in a steady stream, and the night passed quickly in a heady rush.

Concertgoers floated in and out of Leda's apartment: admirers, coworkers, musicians, lovers. Eon, the ethereally beautiful guitarist Leda had been dating for the past year, curled up on the couch and plucked out a new tune on one of Leda's guitars. Once Luis's rounds were over, he arrived to corner Leda in the kitchen and kiss her soundly, then started talking to another club staffer about trading shifts. Neither of Leda's partners seemed to mind each other's presence at all. Luis even offered to walk Eon to their car when they got up to leave.

Leda presided over everyone, resplendent in her glitter makeup. Watching her accept kisses and offerings from her devotees, David remembered just how much he loved his sister. As a child, he'd truly believed there was nothing Leda couldn't do. And even when it had become apparent that she was not a beautiful witch riding in to save him from his father, that she was just another fucked-up magical kid like him, he'd still idolized her.

Unlike Moira, who was making new friends aplenty with a drink in one hand and a slice of cake in the other, Rhys was no social butterfly. But after a half hour of observing the proceedings from his stiff seat on the couch, he grabbed a drink and started to talk to people. Leda descended like a vulture and enticed him into some private conversation. David eventually caught a few animated snatches when he wandered into the kitchen for another sparkling water.

"How can you ensure results if you change the process every time?" Rhys was saying. He was cradling a beer bottle to his chest, probably his second, judging by the wide look in his eyes. Whatever Leda was telling him had him rapt, the twin furrows of academic interest deep between his brows. "You're introducing too many variables."

"I take meticulous notes!" Leda insisted. "I work towards results, not process. I don't know how you can say the same incantation over and over again, waiting for something to happen. I'd die of boredom."

"The spell isn't the whole working, it's just a controlled environment. But I don't expect you to get that; chaos magicians are magical anarchists. No gods, no masters, right?"

"No gods doesn't mean no discipline, or no faith in your own abilities," Leda countered, eyes twinkling merrily. She was having the time of her life, caught in one of the intellectual dances that had baffled all her tutors growing up. "Dogmatism is a magician's greatest enemy. I can throw together a spell through spit and a cigarette-smoke sigil and have a record contract knocking down my door any day I want to."

"The first demon I summoned got me an internship with zero experience and a walk-in interview," Rhys shot back. He knew the steps to this dance, the little one-two step of one upmanship. It was occultism's oldest pissing contest.

"Hey, that's not bad!" Leda crooned, nudging Rhys with her shoulder. "Does that demon have a sister I can talk to?"

"Not on your life," Rhys said with a laugh. There was a boyish quirk to his mouth that made something buried deep inside David's chest ache. When was the last time he had seen Rhys smile this much? Leda had that effect on people. Her presence was permission to act out, to unwind, to slough off any societal conventions that fit too snugly.

David sifted through the bottles and cans in the fridge while he eavesdropped. Rhys and his sister were wedged in a corner of the kitchen, only barely aware of his presence. It would be easy enough to palm a beer to nurse in a dark part of the house, or deftly slip a shot of white rum into his seltzer when everyone's back was turned. That knack for secrecy, for refilling his glass when no one was looking or when everyone else was too drunk to care, was a habit that was hard to break.

David swallowed down the urge and grabbed a sparkling water. He was only feeling tempted to drink because he was in a party environment. The energy was lighting up parts of his brain better left dormant, pressing against old self-soothing mechanisms that would never fully die, not really. He knew all this rationally; his therapist had told him as much.

David cracked open the tab on his drink and threw the water back hard, hoping it would burn. Wishing that it hurt like vodka, like bottoming out but at least feeling alive on the way down.

"Once you get past the mental blocks of right and wrong," Leda was saying, "that's where the real magic happens. Losing control every once in a while is good for you. The maenads knew that."

"But no one can be a maenad every day of their lives," Rhys said. "Eventually, you come back down from the high and then there's just blood and spilled wine to clean up. That's what happens when you let yourself go too far."

"True, that's where balance lives. I'd say that's where magic comes from, our ability to taste extremes and choose for ourselves what serves us best. Most people, when left to make their own choices without being shamed for it, choose a sustainable middle ground between ecstasy and asceticism." Leda spared a fond glance to Eon, who was in the living room flickering her a come-hither glance with eyes highlighted by white mascara. "Then again, I've always been a bit of a hedonist."

Rhys followed her gaze, dark eyes as bottomless as the far reaches of space. "How do you know?" he said suddenly. "That you love them both? At the same time, I mean."

Drunk. He was only uncalculated when he was drunk. A shadow passed over his face like he had just let some terrible secret slip.

Leda smirked at Rhys with a knowing that made David's stomach twist. "How do you know you love anyone?" she asked.

"There's no not loving them," he said, exorcising himself of the words. "It's like an invasive species; you could cut it down, but it'll just keep coming back."

"Sounds like you know already, then."

Rhys looked down at his glass and glowered. Disappointed in himself, then. "I'm sorry, that's a rude thing to ask."

"It's not the weirdest thing people have asked me about being polyamorous, no worries. People have questions, I get it. They usually have a couple more when they find out I'm also sleeping with my ex-therapist and her wife, and currently in talks with this dreamy rope top in Brooklyn who might tie me up, if I play my cards right."

Rhys immediately flushed scarlet and stammered something incoherent before Leda's ringing laughter cut him off.

"He was right when he called you a consummate Catholic! So cute."

"Excuse me," David muttered, brushing past them both. Leda tried to say his name, to entice him back into the kitchen and into good spirits, but he pretended like he didn't hear. He just found a quiet seat in the lively living room, doing his best not to look back at Rhys.

Leda sent everyone home after a few hours, though David got the impression that on any other night the party would have raged on well into the night. Moira gave David a kiss on the cheek before she left, and Rhys, perhaps emboldened by the beer or the late hour, followed suit before gathering up his coat and wallet. They went home to Jamaica Plain and left him to Leda's hospitality, and David couldn't help but notice that the apartment was a little dimmer without them in it.

The Murphy bed was a piss-poor substitute for his ergonomic Swedish mattress, but he made do. He managed to snag a few restless hours of shuteye, then hauled himself out of bed early for a scalding hot shower. He itched for his routine, for his morning protein shake and HIIT session, but the shower soothed the worst of his nerves.

When David emerged into the kitchen, Leda was standing at the stove in sweatpants and a slouchy men's tank top, briskly scrambling eggs. She smiled at him, her labret piercing winking. "Morning. You hungry?"

"I am, actually," David said, leaning against the counter. "Coffee?"

Leda pushed him a full mug. Unsweetened with a splash of cream.

"How did you sleep?"

"As well as I ever do in someone else's house."

"Like shit, then. You're looking pretty rough around the edges."

Tossing a hand towel over her shoulder, Leda began to portion out two plates of eggs. She looked him over, her piercing gaze cutting right through any lies he could muster. It reminded him of his father, if his father had ever looked at him like that out of love, not bottom-line appraisal.

"I think we need to pick up our conversation from last night about you not doing so hot. What's been going on?"

David sipped his coffee and stabbed at his eggs for a minute, working up the right words. Asking for help was not his strong suit. Asking from one of the only people he actually admired felt like adding insult to injury. "I can't channel, I can't sleep, I'm exhausted all the time... And I keep having these blackouts. I'll be fine, and then I'll start getting lightheaded and sick to my stomach and seeing things..."

"What kind of things?" Leda said, all the sparkle gone from her eyes. She was worried about him. That somehow made the conversation harder.

"I don't know. Memories, I think. Memories that aren't mine."

"And you think this has something to do with that old story Dad used to tell to scare his business partners?"

David's eyes skimmed hand-drawn sigils taped to potted plants and appliances, her tiny household altars of pennies and red thread and pinches of tobacco meant to draw and trap energies to be used to power spells later. If anyone could believe what he was afraid to even let himself consider, it was Leda.

"Deals have two sides to them. Everything comes with a price," he said.

"If that's the case, why didn't the deal take Dad? Or his dad or his dad?"

"Contracts have loopholes. Trust me, I'm a lawyer."

"Ass," Leda murmured, doctoring her coffee with powdered creamer and a shot of vanilla syrup.

"The contract was full of lots of esoteric bullshit," David said, following her into the living room and taking a seat on the ottoman. "Something about a demon named Baelshieth. Ring any bells?"

"None."

"Rhys found the name scattered through Evgeni's records."

"And you think this Baelshieth character is crawling around inside your head? That sucks, man."

"You don't seem worried about your own health at all," David countered, bristling.

Leda let out a triumphant cackle of laughter. "I'm no Aristarkhov son. Just because Dad's blood is in my veins doesn't make me a viable heir to any grandfathered demon contract. I never thought I would appreciate medieval sexism, but here we are. I'm assuming you all came here because you need my help? No offense, David, but you aren't really one for social calls."

"None taken," David said.

Leda tapped a short black fingernail against her lips, ruminating. "I wish I knew more about demons, but I just don't work with them. I can commend you to some wonderful Satanists, although most of them don't really believe in the Devil in the traditional sense. My tattoo artist does, though, and he knows his way around an unhallowed bargain."

"Rhys has got the research covered," David said. "I was hoping you might be able to give me advice on how to, I don't know, handle this? Is there any avenue we haven't explored yet? I can't keep getting sicker, Leda. I can't."

"Well, have you tried to talk to it? You don't really know what it wants, do you?"

"It wants to wreck my life," David muttered, and the venom in his words surprised him. He hadn't realized how much he hated the thing growing inside him until that moment.

"It sounds like you've only tried to repress this spirit, and that isn't working. Sometimes the best way to face darkness is to walk right into it."

"Yes, well, I'll keep that in mind," David said. His headache was starting to come back, building in his ears like the pounding of a distant war drum. The dizziness would follow, and if he was lucky, that was all that would follow. He passed a hand over his face and pinched the bridge of his nose.

"Just think it over," Leda said. "There's no need to rush. Kick back, my place is your place. Just let me know if you decide to summon any demons; put a sock on the door or something." She stood and gathered up their dishes, and hummed to herself while she wandered back into the kitchen.

David was left with nothing but silence, until Leda poked her head around the corner of the room and said, almost as an afterthought: "I guess we'll figure out how serious this thing is on your thirtieth, huh? Live through that and you're probably fine for life."

The muscles in David's stomach clenched. "What do you mean 'on my thirtieth'?"

"The timeline," Leda said, looking genuinely confused. "On the curse?"

"What timeline?" David demanded.

"Oh God, I thought you knew!" Leda exclaimed, black eyes going wide. "It's part of that old story. Maybe you just forgot. Or, you know what, maybe I heard about it when I went flipping through dad's journal looking for juicy blackmail."

He wanted to grab her by the shoulders and shake her, but he wasn't sure his legs were trustworthy at the moment. *What timeline?*

"The demon is supposed to come to collect when the Aristarkhov turns thirty. That's the terms and conditions of the soul-snatching. At least according to folklore."

David's mouth was dry as ash, and there was a tinny ringing in his ears. "My birthday is in a week," David said tightly.

"It's an old story," Leda sighed. "Details get exaggerated. Demon deals don't just kill people, and I've never heard of one being transferable anyway."

"One minute ago, you were on board with the idea."

"I can hold multiple potentialities up here without committing to any of them," Leda said, tapping her forehead. "Chaos magician, remember? We operate in multiple realities at once. In one reality, there's a demon out for your soul. In another reality, you're overworked from playing psychic since you were a kid and will probably be fine. No use committing to one until we know which one we're living in."

"Fine, fine," David muttered. In that moment, he wanted Leda to disappear. He wanted to be left alone with the darkness and his own despair, to mourn the thirties he might never get.

But that, he reminded himself quickly, would be unproductive. He had to focus. He had to force himself through.

"I should get going," he said, pulling himself to his feet and reaching for his coat. God, his head was killing him.

"David," Leda started, looking injured. David didn't let her get any further. If she tried to press him to stay, he would give in. It was too tempting to curl up in Leda's house and let his sister fuss over him while the world went on turning outside his door. He needed to get back to Rhys and Moira, he needed to get back to his day job, and he needed to keep working to unravel his curse. He didn't have any other choice.

"I'm fine, Leda. Really."

Leda pressed her lips together skeptically, but then she nodded. "I just hope you know what you're doing."

David gave his sister a brisk kiss on the cheek before gathering his keys and his wallet. They had never been big on sweet talk and physical affection, not even when they were children, and David was still getting to know the woman she had grown into, but she accepted the small gesture of familial love graciously.

"Me too."

CHAPTER THIRTY

DAVID

David tried to return to his life at the firm to the best of his ability the next day. His employer threatened to put him on extended leave, but David, through a mixture of slick talk and no small amount of charm, managed to wiggle out of the worst of the discipline and got away with a slap on the wrist. He put on his favorite suit, smiled with all his teeth at anyone who insinuated that he should take some time off, and threw himself into his work with an enthusiasm that bordered on feral. Psychic breakdown or no, he was not going to fall behind. He was not going to sacrifice all he had worked so hard to build. He made it two days before the spirit sickness caught up with him. He ended up falling asleep on his lunch break in his car dreaming of Rhys's steely eyes holding him steady in place, Moira's warm fingers curled around his own. He ached for both of them in different ways, and as his condition continued to worsen, there seemed to be no use in fighting it. He didn't have the energy for ego anymore, or for denying himself.

In the end, David only lasted until the end of the work week before picking up the phone. When he heard Rhys's "hello" on the other end, prim and crisp, relief washed over him.

"Rhys. Yes. Hi." God, he sounded desperate. David pulled it together. "I hope I'm not interrupting anything."

"Nothing important," Rhys said, with a shuffle of papers that said he was lying. "What do you need, David?"

It wasn't an irritated question. It was broad and open, inviting even. If David didn't know better, he would have said that Rhys was happy to hear from him. David was still getting used to that.

"I was hoping we could pick back up where we left off before my little... incident."

"It's been more than one incident, David," Rhys said, and oh *no*, he sounded concerned. David could handle a lot from Rhys: rivalry, arguments, sexual tension so thick you could cut it with a knife. But kindness was too much. That was too close to something real, something David knew he could never have, no matter what Moira was willing to allow. Real closeness between Rhys and David was a live wire capable of setting the world on fire, and it was only a matter of time before the sparks between them grew into a destructive, out-of-control blaze.

"I was thinking of going back to Lorena's," David said. "She's one of the smartest magical people in the city. If she can lift the curse, then our problem is solved."

And then we won't have any more recourse with one another, David thought. It was sobering. Even though he would give anything to be well again, the thought of losing all the ground he had gained with Rhys and going back to icy professionalism wasn't pleasant.

Rhys cleared his throat on the other end of the phone. Maybe, David mused dangerously, Rhys was thinking the same thing.

"Moira and I can meet you there. Just say when."

"Can you come tonight?" David asked, and there was that pathetic desperation again, worming its way into his voice. An Aristarkhov was never desperate, but David was now. If you had asked David how he thought he would face death before all this happened, he would have said that he would go down alone, with a sneer on his face and a haughty tilt to his chin. But it turned out that the prospect of dying was actually fucking terrifying, and it made David want to barricade himself away from the world with the people he cared about. That number had always been pitifully low, and Rhys McGowan had always been on the list, no matter how much David tried to cross out his name.

"Moira works until five. It wouldn't be fair to ask her to skip out on her job."

"I want to see her," David said. And why couldn't he just *stop talking*? He had barely been able to tolerate Moira not three months ago, and now he didn't feel like he could make it to the end of the week without a hug from her. The spirit sickness must be rotting his brain, lighting up adolescent needs for affection and approval that he had thought long ago smothered. Or maybe this was who he really was, under the bravado and the money and the glossy job: a scared child who couldn't do anything by himself. "I can wait until she's free."

"I'll bring her," Rhys said, in a warm, soothing voice that settled low into David's stomach. "We're going to figure this out, alright?"

David closed his eyes and pressed the phone tighter to his ear, savoring the sound of Rhys breathing on the other end. Rhys was his High Priest now, and he was probably only being gentle out of obligation, or pity. But David wanted to pretend, just for a moment, that Rhys's kindness meant something more. That whatever was left between them wasn't soured and unsalvageeable.

"David?" Rhys asked.

David's eyes flashed open. "That sounds good to me. Just text me when you're headed over and I'll meet you at the botanica."

"Take care of yourself until then, please."

And with that, Rhys hung up and left David feeling hot and cold all at once.

Moira and Rhys met David on the sidewalk outside Lorena's botanica. David, who had been nervously smoking through a pack of cigarettes for the last fifteen minutes, couldn't help the physical reaction that overtook him when he saw them striding across the street. His heart leapt into his mouth at the sight of Rhys's black curls, and his arms opened instinctively to Moira, who stepped right into his embrace like she belonged there. David closed his eyes and breathed in her sandalwood perfume, allowing her energy to wash over him. David rested his chin on the crown of her head and rubbed a circle between her shoulder blades, sending her soothing signals through the point of contact. *I'm alright,* he was saying. *I'm not dead yet.*

Rhys stood a polite distance away, trying not to look at them. There was a line of confusion between his brows. Confusion, or anguish.

"Shall we go inside?" Rhys asked.

David nodded, opening the door for them both. Rhys usually scowled when David tried to do anything chivalrous for him, but this time he stepped through the door without complaint.

The botanica was blessedly empty, probably because it was a rainy evening and almost closing time.

"Lorena?" David called.

"I'm here, mijo," Lorena replied. The trio turned a corner to find Lorena standing at the counter, fingers hovering over three gilt-edged tarot cards. The High Priestess, The Chariot, and the Hanged Man. "And you all are right on time."

If David had been raised in a different family, he might be a little spooked by Lorena's uncanny abilities, but he knew her too well to be surprised. Of course she had divined they were coming.

"Hello, Lorena," Moira said courteously. Rhys echoed her, obeying the sort of unspoken protocol that came with conversing with someone exponentially more powerful than yourself.

Lorena flipped the cards back into the deck and shuffled idly while she looked David up and down. "Have you finally come to your senses and decided to let people help you?"

David considered arguing with her, but there was no point. She could see with naked clarity how hard he was leaning on Rhys and Moira, and she knew he needed her expertise. So, he just nodded, making the gesture as deferential as possible.

And he told her about the curse, all of it, down to every scrap of conflicting information. Lorena just listened with calm, dark eyes, because of course the cards had already told her everything she needed to know.

"We haven't made any progress on breaking the curse," David finished. "I'm out of my depth, and I'm running out of time."

"Time?" Rhys echoed, shooting David a dark-eyed look.

David swallowed hard. "When I talked to Leda, she reminded me about a part of the legend I had forgotten. The Devil is supposed to come to collect on the Aristarkhov deal when the heir turns thirty."

Rhys went a bit ashen. "David, your birthday is in five days."

"I know, I know," David said, gritting his teeth against another wave of nausea. The room spun for a few minutes, then settled. "I just found out, and I wasn't even sure it was something to be taken seriously. But now I'm willing to consider any possibility, so long as it helps me."

Moira's eyes gleamed strangely in the dim lighting of the botanica, and for a moment David thought she was going to cry. But then she stepped forward and pressed her palms against the glass countertop, fixing Lorena with a steely look. "You *have* to help him, Lorena."

"Very bold of you to say," Lorena said.

"She doesn't mean any disrespect," Rhys said quickly.

"I'm sure she doesn't. Even the Syrophoneician woman asked Jesus for what she wanted, isn't that right?"

"Right," David said encouragingly, even though the Biblical reference was lost on him.

"Please," Moira added, with unashamed earnestness that made David want to hug her all over again.

Lorena looked at her hard for a long moment, then reached under the counter and produced a little wooden box. She waved David closer and began to study his face as though for signs of sickness. Rhys stood awkwardly next to Moira, shifting from foot to foot as Lorena completed her examination.

"Why didn't you come to me sooner?" Lorena murmured, turning over David's hands and examining the lines of his palms. All at once, she wasn't the most powerful person in the room, she was just the Lorena he had grown up with, the surrogate mother who had bandaged his scraped knees and listened to him whine about boys.

"I don't know," David muttered, wincing against an oncoming headache. "I wanted to fix it myself."

"Like a chicken trying to find its own severed head," Lorena snorted. "It looks like you've let this go untreated for months."

"Can you fix it?" David pressed. "Don't you have some kind of uncrossing oil or curse-breaking powder?"

Lorena opened up the wooden box and tipped a handful of small pink seashells into her hands. She shook them as though they were dice, muttering in Spanish, and then tossed them across the counter. They spilled towards David like grasping tendrils of seafoam.

Lorena sorted through the shells with her long acrylic nails and frowned. "No," she pronounced. "I can't fix it. This isn't your garden variety evil eye or hex from a neighbor. This is old, nasty magic, passed down through the blood. I can make you more comfortable, but this is a thing you have to fight off yourself. Only blood can rewrite blood. The answer has got to come from you."

David sagged against the counter, feeling entirely defeated. "I don't have the *time*, Lorena."

"I just don't get it," Moira muttered. "It isn't fair. He didn't even make the deal. Why should he suffer for something his ancestor did?"

Lorena just shook her head. "We don't choose our families. Sometimes, they leave us with horrible messes to clean up. That's just the way of the world."

"But the terms of the contract have already been fulfilled," David pressed. "So, there's got to be some mistake here. Deals aren't hereditary; there's got to be some way out."

Lorena looked at David with a heavy sadness in her eyes. "Oh, David. You still don't realize what he did, do you?"

Dread trickled down David's spine. He had spent months trying to unravel the mystery of this curse, but now that it was right there within his grasp, he wasn't sure he wanted it. The truth, oftentimes, was much more terrible than any fairy tale.

"I'm so sorry, mijo," Lorena went on. "We all thought he had told you. He must have died before he was able to. I would have told you myself, if I knew you were going through this. I wish you had reached out before now."

"Who?" David demanded. "What are you talking about?"

Lorena took his face between her weathered hands. "The old story, David. Try to think. The demon thought it was getting your ancestor out of their bargain, but the deal was made in exchange for the life of the youngest Aristarkhov heir. Anatoly was the last of his line, but Aristarkhovs have always found a way to survive. He sired sons."

David stared at his old mentor in bafflement. The implications weren't sinking in, but they loomed just out of reach.

"It's a loophole," Rhys breathed. "Anatoly wrote a loophole into the contract. But that means–"

"Jesus Christ," David said, prying off Lorena's hands and leaning hard on the counter. He looked like he might lose consciousness again, but not from demon-sickness. From total and utter despair. Of course. *Of course.* He had been an idiot not to see it. "Evgeni found the same way out. The son of a bitch."

"David," Moira said quietly, but he barely heard her. His mind was a maelstrom.

"Oh God, Leda," David moaned. "He abandoned Leda because she wasn't what he was looking for. He needed a boy. Lorena, why didn't you *tell* me?"

The priestess looked at him with a mixture of piteous love and unshakeable poise. She looked like one of her saint statues, high above the realm of human squabbles.

"You never call, David, you never *asked*. I wasn't even sure there was any truth to the curse, until I found out you were sick moments ago. Give me a little credit. I only ever heard of the curse in rumors; you know how sorcerers love to gossip. I assumed it was just Evgeni trying to bolster his own reputation."

"So, this is how my family has always done things? Sacrificing their fucking kids?"

"If the youngest son sires sons before their thirtieth birthday, the curse gets grandfathered down and the cycle repeats. That's the bedtime story, anyway. It could go on indefinitely."

"Well, I don't have kids," David spit. "I don't want them. And even if I did, I would never use them as bait!"

"You'll find your own way through this. You're smart, and you have some of the strongest supernatural abilities I've ever seen–"

"No, I don't!" David exploded, with a ferocity that made Moira jump. "None of those abilities belong to me; they're just the side effects of some sick family curse. Evgeni knew about this, he *knew,* and he still tried to wring every drop of value out of me before turning me over to a goddamn demon. I was bred to be slaughtered, like an *animal*."

Lorena was unimpressed with his outburst. "Well, you had better just lay down and die, then," she said, slate eyes hard. "Or you could keep shouting at me; I'm sure that will help things."

"Lorena–"

"You are what you choose, David. You can choose to be your father's son, or you can choose to be a sheep waiting for the butcher, or you can choose to fight this. Nobody else can make that decision for you. But I very much hope that you choose to fight." She swept the seashells back into their box. "I'll pray to Santa Muerte for you."

"I'm not sure how prayers are going to help me now," David snapped.

Lorena swatted him on the shoulder. "Don't let her hear you being ungrateful! When my husband and I travelled from Guatemala, she was there. When I had my gender reassignment surgery and went to the courthouse to change my name, she protected me. And she's protected you too, David, ever since you were a child. I pray to her for you all the time. Go apologize."

David slunk off to the saint's shrine and slapped a couple of dollar bills down on the altar. Then he stalked out the door, letting it slam shut behind him.

He didn't know how long he stood out there on the street, gulping down burning breaths while his eyes stung treacherously. Leave it to Evgeni to screw his progeny from beyond the grave, and leave it to David to be the one left holding the short end of the stick. He should have put it together sooner. He should have done something before now, asked for more help, something. He should have–

"David," Rhys said, settling his hand on the other man's shoulder.

David flinched back. He didn't want to, but he couldn't help it. Human contact was too much for his raw nerves. Moira was lingering behind Rhys, a line of concern between her perfectly penciled brows.

Rhys pressed his lips together in a displeased line, and for a terrible moment, David thought Rhys was going to leave him there alone on the curb, out of hope, out of options. But then Rhys fished his car keys out of his pocket and said, with unimpeachable surety, "You're coming home with us. Let's go."

David thought about arguing. He thought about digging his heels in and insisting that he could handle this, that he didn't need to be monitored. But, for once in his life, all the lies evaporated on his tongue. Instead, he just dropped his head and nodded. "Alright," he said, voice hoarse.

"We've got a guest room," Moira said, circling her fingers around his bicep and leading him across the street. "I suggest you use it."

David didn't have it in him to argue. And, though he would never admit it, he was so, so grateful.

CHAPTER THIRTY-ONE

MOIRA

David spent much of the next few days at the McGowan-Delacroix residence, leaving only to drop off papers at the office and gather some clothes and toiletries from his condo. Moira set him up on a futon in her meditation room, then warded and blessed the room with Florida water and frankincense. David slept in a cocoon of her magic, which managed to take the edge off his suffering. But it didn't stop him from getting paler and more lethargic with each passing day.

The effort to break his curse was a round-the-clock affair, and none of them left the house much. They spent long hours in the study, Rhys stalking around flipping through ancient texts, David curled up in the armchair scrolling through exorcism case studies on his tablet, Moira sitting on the rug trying to divine a solution with tarot cards. No answers presented themselves, no matter what incantation or ritual they tried. Moira chalked out so many different ceremonial circles on the hardwood floor that her knees developed twin bruises, and David subjected himself to Rhys's ministrations over and over again. None of the rituals had any effect. If anything, they only seemed to make David sicker as the demon inside him rebelled. During various rituals, he was thrown to the ground, assaulted with a pounding headache, or made violently ill.

David slept in increasingly erratic, drawn-out bursts, and Rhys barely slept at all, living off coffee and whatever little bits of takeout Moira encouraged him to eat. To her knowledge, he only ever paused to call Leda a handful of times and give her a sugarcoated update on her brother's condition, and to make an appointment with that therapist he promised her he would get. Leda, for her part, mobilized the network of chaos magicians she held sway over to try and uncover any answers they could about the curse, and she offered to come sit vigil with David, but David wouldn't hear of it. She tried to push, but in the end, her time-worn distance from her brother won out.

Rhys was relentless in his pursuit of an answer, forging ahead even when Moira and David succumbed to exhaustion. Moira had never seen her husband so possessed by any single-minded pursuit, and she knew, without him having to say anything, that he was absolutely terrified of losing David.

The two men circled each other in tighter and tighter orbits. Rhys always chose the chair nearest to David, sitting close enough that their knees touched, and they would discuss possible rituals in quiet voices in the kitchen, their shoulders pressed together. Once, Moira walked in to find David sitting on the kitchen island with his feet dangling, Rhys's hand spread across his knee.

"Try one more time for me," Rhys was saying. "Just one more ritual. Please. I think I've got it this time."

"Rhys, we've tried everything," David sighed. "Lorena said herself this curse could only be broken by an Aristarkhov. My father's dead and Leda is illegitimate. You're a great sorcerer, but you aren't blood."

"Let me try," Rhys said through gritted teeth. "You can't just expect me to stand by and watch you die. Not after everything we've been through."

Moira thought about announcing her presence, but she got the impression that she was interrupting something, so she stood still in the doorway. Allowing romance to blossom between her husband and his ex had seemed reasonable under the circumstances, especially in light of the special connection she had with David, but seeing it in practice was something different. Conflicting emotions warred in her chest: anxiety jousting with jealousy while love watched from the sidelines.

David moved to cover Rhys's hand with his own, then thought better of it and braced his hands behind him on the counter, safely out of sight and mind. "Just because we have a past, that doesn't mean you're beholden to me. We're even."

"This isn't about getting even, David. It's not about repaying a debt. I'm doing this because I care about you. You have to know by now that I–"

"Don't," David said quietly. "Please don't."

Rhys scowled and withdrew his hand, flexing his fingers as though they ached. "Fine. We'll go on not talking about it – forever, if that's what you want. But at least let me try another exorcism."

"I don't think that's a good idea," Moira said, finally breaking the spell.

Rhys spun around with a little start. "Why not?" he demanded, putting an extra foot between himself and David.

Moira padded into the kitchen, pulling her knit shawl closer around her shoulders. "He's worse off after every ritual. I don't think his body can take much more, baby. At this point, we're doing more harm than good."

"We can't just give up," Rhys said, agonized.

"I'm not suggesting that. I'm just saying that attacking the problem head on isn't working. David, you're going to need every ounce of strength to fight this thing on your birthday. I don't want to weaken you any more than we already have."

"I appreciate that," David said, and he sounded so tired.

Moira stood between David's legs, wrapping her arms around his middle. David hugged her back, his strong arms secure around her shoulders. Rhys watched them both with jealousy simmering in his eyes, but Moira refused to be made to feel bad. If Rhys wanted to torture himself by not allowing himself to be close to David in the way he truly wanted, that wasn't her fault. She would take her comfort where she could find it. And if Rhys felt the sting of what it was like to watch the person they loved most wrapped up in the love of someone else, maybe that would teach him a thing or two about what it felt like being in her position.

"Well, I'm not giving up," Rhys said, and stormed off to his study.

Moira sighed. "He's impossible."

"He's scared," David replied, squeezing her a little tighter.

"So am I," Moira whispered.

The next forty-eight hours slipped past in a haze of research, sleeplessness, and failed spells. Rhys continued to come apart at the seams, and David spent most of his days in bed. Moira felt frayed, like a rope pulled too tight. July 25th loomed over them, oppressive and inevitable, until all of a sudden, it was the 24th.

On the eve of his thirtieth birthday, David collapsed in the upstairs hallway. Moira emerged from her room to find him face down on the floor, pale and entirely unresponsive.

"Jesus," she breathed, and darted to his side. He was limp as a corpse, but when she turned him over onto his back, she saw that he was still breathing.

"David," she pled, cradling his face in his hands. "Come on, David, wake up. Wake up."

For a long moment, there was no response. Moira debated running to fetch Rhys, who was deep into his research in the study, but she didn't want to leave David's side.

Then, David's eyelids twitched. They were latticed with tiny blue veins, so much more visible than usual.

Moira raked her fingernails through David's hair, leaning in close. "David?"

David muttered something incomprehensible, then attempted to push himself up onto his elbows. It didn't go very well.

Moira looped her arm through his and hauled him to his feet, supporting nearly all his weight as he sagged against her.

"You need to lie down," she said, and found that her voice was thick with tears. For a moment, she had thought he was really gone. "Come here."

She guided him into the nearest room and sat him down on the edge of her and Rhys's bed. David kicked off his shoes and curled up on his side, shivering like it was the middle of winter.

"I'm alright," he said hoarsely. His brows were drawn together tightly.

"Like hell you are," she said, voice breaking. "I'm getting Rhys. Don't move."

David's hand darted out and grabbed her wrist, surprisingly quick despite his sapped strength. His weariness went through her in a heavy wave, followed by a thin, cold thread of fear. He was scared of being left alone.

"Stay," he said. "Please?"

"Rhys–"

"I just want to be with you right now, if that's alright."

Moira sat gingerly down on the edge of the bed. She latticed her fingers through David's. They were cold to the touch. "You don't mind me seeing you like this?"

David cracked a weak smile. There was still a dull gleam of Aristarkhov charm in it, despite the circumstances. "I've never been able to pull one over on you. You know exactly how fucked up I am. You can feel it. I can't hide anything from you, Moira."

Moira rubbed her thumb in a soothing circle over David's wrist. He was right, of course. She could feel the sickness radiating off him, and it made her skin prickle. But she could also feel something else, under the exhaustion and dread. It felt like a warm pulse, and she had sensed it before, in hugs from her mother or kisses from Rhys.

"Is this the part where you tell me you love me?" she teased, despite the lump building in her throat.

David kissed the back of her hand, his smile taking on a sarcastic edge. For an instant, the David she knew peeked through the haze of illness, like sun on a stormy day. "We'll have a spring wedding and then honeymoon in Saint Tropez."

Moira rolled her eyes and gave a little snort. "I'm a married woman, Mr Aristarkhov."

David's disposition sobered a little bit, and when he spoke again, it was quiet and honest, stripped bare of any bravado. "I didn't know it was possible to fall for someone without wanting to take them to bed. But you proved me wrong. I'm sorry I underestimated you. And I'm sorry it took me so long to realize how important you are to me. I wasted so much time."

"You've got plenty of time left," Moira urged.

"No, I don't," David said with a bitter twist to his mouth. "You don't have to pretend for me."

The tears finally broke through to the surface, and Moira threw her arms around David. To her surprise, he didn't stiffen or push her away. He actually pulled her onto the bed next to him. Dying men had no use for pride, it seemed.

"It helps," he explained with a huff. "Touching you takes the edge off."

"I know," Moira said, snuggling up and tucking her legs against his. Her bare feet brushed against his socked ones, and his breath stirred the baby hairs at the nape of her neck. "It feels good to me, too."

She had never been this close to him before, and she was enveloped in the sea of his emotions. The fear was quieter now, and the warm pulse of affection was stronger, lulling her into drowsiness. She tried to quiet her mind and offer him as much peace as she could through their strange psychic bond.

David draped an arm over her waist. "Is this too much?" he asked, voice muffled by her shoulder.

Moira shook her head. "No. You're cozy."

"Thank you for this," David said, eyes sliding shut. "Just... give me a minute or two."

He was asleep moments later. Moira considered slipping out of bed and going to update Rhys on David's condition, but she hadn't been sleeping well lately, and David's rhythmic breathing was so soothing. She could spare a few minutes to rest her eyes.

Moira woke up hours later, when the room was dark and the house was silent. It took her a moment to realize that it was David, not Rhys beside her, and to remember how she had come to fall asleep in another man's arms. David was still fast asleep, his breath shallow. She was just about to drift off again when a movement in a corner of the room caught her eye.

It was Rhys, sitting in the reading chair and unlacing his shoes. The sleeves of his rumpled shirt were pushed up past the elbows, and his hair was disheveled, like he had been wrestling a demon for the last hour. Knowing Rhys, it was entirely possible.

"Baby," Moira murmured, lifting her head off the pillow. She wondered if the scene she was caught in needed some sort of explanation.

"You're fine, love," Rhys said, with a bone-deep weariness in his voice. Exhaustion sat heavy on his shoulders, and he all but staggered over to the empty side of the bed.

"I can move him into the meditation room," Moira said, so quiet it was almost a whisper.

"Let him sleep," Rhys said. "God knows we can all use some rest."

"Were you able to make any more progress?"

"No. Just more dead ends."

Rhys propped himself up on his elbow and surveyed David's face, then dropped a small kiss to his shoulder. Under other circumstances, Moira would have felt like Rhys had walked in on something too private to share, or that she was witnessing something she shouldn't be, but she found that all she felt in bed with both of them was relief, and an overwhelming sense of protective affection. Together, all their sharp edges slotted together perfectly.

It was so unfair that it had taken them all this long to realize that.

"We're losing him," Rhys muttered.

"He isn't gone yet. We'll figure something out. I promise."

"We can try the new ritual I found tomorrow. If he'll let me."

Rhys settled down next to David, close but not quite touching. His eyes slid shut in the dark, and for a moment Moira thought he had fallen asleep.

"Moira," he murmured after a moment.

"Yes?"

"I love you."

Moira swallowed down the lump in her throat. "I know. I love you too. Get some sleep, baby."

She didn't have to tell Rhys twice. Within minutes, he was fast asleep.

Moira slept through almost the entire night, only waking as the peachy dawn light was creeping in through the windows. She rolled over to find Rhys out cold, his black curls in his eyes, but something was wrong.

David was nowhere to be found.

Moira pressed her palm to the sheets where he had lain. They were cool to the touch. When she peered out the window, she saw that his Audi was missing from the driveway.

"Rhys," she gasped, nudging her husband awake.

Rhys murmured David's name, either in some dream or because he thought the other man was still asleep next to him. Then, his eyes flickered open.

"He's gone," Moira said.

"Shit," Rhys said. Then, looking at his watch and marking both the time and the date, he repeated even more resolutely. "Shit."

"Why would he leave?" Moira said. The world suddenly seemed to be spinning very fast. "He can barely stay upright, much less drive."

Rhys was out of bed in an instant, yanking on his shoes. "He slunk off like a cat to die alone, and I can't, I won't let that happen."

"Where would he even go?"

"Back to where it all started," Rhys said, snatching up his coat. "Beacon Hill."

Moira hopped to her feet and reached for her cellphone. "I'll drive."

"He better be in one piece when we get there," Rhys said darkly. "Or else I'm going to kill him myself."

CHAPTER THIRTY-TWO

RHYS

Rhys knocked back half a sparkling water and three anxiety meds on the drive to Beacon Hill, and by the time Moira parked on the street, there was a layer of fuzzy numbness over his terror and anger. Somehow, it didn't make him feel any calmer.

Rhys kicked open the car door as soon as the Lincoln came to a stop, then grabbed Moira's hand and hustled her across the street. A summer storm was rolling in overhead, and the Beacon Hill house looked craggy and dilapidated in the thin gray light.

Rhys jammed the spare key into the lock and stormed into the house, Moira hot on his heels.

"DAVID," he thundered.

Silence.

"He's here," Moira said. "I can feel him."

"Split up," Rhys said. "I'll take the second level; you take the first."

Rhys darted up the stairs two at a time, his skin buzzing with nerves. He threw open every door in the hallway, calling David's name. Downstairs, Moira's voice echoed the refrain. Rhys checked the library and Evgeni's destroyed room, then strode towards the small door in the eastmost wing of the house. David's childhood bedroom.

The door was locked.

"David!" Rhys shouted, pounding on the wood. "Open the goddamn door!"

There was no reply, and somehow this was worse than any snide comment or demand to be left alone. Terror seized Rhys's heart in a vice, cutting through the haze of medication like a hot knife through butter.

"David, let me in. Please." Rhys's voice broke. "Please be alive."

"Did you find him?" Moira called from somewhere else in the house. By the sound of it, she was hustling up the stairs.

"He's barricaded himself in his room," Rhys called, crouching down to examine the doorknob. If he stole a bobby pin from Moira, he might be able to pick the lock, just maybe. He suddenly wished that he had misbehaved more as a youth and acquired any useful breaking-and-entering skills.

"Move," Moira said behind him.

Rhys pushed himself away from the door just in time to see Moira swing a heavy candlestick and absolutely obliterate the doorknob. It fell to the ground, dented and useless, leaving a gaping hole in the wood.

"Desperate times," Moira said primly, and then shoved open the door.

The room was dusty and dark, a graveyard of abandoned teenage paraphernalia. For a moment, Rhys thought the room was empty. But then he caught sight of a lump curled up in the corner of the twin bed.

"David," he breathed, rushing over.

The lump shuddered and then stuck out a hand, stopping Rhys short.

"Get out," David rasped. As Rhys's eyes adjusted to the dark, he could see that David's wavy hair was stuck to his forehead with sweat, and that his eyes were rimmed with red. He looked like he was burning up with fever.

"No," Rhys said, swatting his hand away. "You're coming with us."

"Just leave me alone," David said, then shuddered as his body was wracked with chills. He coughed and dry-heaved, and Moira gave a little gasp, taking a step forward.

"Why did you run?" Rhys demanded. "We were going to take care of you. We were going to be…" he didn't know what he meant to say next. *Alright. Together. A Family.* They were all shattered hopes, now.

"You've done everything you can do," David said. "This is my curse. It's mine to bear. I don't want you here when it comes for me."

"Bullshit."

"Get *out*, Rhys."

"No."

Rhys bunched David's shirtfront in his hands and hauled the other man into a sitting position. David swayed dangerously, but he managed to stay upright. His eyes were glazed over, and he looked half delirious. Rhys didn't know exactly when the Devil would come to collect, but he got the impression they didn't have much time.

"Help me get him into the library." Rhys said, hooking one of David's arms over his shoulders. "I've got one more ritual we can try."

Rhys would have preferred carrying out the magical operation in his own study, close to his own supplies and books, but they did the best they could with the materials at hand. Moira laid out a ring of flickering candles on the library floor and whispered a prayer to keep the magical circle strong. She knelt in the middle with David, cradling his head in her lap while she wiped a damp washcloth across his burning brow. As she pressed her hand to his temple, Rhys stripped off his jacket and pulled up the latest ritual he had found on his phone. It wasn't ideal, but it would do.

"He's fading," Moira said. "Rhys, I don't know if he can handle another exorcism."

"We don't have a choice," Rhys said, rolling the sleeves of his shirt up past the elbow. "We have to try. This rite is from the same time period and region as the original Aristarkhov contract; I think it could work. I know it could."

"I believe in you, Rhys. But I don't feel good about this."

"Will you help me?" Rhys asked, raking his fingers through his bedraggled curls. Exhaustion was singing in his limbs, but he had to push through. For David. For all of them.

"Yes. Just tell me how."

David shivered and moaned something incomprehensible, and Moira shushed him quietly. She dropped her forehead to his and muttered something soothing, and Rhys was once again struck by their easy intimacy. He had been that close to David, once, and that close to Moira, too.

God, he had wasted so much time being jealous. So much time denying himself what he really wanted. And now he was going to have to stand there and watch David slip into oblivion.

Rhys balled his hands into fists, his fingernails cutting half-moons into his skin. No. No, he could not afford to think like that. Failure was not an option. He was strong enough and smart enough to figure this out. He was High Priest, for God's sake. If he couldn't save David, no one could.

"If I do this right, I should be able to draw the demon out of him. But it won't be pretty."

"Do what you have to. I'll handle David."

Rhys dimmed all the lights and drew the curtains closed until the only illumination came from the flickering candles in the center of the room. David looked especially wan in the eerie light, even with Moira bending over him.

"It's time," Rhys said. "You've got to let him go, Moira."

Moira did as she was told, stepping outside of the circle and leaving David alone inside. Rhys crossed himself, muttered a quick prayer to Saint Michael, and then looped his arm around Moira's waist and crushed a kiss to her mouth.

"I love you," he breathed against her lips. "Whatever happens, I love you."

Then he took a step back and straightened his posture, adopting the bearing of the sorcerer. He planted his feet firmly on the ground, shoulder width apart, and raised one commanding hand.

"In the name of the Creator of the Universe, I command you to come out of him," Rhys began, threading as much authority as he could through his voice.

David convulsed in the circle, curling in tight on himself, and when he looked back up at Rhys, there was very little left of him in those watery green eyes. Something else was rising to the surface, appearing to defend its claim on David's soul. It bared David's teeth in a horrible grimace, contorting his face.

"You stop that," Moira snapped with surprising ferocity. She lit a candle and cupped it in her hands, whispering her own incantations into the flame. David shook violently and then hit his knees, his palms smacking against the hardwood. Moira's magic pinned him down, making it harder for the manifesting demon to hurt David or anyone else. Between the two of them, Rhys hoped they would be able to keep David alive long enough to banish the demon.

Rhys flipped to the ritual on his phone. It was in German, which wasn't his strongest language, but he could get through it. For David, he could do anything.

Rhys launched into the incantation, pouring every ounce of his magical strength into the ritual. He didn't care if he was wiped for weeks after this, or if the working took years off his life. All that mattered was saving David and keeping Moira safe. He had to get this right. He only had one shot.

David screamed as the magical words poured over him, and now it really sounded like him, like a man suffering in agony. Moira trembled next to Rhys, a single tear trickling down her cheek, but she kept driving down the demon with the magic her grandmother had passed down to her. Her fingers were shaking with the effort.

Rhys reached the climax of the spell just as David, or the demon possessing him, collapsed to the floor in a shuddering heap. Close. They were close. Rhys just had to push a little harder.

"We're losing him," Moira cried, then skittered over and dropped to her knees at the edge of the circle, perilously close to David.

"Moira!" Rhys snapped. "Get away from him!"

"I can handle him. Keep going!"

Rhys applied himself to the spell, perspiration trickling down his temple, as Moira spoke directly to David.

"David. David, you look at me."

Burning green eyes cut over to Moira.

"You've got to fight this," she said, leaning in close. She was so near to the circle that the candlelight illuminated her face like a saint's halo. "Ground like I taught you. *Breathe*."

"I can't," David gasped. It was really him this time, surfacing for a moment. Fat tears fell from his eyes and splashed against the ground. "He's too strong. I can't."

"I need you to. I need you to find that last bit of strength in the bottom of yourself and fight this, do you understand me? Hold the line, David."

David tried to push himself to his knees but fell onto his back, where he covered his hands with his face and let despair take him. Sobs rattled his shoulders, rolling through him along with waves of pain that made him cry out and arch his back against the ground.

"God, just let him take me," David managed. He sounded like a terrified little boy. Rhys's shoulders shook with the effort of holding the spell together and the overwhelming desire to gather David into his arms, but he stayed resolute. "There's nothing left for me. I'm nothing without him. This is all I'm good for."

"You stop feeling sorry for yourself and you fight this son of a bitch, David Aristarkhov," Moira said. "There are too many people who love you for you to give up now. Leda, Lorena. I love you. Rhys loves you. Do not prove your father right at the bottom of the ninth. *Fight.*"

David let out another scream as Rhys spoke the final words of the ritual. This was it. It had to be.

To Rhys's horror, nothing happened. David's fever didn't break, his convulsions didn't cease, clarity didn't come back into his eyes. He just writhed on the ground, tottering on the brink of death, in excruciating pain. Pain that Rhys had put him in.

"It's not working," Rhys said, his heart hammering in his chest. Panic was starting to set in, blackening the edges of his vision. "Moira, the spell's not working."

"David, stay with me," Moira said, voice rising in desperation. "Listen to my voice. Stay."

Cold numbness crashed over Rhys in a wave, and he dropped his phone onto the ground. Failed. He had failed. All the power and fancy titles in the world meant nothing when it mattered most, and now he had to watch David die.

In the circle, David's eyes rolled back in his head, and he started to shake.

"He's having a seizure," Moira cried. "Rhys, call a doctor, do *something*!"

"I–" Rhys stammered. He knew instinctively that by the time ambulance arrived, David would be dead. They were out of time and out of options.

The room tilted on its axis, and Rhys lost a precious few seconds to crushing nausea. In that moment, he would have done anything to keep David alive, he would have killed, even. But there were no options left to them.

Rhys squeezed his eyes shut. "Think, McGowan," he breathed. "Think."

Rhys shut out Moira's cries and David's gasping for breath and retreated deep into himself, flipping through possible spells and solutions at the speed of light. He turned over the details of the contract in his mind like a twelve-sided dice, looking for any possible loopholes.

The only way out, he concluded, was to do what Evgeni and his forefathers had done. Offer up one life in place of another.

Rhys had always been selfish, and he didn't apologize for that. His whole life, he had pursued what he wanted relentlessly, whether that was money, power, or station. But right now, the only thing he truly wanted was David alive and well, and that might just require an act of selflessness.

Rhys's eyes flew open.

He staggered towards Evgeni's desk and snatched up the ceremonial dagger from its decorative holder. Then he ran to the circle and hauled Moira to her feet. Her lovely face was stained with tears. His heart constricted at the thought of what he was about to put her though. But it was the only way.

"You're my whole world," he said. "And I pray to God you can find it in your heart to forgive me."

"What are you talking about?"

"I know how to save David. But I need your help," he rasped, gripping her by the shoulders.

"How?" she demanded. "Just tell me how."

He told her. He pressed his forehead to hers and told her what he intended to do, outlining every step with damning clarity. When he pulled away, Moira's eyes were shining with tears.

"You can't," she said, shaking her head so hard her curls bounced. "There has to be another way."

"It's our only shot. And there's no more time."

Moira pressed her lips together until the color drained from then, then she knotted her fingers into Rhys's shirtfront and hauled him towards her. She kissed him with a desperate finality, a kiss like drowning, like dying, and then she let him go.

"You do this thing," she said, voice dark. "And you come back to me; you hear me Rhys McGowan? *You come back.*"

"I swear it," he said, heart pounding like a drum in his chest. "I swear to any God who will listen. I'll come back to you. You remember that old story? Tam Lin?"

Moira nodded in a daze. "I remember."

"Good. I need you to hold down David. And for God's sake, be careful. It's not just him you're dealing with in there. Don't let him go, Moira, no matter what happens."

Moira nodded breathlessly and stepped into the circle.

David's face snapped over to her, and Rhys watched with lead-stomached horror as all the personhood drained out of his eyes. It was replaced with a sharp, serpentine hatred. Baelshieth.

Baelshieth lunged for Moira, but Moira didn't run away from the ferocity. Instead, she threw herself right into it, wrapping her arms around David and clinging to him for dear life. Rhys shoved David to the floor, pinning his arms at his sides. David writhed and spat, trying to scratch at them both, but Moira wrestled him down with the sheer force of her arms and will. He was strong, but she was tenacious.

"You don't scare me," Moira declared, even though her voice was shaking. "And you can't have him. He's ours. I won't let him go."

"Give me his hand," Rhys said.

Moira managed to peel one of David's hands away from his body. He was struggling in waves now, at one moment trying to throw her off, in another moment clinging to her like she was the only bulwark between him and death. It was hard to say whether she had more of David or Baelshieth in her arms.

Rhys sliced open David's palm with the knife. A little trail of blood ran down his arm and across Moira's fingers.

Rhys then cut his hand to match, a long incision that bled freely. Blood smeared on the knees of his chinos, on the ground between them.

The muscles in Moira's shoulders shook, threatening to betray her at the last minute.

"Rhys," she pleaded. "I can't hold him."

Rhys seized David's hand and smashed his palm against it, mingling their blood.

"Through the binding of blood, I, Rhys McGowan, am adopted into Aristarkhov line," he pronounced, solemn and final.

"I bear witness," Moira said, just as he had instructed her to.

Overhead, thunder rumbled.

The hanged man

CHAPTER THIRTY-THREE

DAVID

David came back to himself with a gasp, like he was surfacing out of deep waters. The shadows and contours of his study came into sharp relief, searing and vibrant even in the dark. He had forgotten what it was like to be well after so many months of being ill, but now there was strength in his arms and clarity in his eyes, not to mention the sharpening of his psychic senses. Baelshieth was gone, really gone, and the darkness clinging to the corners of his mind had been exorcised once and for all.

He was tangled up with Rhys and Moira in the ceremonial circle, and they were both shaking. David could tell from Moira's touch on his skin that it was because she was terrified, but he had never known Rhys to tremble.

"Rhys," David gasped. "What did you do?"

"Listen to me," Rhys groaned, pressing a hand to his chest. He was doubled over as if in pain. "Both of you. You're the only two people I've ever loved. I trust you with my life."

Moira stood up and stepped out of the circle, pacing a tight, worried pattern on the floor.

"Fight for me," Rhys urged.

Fear trickled down David's spine. "What did you *do*?" he demanded again.

Rhys clutched David so tightly, so close. Rhys's eyes were as dark as a night without stars. *"Fight* for me."

Then he shoved David out of the circle.

David's back hit the hardwood the same instant Rhys let out a gut-wrenching cry, his fingers tangled in his black curls. David had never heard Rhys in pain like that, not even when he broke his ankle after jumping out of the second story window of their dormitory one night to evade the RA. The sound sliced right through his heart, making it hard to think, hard to breathe.

Moira's forehead was shining with sweat, her chest heaving with exertion. She had held him down, David remembered dimly. She had held him down and told him she loved him, and Rhys...

There would be enough time to dwell on what Rhys had said later.

David took Moira's shoulders in his hands, sending her as much surety as he could manage. "Moira, what did he do?"

"Some kind of bastardized adoption ritual," Moira said, her eyes cutting wildly between David and Rhys. She placed her hands on top of David's, tangling their fingers together. Terrified. She was terrified. "He's the younger of you two, so if the demon thinks you're brothers, it will attack him instead. He was trying to buy us time, he said–" Fat tears began to roll down her cheeks. "God, I should have never let him."

This, David knew intimately, was the sharp, biting edge of loving Rhys McGowan. He would always push himself beyond the breaking point to achieve his goals, and you would be left standing there like a fool with your heart in your hands.

"Rhys wasn't able to break the curse, but I might be able to," David said, steering her back on track. His thoughts were coming lightning fast. He had been in such a fog for weeks that he almost felt high on the clarity. "Especially with your help."

In the dim light of the study, with tear tracks down her furious face, Moira really was every inch a goddess, every inch as awful and vulnerable and magical. And David needed all of her power and poise to get through this. He wouldn't survive it without her.

"Alright," she said, taking a shaky breath. "Alright. Just tell me what to do."

Rhys gave another horrible cry, and Moira started under David's hands. David squeezed his eyes shut and swallowed hard, blocking out the sound to the best of his ability. He didn't have time to lose it. He needed to focus.

"I'm going to try and exorcise him. I need you to keep him alive long enough for me to do that."

There was an awful scrabbling sound from the circle, and David turned to see Rhys – or Baelshieth, it was impossible to tell – trying to claw his way out of the circle to no avail. Rhys's fingernails were splintering down to the flesh.

"Stop it!" Moira thundered, throwing out a hand. "You will *not* hurt him, do you hear me?"

Moira raced over to where Rhys's messenger bag was lying discarded in a corner and retrieved a small plastic vial that David recognized immediately. It was the holy water Rhys carried around with him, either out of superstition or because he enjoyed the irony, it had always been hard to tell.

Moira walked right up to the edge of the circle, uncapped the holy water, and splashed it across Rhys's face. He convulsed and screamed like she had just shoved a hot poker down his throat. David had witnessed some scary shit in his day, but even his stomach clenched at the sound. Whatever had its claws in Rhys was old, and ugly, and strong. And it was David's fault Rhys was in that circle instead of him.

"David, there's no time left," Moira pled. She was pushing through the terror and the tears, weaving symbols in the air with her fingers as she muttered incantations under her breath. If she could get through this, so could David.

Lorena's voice reverberated through his head.

Only blood can rewrite blood.

"Listen to me, you son of a bitch," David growled, addressing the spirit. "You're in my house now, and you do what I say. And I say you're going right back to hell."

Rhys's back arched off the hardwood, so far that David feared it would snap. David shoved the sleeves of his Henley up past his elbows, revealing his tattoo. If it was Aristarkhov blood this demon wanted, it was Aristarkhov blood he was going to get.

David flung his cut hand over the circle, splattering droplets of red across Rhys's sweat-slick collarbones and flushed cheeks. Immediately, Rhys's eyes rolled back in his head.

Blood magic was volatile and dangerous even with proper preparation, but David was running on pure instinct, unravelling the curse with power of sheer, indomitable will. No Aristarkhov had ever been able to break the pact before, but none of them had been David, and none of them had ever watched the life drain out of the eyes of the man they loved.

Love, David thought with awful clarity. *Oh God, I love him.*

If he wasn't able to save Rhys, he would never be able to live with himself again.

"He doesn't belong to you," David declared, hand outstretched, bloody fingers spread. "He belongs to *me.* Blood of my blood, flesh of my flesh."

Rhys scrubbed violently at the blood on his face, but it did no good. He was marked by it, and the demon was bound by whatever dark magic David had inherited.

"He's my family, do you understand?" David pressed on, even as he began to feel lightheaded. This wasn't the spirit sickness of a demon draining him of his lifeforce slowly, it was simply supernatural burnout, onrushing as fast as a freight train. David gritted his teeth and tried to hang on. He had walked away from harder rituals before; he could do this. He didn't have any protection, or any plan, but damn the consequences. Rhys was more important. And he'd rather walk into the ocean than be the reason Moira had to watch her husband suffer an instant longer. "But he's not Evgeni's son. You have no claim on him."

Rhys screamed, really screamed, and for one shattering moment David thought he had broken Rhys beyond repair. But when Rhys opened his eyes, they were a little clearer, a little closer to the stormy black that David knew so well. It was working.

A staticky feeling started crawling along David's tongue, along with numbness in his right side. This wasn't a ritual anyone was ever supposed to try; it was made up of loopholes and prayers, held together with spit and sweat and blood. He was being sapped of his strength, fast. If this was any other ritual, David would tap out. But he couldn't stop. Not when he was so close.

"David!" Moira cried, and it was only then he realized he was swaying. He nearly hit the ground but caught himself on one knee at the last moment. A searing pain ran through his ocular nerve.

"I'm fine," David said though gritted teeth, but he was most certainly not fine. He felt like his insides were liquified, being boiled alive by the sheer heat of all the power in the room. Severing a demon deal without paying the price was an insanely stupid ritual to attempt, but David had never been one for caution and good sense.

Moira latticed her fingers through his uninjured hand. Immediately, David's system was flooded with vitality and power, more than Moira had ever lent to him before.

More than she had to spare.

Moira sagged against him until she was on her knees beside him, her fingers still tight as a vice against his as her face went ashen.

"Moira, let go," David ordered, suddenly buzzing with life. His headache evaporated. If anything, she clung to him tighter.

"No," she gasped, her breaths coming fast and shallow.

"*Moira*," David pled, trying to free his fingers. He couldn't lose them both. He could *not*.

"You're the only one who can save him," Moira said, sending him another wave of power that sent an electric jolt up David's spine. "But I'm damn well going to do everything I can. Don't let me down, indigo child."

David was caught between them both, his bleeding hand suspended in midair, holding the demon in place, while Moira fed him her lifeforce through the other. Rhys convulsed on the ground, teeth chattering, and David felt the magical tension in the air pull tight as a bowstring.

Something was going to snap any second. He just prayed it wasn't the three of them.

"Baelshieth," David ordered, layering Moira's magic over his own medium prowess in a heady cocktail of dominance and power. "Come out of him. *Now.*"

The enchantment in the air crackled and simmered, burning so hot David could taste it on his tongue.

Then, with a shudder and a groan, Rhys collapsed on the ground. His body was entirely limp, his lips alarmingly pale.

David released his grip on the magic in the room with an aching shudder. He tried to pull himself to his feet and failed. There was no strength left in his limbs. Moira was in no better shape, so they crawled into the circle, their knees disturbing the ring of candles, and descended upon Rhys.

"Baby," Moira said, cradling his cheeks in her hands. "Baby, please wake up."

"Rhys," David said, voice hoarse as he eased Rhys onto his back and slipped a hand under his skull. He threaded his fingers through Rhys's curls, rubbing a circle against his temple with his thumb. "Don't do this."

For a long, awful moment, there was silence.

Then, Rhys's eyes skittered behind his eyelids.

Moira let out a little cry, tears streaming freely down her cheeks, and threw her arms around her husband. She kissed him soundly, wetting his face with her tears. The couple embraced tightly, reunited against the threat of death.

"Don't you *ever* do something like that again," Moira sobbed.

Rhys clutched her closer, squeezing his eyes shut. "I'm sorry," he said, voice thin.

David suddenly felt the need to put space between himself and this display of spousal affection. He released his grasp on Rhys without being told, because he had no right, because that wasn't his place, because–

Rhys hauled David closer and kissed him on the mouth.

Rhys tasted like candle smoke and the salt of Moira's tears and David's own blood, and David was so taken aback by the tenderness that he didn't even return the kiss; he just sat there in shock. He was alive. Rhys was alive. And the Aristarkhov demon had been snuffed out once and for all, or at least kept at bay. Somehow, they had all cheated the Devil.

Only time would tell if the Devil would let them get away with it.

Rhys wasn't able to stay sitting up for long, and soon slipped down against the floorboards with a thud.

"I would like to lie down, please," he rasped. Then, he promptly lost consciousness.

The hanged man

CHAPTER THIRTY-FOUR

DAVID

Rhys's ascension was on a Sunday, at an hour in the morning when decent people were either in church or still asleep in bed. But David had never been decent, and he wouldn't miss this ceremony for the world.

He double-parked the Audi outside the Society headquarters, trusting the charm hanging from the rearview to prevent anyone from ticketing him, and took the steps two at the time, a Neiman Marcus bag swinging from his arm.

The lounge was more crowded than David had ever seen it, with Society brothers mingling with guests, some familiar, some foreign. David nixed the pleasantries and cut down the hallway to the High Priest's office, nearly colliding with Antoni in the process.

"Antoni," David said, putting a steadying hand on the other man's shoulder. "Where's Rhys?"

Antoni nodded towards the High Priest's office. "Still getting ready."

David headed down the dim hallway and eased open the door. Rhys was standing with his back to David, fussing with his necktie. David watched him for a moment, savoring the small pleasure of the thing.

"Need some help with that?" David asked.

Rhys turned at the sound of his voice. He had dressed for his ascension in a deep plum suit, narrowly cut with an iridescent kerchief blooming out of the breast pocket. He wore rings on nearly every one of his fingers, and there was a blink-and-you'd-miss-it smudge of khol along his lash line. His curly hair had been corralled into submission and set perfectly.

"You shouldn't be in here," Rhys said, an irrepressible smile tugging at his lips. He wasn't upset. Quite the opposite. "It's bad luck, you know."

"I think you're getting your ceremonies mixed up," David said, shutting the door gently behind him.

They hadn't spoken much since Rhys had recovered in the Beacon Hill house after his brush with death. He had spent only one night under David's care before returning to work, and then he had disappeared almost entirely into the strange machinations of running the Society. David didn't go hunting for him. Rhys had a lot on his plate, and David didn't know what he was supposed to say to him except thank you, and a whole host of other things that would be incredibly stupid to speak aloud. He hadn't texted Moira much either, because he couldn't help but feel as though he was intruding in her life, somewhat. They had kept their promises to one another, and now he wasn't sure whether he had a place in her life at all.

David crossed to Rhys and set the bag down on the desk. He reached for Rhys's tie, deft fingers untangling the silk as Rhys stood still and let David attend to him. A month ago, this would have been unthinkable, too preposterous for even his wildest dreams. But now, Rhys was close enough that David could smell his verdant cologne, and David was diligently straightening his tie as though this sort of thing was allowed. David kept his eyes on his work and kept his touch perfunctory and professional, but it was impossible not to remember the last time they had been this close – when Rhys had kissed him, firmly and unapologetically, like David was something worth fighting for.

The only two people I have ever loved, he had said. The tense of that statement got under David's skin. It left the current status of Rhys's feelings up to interpretation.

"What's in the bag?" Rhys asked, pulling David from his reverie. He took a steadying step back, putting a few inches of saving grace between him and Rhys.

"I already threw the receipt away, so don't bother trying to tell me to take it back."

"David…" Rhys warned. His voice was stern, but his eyes were hungry as they travelled over the bag. He could pretend all he wanted to, but Rhys had always loved gifts. He just didn't like feeling beholden to the giver.

David held up a hand, silencing his protests. "Just so you don't feel guilty, this is your ascension present. I'm well within my rights to get you something. It's the one time of year when bribing your High Priest is allowed."

It was a joke, of course, but there was a grain of truth in it. Rhys had been showered in free dinners, cufflinks, fountain pens, and tie pins. Antoni had demonstrated his friendship with a bottle of brandy and a first edition of one of Rhys's favorite books, and Cameron had cemented his loyalty with an eye-wateringly expensive wristwatch. David suddenly felt very exposed as he realized he wasn't trying to smooth over any lingering hard feelings or curry favor with this gift. He was giving it simply for the pleasure of watching Rhys open it.

Rhys looked pained for a moment, then he swallowed. "Fine, fine. Let me see."

David slid the bag across the desk, making sure the paper was arranged crisp and straight. Their fingers brushed as Rhys accepted the present.

"Enjoy the experience," David said. "You only have one first time."

Rhys paused, fingers hovering over the bag, and then reached inside and removed a taupe shoe box. A Christian Louboutin label was embossed into the top in swirling cursive letters.

Rhys's breath caught visibly, and a surge of delight flooded through David.

"You did not," Rhys said.

"I did," David replied. "Open it."

Rhys lifted the lid delicately, as though he was worried about leaving fingerprints on the pristine packaging. Nestled perfectly inside were a black patent leather pair of red-bottom men's loafers. They were iconic, and they retailed for close to a thousand dollars.

"I can't think of anything that radiates power and status more than those shoes," David said. "You're High Priest, now; you deserve them."

Rhys gingerly set the box down on the desk and pressed his knuckles to his mouth, looking at David hard.

David just looked right back, completely unremorseful. "I'm sorry I was a dick about the Priesthood. But Wayne was right to choose you. We're lucky to have you. I…" He caught himself and swallowed, thinking better of getting too vulnerable. "Yeah. We're all lucky."

"Thank you," Rhys said.

David nodded, forcing one of his careless smiles. "Honestly, I just got tired of looking at those terrible old loafers."

Rhys gave a laugh and began to pull off his battered dress shoes, lining them up next to his desk. Then he carefully removed the paper from the Louboutin's and unlaced them with an archivist's steady hands. David watched, satisfaction blossoming in his chest, as Rhys slipped them on and laced them up.

"Feels pretty fantastic, doesn't it?"

A boyish smile burst across Rhys's face, and David felt physically pained.

"Better than fantastic."

"Good. Well, I had better get out of here and let you finish getting ready. I just wanted to make sure those got to you before the ceremony. I figured you'd want to wear them."

David turned to see himself out, but Rhys caught him by the wrist. The touch seared against David's skin, kicking up his heartbeat.

"Have you been alright?" Rhys asked, and he almost sounded nervous. "Since that night?"

"Alright as anybody can be," David said, honestly. He kept talking, because Rhys's fingers on his wrist were warm and real and he didn't want the contact to end. "I take my vitamins, I see my therapist, I get through it. I've been keeping sober, throwing myself into work to make up for lost time. How have you been?"

"A little weak, but no worse for wear. I should be fine for the ceremony today."

"What you did," David began carefully. "You saved my life, Rhys, but you gambled yours. I know we managed to pull you back from the brink when you were in the circle, but if the curse really has been grandfathered onto you, then the terms still apply. You've got until you're thirty to find a way to end this. And the years go by fast, trust me."

"We'll figure something out," Rhys said, squeezing gently. *We.* The word coursed through David like electricity. Rhys imagined a future with David in it, but in what capacity, David wasn't sure. "But I don't want to talk about that today. Today is for celebration. Can you still... do you still have your gifts? I know you were worried about losing them once the curse was lifted."

"I haven't totally lost my touch, thank God. Things don't come quite as easily as they used to, but the skills are still there."

"Good. That's, um. That's good."

Rhys was obviously nervous now, and he just kept holding David like he was going to pull him closer at any moment.

"What's going on, Rhys?" David asked quietly. He could hear low voices outside the door, the scuttle of footsteps as the Society made preparations, but he didn't care. This cramped little room was the only place on earth that existed, as far as he was concerned. Rhys opened his mouth to respond, but he never got the chance, because the door clicked open, and Moira walked inside.

"Am I interrupting something?" she said, with mirth in her eyes.

Rhys rolled his eyes and beckoned her closer. "Neither of you are even supposed to be back here. Breaking rules on my first day."

"Expect plenty of it," Moira said, sauntering over. She was wearing a huge lavender fur coat over her black dress.

David expected Rhys to let go of his hand, maybe put a little distance between them, but Rhys kept holding him as Moira pushed up on her tiptoes and kissed her husband. Rhys slid his thumb down into the soft center of David's palm and pressed gently, and the sensation nearly made David weak in the knees. Rhys didn't let go until he was done kissing Moira thoroughly.

"Is this new?" Rhys asked, gesturing towards the coat. "This looks like that Gucci coat you're always going gaga over."

"Brand new," Moira purred, looking pleased as a cat with cream. Something in her expression tipped Rhys off. He blanched and peeled back the collar of her coat to look at her label. Moira burst into a peal of laughter, and David couldn't help but smirk.

"David," Rhys began. "This is…"

"What she deserves," David provided. Moira slid her arms around his waist and hugged him. He was struck for the dozenth time by how natural it was to pull her in closer, to breathe in her floral scent and bask in her body heat. David usually couldn't see auras on people unless he was trying hard, but her aura was so bright today, so electric with excitement and joy, that she radiated an amethyst glow. He had shipped the coat directly to her house with a note, not sure if she would have taken kindly to an unannounced house call, but now he saw that she would have been undoubtedly delighted to see him.

Rhys looked at them both with a strange expression, odd only in how open and vulnerable it was compared to his usual standoffishness. David couldn't tell how he was feeling, exactly, but he seemed slightly overwhelmed.

"You both really should go get in your places," Rhys said. He gave David an apologetic look. "I'll catch up with you later. Thank you for the gift."

The ascension ceremony was usually a private affair, strictly for Society initiates, but Rhys had rebuffed tradition in favor of an open ritual. Select guests were allowed, including some close friends and family of Society members and representatives from other occult groups. The Society members – David couldn't strictly call them 'brothers' anymore, since Kitty had just started her initiation exams – were gathering on a chalked circle in the middle of the room, chatting quietly as they took their places.

Leda was here for her own whimsical pleasure, but also, David knew, as a representative of the shadowy cabal of interconnected chaos magicians she presided over. She had traded out her leather jacket for a slouchy blazer, although the clothes underneath were still as black and low-cut as ever. She cut a striking figure standing next to Moira, leaning down to whisper something in the other woman's ear that made her grin.

There were other people in attendance David knew only by reputation, including the head of a major Wiccan coven from Salem and the married leaders of a local Rosicrucian chapter.

"I didn't realize we were going to have such an audience," he said, sidling up to Leda. "I didn't think Rhys had this many friends outside of the Society."

"He doesn't," Moira said. "But he's smarter than Wayne was. He knows the Society can't thrive in isolation anymore."

"I think we've done just fine for ourselves," David said, adjusting his cufflinks.

Leda shot him a smirk. "Have you? Eating away at the endowment in your basement ritual room and doing the same old spells over and over again?"

"Alright, maybe things have gotten a little rote."

"You've got no political power in Boston anymore. If Rhys keeps making the right connections and schmoozing the right people, maybe someday you will, again."

David just shook his head, baffled. He would never have considered doing anything with the High Priesthood except sitting on power and dolling out nepotistic favors to his favorite people. But Rhys was expansion-minded; he had genuine aims for the Society as a whole, with obvious plans for how to achieve them. It was his first day acting in any official capacity and he was already a force to be reckoned with pulling strings behind the scenes.

David was convinced in that moment of how truly right Rhys had been for the Priesthood, and he was struck with a reckless sort of admiration for his oldest friend. Rhys was always at his best when he was designing some scheme. The Priesthood gave him all the resources and leverage he needed to shine.

David gave Leda a nod and squeezed Moira's hand before he took his place in the circle, right between Antoni and Cameron. The lights dimmed until the only illumination came from the candles Kitty had lit at strategic points around the room, and everyone fell silent.

Rhys appeared through the doorway and took his place on the raised dais in the center of the circle. In the flickering light, he looked otherworldly, like a prince of demons taking the shape of a man.

David stared. He had been rebelling at the thought of having to kneel for anyone as part of this ceremony, but suddenly he didn't have any trouble imagining getting on his knees for Rhys. If anyone deserved obeisance, it was him.

Generally, the ritual would be led by the former High Priest, but Wayne was somewhere tropical with his ringer off, and so Rhys led it himself. He spoke the words of invocation clearly and confidently, summoning his own spirit court to witness the momentous occasion. The performer in David found that he enjoyed having a larger audience than usual, and he savored the awed gasps that rippled through the crowd as the spirits swirled into visibility in the shape of shadows and floating black masses. Rhys held them all at bay with a sharp word and the angle of his outstretched hand, and David's psychic intuition tingled as they settled in to watch from the corners of the room.

The fealty ritual came next. One by one, each Society member entered the circle, stepped up to the dais, and took a knee in front of Rhys. Everyone else held the energetic circle open.

When it was David's turn, he swept into a low bow in front of Rhys, dipping his head and averting his gaze in deference. He usually scoffed at ceremonial playacting, but he really tried to mean this one, to bring his heart in alignment with the ritual. Rhys's hand swept lightly over his head, his thumb touching David's forehead as if in blessing. It felt holy and profane at the same time, and David's skin prickled at the touch.

Afterwards, when the candles were snuffed out and the lights turned back on, applause and cheers rippled through the crowd. The Society members jostled forward to clap Rhys on the back and pump his hand, and David fell back to watch it all unfold. He took a private, simple pleasure in watching Rhys bathed in all that adoration, getting everything that he had ever wanted.

A twist of pain intruded on the reverie, reminding David that Rhys's life was full to the brim with satisfaction now. He had the world. Now that he was High Priest, there was very little David could offer to Rhys except his friendship and his talents as a scryer.

David excused himself early and headed over to Beacon Hill to finish preparations for the afterparty.

The cleaners had entirely transformed the townhouse. The furniture and rugs had been vacuumed until they shone in new colors, and the heavy curtains had been beaten clean and drawn back to let light spill into the house. The sun brought out the shades of gold and mahogany in all the dark wood and made the picture frames gleam. It was barely recognizable as the forbidding place he had grown up, when the ceilings seemed to stretch into black nothingness while the walls pressed in suffocatingly. Now the foyer almost felt welcoming, like a grand old hotel throwing open its doors to new clientele.

This was his house, he thought as he welcomed in Antoni and Nathan and all the rest who trickled in wearing their best suits, women and men decked out in silk and gold on their arms. This was really his house, his responsibility, his legacy. It wasn't his father's anymore and hadn't been for a long time. Moira had been right when she sent his ghost packing. But it had taken David a while to warm to the prospect.

Hosting Rhys's ascension party seemed like the right way to extend the olive branch of peace to the man who had beaten him out for High Priest, but it also felt like a renaissance of sorts. For the house, and for the Aristarkhov name. David found he didn't hate carrying it around quite so much now, even if he wasn't exactly proud of the legacy his father had left behind. Besides, he liked having an excuse to show off.

He had cauldrons of fresh flowers and foliage brought in and arranged next to buckets of imported champagne on ice. The wooden floors shined underneath all the loafers and high heels milling about, taking in every room. David had gone the extra mile and opened up the entire ground floor of the house to partygoers, so they could drift from room to room and find their preferred divans and alcoves to cozy up in.

"Dude," Antoni said, eyes swimming with golden light and the third glass of champagne he was on. "I knew you were rich, but I didn't know you owned the damn Smithsonian."

David just smiled, sipping his mineral water, and thumped Antoni on the back.

Despite the glamour, the evening was not particularly formal. There was generally milling about and drinking with impeccable small bites passed around on silver platters, with Rhys set to make a brief speech later in the night. He and Moira took their time getting to the house, of course, probably being swamped by well-wishers at the Society. When they finally arrived, a big cheer went up through the foyer.

Rhys still looked like a conquering prince, and Moira had changed into an evening dress stitched entirely from black lace and sparkling beadwork. David was reminded of her wedding day, when she had worn eggshell lace, and now she looked every inch the chosen consort of an occult leader. David raised his voice with the others when the couple arrived, clapping briskly, and tried to ignore the twinge in his heart at how perfect they looked together.

This night was not about him, he reminded himself. This was about Rhys.

He managed to give Rhys a wide berth for most of the party, and even managed to avoid the temptation to drink or eat carbs or do anything else to take the edge off. But eventually, Rhys found him. Just like he always did.

"Am I making things up or have you been avoiding me?" Rhys asked. He had ambushed David on the landing of the stairs, where they could enjoy a birds-eye view of the party without being overheard. David turned to look at Rhys and could barely remember how to breathe. He looked so perfect standing there with one hand in his pocket, his weight resting casually on one hip. He looked like a head of state, like somebody who didn't need David turning his life upside down with personal crises and family curses anymore.

"I'm just letting you have your moment," David said, leaning against the staircase banner as casually as he could manage. Rhys came to stand next to him, close enough that David could smell the incense notes in his cologne. He was not going to survive this night.

"I had hoped that we were beyond lying to each other," Rhys said.

David swallowed, Adam's apple bobbing. A month ago, he'd gleefully challenged Rhys at every turn, talking back in conclave and going out of his way to get a rise out of him during social hour. Now he could barely look him in the eye.

So instead of looking at Rhys, David cast his gaze out over the parquet floors. Moira was dancing with Nathan, her face alight with a smile as Nathan twirled her clumsily. David wanted very badly to be the one dancing with her.

"Do you miss her?" Rhys asked.

David's eyes flickered over to Rhys's, just for a moment. "Maybe I do."

"You can reach out to her, you know," Rhys said. "She can still be in your life, if she chooses to let you have her. You can have me, too."

"Rhys," David said, voice low with warning. "Don't–"

"Don't tell me what to do, please," Rhys said mildly, holding up a hand. "Just let me finish. I've had a long time to think about this, and if I don't say it all at once, I'm afraid I never will. Just listen."

David was a bit taken aback by being ordered around, but there was only one man alive who David let give him orders, and that was Rhys. So he swallowed down his arguments and waited patiently.

Rhys clenched and unclenched his hands at his side, the only indication that he was horribly, terribly nervous. "I know we've never been good at being good to one another, but I'd like to think that these last weeks... We've both grown and changed, and things are different between us now. I've been thinking a lot about what I want, what I really want, and David..."

Rhys trailed off, pressing his lips together until they turned white.

"Yes?" David prompted, leaning in despite himself.

Rhys looked up at him, pinning him in place with his dark gaze like a butterfly under glass. He took David's hand in his own and pressed a warm, openmouthed kiss to the pink scar running along David's palm.

"Brothers," Rhys said, voice hoarse. "That's what you are to me, do you understand? Family."

"You're carrying around a curse with my name on it. I'm amazed you still want anything to do with me."

"I won't accept a world without you in it, David. I don't care how I have you, I just want you close."

"What are you asking me, Rhys?"

"You *know* what I'm asking," Rhys said, voice agonized.

"If you're going to ask me, do it right," David said, heart beating out of his chest. He needed to know that this was real, that he wasn't hallucinating what was happening. "I deserve that, at least."

Rhys looked down at the ballroom, and in that moment, he really looked like a High Priest, regal and austere. Despite the raucous celebration happening below, it felt like they were the only two people in the room.

David loved him so ferociously that his chest ached.

Rhys turned to David and put his mouth close to his ear. There was no bravado in his voice when he spoke, no command, just the honest desperation of a man undone.

"I want you to be mine, David Aristarkhov."

"Are you asking me to be your boyfriend, McGowan?" David quipped, but it was only to cover how fast his pulse was thrumming in his jugular. Impossible. This was impossible. But somehow, Rhys was really standing there with him, his hand hovering over his bicep like he was afraid to touch David. Somehow, they had come to this moment in time together, and a possible future was unfolding at their feet like a flower.

"Are you saying yes?"

David kissed him in lieu of an answer. It was a firm, unapologetic kiss, strong enough to be a pact. Rhys curled his fingers around the nape of David's neck and kissed him back, right there in front of God and everybody.

When David broke the kiss, seconds or minutes later, his head was swimming with the taste of Rhys and the possibility of a life that felt like this, just this good, every single day.

"Come with me," David said, grabbing Rhys's hand and pulling him down the corridor.

"What are we doing?" Rhys said, but the deliciously dark cast in his voice made it quite clear he knew exactly what they were up to.

"Making up for lost time," David said, and pulled him into a spare bedroom.

The hanged man

CHAPTER THIRTY-FIVE

DAVID

Rhys was on him in an instant, crushing his mouth in a hungry kiss. David sloughed off his dinner jacket without worrying about it getting creased on the floor, gripping Rhys tight by the lapels and pulling him in closer.

Rhys threaded his fingers through David's hair and yanked, tipping David's chin towards the ceiling and exposing his throat. David hissed in pleasured pain, taking a gasping breath.

He had missed so much about Rhys for so long, but his firm hand in the bedroom ranked high on the list.

"You started something in my office," Rhys said, holding David in place. David's pulse pounded in his neck. Slowly, Rhys tugged David to the floor. "Finish it."

David smiled up at Rhys from his knees, delirious with desire and the delight of being kissed so soundly, handled so perfectly roughly.

"Yes, High Priest," David said, less for his own gratification than for Rhys's, because he knew it would get Rhys unspeakably hot. Sure enough, Rhys let out a groan, and David hadn't even touched him yet.

David set about rectifying that promptly, unfastening Rhys's belt and undoing his zipper. He pressed a hot, openmouthed kiss to Rhys's length through the thin fabric of his boxer briefs, like an act of worship. Rhys made an agonized noise, blindly reaching for the nearest piece of furniture to steady himself.

"David," he breathed.

"You know I like it when you say my name while I get you off," David murmured, running his hands up Rhys's thighs. "That much hasn't changed."

"I missed you," Rhys said, voice stripped bare of any lie in the dark. They hadn't bothered with lights, but David could see the contours of Rhys's face in the moonlight streaming in through the bedroom window. Rhys looked absolutely rapt, like he was witnessing a miracle.

"I missed you too," David said, squeezing Rhys's thighs so he would know that David wasn't just saying that, that he meant every word.

Then he took Rhys into his mouth.

Rhys's hands found his hair again, guiding him with a touch that oscillated between gentle and merciless, depending on what David was doing with his mouth. David savored the weight on his tongue, the ache in his jaw, the needy desperation with which Rhys urged him forward.

This was their favorite game. Pushing each other until the other pushed back, until they ended up in a tangle of limbs and flurry of kisses on the bed.

Or the ground.

"David," Rhys panted, sweat shining in his clavicle. His rhythm was becoming more erratic, more selfish. "David, David."

David made a humming noise of approval, and sucked harder.

Rhys came almost embarrassingly quickly, gripping David's hair so tight that euphoric tears stung David's eyes. David swallowed down every drop, blissed out and happily used.

"Up," Rhys said, with barely anytime to catch his breath. "Bed. Now."

"Bossy," David quipped, but he laughed when Rhys hustled him over to the bed and shoved him down on the coverlet. In an instant, Rhys was over him, pressing him down onto the bed with his hands bracketing David's wrists.

Rhys took a deep, shaky breath, then leaned down to press his forehead against David's.

"I should have never left you," he said, voice thick with emotion. His grip was almost hard enough to bruise, like if he could only hold David tight enough, maybe he would never lose him again.

"Yes, you should have," David said, in a rare moment of coital clarity. "We were both better for it. But you came back. And that's what matters. Now kiss me, already."

Rhys, for once, did as he was told. He kissed David until both their lips were swollen, until David was so hard in his dress pants, he thought he might die from the sweet agony. Then, just as David was about to beg to be touched, Rhys released David's wrists and palmed him through his slacks. David bucked his hips into the touch, chasing heat and friction.

"More," David demanded.

"I'll take my time with you, and you'll like it," Rhys said simply, like their dynamic, David's brattiness and his calm control, was the most natural thing in the world. And in some ways, it was.

"Easy, tiger; get me too wound up and all your party guests might hear me."

"Don't act like you don't like the thought of that," Rhys said, and tossed David's belt aside. Then, suddenly, Rhys's hand was wrapped around David's bare, throbbing cock, and David really did have to bite back an embarrassingly loud moan.

"I never got you anything for your birthday," Rhys said, a mischievous smile playing at his lips as he toyed with David, torturously slow.

"You saved my life," David managed between breaths. "That's gift enough."

"Maybe. Or you could consider this the first present of many."

Rhys gave David a few rough strokes, running his thumb along David's slit, and then lowered his head and wrapped his lips around David. David squeezed his eyes shut, losing himself in the sensation of that perfect, cruel mouth pleasuring him with brutal efficiency. His hands, now free, roamed over any part of Rhys's body he could touch, digging into shoulders and tugging on clothes.

"Rhys," he said, gasping. "*Jesus Christ.*"

"Blasphemy," Rhys chided, pausing in his efforts only long enough to fix David with a stern look and drag his tongue all the way up David's length. "Watch your pretty mouth or I'll find new and inventive ways to shut you up."

David didn't know if he wanted punishment or reward more, but he decided to behave himself, since what was currently happening felt too good, too electric, to interrupt.

In the end, David didn't last much longer than Rhys. Years of pent-up lust broke open inside his chest, and within minutes, he spilled into Rhys's hot, wet mouth. Rhys licked him clean and then clambered on top of him again, kissing David sweetly. The kiss tasted like champagne and salt and everything David had been denying himself for years.

"Come here," David said, and yanked Rhys down next to him and into an embrace.

He wasn't sure how long they laid there on the guest bed together, tangled up in the moonlight, but eventually, David came back down to Earth and became once again aware of the sounds of the party filtering in through the door.

"We should probably get back out there," he murmured, winding one of Rhys's curls around his fingers. The very sappy and very uncool thought crossed his mind that he would like to catalogue every single one of those curls, never to forget a single one.

"You're probably right," Rhys said into his chest. He lifted his head and looked David in the eye. "Promise me something."

"Anything."

"No more close calls with death, please. At least not in this calendar year. I don't think I can take it."

"I promise," David said with a chuckle. "Now come on. I'll help you get dressed."

A few minutes later, the two men emerged from the bedroom, hand in hand and only slightly rumpled. They found their way back onto the landing and peered down at the party, which was still in full swing below. Thankfully, it didn't look like they had been missed.

David glanced down at the first floor and found Moira looking up at them both, her brown eyes sparkling. She broke away from the animated conversation she was having with Leda and made her way to the staircase.

Rhys extended his hand to his wife, and she ascended the stairs like a storybook princess, holding her dress daintily in her hands. The moment she was in reach, Rhys pulled her in close and pressed his forehead against her own. David laced his fingers through Moira's, sending her so much gratitude.

They stood like that for a quiet, perfect moment, hands linked, until Moira asked, "Did you two sort things out?"

"I think we did," David said, squeezing her fingertips and sending her a little jolt of excitement. She beamed at him.

"Very thoroughly, it seems," she said, smoothing David's disheveled hair. "That wasn't so hard, was it?"

"Don't tease," Rhys said somberly, but there was a small smile pulling at the corner of his mouth.

"I guess our work isn't done, huh?" Moira mused, leaning her hip against David like it was the most natural thing in the world, like they had been friends since childhood. "Looks like we're all gonna have to spend some quality time together over the next few years to figure out how to put that demon in the ground for good. David, are you okay with extending our little deal for a while more? I think we've still got a lot to learn from each other. You've still got to teach me how to channel, and I'm not done with your spiritual self-defense education yet."

"I'm more than okay with it. But you two should be getting back down there," David said, still leery about monopolizing too much of Rhys's time. Especially after their little escapade. "The people will be missing you. I see a couple of sharks circling down there, spreading gossip behind your back."

"I have the rest of my career to squash dissenters," Rhys said.

"People might talk," Moira murmured, surveying the ballroom with her keen magician's eyes. "You'll need a strong second in command at your side to survive, and support on the home front."

"Luckily, I have both of you. And a few rumors won't kill me. I want to enjoy tonight."

"Then stay," David said, and he could barely believe the words coming out of his mouth. A month ago, he would have refused to set foot in this house, much less invite his Society rival and his wife into it. But now he couldn't imagine reclaiming the hallowed halls of the Beacon Hill house with anybody else. "Stay the night. With me. Here."

Moira glanced at her husband, quirking an intrigued eyebrow.

Rhys shot David a little smirk that made his stomach flutter. "For once, I think I'll take you up on your hospitality."

"Great," David blurted, face flushed.

Moira started tugging both men back towards the stairs, a spring in her step. "Come back downstairs. I want to dance with both of you."

"At the same time?" Rhys asked with a little laugh. "I don't think I know the steps for that."

"We'll figure out the steps as we go," Moira declared, making her way down the stairs with their hands in hers.

David glanced over at Rhys, and the two men shared one of their unspoken exchanges as they delved back into the fray of the party.

Yes, the exchange said. *I think we will.*

THE HANGED MAN

An enigmatic card. The Hanged Man hangs upside down and assumes a strange position, but he doesn't look unhappy about it either. Some traditions call him a traitor and compare him to Judas Iscariot, but that doesn't always seem like the right interpretation. Maybe it's this and more. The Hanged Man follows his own course and doesn't need approval from anyone, but he is also watching and waiting, taking a neutral position as he languishes in an in-between state. He calls back to the Norse god Odin, who hung from the World Tree, waiting to receive the magic of the runes.

The Hanged Man doesn't mean that things are easy but it's an encouraging card: avoid making rash decisions and be wise, and everything should be alright.

THE CHARIOT

Chariots have speed and energy, so can carry you forward, often very quickly. They can also take you upwards into heaven, as we see in Ezekiel's vision from the Old Testament. The Chariot image usually faces you head-on, so it can be cocky and ostentatious, but many of us need some of that confidence. Still, it's not always straightforward: in many card iterations, the Chariot is drawn by the mysterious figure of the Sphinxes. Sphinxes are well-known for their riddles, so your forward motion won't necessarily be instantaneous or easy. Chariots were included in a victory parade, especially in Ancient Greece and Rome, and they are useful in battle.

The Chariot is a card of success.

THE HIGH PRIESTESS

The High Priestess is full of mysterious imagery. She conveys an inner power – not masculine might or anything that overpowers – but energy in deep currents and dark places. She is an initiator, and she sits in front of a veil emblazoned with pomegranates which are the fruit of Persephone, the Greek goddess who spends six months of the year in the Underworld. She has transcended the mysteries of life and death. She is the patron saint of "I can't explain why" when we try to explore our motivations. She sits between the black and the white pillars of the Temple and is quite comfortable holding that space in between. Finally, behind the veil – behind everything – are the waters of the unconscious.

With her, you will go deep, find out something surprising and learn from your intuition and your instincts.

FOLLOW THE SUMMONER'S
CIRCLE THROUGH THE EYES OF
ITS ENCHANTING CHARACTERS:

RHYS'S STORY IN
ASCENSION,

MOIRA'S STORY IN
DIVINATION,

AND LEDA'S STORY IN
TRANSFIGURATION.

ACKNOWLEDGMENTS

Writing acknowledgements is always a daunting task, because so many people inspire, support, and touch a book before it gets released into the world. This time, it's especially daunting, because this book has been in development for nearly seven years.

I would be remiss not to thank Kit, without whom this entire series, and Rhys in particular, would not exist. He has held loving space for me and this story since its inception and has helped me navigate plot holes aplenty. His presence in my life re-oriented my entire worldview and led me to a love for romance in all its forms, so I truly have him to thank for my career in its current iteration.

Thank you to Devin, for keeping me sane and grounded, and to Chris, for always cheering me on and cheering me up. Thank you to everyone who read early versions of this book and encouraged me to keep going, especially Lyndall, Genevieve, Eliza, and Sarah. Thank you to Ellie, who kept me from giving up through her sheer enthusiasm about what was working and laser-sharp insight into what needed to be fixed, and to Elias, who was always there to listen in love. Thanks to the sprinters in the word camp discord, who encouraged me to squeeze in one more sprint, and to never give up.

Thank you to the phenomenal team at Angry Robot, especially Eleanor, Caroline, Des, and Amy, who consistently put in the time and work to help take my books to the next level. There was a time when I truly didn't think this book was going to get picked up, and I'm still over the moon that not just the book but the entire series has found such a good and loving home. Thank you to Tara, my marvelous agent, who always has my best interests at heart and is always there when I need her.

In addition, I want to thank the myriad of occultists, astrologers, magicians, witches, and clergy people who I have learned from over the years, who helped lay the foundation for the magic system in this book. Too many people to name have been gracious and welcoming of my questions and curiosity, and they've helped keep my personal spiritual fire burning as well. Thank you to my friends in grad school who indulged my camping out in the occult section of the library and studying magic when I was supposed to be studying for my theology exams, and thank you to my parents for not getting onto me for writing during my visits home.

Thank you to the Divine, in whatever shape or form it chooses to take when it touches my life. My search for a glimpse of God has led me down many winding roads, but I'm so grateful that it led me to this book, and to these characters I love so dearly.

And finally, thank you to the readers who keep showing up and making space for me to try new things and take narrative risks. It's truly a privilege and a pleasure to tell stories for a living, and it's something I hope I never take for granted. Thank you for being here, and for believing in magic.

We are Angry Robot, your favourite independent, genre-fluid publisher, bringing you the very best in sci-fi, fantasy, horror and everything in between!

Check out our website at www.angryrobotbooks.com to see our entire catalogue.

Follow us on social media:
Twitter @angryrobotbooks
Instagram @angryrobotbooks
TikTok @angryrobotbooks

Sign up to our mailing list now: